Lord of the Mountains

The Viking Lords series by Sabrina Jarema

Lord of the Runes

Lord of the Mountains

Lord of the Mountains

Sabrina Jarema

LYRICAL PRESS
Kensington Publishing Corp.
www.kensingtonbooks.com

LYRICAL PRESS BOOKS are published by

Kensington Publishing Corp.
119 West 40th Street
New York, NY 10018

First Electronic Edition: March 2017
eISBN-13: 978-1-60183-881-0
eISBN-10: 1-60183-881-6

First Print Edition: March 2017
ISBN-13: 978-1-60183-884-1
ISBN-10: 1-60183-884-0

Printed in the United States of America

ACKNOWLEDGMENTS

Writing is a solitary endeavor, but behind each author there are people who provide encouragement, advice, and shoulders to lean on.

I want to thank my agent, Nalini Akolekar, for backing my decision to write stories about the Vikings I've loved so much all my life. Your efforts are helping me live my greatest dream.

Thanks to my editor, Martin Biro, for saying yes to this series, and for being so enthusiastic about it. You gave me the shove I needed to make this book the best it can be.

I cannot express enough appreciation to my critique partners, Karen Fleming, Carol Post, and Dixie Taylor. You lifted me when I fell, honored me with your cherished friendship, and gave me the critiques that made this possible—Skittles and all.

My gratitude also goes to the members of the Tampa Area Romance Authors chapter of the Romance Writers of America. Each meeting is an advanced course in all aspects of writing, and a warm group hug from incredible writers. Tarans rock!

And finally, thanks to my close friend and first reader, Teresa Pierpont, for being with me every step of the way. When I told you I wanted to write a romance novel, you said, "Go for it."

So I did.

He would stand on the back of a dragon, coming to her in the time of war, with his arrogance and his weapons and his hate. His blood would run into the ground of her homeland. And it would mingle with hers.

—from the vision of Silvi Ivarsdottir

Glossary

Aifur—Area of dangerous rapids in the Dnieper river.

Arrha—A down payment on the bride-price of a woman, made to show good faith during marriage negotiations.

Asgard—One of the Nine Worlds in Scandinavian mythology. Home of the Aesir, the gods who represented war and martial ways.

Blótgythiur—Priestesses who made blood sacrifices in the temples.

Draugar—A spirit of the dead.

Einvigi—An unregulated duel of honor, fought with any weapons and no rules or judges.

Faering—A small, four-oared boat.

Fjells—Mountains.

Folkvang—The realm where the goddess Freya's hall, Sessrumnir, was located. Half the warriors who fell in battle came here.

Fylgjur—Personal guardian spirits in the form of animals. Seeing one indicates death is near, but not always that of the person being guarded.

Handsal—A ceremony sealing the marriage contract. It must be witnessed by at least six men and the agreement is in effect as long as any of them are alive.

Heiman Fylgia—The bride's "accompaniment from home," or dowry. It remains hers as a sort of life insurance policy in case she is widowed or divorced.

Hólmgang—A duel of honor with specific rules and customs, overseen by judges.

Hólmgangustadr—A bounded dueling area.

Hóvgythiur—A temple priestess.

Kasa—A drinking vessel with two handles often used at weddings.

Kennings—Highly complex poetry of ancient Scandinavia.

Knörr—A merchant vessel, partially enclosed with a lower deck for carrying cargo.

Landvaettir—Land spirits.

Midgard—Earth, the land of mortals. One of the Nine Worlds.

Miklagard—Viking name for Istanbul. The "Great City."

Mjölnir—Thor's hammer.

Mundr—The bride-price paid to the family of the woman to compensate them for the loss of her labor.

Nithingr—A coward, without honor.

Ragnarok—"The Twilight of the Gods." The battle in which the gods give their lives for the world they made. A beautiful new world is born from the old one.

Saydalani—Highly skilled pharmacists in the ancient Middle East.

Seax—A long knife, worn horizontally below the belt.

Seith-kona—A practitioner of shamanistic magic.

Sjaund—The "funeral ale." Seven days after a person died, the heirs gathered at a feast, drank ale, and settled his affairs. After this, the deceased was considered truly gone.

Staraya Ladoga—A major settlement east of the Baltic used by the Scandinavian people traveling to and returning from Constantinople and the East.

Tafl—An ancient Scandinavian board game played by both men and women. The full name is *hnefatafl*.

Thing—A regional assembly of free men who met to consult on important matters and to administer justice.

Vargamon—A wise woman who relates to wolves.

Völur—Plural of *völva*.

Völva—A practitioner of indigenous magic and prophecy, normally an elderly woman who had released herself from family bonds.

Wergeld—Amount of money each person's life was worth according to rank.

Wyrd—Fate, destiny.

Chapter One

The village of Haardvik
Hardangerfjorden, Hordaland, Norway
851 A.D.

The sound of steel on steel shattered the calm beauty of the early spring day.

Silvi Ivarsdottir paused, listening to the clash echoing through the trees and the mountains. She didn't need to reach out with her thoughts to know what was happening. The reason for the disruption was obvious. Her brother's weeklong wedding celebrations were still going on in the village, so beer and weapons were inevitable. Anticipated, in fact. It was what men did best.

The sound of combat didn't come from the village. She tilted her head, seeking the source of the disturbance. Her breath stilled. They wouldn't dare. It came from the place where the gods walked, the sacred grove. No one brought weapons there, the same as in the great temples. It was sacrilege.

Her stomach twisting, she rushed toward the clearing. She didn't fear facing down warriors. Rather, they should fear *her*. After all, she'd had the gods on her side since birth. She would defend and honor them until she went to Freya's hall in the afterlife.

She burst into the clearing and skidded to a stop. Two men circled each other. They were bare to the waist. Their long, dark hair swirled around their broad shoulders as they came together in an explosion of steel and sparks. They were both massive, men in their prime, fighting with all the skill that made their people so feared throughout the world. They moved with the masculine grace inborn to all the finest warriors as they surged through the clearing like water rushing in a river.

Her cousin Rorik laughed aloud as he swung, his black hair sweeping over his shoulders and down his chest. White teeth flashing, he smashed his shield against his opponent's arm, trapping his blade. Rorik thrust, but his blade met with air as the other man stepped to the side and brought his own shield up, deflecting the deadly edge.

Magnus.

He pressed Rorik back several steps with his wicked, fast sword strokes. His hair was so dark, it looked almost black, except for the deep golden lights in it. Moving with the skill of a predator, he surged forward, taking his advantage.

Her heart stuttered. As she watched them, her body heated, her breath quickening. Maybe it was only because she had just run a fair distance. The sun glanced off Magnus's sculpted arms as he swung his sword in a deadly arc. It smashed into the other blade with an explosion of sparks. She held her breath. If she called out, it could distract them. An instant's hesitation might mean death to one of them. Her anger at the sacrilege was not worth the risk. She could do nothing but watch.

Rorik disengaged, then hit Magnus's sword with his own, nearly knocking it out of his hand. He shook his black hair from his face and laughed as he brought his sword around for another blow. Magnus hit the ground, rolled, and came to his knees. He swept his shield horizontally, aiming for Rorik's legs. Rorik leaped over it with a yell, and before he landed, Magnus was on his feet. He struck Rorik with his shield and knocked him onto his back.

It wasn't over yet, though. Rorik threw his shield, edge first. Magnus spun out of the way, arching his back as it knifed past him. It gave Rorik time to leap up and charge him. He drove Magnus back until he could grab his own shield and reposition it on his left arm.

They circled each other, grinning. Their bodies glistened with sweat. Rorik's stomach was rippled and flat. Magnus's was the same, save for a wicked, jagged scar crossing his lower abdomen. Both were slim hipped, broad shouldered, tall and powerful. But it was Magnus she watched. Rorik laughed and danced as he fought. Magnus stood solid, every move weighted and purposeful. His cuts were clean, direct, with no wasted energy or movement. His strength radiated from him like a storm rolling over the mountains.

She'd seen him in a vision before he'd come with her brother, Eirik, to set her village free of the marauders who had held them captive all winter. She'd tended his wounds, and while his blood flowed onto the ground, he'd stared at her as one thunderstruck. He'd continued to watch her through the following days. Now Eirik was married to Magnus's sister, Asa, so Magnus was family of sorts. She'd have to see him many times in the future. At least, until she went to live at the great temple at Uppsala. Then she would see no one at all.

She shook herself out of her reverie. This was wrong, that they should bring weapons into a sacred place. They were still feinting, no doubt resting for a final onslaught.

"Rorik." Her raised voice stopped him short and he jumped away from Magnus with a guilty wince. "How dare you fight in the grove, Rorik? Not even you could be that sacrilegious."

Instead of answering her, her cousin clapped Magnus on the shoulder and said, low, "Run. *Now*." He bounded into the shadow of the trees, leaving Magnus standing alone.

She started after him. "I heard that, Rorik. Get back here."

Magnus lifted his sword in a question. "Rorik, what are you doing?" He turned toward Silvi as she bore down on him. "We were just training a bit, Silvi. How could we know this was your grove?"

"It's the gods' grove, not mine. Rorik knows. He's been here before." She shot Magnus a glare. "As for you . . . Don't you scent the breath of the gods here? Don't you feel their power in the very ground? Or has your dishonor chased them from here?"

"I scarcely think a little swordplay would frighten them from here. Perhaps they're away for the day, seeing to other matters." He sheathed his sword.

She bit the inside of her cheek to keep from cursing. "How can you be so irreverent? The gods will surely smite you for such talk."

He swallowed and looked away from her. "I've seen what comes of too much involvement with the gods. Even as Eirik stayed the winter with us in Thorsfjell, I saw how he was pulled between Odin and Thor, but he balanced them within him. I don't have that knowledge. I know only the steel of my blade and the silver of my coins."

"Thorsfjell, Thor's Mountain. Even your home bears his name, and yet, to you, it is just a name. The gods' power slides past you, never going more than skin deep. Instead of their voices, all you hear is the clink of coins." Her heart sank. Just as he had watched her this past week, so she had been aware of him. And her dreams at night . . . But it could not be. She wasn't meant for the hearth, a husband, and children. And even if she were to follow that path, this irreverent warrior was not for her. They walked in two different worlds.

Her soul twisting, she tried to rush past him, but he caught her by the arm. A spark shot between them and she gasped. His eyes widened and he let her go.

"No man may touch me," she said. "I am meant for the gods. They saved me this past winter from the marauders."

"Then they know I pose no such threat to you, Silvi. Just understand that while you dream, enemies could overrun you, as Hakon and his outlaws did last winter."

"The runes will warn me."

"As they did then?"

She firmed her resolve. "The runes showed my mother and me that we'd know great change and loss. It was our own shortcoming preventing us from understanding what the gods tried to tell us."

"And yet, for all your efforts, the gods took your father, and so many of your warriors and people."

"My father was weakened from the wasting disease. He died in battle with a sword in his hand, as a warrior would want, instead of as a shell of a man wasting away on his sickbed. In that, the gods blessed him. At the moment of our births, the Norns decree when we each will die. No one, not even the gods themselves, can stop that. It was their time. In all else, the gods will provide."

"The gods favor the strong." His voice was sharp, like the honed edge of his blade. "Don't forget, the blood of warriors guards you. Silver gives you the privilege of food in your belly and a warm house in which to dream your dreams. All the gods do is watch us from Asgard in the same way we watch ants scurrying on the ground."

A shadow came over them as a cloud hid the sun. Were the gods displeased at his words? Silvi shook her head at his blindness. If he did not recognize the gods, as he should, how could they bless him? How could they smile on him if he didn't look up to see them? He was lost, like a ship at sea without a sail, and he didn't even know it. She raised her hand toward his arm, then dropped it to her side without touching him. "There's an imbalance in you, Magnus. The answer is not one thing or the other, but a mix of our world and that of the gods."

He gave her a gentle smile and looked into her eyes, something no man except her brother could do. "Then you should heed your own wisdom, Silvi. I know you want to go to Uppsala to become one of the priestesses there. Where's the balance in that? You shun the things of this world, seeking only the starlit realms. Your beauty will be wasted there among the men who dance like women. The strength I've seen in you these past days will thin into insipid chants and rituals." He lifted his hand to her cheek but didn't touch it. Yet she trembled as though he had. He stepped back and took a deep breath. "Perhaps you're right. I shouldn't be here. Not with the thoughts I have in my mind. Thor's bolt will find me if I remain here any longer."

She watched him as he strode out of the grove toward the village. He was strong, beautiful, deep, like the roots of his mountain. Crystals sparkled in his blue eyes, his hair was like the night caressing the slopes of his shoulders. The gods had been so pleased when they'd created him that they'd made another who looked like him—his twin brother, Leif. Leif was the breeze swirling up the sides of the mountains in the spring, light and free, to career off the peaks and be gone, uncatchable.

Magnus bore the weight of that mountain. His people, his trading business, his world. He deserved a woman who could be a true wife to him, seeing to his people while he was gone, ruling over the household, warming his bed and bearing his children.

Her body clenched. He was everything any woman wanted in a husband. But she was not just any woman. She must keep remembering that.

"So how bad was it?" Rorik grinned at him.

"I'm not certain." Magnus sank down on a barrel in front of the longhouse with a sigh, running his hand through his damp hair. He'd kept in fighting condition during the winter, of course, and had defeated the outlaws who had attacked Thorsfjell. Then there had been the battle with Hakon and his men here at Haardvik. He wasn't quite as skilled with the sword as Rorik, even though they'd only been sparring. He'd be sore tomorrow, but it felt good. He glanced at the black-haired warrior.

Rorik sat on a fallen log with a giggling serving girl under each arm. They caressed his bare chest and arms, their hands drifting lower. He gave each of them a quick kiss. "Go about your duties or

Eirik will have my head. Meet me tonight in my chamber. *Both* of you." As they sauntered away, laughing, one of them winked at Magnus. Rorik certainly worked fast.

"That's the way it usually is with Silvi," Rorik said. "I never know what she's talking about. Between her visions and those strange eyes of hers, I stay clear. I love my cousin, but I'm a simple man with simple . . . tastes." He eyed another woman who walked past them.

"Aren't we all?"

"I tried to warn you to leave, but you were too slow." Rorik chuckled. "Or perhaps you meant to stay behind?"

Magnus kicked a small rock with the toe of his shoe. "It's obvious I find her beautiful." What man wouldn't? With her white-blond hair and eyes the color of a fine sword's blade, he'd felt shield-struck when he first saw her during the battle for Haardvik. Since then, he couldn't help but watch her, giving Leif much fodder for jokes. "She claims she's meant for the great temple at Uppsala. I need a woman who can run my village when I'm not there, bring me political connections, and give me a bit of wealth. I do well enough for my people, but we live a difficult life in the mountainous interior. We can't grow much for ourselves. Our summer is shorter than here on the coast, so we don't keep as many animals. We hunt for much of what we eat and have to import the rest. That's expensive."

"When Leif was at my village, he said your people spend all winter making textiles, jewelry, and carvings for you to take to the markets come spring. That's resourceful."

"It brings in what we need. Barely. Thorsfjell needs so much more." He stopped. Rorik didn't need to hear of his weaknesses. "I require a woman who is strong and self-sufficient. One who can guide my people, make judgments, run a household, and stand beside me in every way."

"All of which Silvi has been trained to do."

He blinked. "I thought she was going to be a priestess."

Rorik snorted. "That's what she wants. But Eirik said it will only happen if he's dead. Even their mother, Lifa, said she doesn't want that for Silvi—and she's a respected rune mistress herself, trained at the temple. Silvi knows about running a household, wielding power when the men are away raiding or trading, and keeping the accounts."

"Then why isn't she married yet? She's long past the age."

"Men can't look into her eyes, for one thing. She's too strange

with her visions and knowledge of the other realms. Eirik has the right
to make her marry, but those arrangements seldom turn out well. It's
too easy for women to divorce their husbands if they're not happy. Apparently, Lifa had a vision long ago of Silvi at Uppsala, and my cousin
has hung on to that as proof it's where she's meant to be. It's been a
running argument for years between them. As to why she wants to be
there so badly, that's something she'll have to tell you herself. I don't
look too deeply into these things."

A familiar laugh drifted to them across the village. Near the well,
Asa, Magnus's newly married sister, stood with a group of women,
her red hair blazing in the spring sun. She stood taller and straighter
than the others, but then, years of sword training made that so. Would
she remain a shieldmaiden now that her life was here with Eirik? Or
would she take the path of other women and settle for children and
the hearth?

He shook his head. Not Asa. Not yet, anyhow. She had blossomed
under Eirik's love, and was happy, finally. Eirik stood between her and
her past, slaying anything that might threaten her, as he had killed
Hakon, the *nithingr* who had brought such pain to them all. Magnus
rubbed the scar on his stomach.

Rorik followed his gaze. "Ah yes. The gods finally smiled on Eirik.
Your sister is as beautiful as my cousin. Yet, they could not be more
different. One like a sword, the other a deep pond covered in thin ice.
Both just as dangerous. After all, they *are* women." He stood. "We'd
all like to see Silvi married and happy. Lifa always said that if any
man can look into her daughter's eyes, he might be the one for her.
My aunt, like others who walk with the gods, often says such things.
I prefer to speak plainly, with my sword."

Another woman glanced over her shoulder at him as she passed.
He chuckled. "Both my swords. I'll see you at the evening meal." He
followed her toward a small house, calling back, "Perhaps."

Magnus looked at Asa as she talked with the other women. Eirik
snuck up behind her, grabbed her, and flung her over his shoulder.
She shrieked and pounded on his back in mock outrage as everyone
in the yard called out encouragement to the new bridegroom. With
Asa's propensity for weapons, he might need it. Her throaty laugh
floated on the air as Eirik carried her into the longhouse where their
private chamber was.

With the wedding festivities ending tomorrow, Magnus would

head back to Thorsfjell soon. He had goods ready for the market and had to return. Without his sister. He, Leif, and Asa had been together so long, having only each other, that he couldn't imagine her not being there. But this was best for her, and even for him and their people.

Asa's bride-price had brought in a great deal of gold. Enough, perhaps, to set aside some to purchase another *knörr*. The merchant ships were slow, meant to hold a large amount of cargo. He gazed out over the fjord cliff to where Rorik's vast fleet of beautiful, sleek warships lay anchored near the narrow beach. If only he could afford a longship. Then he could outrun the pirates who threatened all on the seas. In the past, he could do no more than stand and fight. And he had. Between Leif, Asa, and him, they had held their own, not losing any cargo or their lives. Yet.

If he had one of the blade-sharp ships to cut through the waves, he could outrun his enemies, make more trips, and earn more money for his people. It was a luxury, though, and they had so many other needs. He had to put aside his dreams for the good of his people. He looked away from the tempting ships.

White-blond hair caught his eye. *Silvi.* She entered the village from the direction of the sacred grove, moving with her head down, toward the longhouse. She was so slender, her skin so pale, she appeared little more than an apparition. Her hair curtained her face and she met no one's gaze as she walked. What was it Rorik had said? That if any man could meet her eyes, he was the one for her? Why was that difficult? Her eyes were so beautiful, he could fall into them forever. Was that why no man met her gaze? Could she see into them too clearly?

In the grove, she had come too close to his secret. Something no one else knew. Something he had not even told his twin, Leif. The truth would undermine his rank as jarl.

A woman with an infant approached Silvi. As they spoke, Silvi put her hand on the babe and nodded. They went into the building together. No doubt the child ailed and needed herbs. Was it true Lifa had made certain Silvi knew how to be a wife? She was certainly versed in healing and medicine. He had seen her skill all too well after the battle with Hakon and his outlaws. When she had tended to his wound, he'd thought his head injury was making him see things. He could barely think straight as he'd breathed in her sweet scent.

He'd spoken with her several times over these past days. They were so far apart, it was as though he stood on Midgard, their own world, and she'd come from Alfheim, the realm of the Light Elves, near to Asgard.

He blew out a harsh breath. Perhaps she was the wisest of them all, wishing to retreat from a world filled with so much pain and horror. Who was he to hold her here to wither and fade in a life where she was not meant to be? As the daughter, and now a sister, of a jarl, she had been raised in relative luxury. Though he was a jarl as well and could give her every protection, Thorsfjell was rugged and windswept, the winters longer and colder than here near the coast. He would do her a disservice to bring her there. Let her go to Uppsala and dwell with the gods, as close to Asgard as she could come in this world.

He'd go back to his sword and his silver, as she had said, and keep his secrets to himself. Until the gods discovered what he hid in his heart. When that happened, he'd not drag her down with him as they descended on him with their fury.

Even though he could look into her eyes.

"Are you certain you don't want to stay a few more days?" Eirik took a sip of his mead. He and Asa would continue to drink the honey wine for the next three weeks to sweeten the first month of their marriage.

Magnus joined him at the table and poured ale into his cup. Mead was fine on occasion, but not every day. "Rorik is leaving tomorrow and offered to escort me to the entrance of the Sognefjorden. I didn't want to slow him down with my *knörrs*, but he said he'd be skirting the islands anyhow, where it's slower sailing. We'll pick up the southern current, to help speed the journey. I have to load my ships and get to the markets in Kaupang. Since you claimed Asa's dragonhead prow ornament as her dowry, I have to avoid Hedeby, where King Horik often is. He wanted that dragonhead and isn't going to be pleased. I may have to lie low for a time." He grinned and took a large swallow.

Eirik laughed. "Starting next year, you'll stop here and pick up the carvings she did during the winter, as we agreed. Including one dragon. Though I'll make certain the one I have for my ship is the best one, of course. She'll do a magnificent one for the king. He'll just have to wait another year. Then you won't have to avoid Hedeby, the largest market. I don't think he'd go so far as to attack your ships, though, so you don't need an escort."

"I wasn't concerned about the king."

"Then why do you want to sail with Rorik?"

"I don't think the outlaws who attacked Thorsfjell during the winter did so on their own." He swirled the ale in his cup. "A coward called Toke, who is more raider than merchant, took over Bygvik, the village in the next valley. He killed their jarl. I didn't do anything about it, for I didn't know the old jarl. I thought his family would take vengeance, but no one ever did, so Toke remained in power. The fjord entrance is next to mine. His men sail the Sognefjorden, harassing and pirating other merchants and jarls living in the villages on the shores. Word among the merchants in the region has it that he's jealous of the prices our goods bring. I can't help but feel he had something to do with those attacks. Perhaps he put the outlaws up to it. He may have paid them. With Thorsfjell's goods destroyed, he could charge more for his own."

"Asa saw a dark rider in the woods after that last battle."

"Yes. And my stable hand, Sjurd, saw him as well."

"Do you think it was Toke?"

"I don't think he'd get that close to a battle. He's known as a *nithingr*, without honor. Which sometimes can make a man more dangerous. More unpredictable. He won't have principles to guide his actions." He took another swallow of ale. "Eventually, I'll have to travel to the market at Kaupang on my own, but if I have the chance to journey home with a larger force, I'll take it."

"Because Asa is your sister, Rorik would likely allow a ship or two to remain with you, as a matter of family."

Magnus shook his head. "I'll not be beholden to anyone. And he may need his ships. He's heading off to meet Ragnar Lothbrok, which surprises me. I've heard there's a massive fleet of our ships farther south, near London. Almost three hundred fifty of them. They wintered there for the first time at Thanet, attacking the area. Last I heard, they're to head north through Mercia. I thought Rorik would join in the fun."

"Not likely," Eirik said. "We came across the fleet as we sailed home last fall. He thinks there are too many ships and that means less gold and silver for each man. From what I understand, Aethelwulf, the king, is very strong in the area and may give them a problem. Rorik follows his guts in these instances and he'd rather strike away from so much attention. More spoils for him that way."

Magnus nodded. "Makes sense. Lothbrok's amassing a smaller fleet to sail up the Humber River. Rorik may need all his ships for that. Besides, Leif and I have plenty of experience fighting on the water. We've never been taken and I don't intend to learn what it's like, although we're somewhat weakened without Asa with us."

"She is quite skilled. With a blade." Eirik smiled into his cup and glanced to the other side of the room.

Magnus winced. "This is my sister we're talking about."

"And this is the wedding celebration, so there's always such talk throughout the week."

He followed Eirik's gaze. Asa sat with Eirik's mother, Lifa, and several other women, runes on the table between them. Silvi was there as well. Lifa had agreed to teach Asa about the ancient symbols to help with her carving, so of course her daughter would sit in on the session.

Her white-blond hair glowed in the soft firelight of the central longhearth. She smiled at something her mother said. Magnus's body tightened and his breath hitched. He shifted on the hard bench. Silvi's smile was so rare, it caught him off guard.

"Of course, there's a way for you to get the longships and warriors you need to be a force on the seas yourself."

He dragged his attention away from Silvi and focused on Eirik. "How?"

Eirik nodded toward her. "I've never actually set a dowry for her, but that can change. Warships and the men to sail them and fight for you. Isn't that what you need?"

Was he that transparent? "That takes gold."

"And gold." Eirik set down his cup. He fixed him with a hard look.

Magnus's head spun. And it wasn't because of the ale. "You want me to marry your sister."

"*You* want to marry my sister. We need to lay out the terms so we understand each other. I have several longships on the beach in a cove just up the fjord. I won't be going anyplace this year. I have to establish my jarlship, gather warriors to fight for me, and settle my household. And see to my wife." He grinned. "Rorik's shipbuilders can work on other vessels for me this year and the next. The women will work on weaving the sails, which takes just as long. In the meantime, three of my ships will be sitting idle. They could be yours.

Now. I'll give you the men you need until you can gather more of your own. Your *knörrs* call for five or six men to sail each of them, but longships require more."

"Actually, that's fine for coastal ships, but I have oceangoing vessels. I need at least twelve men to crew each of them. I put out word about where I'm trading. People in my area rent space on my ships for their cargo in exchange for working as the crew, so I don't need to support all those men."

"I know warships, not merchant ships." Eirik shrugged. "They need more men to sail them. With the fleet you'll have, you'll attract more warriors and that will bring your enemies to heel, including Toke. Rorik would be your ally. He'll contribute men as well, and back you however you need. You'll have power, with him in the north and with me in the south. And no one has more power and wealth than Rorik. Not even the Danish king, Horik. No one crosses him on land or on the seas. You have our support because of my marriage to your sister, of course. But with you married to Silvi, it would double the ties between us."

If his mind started functioning, he might be able to form an answer. Instead, he stared at Eirik. He could have the ships he'd dreamed of, the power to become a major force along the trade routes, and best of all, Silvi. In one moment, his world expanded. It all sounded good, but there was one small problem.

"I understand she's to become a priestess at Uppsala. I won't come between the gods and Silvi." He didn't need any more trouble with them than he already had.

Eirik grimaced. "You mean between Silvi's foolish dreams and Silvi. A *hóvgythiur*. That won't happen while I have any say. She's never been farther away from Haardvik than a half day's ride, when she visited outlying farmsteads with our mother. She has no idea of life yet. My mother wants her to live first, experience all she can. Gather wisdom. So do I. Her heart is too full of love to lock it away like that. All her love should go to a fine man, not distant gods. She should whisper words in the night to her lover, not to an unhearing statue." He held his hands up. "I'm not disparaging the gods, mind you. I'm pleased she hears them so clearly and they speak to her. But it's not all she's meant for. They gave her great gifts, and she needs to use them for the people she loves. You don't have a rune reader any longer, remember."

"No. We lost the one we had at Thorsfjell all winter." He made an effort to smile. His stomach was twisting like a loose sail in a stiff breeze.

"You could have a better one than I was. I do well enough with the runes, but Silvi is far more skilled." He nodded toward the women. Asa held up a rune and spoke to Lifa, no doubt telling her what it meant. Lifa nodded and showed her another one.

"And your healer woman, Ingeborg, is getting old. How many more winters will she be able to travel to the homesteads to see to the ailing? Silvi is well versed in all medical skills, as you've seen." He looked at the healing wound at the edge of Magnus's scalp. "It's not a decision to make lightly, I know. Go home. Think on it. The offer will stand."

"Why, Eirik? Why me? There are other men who are wealthier, more powerful than I am. Men who can bring you political connections I cannot."

"I don't need them. I have my own. And I have Rorik as family and an ally. I admit I can use your trade routes and connections at the markets. Besides that, I want what's best for Silvi, even if she doesn't see it herself. You're the only man I've seen her speak to for any length of time during this past week. She watches you when you're not staring at her."

She does?

"And don't forget, I lived at Thorsfjell all winter. I know the manner of man you are. With your honor and steadfastness, you would be the type of husband I want for her. You're a man of the world. You may well be the only one who could hold her to the earth so she doesn't float away to Asgard one day."

Eirik downed the rest of his mead and set the cup on the table. "Sometime this summer, Asa and I will return to Thorsfjell for her things. We prepared for battle when we came here. She left her fine clothes, jewelry, carving tools, and her personal items behind. I'll bring Silvi with us, and I'm certain my mother will want to come as well. She'll see to the spiritual welfare of your people. We can talk further on this then. Silvi needs to experience more of the world she's so determined to retreat from. She needs to see the best of it." He rose and went to the table where the women still studied the stones. Sitting down, he drew Asa close to his side and she leaned on him with a smile.

Could he have such a marriage with Silvi? Or would she resent him for pulling her out of the life she longed for? At least he had some time to think on it, but it would be best if he consulted with her. Not now. When they came to Thorsfjell, he'd show her all he could offer her. Once she saw the peace of the village and the creativity of the people, she would understand better. And perhaps fall in love with it all.

And with him? He shook his head. He was getting ahead of himself. Love wasn't necessary in a marriage, just respect and consideration. But if she ever looked at him like Asa looked at Eirik, he could rest assured he hadn't torn her life apart.

As for his own life, it was already in a shambles where Silvi was concerned. He'd fallen in love with her the first time he saw her. And if she couldn't return his feelings, it might be better for him to be alone in life than alone in love.

Chapter Two

"I came to say farewell."

Silvi spun at the sound of Magnus's voice, and nearly lost her balance. The herbs she'd been grinding scattered across the table. He put out a hand to steady her, hesitated, then pulled it back. She hadn't planned on seeing the fleet off. She had too much work to do to replenish the herbs they'd used throughout the winter. Rorik had already come by to say farewell, so she had no reason to go down to the beach.

Magnus stood before her, his dark hair washed and shining in the firelight of the longhouse, his sword at his side. Strength radiated from him. Though she was drawn to that strength and the protection it held, she took a step back.

"May the gods grant you a safe journey, Magnus. With Rorik's ships surrounding you, it can be no other way."

"He is truly the lord of the seas. I'm honored to travel with him. As I am honored to have come here and fought for Haardvik." His blue eyes were deep, like the fjords in the summer. "I hope you'll come with Asa and Eirik to Thorsfjell when they journey there in a few weeks."

She glanced away from him to the herbs on the table. "I heard they're returning there to get Asa's things. My mother is looking forward to it. I'll likely be gone by then to Uppsala to begin my studies. It takes many years. We may not meet again, unless you come there during the great festivals." Her throat closed and her eyes misted as she spoke the words. How strange. The thought had always filled her with such joy. But happiness could cause tears as well.

"Perhaps you could delay your journey there and come with your brother. I think you would like it at Thorsfjell. We create many works of beauty. Carvings of wood and soapstone, jewelry of silver and gold and amber, beads of multicolored glass, weavings and cloth the merchants fight over. It's peaceful in the mountains, with a stark, strong beauty. We're isolated, but there's no place like it in all of the north."

His gaze was focused, intense. This time, it was she who couldn't meet his eyes. His scent came to her through the smoke of the central fire, that of leather, steel, and masculine power. Her body responded in her deepest core. Something in that depth woke, like a dragon in the darkness of the earth. It rose, molten and strong, driving her breath from her.

She took another step back. "I have already waited too long." The words came from her as though someone else spoke them. As though they held another meaning altogether. Did the gods influence this time? Why? It was a simple farewell between her and a man she might never see again.

"I hope you'll consider it anyhow." He inclined his head, his gaze slipping to her mouth. "Be well and happy."

As he left, she leaned against the table, the strength draining from her body. She nearly sat on the bench, but instead put down the grinding stone and followed him outside. When she broke out into the light, he was far ahead of her, striding down the path leading to the beach where the ships waited.

The breeze blew her hair behind her as she walked to the edge of the cliff overlooking the fjord. Several ships had already left the shore, their oars cutting the water like knife blades. Magnus jogged down to the water's edge and waded out to one of his *knörrs*. One of his men helped him climb up the side. He looked up and stilled when he saw her. She lifted her hand as the wind whipped her hair around her. He didn't return the gesture, but watched her for a moment longer. Then he called out orders to his men and they scrambled to the oars. As the ship pulled away from the shore, he did not look back.

"The hands of the Norns have stirred this time." Lifa stopped beside her.

Nuallen, tall and silent, stood near Lifa, as always. He'd been wounded and captured in battle in Northumbria the summer before last. After he had recovered, he had lived as Lifa's slave. Eirik freed him after the fight for Haardvik, but he'd chosen to remain with them as a free man, and as Lifa's bodyguard. He wore the wide silver arm ring Eirik had given him as a token of his service. Whenever Lifa left the longhouse, he was just behind her, always watching, always attentive.

Silvi smiled at him. They had all become close during the winter when Hakon and the marauders had taken over the village. His focus remained, though, on Lifa. He loved her. Silvi had seen it long ago. The light in his eyes when he saw her was the same as when Magnus looked at Silvi. But it couldn't mean the same thing. Could it?

"Did you feel it?" Lifa's eyes were distant.

"I felt something. I didn't understand it," Silvi said. Was it the gods, or was it Magnus she'd sensed? The energy that had twined between them still rocked her body. She tamped it down. She couldn't lose sight of the destiny that had always been hers, because of some mere physical attraction.

"We must cast the runes tonight to see what they tell us. This is a time of transition. We must be prepared for whatever comes," Lifa said.

"Mother." Silvi turned away from the cliff edge and faced her. "I feel as though I'm suspended now between what was and what should be. Asa is the new mistress here at Haardvik. You have your work, as always. People come to you for healing in the mind and the body, to find answers for their futures, and to seek your wisdom. I cannot walk in your shadow any longer. I want to find my own path, and that path leads to Uppsala. It is time."

"I see." Lifa continued to watch the departing ships. "And what of Magnus?"

She might as well have struck Silvi with a war hammer. Had Lifa felt the power passing between Magnus and her? There was no telling what her mother could sense. Her wisdom ran so deep, Silvi sometimes felt as though she would drown in it.

"What—what of Magnus, Mother? He has left for his own world, that of markets and trade and weapons. That's no place for me."

"And how would you know, my daughter?"

"I aim higher. A woman's place is the hearth, and children, and spinning. The things of mundane life."

"Tell that to Asa. I've heard tales about her battles with looms." They both smiled. "And you know a woman need not be a priestess to wield power. She does so in her weaving and the power of life she brings. All things in the home are centered on her, and that includes things of magic. A wife can control destiny with her loom and her spindle, like the Norns control our fates with their spinning. Don't underestimate such magic, Silvi. By loosening a knot in the weft of a loom, any woman can free her lover in battle, or by tying a knot there, she can stop the enemy from moving. It is for this reason we bury women with both weapons and weaving tools."

"Why should I love a man when he'll only leave for trading and raiding, and perhaps die in some faraway place, like Magnus's father did? If Leif hadn't escaped the raiders in the rapids on the Dnieper river, no one would have ever known what happened to their father."

"We can die just as easily here, as we saw this past winter. As your father was killed defending us." She lifted her chin. "I have been greatly blessed. I have had the love of a fine man, the gods gave me the gift of the runes, and I have had two children, both of whom survived. Should you have any less than that?"

"But you lost Father."

"Death is as much a part of life as is birth. And his passing was between him and the gods. Not me."

"It was the gods who made me the way I am, Mother. While other girls dreamed of fine husbands and children and snug, tidy houses, I dreamed of the night, the runes, and of the peoples who dwell in places even farther away than the Nine Worlds we know of. I have always ventured deeper into the shadows of the gods than others. The knowledge that they have touched me is as much a part of me as my hand."

Lifa turned to her with a slight smile and brushed back Silvi's hair. "I've often felt you see things even I cannot in the realms of the gods. But I see this world so much more clearly than you ever could. It is in this world that we live." Lifa kissed her forehead. "Tonight we cast the runes. Be prepared." She headed back toward the longhouse with Nuallen walking beside her, his auburn head bent to listen to something she said.

Silvi looked back out to the fjord at the retreating ships. If only she could become like the eagles that soar above the mountains and the waters. Then she could follow the fleet and watch them as they unfurled their striped woolen sails, catching the uncatchable winds. The longships would knife through the seas, skimming above the waves, bending to the power around them but never breaking. She could stand on that deck, the spray in her hair, and Magnus would put his arm around her to steady her . . .

No. The ships were gone and so was he. So it would be if they married. She'd spend her life wondering if he'd return to her or if the goddess Ran had dragged him down to dwell in the depths of the sea. It would be no life for her.

Uppsala. The name rang like thunder in the mountains. Long ago, her mother had told her how the temple stood on a vast plain, surrounded by mountains and ancient burial mounds. A gold chain wrapped around the gables so all who approached could see it shine. Three statues stood within—Thor, Odin, and Freyr. Beside the temple grew a tree that remained green all year long. Such was the power emanating from there.

Yet, for some reason, she had always had a vision of it as an island, a place of peace amidst a sea of storms. The visions had started when she was very young, but the island had been too far away to see it clearly. Through the years, she'd been able to call the vision at will and, little by little, she had drawn closer to the island. The mountains rose above her, green and lush, and on them, she could see buildings. They were as the halls of Asgard were said to be—tall and gleaming like purest gold. The entire place was radiant, until sometimes it hurt her to look at it. Still, she longed to be there with every part of her being. In the past few months, the currents on the sea had brought her so close, she could smell the scent of the land. Just a bit farther and she would be where she had always belonged. Uppsala was her destiny.

Far better the peace of the temple, where she would study and one day become one of those who sit above the others and tell of what would be. Separate. Singular. Respected.

Not the wife of a man, but the wife of a god.

The lamps burned low, casting shadows into the far reaches of Lifa's private chamber. Outside, in the common room, the people were quiet out of respect for the power the rune mistress would command this night. Only Lifa, Silvi, Eirik, and Asa sat around the small table, Lifa's bag of runes between them. Nuallen stood aside in the darkness, his arms crossed over his chest, watching everything with his verdant eyes.

Lifa didn't reach for the gem-encrusted bag. She sat with her head down, staring at the flame of the lamp on the table. Silvi met Eirik's gaze. He shook his head. They would wait.

The flame danced, though no one moved. Then Lifa drew a breath and put her hand into the bag. She took out a rune but did not glance at it, and laid it on the table. Laguz. The rune of intuition, of other senses. Of visions.

Lifa should pick other runes and place them in patterns, then read their meanings in relation to each other. But she made no move. She never looked at the symbol, only at the light of the lamp. A chill shot up Silvi's spine.

"I see Yggdrasil growing before me. It is, and is not, the World Tree. It is our family, the roots deep, going back to the days when the gods walked freely among us. The branches are wide and strong, reaching outward until I cannot see the length of them. One branch outshines all the others. Many branches from other places, other times, touch it. They gain strength from it, and it grows and splits, becoming longer and more numerous until the tips spread among the very stars. It is Silvi's branch, and that of the generations that should spring from her."

Silvi drew in a harsh breath. That could not be. Why would she see this? Long ago, Lifa had had a vision of her at Uppsala, and that was what drove her entire existence. Why would her path change now?

"Mother?" Eirik leaned forward, his voice low. "Will we become as gods, then, to walk among the stars?"

"Not gods, but men who will journey to other worlds and explore them as we explore the seas." She touched the rune on the table. "These branches, Silvi's branches, are beginning to wither and die. I see it. They shrivel and fall from the tree, decaying into the ground as though they never existed."

"What of Eirik's branch?" Silvi clutched her trembling hands together. The entirety of their family's future could not ride on her.

"His time of transition has passed. He walks his destined path. Laguz only shows me yours, Daughter. And . . ." She looked up at Nu-allen, her eyes wide. He gazed back with his usual calm, inscrutable expression. Her eyes dropped. "And little else."

"Will you not complete the casting?" There had to be more. The meaning of runes often depended on each other and how they were positioned together.

Lifa stood. "The runes have no more to tell this night. I would speak with Silvi alone."

Why did this have to come now? Just when she had declared her independence to her mother and decided it was time to leave Haard-vik. How could both visions be right? She wrapped her arms around her waist as the old, dreaded pain rose in her stomach.

After everyone left, even Nuallen, Lifa did not go to her. Instead, she crossed to the large table in the corner and poured out a measure of a medicinal infusion. She mixed it with water and honey and brought it to Silvi. "Drink this. It will ease the pain."

Of course Lifa would know she hurt. She always hurt, just from being in this world. When the sadness swelled in her, her stomach burned like she had swallowed fire. She drank the familiar ginger brew.

Lifa sat and held out her arms. "Come here to me, Silvi."

"Mother, I'm a woman grown. I don't need coddling like a child." She set the empty cup down.

"You're still my child. We all need the arms of another around us from time to time. It is no childish thing. And even if you do not need me to hold you, *I* need to feel you in my arms."

Silvi nodded, knelt beside her, and laid her head against her mother's breast. She closed her eyes as Lifa embraced her. The warm scent of herbs and wisdom surrounded her. A little of the fire in her stomach subsided.

"I don't know why you would see such a different vision for me than what you've seen before."

"Not so different. The vision I had of you at Uppsala only showed me that you would one day be there. Not that you would live there throughout your lifetime. You would have to be there at some time, since we go there for festivals. Especially the great festival of the sacrifice every nine years. You chose the interpretation."

"I feel like a ship at sea without a sail." Hadn't she thought that of Magnus only a few days ago? Sorrow welled up in her, a great, chok-ing pressure, and she sobbed once as she held it in. Lifa gathered her closer.

"Cry, Silvi. Let it out as I've always told you. Grief is not a bad thing in itself, but if it builds up within you, it can eat away at you until there is nothing left."

She shook her head. She couldn't forever go crying to her mother like a babe. If she became a priestess, no one would touch her, out of respect and out of fear. All that veneration would be little comfort on solitary nights when the pains of this world ate into her. She'd have to be there for others, but who would be there for her?

She couldn't hold it back. Great, wracking sobs tore from her. The certainty and joy she'd felt in her future were gone, leaving only questions. "Why, Mother? Why won't the gods give me answers? If they want me, why won't they clear the way for me to leave? You and Eirik stop me, I had these strange feelings within me when I spoke to Magnus, and nothing is certain any longer. And yet, the island in my visions, the temple, is so much closer now."

"Look at me, Silvi." Lifa placed her hand under Silvi's chin and lifted, giving her no choice. Lifa's dark-haired image swam in tears. "I want you to listen to me. Forget the gods."

What? Silvi gasped and pulled away.

Her mother caught her shoulders and held them. "Forget the runes. Forget signs and portents and visions in the night. A warrior asks the runes if he will survive the coming battle, but in the end, it is he who fights with his weapons and his skill in the light of day and reality.

"You can rely on all our prayers and visions, but you are the one who sets your feet upon the path you'll travel. Listen to the one thing that matters, the one thing that will never fail you. Listen to your heart."

Lifa held her to her breast again and Silvi bowed her head, letting her tears fall. What was her heart telling her? She had never listened to it much, for her mother's vision, and her own, had guided her ambitions. She had walked through her life with such certainty, but now . . .

A tiny corner of the foundation that had always held up her world cracked.

At the mouth of the Sognefjorden

Magnus raised his sword in thanks as Rorik's fleet peeled away from his two *knörrs*, continuing northward. As they became a dark shadow in the distance, he drew his ships toward the channel near the islands guarding the entrance to the fjord. From there, he would follow it to the Lustrafjorden, where he beached his vessels. It was the closest place to his inland village.

They'd had a fair wind during the voyage up the coast. The southern current had run swift, so they'd made good time in only about two days. Of course, Rorik's ships could have made it faster, but the *knörrs* had slowed them down. Still, it had been a pleasant enough trip. Magnus sighed in relief as he saw the familiar islands before him, the mountains rising from the fjord beyond them.

He turned away to direct the adjustment of the sails for the tight maneuvering past the islands. He didn't use the oars except for landing the *knörr*, unlike a longship. The wind had been growing all day and now it blew harder as they skirted the islands.

"Magnus, ships." Leif stood on the prow of the other vessel, pointing ahead of them.

Two *knörrs* slid out from behind the island, heading for them. This wasn't good. They should give a wide berth if they were passing by. But they continued coming. He shaded his eyes with his hand while his helmsmen turned his ships toward each other.

He clenched his jaw as he recognized the other vessels. "It's Toke. How could he know we would be here?"

As his ships came alongside each other, Leif said, "He couldn't have. He might have been lying in wait for anyone entering the fjord. He saw Rorik's ships break off and is taking advantage of it. We'd best prepare for battle."

"Sail toward the lee side of the island. It's calmer and will give us more stability." Magnus took the steering board while Leif did the same on the other boat. They curved around the shore, using the land to protect them from the fast currents. Toke's ships closed in on them. Magnus's seafaring craft held more men and were heavier than Toke's coastal *knörrs*. While Magnus couldn't outrun him, he did have greater numbers.

They slowed and he guided his ship alongside Leif's, turning until they faced Toke's ships with their backs to the sun. Leif and several other men jumped across, carrying mooring lines, and tied the two ships together. They lowered the sails so the wind couldn't shift the boats.

As the men gathered their weapons, Magnus said, "Remember, minimal chain mail. If you fall over, it will drag you under. . . If you do fall in and can't get back aboard, make for the island."

"We won't desert you." One of the men raised his sword and the rest followed suit. "We stand together."

Magnus nodded his thanks. "They'll want the ships, so they won't damage them. They're drawing close enough to fire arrows. The sun should hinder their aim. Ready your shields and your bows. May Odin grant us victory."

They all murmured agreement and Magnus hefted his shield high on his arm, tightening his grip on his sword. The first volley of arrows should come right about . . .

"Now." He and the other men knelt and raised their shields. They formed a wall of wood and leather, the edge of each shield solid against the boss of the next. The arrows hit, biting deep, but no one was injured. His men stood and fired their own arrows back. Screams filled the air. Magnus exchanged grins with Leif. Toke's men, likely all outcasts, weren't as skilled as his were, and now the fool had even fewer of them.

Magnus looked over the edge of his shield. Toke's ships were almost upon them now.

Leif also peered over his shield, then ducked behind it as more arrows hit. "I think I saw Toke there, cowering in the back of the boat."

"Are you certain? He has always had others fight for him."

"I'm not sure why he'd be there, but when they saw us, he couldn't back down in front of his men." Leif chuckled. "This will be amusing."

Magnus raised his voice over the next barrage of arrows. "Don't underestimate the danger of a coward." The ship rocked as Toke's *knörr* rammed it. "Let's give the gods a good show this day."

"When do we not?"

They stood just as the first wave of attackers landed on the deck. They met with yells and the ringing of steel.

Magnus deflected the spear of an attacker with his shield, swiping it to the side and thrusting his sword into the man's chest. He twisted the blade free and pushed him over the side. At the sound of boots behind him, he jammed the pommel of his sword backwards. It slammed into a shield, shattering it. Magnus brought his own shield around, hitting his attacker in the side of the head. The man dropped. Magnus ran him through and stepped over him toward a knot of men fighting. A man came at him. Magnus drove him back into the cluster of combatants. He pushed his shield against the man's sword arm, trapping it against his body before running him through.

He stepped back. Where was Toke? This had to stop now. He had gone too far, ambushing them from behind an island, attacking for no reason. He looked for the *nithingr* but couldn't find him. Another man leaped at him. Magnus let him come. He stepped aside at the last moment and grabbed his helmet. The chinstrap held it on his head as Magnus swung him off the ship and into the water. That was why he didn't wear a headpiece. He looked around.

Leif fought on the other ship, his sword flashing in the bright sun. As he gutted his opponent, he yelled to Magnus, "Rorik's returning."

Magnus looked to the north. The dark shadow on the water was growing larger as the ships approached. The other men heard Leif, and Magnus's men cheered. They were winning, but the size and power of the fleet would make Toke's men wither away and run. Already the cowards were abandoning the battle and leaping back on their own boats.

Magnus saw him then. Toke stood on the deck of his ship, never having left it. He shouted at his men to keep fighting, but they didn't listen. They swarmed over the sides and shoved their boats away, leaving Magnus's forces laughing and jeering at them.

Leif turned back and grinned, but then his eyes widened. "Behind!"

Magnus didn't stop to look. He dropped and brought his shield up, angling it so it caught the wind. With the added power, he swept it behind him, hitting his attacker hard. The warrior stumbled toward the low edge of the ship. Magnus's heart froze. It was a youth, little more than a boy. And he was wearing mail. Flailing his arms, the whelp dropped his sword and flipped over the side into the sea.

Magnus threw down his own weapon, fell to his knees, and reached into the cold, dark waters, trying to find him. His hair trailed into the sea and the spray from the side of the boat caught him in the face. The lad was too young to fight. What was he doing there? What idiot gave him mail to wear in a sea battle? He never had a chance. Magnus leaned over farther, searching, the water up to his shoulders, and almost fell in. A strong hand yanked him back by his belt.

"Magnus, he's gone." Leif peered into the water. "Ran embraces him now, and she doesn't give up what she holds. Let it be."

"What fool let so young a boy fight?" Magnus's hands shook as he picked up his shield and sword. To kill a hardened man was one thing, but this was little more than a child.

An agonized bellow echoed across the water.

"My son! You drowned my son." Toke's scream rang from the other ship as he sailed past.

"I don't kill children. Nor do I bring boys to fight with men. What were you thinking, Toke? He wore mail. You shouldn't have taught him to attack from behind like the *nithingr* you are."

Toke shook his fist. "By right of law, I can kill you for saying that."

"You can try. But you won't. You lack the bollocks for it." Magnus took a harsh breath to bring his anger under control. "A sea battle is no place for a boy. You should have kept him home where he belongs, not leave him behind as you flee for your miserable life. His death lies at your feet, not mine."

"I saw you. You were hanging over the side, pushing him under. Holding him there so he drowned."

Magnus sheathed his sword. "I tried to find him, to pull him back up."

"No. You drowned him." He raised his sword high. "I vow by all the gods that, as you destroyed what I love, so I will annihilate anything you hold to you. Watch your family, your village, your life, Magnus. I'll obliterate them all."

While Toke's ships headed toward the fjord opening, his screams still carried across the waves.

"I should have gone in after the boy." Magnus ran his hand through his dripping hair.

"And Ran would have salivated over a warrior like you." Leif helped toss the body of one of Toke's men overboard. "Even if you didn't drown, she would have come for you herself and pulled you down. The boy is lost because of his father's foolishness. There's no one to blame for his son's death but Toke himself."

"You heard his vows. The rivalry between us will grow into a full-scale war now."

Leif clapped him on the shoulder. "Looks like you may need those other warships and men Eirik offered you as Silvi's dowry after all. Though I don't imagine it would be any hardship to have the lady herself as well."

Magnus said nothing as Rorik's fleet drew closer. All the ships had returned, four and twenty of them, a force as large as any king's army. The splendid sails billowed in the winds, the proud bows rising above the waters. Rorik's flagship led the way. He stood with his feet braced on the prow, his arm wrapped around the dragonhead ornament. Dozens of warriors stood behind the shields lining the low sides. When the oars were in use, the shields wouldn't hang there, but on the seas with ships in full sail, they made a fine display. Thank the gods he was an ally.

Rorik's fleet lowered their sails, slowing the ships a short way off. Their numbers blocked out the northern horizon.

Rorik yelled across the distance. "Trouble, Magnus? The lookout in the last ship thought he saw a battle. We weren't certain how many you faced, so we all returned."

"Just a *nithingr* who thinks to start a war with us. It's been building. He tried to ambush me." Two of his men tossed another body overboard after stripping it of anything of value.

"Looks like he made a mistake."

"That's true of anyone who attacks me on the seas."

Leif raised his stained sword. "We're slow, but we're mean."

"I can see that. Leif, how would you like to come raid with me? Beautiful, willing women, a share of our spoils, the best of everything. Then you could sail on some real ships."

Leif smiled, shaking his head. "Don't you have enough warriors?"

"Never." Rorik swung down off the bow onto the lower level.

"My thanks, Rorik. I'll stay with trading. It's safer." He looked down at the bloody deck. "Usually."

"If you change your mind, I'm sailing to Northumbria with Ragnor Lothbrok. There are some holdings that are ripe for the picking. Good for hostages. Lots of silver and gold there as ransoms. And treasure-filled monasteries guarded by soft-armed monks. Magnus, would you like me to send a couple of my ships with you up the fjord, just to be certain? I can spare them. It's no trouble."

Magnus looked at Leif and his twin nodded. "We must sail past Toke's fjord to get to ours. I don't trust him, especially with what just happened. He's lost his mind."

As Magnus turned back to Rorik, Leif put a hand on his arm. "Make certain one of the ships has Rorik's sister, Kaia, on it. She's . . . a good fighter."

Interesting. The shieldmaiden and his brother had circled each other all week at Haardvik.

Before Magnus could speak, Rorik said, "My sister will command the two ships I send. And they'll stay with you for a time, to increase your strength in case you need it. I know you're accustomed to shieldmaidens."

"I should be. I trained one." Magnus laughed and Rorik joined in. Rorik must have noticed the same thing about Leif and Kaia. He'd wanted Leif to join him. When Leif had refused, Rorik sent her with them. Even more interesting.

Rorik's shouted orders echoed across the water, passed from ship to ship. His men scrambled to obey. Leif jumped back to the other vessel, the men clearing the decks of weapons and the remnants of battle. They untied the ships from each other. Rorik's fleet moved north as two of his warships peeled off.

Magnus called for his men to raise the sail. As they worked the rigging, one of Rorik's longships slipped past them. Kaia stood in the front, tall and slender. She didn't look at them, but her gaze stayed forward, scanning their route. Leif's *knörr* fell in line behind her, and Magnus's ship, along with Rorik's other warship, took up the rear.

Once they got past the islands and entered the fjord, Kaia's ships slowed so that Leif and Magnus could lead the way. The fjord split into other waterways farther up, and she wouldn't know which course to take. The mountains rose high on either side of them.

The fjells of home.

It didn't sit well to take Rorik's charity, but it paid to be sensible. Magnus needed all the help he could get now. As jarl, he'd always had enough warriors for his needs—some to guard his ships, and others to remain behind at Thorsfjell while he and Leif were gone trading.

Rorik was family now, through Asa's marriage to Eirik. So perhaps his help wasn't charity, just what families did for each other. And there was a way to further cement that connection, giving him the warships and fighters he needed.

Silvi.

Chapter Three

Haardvik

The moon darkened.

Silvi studied it, perplexed. The trees of the grove were shadows around her in the night, though the clearing was bright. She'd come to try to ease her mind. In the days since the fleet left and her mother had had the vision, Silvi had been unable to eat or sleep well. Anxiety ate at her, as though the Norns wove a terrible net and now they tightened it. That afternoon, she'd wept, though she didn't know why. She wanted to burst. Her stomach burned and no amount of ginger, myrrh, or cow's milk would soothe it.

In this place, she should have found peace. Instead, a dim shadow passed over the moon, even though there were no clouds. It wasn't like the bite the Fenris wolf had taken from it a year ago during the Ostaramoon of spring. This was the same full moon, but now the tint was more subtle. Few people would notice it. But she did. What did it mean?

Her heart pounded as though she'd run fast. Her mouth dried. She fell to her knees and shut her eyes as the grove swam around her.

A dark dragon with gold-tipped scales swam on the seas, a crimson and ebony sky behind it. Arrows passed through the sky toward it, like a storm. It screamed and lashed its tail, striking them away. But still they came, becoming sharp-beaked birds. They grew until they were as large as swords. The dragon's scales repelled them and it was unharmed. It rose up from the waves and its power swept some of the birds into the churning waters, where they drowned. Another dragon, this one black as night, flew across the waves toward them.

The rest of the birds saw it and fled, leaving only blood burning scarlet on the surface of the ebony seas.

Silvi opened her eyes. Her trees surrounded her, and only the soft sounds of the night wove around her. The moon looked like it always had, bright and full.

How long had she been kneeling here? What did the vision mean? There was only one other time she'd had a vision of a dragon on the seas.

When Magnus had come to fight for Haardvik. The hair stood up on her body. She staggered to her feet and ran back to the village. People were still up, drinking and gaming, but she ignored their greetings. She stopped in front of Nuallen, who guarded Lifa's room as always.

"Is my mother here?"

"She just returned from visiting a sick child and told me to watch for you." He opened the door.

It came as no surprise that Lifa would see this time. Silvi nodded to him and stepped inside. "Mother."

Lifa sat at her table, a small oil lamp before her. "The Fenris wolf has passed close to the moon without taking a bite. Only his shadow touched it."

She sat in the chair opposite Lifa. "I was in the sacred grove, watching it. I saw a dragon on the seas, like my vision when Magnus and Eirik were coming here to kill Hakon. The sky was red, like blood, and there were arrows in the sky that became lethal birds. The dragon defeated them. Magnus and Leif should have reached their home today, if the seas were fair. What if something has happened to them?"

Two rune pouches lay on the side of the table. Lifa pushed one of them across to Silvi. "We need clarification. Take your own runes and pull out only one. Think on Magnus."

"Why can't you do it?" Silvi didn't want to think of him. What would the rune show her mother?

"The gods gave you the vision, not me. They will speak to you this night."

That was true. She opened the drawstring. Reaching into the pouch, she let the wooden disks slip through her fingers, searching for the one that warmed to her touch, that seemed different. Magnus's image rose before her, strong, beautiful, imposing. His blue eyes looked directly at her, into her. Something deep within her melted.

She shook her head. No, those weren't the influences she wanted to bring out.

She bit her lip and tried again. Magnus on the water, in his ship, the striped sails billowing behind him as he stood on the foredeck. His cloak streamed behind him like a storm as he braced his powerful legs on the rolling deck. The ship flexed beneath him, giving to the waves, yet cutting through them. His hand would grip the prow as he leaned into the spray . . .

There. One of the runes felt a bit warm. She pulled it out and laid it on the table. Perhaps it wouldn't tell them anything. Perhaps it would hold many meanings.

Her heart fell. "Raido reversed."

Lifa rose and crossed to the door. As she opened it, she said, "I'll tell Eirik we need to leave as soon as possible. Pack your clothes, Silvi. We're going to Thorsfjell."

We? She picked up the rune. It still warmed in her hand as she considered its meaning. A disruption of a journey, danger during travel. It also indicated reunions, or detours leading to opportunities. Did it show what had happened to Magnus? Or did it warn of what might happen to them if they left Haardvik?

"Mother, there's no reason for you and Silvi to go." Eirik crossed his arms as he stood in the common room. "Asa and I can take my longship. If there's any danger between there and here, I don't want you and Silvi exposed to it. Besides, Magnus and Leif were with Rorik. I doubt anyone would dare approach them. If something did happen, Rorik would send word here. Someone has to remain behind."

"I'll stay." Silvi sat in the shadows on a bench attached to the wall. She had never been farther away from Haardvik than the nearby villages. Never mind that she wanted to travel around Scandinavia to go to Uppsala. She didn't want to go anywhere now. She'd never even been on a ship.

They ignored her.

"Nuallen is very adept at protecting me." Lifa nodded at the man who stood near her.

"It is my honor to see you safe in all situations." He inclined his head to her, a slight smile curling the side of his mouth. He was of an age with Lifa, in his forties, but he was still an imposing man. And during the winter, they had found out how deadly he could be.

"The danger in Silvi's vision was to Magnus, not to us." Lifa's voice was firm.

"I said, I'll stay here." As they continued to argue, Silvi leaned back. What was the point? No one ever listened to her. If they had, she would already be several years into her studies. Instead, she remained in her mother's shadow, always the daughter behind the treasured son. Not that her parents hadn't cherished her. They could not have loved her more.

Sometimes, that wasn't enough.

There was no point in remaining. She had no say about their decision. They'd tell her when they finished debating, but it was obvious what the answer would be. No one could deny her mother, not even Eirik.

Sighing, she walked outside. She wrapped her shawl around herself, against the coolness of the early spring night. The moon was as it should be, bright, full, and shining. She lifted her face to it.

The love of her parents and her brother had shone on her all her life, just as the moon's light did. It was all that stood between her and the pain of living in this world, a pain so overwhelming it bit away at her from within. And now, they wanted to drag her out into that world. The great temple would have shielded her, so the thought of traveling to it had never frightened her. But this, this was different. In this journey she would not only travel through the unknown, but the destination, Thorsfjell itself, was also the unknown.

Asa had told her about the village. It sounded like no place else she had ever heard of with its windswept tundra in the heights above it, and the deep forests around it. Cool winds played off the glaciers in the distance. All was serene, and one could feel the power in the mountains. The land itself pulsed with the footsteps of the gods. Or so Asa claimed.

And then, there was Magnus. A few days ago, she'd faltered in her resolve. No longer. Eirik would never force her to marry. Even in the ancient stories, whenever a woman was made to wed, it never ended well. She had that defense, if nothing else. And there was another ultimate type of defense every woman had against a marriage she didn't want. Divorce. All men knew it.

The breeze picked up. Strange. The night was so clear, and it had been calm only a moment before. Perhaps it was a sign.

If she had the nerve, if she could hold on to her dreams hard enough, she could be free. Of brothers, husbands, everyone. She would have the gold she'd need to travel to the temple, and there she'd have the life she'd always wanted. After she studied, and learned, and became what she was destined to be, no one could tell her what to do.

For once, and forever after that, everyone would have to listen to her.

Approaching the village of Thorsfjell
Lustrafjorden, Sognefjell, Norway

Now Silvi knew what it was like to fly on the back of a dragon.

All the way up the coast, they'd flown over the waves in Eirik's ship, faster than she'd ever thought possible. Eirik told her that the square sail lifted the vessel up and the tiny bubbles of air that became trapped under the overlapped planks on the sides made the sailing smoother. She'd stood on the bow, behind Asa's carved dragon, and imagined herself truly flying. Bending as much as a hand's length, the ship slithered through the water like a living thing. It was sublime, and for the first time, she'd felt free. Seabirds soared alongside them, and great black and white fish that breathed air leaped in the distance.

The ship was open through most of its length. There were only the braces that held the ship together, which the men could sit on to row. But it had a small aft deck for the helmsman to stand on, and Eirik had covered it with a tent of sailcloth for Lifa, Asa, and her to sleep under. He slept outside with his men. On a longship, all were equal. Eirik hoisted sails along with the crew, and rowed when they moved through the tighter areas of the fjords. He ate with them and even gamed alongside them, but no one could doubt that he was the jarl. The respect his men showed him proved it.

Two years ago, Eirik had commissioned Rorik's shipbuilders to make the vessel for his father. Ivar had not lived to see it. The marauders killed him when Hakon invaded Haardvik, and now that Eirik was jarl, the ship, *The Wind of Njord*, was his. It was massive, with twenty pairs of oars, and any ship they'd seen on the seas had given them a wide berth. He'd allowed Silvi to hold the steering board, set on the right side of the stern. The ship had responded to her slightest touch. The feeling of power under her hand stayed with her even after she'd relinquished the helm back to Eirik.

Silvi wanted to stay outside, even to sleep, not wanting to miss anything. But that wouldn't be seemly. So she stayed under the tent with Lifa at night. During the day that they were on the ocean, though, she took in the sea, the sun, and the wind that carried them farther north.

She'd been so afraid of this journey. She'd never dreamt their land was so large. They'd sailed for more than a day between the fjords, and still the coast, and the islands guarding it, continued north into the distance as they'd turned inland. If only they could sail on forever. Who'd have thought she'd love the sea so much? But then, she was Norse and they did have the sea in their blood. Her life had been so limited. What else had she missed? And what else would she never experience if she retreated to the temple to live out her life? She might experience this only once more—when she traveled to Uppsala.

Now, the journey was almost ended. They lowered their sail as they approached the beach at the end of the fjord. Silvi moved to the bow along with Asa and Eirik. The *knörrs* were there, on the sand, and looked undamaged. Two longships sat on the beach beside them.

Eirik nodded toward them. "Those are Rorik's ships. Kaia commands one of them. That they're here means something happened. He wouldn't have parted with them otherwise, when raiding season is upon us."

Several men stood beside the vessels, watching, their swords unsheathed.

Asa stepped in front of him. "Those are Magnus's men. They don't know who we are." She climbed up and hung on to the dragonhead prow piece, waving to them. They stared at her for a moment, then sheathed their swords and raised their arms, yelling a greeting.

The great ship slid onto the beach and the men took the lines to pull them up farther.

Eirik and Asa jumped into the shallow water. Magnus's men pulled a high-wheeled cart alongside the *Wind* for Silvi and Lifa to disembark on. Nuallen helped Silvi into it, but he picked up a protesting Lifa and carried her.

"Nuallen, I'm not so old that I cannot climb out of a ship."

"You're not old at all, Lifa. But it's my duty to guard you, and that includes making certain you don't drown." He set her down in the cart.

She brushed off her gown. "In knee-deep water?" She was blushing.

The men rolled the cart up onto the shore and helped the women down. The land rocked under Silvi's feet and she swayed.

"Have to get your land legs back," Asa said as she walked to her brother's men. "Amund, how are my brothers? And the warriors? Did they get back safely?"

The red-haired warrior gave her a quizzical look. "Both the jarl and Leif are well, mistress. That whoreson, Toke, attacked us, though. Ambushed us at the outer islands. But it wasn't any trouble. All of us returned with little more than scratches, though we gave Ran a good time that night with Toke's drowned men. We'd already beaten them, but Toke turned tail and fled when he saw Rorik returning with his entire fleet. A sight that was, too. At least Toke only had coastal *knörrs*. If he'd had his longship, he'd have had more men and more speed. We wouldn't have had time to prepare. Of course, if we'd had warships, he wouldn't dare even try."

Asa let out a breath and Silvi murmured her thanks to the gods.

Eirik gathered Asa into his arms and kissed the top of her head. She smiled at him, then addressed the men. "Are there any horses at the farmstead?"

"Yes, mistress. We'll get them for you." Two of them ran off toward a small house at the base of the nearest mountain.

She looked at all of them. "We keep horses here and at the village for traveling back and forth. My family owns this land and most of the valley between here and Thorsfjell, where we do our farming. We'll follow this stream until we reach the path that takes us up into the mountain." She pointed to the shallow brook winding into the distance.

The men brought their belongings off the ship as they waited for the horses. Lifa had had Silvi bring most of her clothing and jewelry. Her runes. Too many of her things, in fact. Just how long were they going to stay here? Asa was to pack her own possessions to bring back to Haardvik, but that shouldn't take long. Lifa and Eirik had brought many things. Why? It wasn't as though they were going to visit a king or anyone else. Unless . . .

Silvi looked out across the fjord waters and gritted her teeth. Her mother and Eirik planned for her to marry Magnus. They would need many fine clothes for the wedding and feasting, and she would need all her most personal things, like her clothing and jewelry. And runes. That was why Eirik had been so insistent that she come with them. She lifted her chin. She had something to say about that.

A cold wind blew off the mountains, sweeping down through the valley. She closed her eyes and breathed deep. It smelled of ice and trees and something wild. This was far more isolated than Haardvik was. There were always traders and allies coming and going back home.

A stillness lay on this land, as though no one had ever walked here before. It was like the world was new, and the gods Odin, Vili, and Ve hadn't created man and woman yet.

She kept her back to the others as they talked and laughed. Now that they knew Magnus and Leif were well, their mood had lightened with relief. Hers, however, had worsened. She had to keep telling herself Eirik would never force her to wed. Magnus didn't seem the type of man to take an unwilling woman. But men did strange things when they desired something, whether it was women, gold, or possessions. Magnus desired her. It lay in his beautiful blue eyes as he looked at her. That might not be enough, and it certainly wasn't enough for marriage. What else could Eirik offer Magnus to entice him to wed her? To keep her from becoming a priestess?

The men brought back horses. They tied their belongings onto the packhorses and mounted. As Silvi gathered her reins, she glanced into one of the beached *knörrs*. Dark stains splattered the inside walls of the vessel. They spread over the floor of the front deck as well. Blood. Her stomach dropped.

The battle hadn't been so easy after all. What was it the man had said? If Magnus had warships, Toke wouldn't be a threat anymore with his slow *knörrs* and single longship.

She tightened her hands on the reins. Warships were exactly what Eirik could offer him.

The king was dead. As usual.

Magnus frowned at the *tafl* board as Leif gave him a triumphant grin. His twin had slaughtered him again. Asa was the only one who could beat Leif, and now, with her gone, he would be insufferable.

"No." Magnus grabbed a playing piece away as Leif set it on the board. "I'm not playing you again. Find someone else."

"Jarl Magnus!" Sjurd, a young man who worked in the stables, ran in through the open front doors. "It's the mistress Asa, and Eirik. I saw them coming up the mountain. Also an older woman and man. And many warriors. They're almost here."

He frowned at Leif as they crossed the common room. "They weren't supposed to be here until later this summer."

"Maybe Asa wanted her clothes. You know how women are."

They strode into the yard. "More likely she left a weapon or two here. They couldn't have heard about the attack already."

Leif chuckled. "I'll wager you Silvi or Lifa had a vision about it. What will you bet? Your ivory-handled dagger."

"That's ridiculous. I'm not wagering you anything." Sjurd had mentioned an older woman, but not a younger one. Could something have happened to Silvi? They would never leave her behind, no matter how well-guarded Haardvik was. Or had she already left for Uppsala? Only a few days had passed, and Eirik had been adamant that she not go. His heart pounding, Magnus lengthened his stride until he came to the head of the path. The group from Haardvik were just rounding the last curve.

There she was, in the midst of the riders. Sjurd might have missed her, but Magnus never would. His heart slowed with relief. Asa saw him and waved. As they rode into the yard, she swung her leg over her horse's neck and slid off. She ran to him and nearly laid him flat as she all but leaped on him.

"Magnus, you're all right? We were so worried, we had to come." She clung to him as though she'd never let go.

Eirik jumped off his horse. "Silvi had a vision. Of a dragon being attacked on the seas. She felt it was you."

Leif barked out a laugh. "Your ivory-handled dagger. I'll get it from you this evening."

"I never bet you . . . Oh Hel." He wrapped his arms around Asa, but drank in Silvi's beauty. She dismounted with her usual grace, ducking her head, avoiding his gaze. A tint of color touched her pale cheek as she patted her horse's neck.

Nuallen helped Lifa down from her horse. He set her on her feet as though she were made of the finest glass. She smiled her thanks.

Magnus carefully pried Asa off of him and gave her a kiss on the forehead. "Come, all of you. Eat and drink. You've traveled long."

With Asa under his arm, he led the way into the longhouse. The serving girl, Birgitta, was already setting out plates and cups, but when she saw Asa, she came to her, laughing.

"I heard you married Jarl Eirik, mistress. I always knew you would. I'm so happy for you." They walked toward the kitchen, arm in arm. The girl had always been more of a friend to Asa than a maid. She would likely follow Asa to Haardvik, and since she and Sjurd were fond of each other, Magnus would probably have to relinquish the young man also. Nuallen hovered over Lifa. Leif had been sniffing around after Kaia and, with as deadly as she was, he would be lucky not to lose an appendage. Of one kind or another.

Was everyone around here falling in love?

Silvi wandered the common room and stopped at one of the pillars. A vine spiraled its way up the post, birds and flowers intertwined in it. She ran her hand along the design, her eyes wide.

Magnus filled a cup and brought it to her. "You must be thirsty. Will you have some ale?"

"My thanks." She lowered her gaze at she took the cup. "Did Asa carve this post? It looks like the dragon on Eirik's ship."

"You have a sharp eye, Silvi. She did all the carvings here in the room. Sometimes she got bored during the summer when she was too young to come trading with us. Nothing was safe from her knife." He leaned his shoulder against the pillar. "So you had a vision of me?"

She colored. "Not exactly you. It was a dragon."

"Is that how you see me? As a huge beast? I would never hurt you."

She raised her eyes to his. "The dragon is not always evil. It's strong and powerful. Its beauty is like that of gold and the stars. Nothing can stand against it. It's—" She looked away. "It's Asa's guardian spirit. So perhaps, because you're her brother, it guards you as well."

"That's good to know."

Asa came to them and took Silvi's arm. "All the food is laid out. Why don't you sit down and eat? After that, I'll show you to the chamber you'll share with your mother, and you can rest if you like." As they walked away, Asa looked back at Magnus and gave him a sweet smile. The little conniver.

He pushed off the post but stayed where he was, watching Silvi as

Asa introduced her to some of the villagers who had come in. Word had spread that his sister was home, and people trickled in to see her. Soon, there would be a wave. They'd better put out more food and drink. Might as well make it a celebration.

He went to the table and took a plate to snag some of the food before it all disappeared.

Eirik joined him. "So when do you want to talk?"

Magnus speared a sausage with his knife. "Whenever you're ready. Do you want to rest until tomorrow, or start tonight?"

Eirik chuckled. "Start? Do you anticipate this taking so long?"

"Depends on what we talk about. The battle, or a wedding."

"Is there a difference?"

Magnus gave a short laugh. "You have a point." He looked toward the door as more villagers and a group of his warriors entered, yelling a greeting to Asa. "I have to play host until everyone has drunk themselves into a stupor. After that, we'll talk in my meeting room."

"I'll watch my own drinking, then. And do you have ale? If I have one more cup of mead . . ." He winced.

"Honeymoon over already?"

Eirik ladled mutton stew into a bowl. "Hardly. A woman must have thought of that wretched custom. An entire month of it? Give me good ale or beer any day."

"I'll tell Birgitta to make certain you get some."

"My thanks. Believe me."

Magnus sat down with his plate as Eirik made his way across the crowded room toward Asa. But Magnus didn't eat. This was it. Tonight held his future. A marriage, an increase in strength and political power, and a war averted. Or at least prepared for. He watched his people gather around Asa. This was the difference between life and death for them. If Toke attacked him every time he sailed past the coward's fjord, it jeopardized Magnus's ability to get to the markets. One of these days, they might lose a battle and their cargo. Trading was essential to their survival.

Longships and warriors were all well and good. But would he be able to afford Silvi's bride-price? He'd been ruthless with Asa's, wanting more for her than a king's daughter was worth. Would Eirik return the favor for Silvi? Magnus had the gold he'd received for Asa. He'd planned to use it to support the village. Now it might go right back where it came from, in which case getting to market would be even more imperative. Of course, at that point, he'd have the longships.

And Silvi.

"How old do you think the boy was?" Eirik leaned back in his chair and propped his ankle on his knee, a cup of ale in his hand.

Magnus sighed. "Not more than fourteen winters, I would say. Our youth often begin fighting by then, but it was a shock to see him. If only I'd looked first."

"If he had been a skilled warrior, and you hesitated, you'd be dead. You did the only thing you could do. React."

"I could have taught him a good lesson and sent him back to his idiot father."

"Even young children have been known to exact revenge killings on their families' enemies. The boy probably would have grown up in Toke's footsteps and continued to attack you."

"At least he would have grown up. I could have handled the rest of it. I'll see his face before me as he went into the water for a long time." Eirik had, no doubt, seen much worse when he'd gone raiding throughout the world with Rorik. When all was said and done, Magnus was just a trader. He fought when he had to, but only when forced. Killing never came easy.

The celebration of Asa's return had gone on until well after dark. Some of the warriors were still drinking in the common room when he'd given up and caught Eirik's eye. They'd left just as a brawl was threatening to start. As they'd closed the door to the meeting room, fists had begun flying. As long as no weapons were involved, or they didn't break too much furniture, he didn't care. The women had gone to bed earlier, so he let the men enjoy themselves.

He'd related the details of the battle to Eirik, including Toke's threat to destroy anything Magnus held.

"I wanted you to know where things stand before we speak of my marrying Silvi."

Eirik inclined his head. "I appreciate your honesty. It makes me uncomfortable to know Toke could target this place again. That is, if he was behind the outcasts' attacks this past winter."

"He lives over the mountain in the valley to the southeast, but he's not strong enough to attack Thorsfjell. He needed others to do it for him, and they're all dead now. Only thugs would follow him, which gave him a connection with those outlaws over the winter. He's too much of a fool for many men to follow him. Besides, he doesn't have the money to attract the honorable ones, and I do. It's part of the reason he resents me."

Magnus took a drink of ale. "Where I'm vulnerable is on the water. Rorik's ships can't stay here forever. The entrance to Toke's fjord is right next to mine leading into the Sognefjorden and he could waylay me again and again. He has smaller *knörrs*, but he got a long-ship from somewhere and can still do some damage to me. This time he got more than he bargained for—a dead son and another enemy. One of these days, though, he could get lucky. Silvi won't be going to the markets with us. If she stays here, she will be safe."

He leaned forward. "I need those three ships you offered me. And the warriors. And the gold to support them. I could put an end to his pirating. All the other jarls and merchants in this region would be beholden to me. That would strengthen my position. If the offer is still open, that is." He waited.

Eirik didn't answer. He drew a pattern in a puddle that their cups had left on the table. He'd done that before, when they were negotiating for Asa. Then he regarded Magnus, his eyes sharp.

"The offer still stands. I think you're strong enough here to repel any direct attacks, as you did with that bunch over the winter."

"I've thought of what you said when you cast my runes back then." The casting had haunted him ever since. "You said I tend to hesitate, and it would cause harm to someone I love. I did so with Asa, and it almost ruined her life. I think I do it because I'm concerned about making the right decision. I've considered attacking Toke first this time, do some damage to him as a warning. But he'd run, and the only thing I'd hurt would be the people of Bygvik. They've suffered enough."

"You could take this to the *Thing* when it meets in a couple of months. All free men will be at the gathering and will hear your grievances. He attacked you with no provocation. They can vote on what should be done to resolve this."

"That's weeks off. I need to get to the markets before then. It's something to keep in mind, yes. Even if they might vote in my favor, it's still up to me to enforce whatever they might decide. I don't see gaining any revenge from them I can't do for myself."

"You called Toke a *nithingr*. He has the right to try to kill you for that. You could let him make the attempt, then slay him."

"He'll never try."

"Then I suppose we have a marriage to negotiate."

"We've already negotiated the dowry. That leaves only the bride-price." Magnus wanted to hold his breath, but Eirik would notice. It would give him an advantage to know how much Magnus wanted Silvi. Eirik also had a lot to lose if Silvi made good on her desire to become a priestess. She would be lost to them all.

Eirik smiled, just a bit. "I know you have the gold from Asa's bride-price, since I gave it to you at the wedding." He paused and their eyes met and clashed. "Half of that. It's not that I think Silvi's worth so much less. Quite the contrary. But the bride-price you wanted for Asa was exorbitant, and we both know it. Though she's worth every coin and then some. Besides, you have need of it. It's still a large sum. It doesn't insult Silvi. In fact, it would even things out, for us both to receive the same amount."

"Done." Magnus shook his head. "Do we have any other female relatives between us? We can just keep on exchanging the same pile of gold back and forth."

Eirik laughed. "There's always Leif and Kaia. But that's Rorik's business, and I'm not getting involved with that."

"Nor I." They raised their cups to each other.

Eirik leaned back and regarded his ale. Magnus waited. He had come to know Eirik very well during the long winter. There was more.

Eirik's eyes narrowed. "I won't force her to marry, just as we didn't force Asa to marry me. It'll be up to you to convince her."

"I'd like to be the one to tell her. After we've had a little time to get to know each other. I'll show her around Thorsfjell, introduce her to the people here. If she can accept them, it might make it easier for her to accept this marriage."

"Don't be too surprised if she already knows about it." Eirik held his hand up, palm out. "I don't mean through visions or runes. She's a very smart, sensible woman. She can figure it out. We had her bring almost all her possessions with her. She doesn't have much. Things mean little to her. But it was more than she would need for a short stay. If she agrees, and only if she agrees, we can have the *handsal*, sealing the contract. With all these warriors staying here, we won't have any problem finding six men to witness it."

"Agreed." He rubbed the bridge of his nose. "I just wish I understood her better."

"If you are to marry her, first thing tomorrow is as good a time to start as any."

"In other words, you don't understand her either."

"I'm not certain I even understand Asa yet, though at least she's a warrior. That puts us on somewhat even footing. Silvi can be practical when she needs to be. She was trained to run a household, but any woman can do that."

"You mean in between doing whatever it is she does for the gods."

"She brings a connection to the gods, yes, which never hurts. She's also a rune reader, a healer, and is versed in the ways of the ancient wisdom and herb-lore. She is wise and compassionate, thinking of others before herself. And I'm certain you've noticed her beauty. She'll be a good wife once she accepts it."

Magnus leaned back. "I thought we started this conversation with me trying to convince you. Now it sounds like you're trying to convince me."

"All that matters is that you convince *her*. And if it doesn't work, my mother may step in. She doesn't want to lose Silvi to these foolish dreams of hers any more than I do." He sighed. "Believe me, my mother may not be a warrior, but she always knows just where to strike."

Chapter Four

"May I join you?"

Silvi looked up from her breakfast straight into Magnus's eyes. They were very blue this morning. His hair was freshly washed and combed, and he wore narrow trousers and a fine linen shirt, open at his throat. His belt had an intricate gold buckle and he wore a gold twisted-wire wrist cuff. He hadn't been dressed so well yesterday, but then, he hadn't been expecting them. He held a plate full of sausages. He must like them; he'd eaten them at last night's meal also.

"Silvi?"

"Of course. Please." She played with the spoon in her porridge as he slid onto the bench opposite her.

"Did you sleep well last night?" He nodded his thanks to Birgitta, who brought him a mug of buttermilk.

"I don't remember climbing into bed at all. I hadn't slept well on the ship, so I was more tired than I thought."

"You didn't hear the brawl?"

"What brawl?"

"The one in here last night. It went on for quite a while. Several of my men won't be reporting for work today. They have splitting heads from either too much beer or too much fighting."

She smiled and ducked her head. "I didn't hear anything. I truly needed to sleep."

"It must have been unnerving being on a ship for the first time."

"That wasn't why I didn't sleep." She set down her spoon. "I was so excited. There were sounds I wasn't accustomed to, like the waves against the sides of the ship, the wind in the sails, the men talking through the night. The rocking should have put me to sleep, but instead I wanted to be out there, standing at the bow, watching the moon's light on the water."

He grinned at her and her heart paused. "You liked being on the ship?"

"Oh, yes. I wasn't certain I would at first. It made me realize how big the world is, and that was a bit frightening. But I soon grew to love it."

He chuckled. "You only sailed for a couple of days, and much of that was along the fjords. That wasn't even a small bit of our own land, much less the world. You could spend a lifetime sailing and never glimpse most of it."

"I know. Eirik sailed with Rorik for three years. He said it took months to get to some of the places. I can't imagine that."

"It takes six months to reach Miklagard. If you arrive there at all. It's very dangerous in the rivers. My father was killed near one of the rapids when they portaged their ship."

"I'm sorry, Magnus. That must have been difficult."

"It was. I was too young to assume the title, but I did what I had to do. And Leif made it home, so at least there was that."

"Your family is very close. I saw it when you were at Haardvik."

"After our father's death, our mother chose to return to her homeland, so we only had each other to depend on. I took what he left us and built on it. I don't travel the eastern routes, as he did. I go only to the closer markets like Kaupang, Birka, Hedeby, and Paviken in Gotland."

"Judging from what I've seen here, you've done very well."

"You haven't seen much yet. Would you like to come with me around Thorsfjell when we're finished with breakfast? I need to speak to some of the people about their cargo for our first trip. It would do you some good to get out and walk a bit after being on the boat. It's not usually this warm so early in the spring this far in the interior, so we'd best enjoy the fine day while we can. We might still have a couple of months of cold ahead of us."

She did want to see the village, but she'd thought she would go with Lifa that afternoon. Her mother was out reading runes for the women until then. Still, if Eirik was going to ask her to marry Magnus, she'd best find out what manner of man he was. Marriage wasn't something she wanted, but it would be difficult to fight both her brother and mother. And Magnus. *If* he wanted her. It didn't seem to matter what she wanted.

"Of course I'll go with you."

He nodded and turned to his breakfast. She nibbled at her porridge. If they were married, would they have other mornings like this? Eating together and discussing the days' events? Would they have arisen from the same bed? Would he have . . .

She lost her appetite. Setting down her spoon, she took a sip of milk. It would calm her stomach. The last thing she needed now was for the pain to begin.

People in the common room interrupted Magnus to ask his advice or to let him know of difficulties they were having. His warriors stopped at the table to receive their orders. He dealt with all of it as though born to it. Which he was. His power flowed from him, as much a part of him as his arms. Strong, well-made arms.

To get away from that particular line of thought, she glanced around the room. Leif and Asa were in the far corner, playing *tafl*, from the looks of it. Leif didn't seem pleased. Asa gave him a smile that made him wince. She'd seen Asa use that smile on Eirik, and it didn't bode well.

Asa made a move, then took one of Leif's pieces. He clutched his chest as though he'd been wounded, studied the board, and moved another piece. As Asa countered his move, Kaia walked past, toward the open door. She was long-legged and tall, as were most shield-maidens. Her black hair was braided behind her and she had her hand on the hilt of her sword.

Leif leaned back against the wall behind him. "Kaia, why don't you come and help me here? My sister has mortally wounded me and my king is threatened. Again."

Without pausing, she said, "I don't heal wounds. I cause them." As she strode out of the door, the other warriors hooted in appreciation. Leif burst out laughing. Silvi smiled as well. Although her cousin intimidated her, she had always liked her.

"You'd think Leif would know how to handle a shieldmaiden since our sister is one," Magnus said.

Silvi shook her head. "There's no handling Kaia. Not even Rorik tries, and you know what he's like. Kings don't challenge him, but she does. I think he likes it, though. But then, she's his sister, so it doesn't count. Everyone else bows and scrapes to him. It must get old. Someone has to knock him back a bit."

"What would he do if he ever found a woman like that?"

"I don't think she exists. They see him and fall at his feet. Do whatever he wants. It's always been that way and he expects it now."

"I agree. That would get old." His smile was warm. "Better a bit of a challenge. That makes it all the more appreciated when it does come."

Heat rose in her cheeks.

He stood and held out his hand. "Are you finished?"

She stared at his hand for a moment. No man touched her. But then, no man other than her brother and her father had ever looked into her eyes before, either. And if he became her husband, he would do much more than that. It wouldn't be wise to antagonize him. She put her fingers on his palm.

He led her out into the bright yard. Young boys ran past them, yelling, brandishing wooden swords. Women and girls sat outside, weaving ribbons on board looms, enjoying the unusually warm weather. An old man sat on a barrel, carving a soapstone bowl. Everyone greeted them, and when he introduced her as Eirik's sister, the women gathered around her.

"Silvi is a rune reader like Eirik is," Magnus said. "I hear she's very good."

One woman pressed a beautiful piece of ribbon into her hands. "Eirik made a rune for my child when he was sick. He got well. I will always be grateful."

"It was my brother, not me." She tried to give it back.

"It is what you do as well. My thanks." The woman stepped away.

Another said, "He read my runes and told me I should speak to a man I've had my eye on. I did, and now we're going to marry this fall."

"He told me I would bear a child this year." A young woman placed a hand on her belly. "I haven't even told my husband yet, but I think Eirik was right."

The women crowded even closer. "Would you read mine, mistress? Please see what my future holds." One of them reached for her.

Magnus glanced at her, his hand tightening around hers. "It has been a long voyage for Silvi. She might not be ready for that yet."

People never came too close to her at home. They loved her, but respected her need to remain apart. These women didn't know that. Didn't know her. Such peace and warmth came from them that she wanted to bask in it. It was strange and wonderful. "It's all right, Magnus. I don't mind. I did, after all, bring my set. I can read for anyone who wishes it."

"In a few days," Magnus said. "When you're better rested."

As the women thanked her, joy filled her. Always in Haardvik, people went to her mother for such things. And why not? She was a renowned rune mistress, trained at the temple, known throughout the south. These women, too, should go to Lifa since she was reading elsewhere in the village. And yet, they looked to her.

Silvi had read for people at home, but she knew all of them. Would that make a difference? Could the runes speak to her in a strange place? Eirik had an innate talent for seeing into people and, no doubt, it aided him. She had little knowledge of people. The runes weren't her strongest talent, as they were her mother's and Eirik's. Still, she had to try.

In the eyes of these women there was the same hope, excitement, and respect that followed Lifa whenever she visited a village. Except this time, it was for her.

They stopped by several cottages and Magnus spoke to the artisans there, introducing her as though it was important they know her. She couldn't remember all their names, but she was amazed at the beauty of their work—the gold- and silversmiths, the stone- and woodcarvers, the weavers and spinners. A glassmaker formed beads with colors swirling inside, and he gave her one of them to close the neck of a gown. Many of the artisans worked outside, if they could, for it was a rare, beautiful day. As they left one of the houses, Magnus took her hand. Her palm tingled where he grasped it.

"There's Ingeborg. She's our healer. One of my warriors was injured in the battle and I want to see how he's doing. He lives down in the valley, but she would know anyhow. I think she knows everything here."

He led her to the front of a small cottage where an older woman was tending an herb garden. "Ingeborg, I've brought someone for you to meet." They stopped in front of her as the woman straightened. "This is Silvi, Eirik's sister."

"I heard he and Asa were back, along with his family. I would know that she is his sister. Their eyes are the same shape. Welcome, child. Please come in, out of the sun." When they stepped into the small house, Ingeborg reached for Silvi's hands, and Magnus had to relinquish his hold on her. "Such soft hands you have. So beautiful. Are you trained in the healing arts, child? You should be."

Silvi drew them gently from her grasp. "I know of them from my mother. I've followed her all my life and helped her. I don't know as much as she does, but I can assist with some things. And I do know herbs."

"That is good. All women should have such knowledge."

"Just don't get a belly wound while you're here, Silvi." Magnus regarded Ingeborg with a straight face. "She'll pour my expensive wine, imported from the Rhineland, inside you, then stuff you full of leeks. It's better, some think, to die and go to Valhalla. At least you'd be safe from her tender mercies there."

"I give you leeks so I can smell if your stomach has been opened. I'm just a humble healer woman, and I do my best to keep all of you from visiting Valhalla too soon. Sometimes I have to wrestle the gods for one of you. Now and again, they let me win."

"And we thank you." His voice was soft.

"Humph." She turned her faded gaze on Silvi. "That would be the day. They come to me with the tiniest splinter, even the strongest of them."

"We do not."

"You'd be surprised who slinks in here, whining about nothing, when no one is about."

He grinned. "I think you spin tales, old woman. None of my warriors whine."

"They whine. And they show me more respect than you do. Don't forget, I pulled you from your mother's womb, though you fought your way past Leif to come out first. I had to push him back inside so you could have your way. Some things never change."

He laughed. "He always says he let me slide by first so he wouldn't have to be jarl one day. He doesn't want the responsibility."

"Then he should thank me for sparing him that fate. And you should be mindful that I gave you the title."

"I think my father had something to do with that. And, at times, I'm tempted to trade places with Leif."

Silvi smiled at their banter. Magnus was so free and easy, his face soft with the affection that came of longtime friendship. What would it be like to see it soften like that for her one day? For him to smile his beautiful smile at her? She drew in a sharp breath. What was she thinking? She moved away from him and perused the bowls and jars of herbs as they discussed the wounded warrior.

Of course he was showing her Thorsfjell. He hoped she would like it and the people. The problem was, she did. They'd already spent the better part of the day going from house to house, as he spoke with the artisans about the upcoming voyage to Kaupang. It was like no place else she'd ever been. Granted, she hadn't traveled far from home, but small villages and farmsteads lay within half a day's ride of it. Her mother and she had visited them frequently. None of them were like this place.

The people here radiated peace. They found joy in their life's work, and their efforts supported their village. From what she could gather as he spoke with them, he returned to them the gold and silver they wanted for their wares and kept a small amount for taking the items to the markets. This, he reinvested in supplies and foods for the village. There didn't seem to be much left for himself, but that didn't appear to bother him. He was looking out for his people.

The idea for the village was unique. She'd never heard of such an arrangement. The mountains kept them isolated and made it difficult to grow food and have enough pasture for animals. They needed for themselves all they could grow and raise; they'd had to create other things they could trade and sell. The things they made provided them with a way to survive.

Except, Toke might be lurking at the entrance to the fjord, blocking the way to the ocean beyond it. They would have to run a blockade every time they left. Before, Magnus and he had been evenly matched with their *knörrs*, though Magnus's were larger and could hold a greater number of men. Somehow, Toke had acquired a warship. If only Magnus had longships and more warriors.

She could bring those to him.

"Silvi?" His voice close to her made her jump. "I'm sorry. I didn't mean to startle you. We'd best be going. You'd probably like to rest before the evening meal."

"That sounds good. I've enjoyed meeting everyone and seeing Thorsfjell, but I am a little tired."

Ingeborg followed them to the door. "Have you taken Silvi above?"

"Not yet. I thought I might tomorrow."

"Why? What's above?" Silvi stepped outside as Magnus held the door open for her. Ingeborg joined them among the fragrant herbs.

"I think I'll keep that a surprise. It's something you'll want to see." He inclined his head to the healer. "My thanks for the good news about Bertil's wounds. They weren't serious, but even small cuts can fester."

"He'll be back with you for the upcoming voyage. He wanted to come here now, but I threatened him with one of my concoctions. He'll stay in the valley and heal."

"A wise man." He grabbed Silvi's hand and pulled her out of the garden as Ingeborg reached for a broom nearby, a look of revenge on her lined face.

But she left the broom where it was. "Come back anytime, Silvi. Just don't bring him. No respect for his elders."

Silvi laughed and looked up at Magnus. He was staring at her, his gaze searching her face. When it came to rest on her lips, she ducked her head, her cheeks heating.

He touched her under her chin with such gentleness, she almost didn't feel it. But it blasted through her senses like a wave striking her in the sea. She had to lift her head to escape the contact. It was what he wanted, for it forced her to look at him.

"Your laugh is so rare. I wish I could hear it more often."

"These have not been the easiest of times. The attack on Haardvik and my father's death. All the people we lost. The terrible winter with Hakon and his men. The depravities our women had to endure." A shudder rocked through her. "The battle to win back our village. Then there was the attack on you and our having to come here so quickly. And now you have this trouble with Toke. I feel all this. It's not been easy. The only light was Eirik and Asa's wedding."

"I know. But the fight with Toke is a problem that you don't need to worry about."

Didn't she? She and the ships she'd bring were the solution to it. He was still looking at her mouth, a strange intensity in his eyes. She lowered her gaze and stepped back. Behind her, Ingeborg chuckled. Silvi glanced at her. The healer was still standing in her garden, watching them with a great smile. "Ah yes, Magnus is the first, as always. But not too long, either, for Leif, I think."

Magnus gave her an indulgent look. "Best take some of your own concoctions yourself, old woman. Your mind is going."

Ingeborg laughed and walked back inside her house, waving her hand in dismissal of his suggestion. They made their way back to the longhouse, but Silvi kept her arms crossed lest he try to take her hand again.

She tightened the one he'd held, her skin still tingling. His touch did the strangest things to her. Not how contact with others usually affected her. She wanted to shrink away from them, afraid to feel what they were inside. They lived in a brutal world, and sometimes that harshness lived inside people. She could always feel it rushing out at her, trying to break into her, to drag her down into its darkness. She had long ago learned to stand against it. To hold herself apart. It was why she'd always envisioned Uppsala as her golden island, alone in a storm-tossed sea.

Everything was different here. Magnus was unique among so many other men, and so was his touch. That was why she couldn't let him touch her again—it was pleasant. Too pleasant. He was the tempest that could blow her off course from where she needed to go. Her island.

Once she got back to the room she shared with her mother, she lay down on the bed, closed her eyes, and called the vision. Always the sight of the island calmed her, letting her see where her destiny lay.

Her stomach knotted. It had been coming closer as the months went by. Now, it was smaller again, its mountains less distinct. The sea was dark, churning. A strong current swirled around her. Why was this happening? Now, of all times?

Magnus. She sat up, staring across the empty room. He was the current pulling her away from the place she'd dreamed of all her life. Or was it the gods? Could they be taking it away from her because she was wavering in her devotion to them? Perhaps they were warning her, telling her that if she wasn't strong enough, the things of this world would sweep her away from them. She wouldn't be worthy of them.

The pain in her stomach hit hard, burning like the sun. She hugged herself, and leaned over the bed furs. Were they punishing her? This happened whenever she had doubts or worries about her desire to serve them. They might be testing her. She had to strengthen her resolve to stand firm for what she wanted. What she had always wanted. Only if she remained determined would she be worthy of them. And of her destiny.

A destiny that didn't include Magnus. He was the tide threatening to carry her beyond her island into the vast unknown. Everyone knew that therein lay dragons.

After Silvi went to her room, Magnus sat at a table with Eirik. He was drinking a mug of ale. Magnus nodded his thanks to Birgitta when she set a brimming mug in front of him.

"Still watching Asa trounce Leif at *tafl*?" He took a long drink.

"Some things never change." Eirik smiled as Asa made a move and Leif frowned at her. "Except it's warmer now, thank the gods. Your winters here are far colder than ours on the coast."

"I'll wager that's not all that's warmer." He glanced at Asa as she laughed at something Leif grumbled. "You are, after all, married now."

Eirik raised his mug. "And that type of warmth isn't up for discussion."

"As though I'd want to know. Asa would have both our heads."

As Magnus chuckled, two of his warriors came in the front doors, supporting a disheveled blond woman who stumbled between them. A boy of no more than ten winters entered behind them, but he was so weak, he sank to the floor. They weren't from Thorsfjell.

Magnus stood. "Amund, Dagr, what has happened?" He went to them as they settled the woman at one of the tables. Eirik, Asa, and Leif joined them.

"We saw her coming out of the woods from the east, Jarl. She's exhausted, and the youth is injured." Amund helped the boy stand. He brought him to the table to sit beside the woman.

"I'm Fastny and this is my son, Jarpi." Her voice was hoarse. "We came around the mountain from Bygvik. Toke sent his men after us. I beg you for sanctuary for my son, if not for me." Tears filled her eyes as she gazed at Magnus.

"Both of you are welcome here." It wasn't the first time people from that village had fled to escape Toke's viciousness. He took her hand as he looked at Birgitta. "Get food, and then send someone for Ingeborg." As the girl left, he patted Fastny's hand. "Ingeborg is our healer. She'll help you."

"Not for me. Jarpi is hurt. Beaten. He needs something for his wounds."

The boy tried to hold his head up, to be stoic and proud. But his chin quivered as a tear slipped down his bruised cheek.

Magnus stepped to the boy. "Where are you hurt?"

After hesitating, Jarpi faced away from him. His shirt was shredded. Blood seeped from the whip marks across his back. That someone would do this to a child . . .

Magnus's blood ran hot, his hands fisting. "Someone get Ingeborg. *Now.*" Amund leaped for the door as everyone spoke at once.

"I'll look at him." Silvi's calm voice cut through the noise. The commotion must have awakened her. The room fell silent as she turned her concerned gaze to Fastny. "With your leave." The woman stared at her and nodded. Silvi smiled. "You'll be safe now. Magnus is a good man, and Thorsfjell will give you peace, as it does so many others." At the sound of her words, Fastny closed her eyes, her body sagging in relief.

Silvi went to the boy. "May I look at your wounds?"

"I'm fine." He threw back his shoulders, then winced. "My mother is weak. See to her first."

"She can tell us what happened while Silvi looks at your back," Magnus said.

Jarpi bit his lip and shifted around on the bench. Silvi didn't react to what she saw, except that her mouth tightened. "You're very brave to have protected your mother all the way here with the pain this must cause you." Her voice was light, but tension underlay it. "Very brave and strong. What a fine warrior you'll make."

"The pain's not so bad." He flinched as she touched his shirt.

"I need warm water and clean cloths to soak the material away from his skin." She continued examining the area.

"How did this happen?" Magnus pulled up a bench and sat facing the woman. "You said Toke's men chased you?" If they were still out there, he'd have to act fast. But first, he needed information.

"I live on a farmstead to the east of Bygvik. Toke took my son as a servant in his longhouse after the others fled. Yesterday, Jarpi spilled ale on the table and Toke beat him because of it. Jarpi ran away, returning to me. We couldn't stay, for they'd only drag him back and it would be even worse for him. I'd heard that others have found safety here. We came around the southern tip of the mountain. The men were behind us until this morning. I'm sorry to have brought them here with us, but I had to come. I'm a widow and we have no one to protect us."

"You do now." Magnus stood. "Dagr, gather any warriors you find and have them meet us behind the longhouse. Leif, get our swords and shields."

"Done." He crossed to Magnus's chamber.

"I'll get my weapons. I'm coming also." Eirik strode toward Asa's old room.

"If you think you're leaving me behind, think again." Asa ran after him.

Magnus grinned. Eirik had been right. Some things never changed.

They all met up near the woods behind the longhouse. "With any luck, Toke's men won't know Fastny and Jarpi have reached us," Magnus said. "They'll still be looking for them at the tip of the mountain. It's narrow between the slope and the fjord. We'll move through the woods and ambush them there."

"Then you'll need me." They all turned to Nuallen. No one had seen him approach from the shadow of the trees. His only weapon was a seax hanging below his belt.

"Since when do you part from Lifa?" Eirik looked surprised.

"Anything that threatens Thorsfjell, threatens Lifa. I must see to it. She's safe reading runes with other women, and Magnus's men guard them well. By going on ahead of you, I can circle around the outcasts and kill one or two. Their panic will drive the rest straight to you."

"You should have a sword." Magnus wouldn't underestimate the Northumbrian. He'd heard what he'd done over the winter in Haardvik, how he could slaughter men without their realizing what killed them.

"I don't even need this." He slapped the seax, then went ahead of them into the woods. The leaves didn't move as he passed. An instant later, he was gone without a trace.

"You owe me a good fight." Kaia stepped into the group and crossed her arms. Her gray-green eyes were hard, like an aged sword blade. "Rorik sent me here to help guard you, when I could have gone raiding this summer. I'm not happy."

Eirik eyed his cousin. "If she's not happy, let her fight. It's safer that way."

Magnus gave a short nod. He'd welcome another shieldmaiden.

Like she-wolves, they could be far more deadly than the men. With his warriors, their number and skill was such that no band of outcasts could escape them.

Traveling silent and swift, they reached the southern base of the mountain without encountering anyone. Dagr found Fastny and Jarpi's footprints, but not those of the outcasts. The whoresons were still east of them. Swords unsheathed, they kept each other in sight as they moved in a line through the trees.

Magus heard the outcasts' panicked shouts before he saw them. He signaled the others to draw in together, to protect each other if need be. They waited.

A group of men ran straight into them, their eyes wide, sweat pouring from their faces. They never had a chance. Magnus slashed the throat of one of them, then spun to face the next man. He fell before Magnus touched him. Leif had already slain him. Hefting his dripping blade, Magnus looked around.

Eirik had moved so fast, he'd slain three of the bastards before those in the back had even skidded to a stop. Asa darted around a large man faster than he could turn to face her, and buried her blade in the back of his neck. She followed Eirik through the melee.

Teeth bared in a savage smile, Kaia was like a lethal storm. Her eyes blazed as she parried a sword strike, then sliced her opponent across the stomach. With a backswing, she cut his throat as he fell. She left him and leaped on the back of another, reached around, and gutted him. Her scream matched his.

Magnus's warriors finished the rest of them off. The shrieks of the dying outcasts echoed off the mountain above. As the others checked the bodies, Magnus surveyed the slaughter. That was the only word for it. His men were, for the most part, uninjured. They had a few cuts and scrapes, but nothing requiring Ingeborg's skills.

"There were twelve of them." Leif sheathed his sword as he walked over.

"Fourteen." Nuallen emerged from the trees. "I killed two. The others stumbled across the bodies. When they found no marks on them, they panicked and ran. They shouted about the *landvaettir* being after them. As I understand your beliefs, those land spirits are offended by violence." He gave a wry look at the carnage around them. "I think this qualifies. We may be in trouble."

"The *landvaettir* are offended by men such as these. I'm protecting my side of the mountain. These are outcasts, and it is my right to slay them, as it is the right of any who come across them." Magnus nodded to his men. "Get their weapons, then leave the bodies for the wolves. When they don't return to Bygvik, Toke will know what happened."

He wiped his sword on the shirt of one of the fallen men, then sheathed it. It was fortunate that the woman and her son had reached Thorsfjell. If this group had found them, Fastny and Jarpi never would have made it back to Bygvik. Nor would their deaths have been easy or quick. He clenched his jaw.

It was unfortunate timing, though. Now that Silvi had seen what trouble lay here, she might be even more against marrying him than she already was. And yet, didn't warfare and rivalry exist everywhere? She must know that. She was the daughter and sister of warriors, but would she consent to being the wife of one?

She'd aided the boy while maintaining his pride, and had comforted the mother. It was her nature. Her beauty and calm strength had soothed them, a great gift to such wounded hearts. She'd acted just as jarl's wife should. Seeing her compassion and innate wisdom made him even more determined to make Silvi his. He wasn't the only one who needed her. His village did, as well. She'd answered the needs of two lost people this day. Would she answer the call of Thorsfjell?

He looked up through the trees to the mountain. There was one place where she could see into the very center of all they were. If that called to her, then with her tenderness and kindness toward all hurting things, surely she would answer.

"Magnus, where are we going?" Silvi breathed hard as she climbed the path winding toward the peak of the mountain the next day. The village lay below them, though she couldn't see it any longer.

"Just a little farther. I promise, it will be worth it." He held out his hand to her, but she ignored it and kept walking. If this was just a way to get her alone, then no, it would not be worth it.

She eyed him as he passed her again and led the way. He walked with the confidence of a warrior, at home in this world and in his own body. His long dark hair flowed down his back, streaming behind him in the wind that had picked up. A storm was coming, but he had assured her they would be back before it hit. She wasn't concerned. The gods walked in storms.

The path flattened out and they were on level ground. Magnus led her through a stand of trees and into a clearing. Energy, subtle yet unmistakable, climbed up her body and she stilled.

"This is your sacred grove, isn't it?"

"Yes. I thought you might enjoy seeing it."

Rune stones circled the place, some very, very old and weathered. To her right, one was brightly colored, taller than the others, and appeared new. The carving of Yggdrasil looked familiar. She went to it and placed her hand on it, bending to read the inscription:

> *Eirik carved these runes for Magnus, Leif, and Asa in honor of their father, Sigrund. He went east in search of gold. On the way back from Miklagard he died in the Aifur with his sword in his hand. May Thor consecrate these runes.*

"Your brother made this during the past winter while he was here, to thank us for allowing him to stay. Our old rune master didn't have the strength to make one for our father. It means a great deal to us, that he will be remembered for hundreds of years to come."

She ran her fingers along the carved symbols. "I recognized his style. He's going to make one in remembrance of our father to set in our sacred grove at Haardvik."

She turned away from it to look behind her and all the breath left her body. A world of white stretched beyond the mountain. Several trees had blocked the view as she'd entered the grove, but from this angle, she could see a vastness she couldn't comprehend. She glanced at Magnus and he smiled.

"It's the tundra. It runs the interior of our land. The glaciers lie there as well. Go take a closer look."

He walked slightly behind her as she moved toward the gap in the trees. When she passed beyond them, she stood on a cliff with the world opened up before her. Below them, trees still grew. But farther north, they thinned until the land turned white with snow. It stretched forever. The storm roiled over it all, the black clouds shadowing the ice, melding with it in the distance until it all blended into one. There was no horizon. A stiff wind blew her skirt back hard against her legs, bringing with it the promise of ice.

She closed her eyes and breathed in the storm.

"So beautiful." Magnus's voice brought her back. But he wasn't looking at the tundra. He was looking at her. She couldn't meet his eyes and he cleared his throat.

"The stories come down to us from our ancestors," he said. "The gods move across the tundra in the storms. They come here to rest for a time in this grove before continuing on their way. That's why we keep this view clear, so they may see where to stop. Of course, it's only an old tale."

"They're still here. In this place, in this storm. I felt it as soon as I stepped into the grove. Don't you feel them? They are coming, even now." She tilted her chin up and spread her arms slightly away from her body. At his silence, she lowered her arms and regarded him. "You don't feel it, do you? Not even here. You didn't at Haardvik either."

He remained silent for a time, as though he wasn't going to answer her. He shifted his gaze back to the tundra. When he spoke, his voice was low. "I haven't in a very long time. No one knows it. Not even Leif." He didn't glance at her.

"Then when you make the sacrifices and perform the rituals—"

"I go through the motions. I feel none of it."

She couldn't wrap her mind around it. "Why are you telling me, if no one else knows it?"

"I need . . ." He drew a deep breath. "I need someone to intercede with them. To help my people where I cannot."

"You brought me here, hoping I'd fall in love with this place."

"Yes."

"And you showed me around Thorsfjell yesterday, wanting me to love the people there."

"Yes."

"And you're spending this time with me, why? So I'll fall in love with you?"

"I think it may be a bit soon for that." Humor colored his voice and he turned to her only then. "I wanted to bring you here so you could see the great temple isn't the only place that holds power. You can find the gods you love here as well."

That was certainly true. Energy buzzed beneath her skin; power still rode on the winds. She wanted to drink it in. "How many long-ships did Eirik offer you for my dowry?"

Admiration shone in his eyes. "Three."

"That's generous. What else?"

"The warriors to crew them until I find my own."

"And?"

"The gold to support them until my trade routes expand. Which they will. Quickly."

"You must want them very badly to consider this."

"Make no mistake, Silvi. I need those ships. You know it and you know why, so I won't offend you by lying. All my life, I've thought of nothing except the welfare of my people. My father taught it to me when I was very young and it has always driven me." He took a step closer to her until he looked down into her eyes. "The ships, the warriors, the gold, are for my people. But just this once, there's something I desire for myself."

Her breath came hard as she gazed up at him. He seemed elemental, a part of the land and the storm. But then, he had been born here and his blood had run into the mountain to protect it.

"What do you want for yourself, Magnus?"

"I want this." He leaned toward her and took her upper arms in his hands. He was so gentle that she could have stepped away. She didn't. He feathered his lips across hers, his hair brushing her cheek. Deep within, her body opened up. She'd thought the land had given its power to her, but it was nothing compared to his kiss. Her hands tingled with the need to touch him, to feel his strength. A shiver passed through her as warmth spread into her thighs. She let out a long sigh, and he took her breath into himself.

He lifted his head, his gaze intense. "This is what I want for myself. You. You must have known it from the first time I saw you at Haardvik."

"I think your people may be getting the better part of this arrangement." She'd seen him watching her. His desire had shone in his eyes. Men often admired her, for they saw only her pale beauty. But once they understood the way she was, they turned away.

Magnus hadn't turned away.

She looked up at the storm above them, anywhere but into his eyes. "Has the *handsal* taken place yet?"

He let go of her arms. "Eirik and I have finalized our agreement, but we haven't done so in front of six witnesses yet. I wanted to speak to you first, give you time to know me, my people, my village. I didn't think we'd speak of it here, now."

"Did you think I wouldn't know what my brother and mother were about by bringing me here?" Anger rose in her, hot and bitter. How could they betray her like this? "You all schemed and planned and are very pleased with yourselves, but you forgot one tiny detail. This is my life as well. Have I no say? Do none of you care what I want?"

"I care. Very much. That's why I'm doing all this. To give you a chance to understand and to agree."

"If you care what I want, then leave me to my gods and my visions."

The wind drove hard into her and she staggered. He reached out to help her, but she stepped away. The clouds descended, swirling around them, and the storm settled into her, sparking in her mind. She ran into the grove, coming to a stop in the center. Her hair whipped around her as the tempest caressed her.

Closing her eyes, she threw back her head and sought the safety of her island. She called the vision and it came. The seas were white with foam while a storm passed overhead. The winds within her collided with the gale on the mountain. But the island was gone.

She cried out, searching for it. The winds only pushed her away, and she stood in the grove once again. What did it mean? Why was it gone? Had Magnus driven it from her with his desire? Had the gods found her unworthy and left her because she was not going to follow them in the temple?

She opened her eyes as Magnus stepped in front of her. He ran a hand through his hair. "I told Eirik I wouldn't take you unless you agreed."

"Then don't take me." She spun and ran back down the path toward the village. Magnus followed close to her.

"Don't run, Silvi. It's too steep. You could be killed."

Perhaps that would be best. Then she truly would be where she belonged. Away from this world and at Folkvang with the goddess Freya, for virgins as well as warriors went there to dwell with her. Magnus grabbed her from behind and swung her around to face him.

She stared at him in shock. No one had ever handled her so strongly before.

"Don't risk yourself like this. If anything happened to you—"

"You wouldn't get your ships. I know. And we couldn't have that, now could we?"

"Didn't you hear what I told you up there? Didn't my kiss tell you anything? Don't my feelings mean anything to you?"

She wrenched her arm free. "They mean as much as mine do to you. Just leave me be."

He followed her all the way to Thorsfjell, but he didn't try to stop her again. At home, she knew places, secret places, where she could go to be alone. But not here. She didn't know the lands well enough yet and she couldn't return to the grove.

A storm was coming, both within her and without, and she had no safe harbor to escape it.

Chapter Five

When Silvi entered the longhouse, Lifa was sitting with a group of women at one of the tables, Nuallen at the next one with Leif. Silvi went to the room she shared with her mother and shut the door. The brazier was still lit. Someone had added more wood to it, most likely one of the servant girls. She sank down into a chair near it and held her shaking hands out to the warm glow.

How could she fight this? Should she even try? Most women accepted the husbands their fathers or brothers picked for them and made the best of it. Eirik could, by right, force her to marry. But would he?

The door opened and she looked up, half expecting to see Magnus. It was Lifa. She closed the door quietly and sat down in the other chair near the brazier.

"Magnus told you."

Of course she would know what happened. "Yes. Not that I didn't suspect it to begin with."

"I'm certain you did."

"The island is gone." She'd told her mother of the visions since the first time she'd seen them when she was a child. "When I was in the grove just now, I tried to see it, to keep me focused on my destiny, but the sea was empty."

Lifa gave her a sharp look. "Why do you think that is?"

"Because all of you have dragged me away from it. The gods see that I'm weak and am not standing up to you. I'm not worthy of them."

"I see. Have you considered that your island may not be Uppsala? That it might mean something else altogether?"

She frowned in confusion. "What else is there, Mother?"

"That's what I mean. You've focused so hard on that one possibility, you've never considered any other. Not in your vision and not in your life."

Her head swam. "The gods gave me this desire from the start. It's everything I've known. Now all of you would drag me from the path they laid before me."

"It's the only path you see because you have always refused to lift your head to see any other. The Norns dictate when we each will die, but until then, we live as we choose. The gods may place a path before us, but there are always forks in it and it is up to us which one we take. The gods have put Magnus before you three times. It must mean something."

"I think you and Eirik have something to do with the second time, Mother. There was Haardvik and now."

"You saw him in a vision before he came to Haardvik. You said he traveled on the back of a dragon and his blood mingled with yours."

"That was only because I cleaned his wounds. He bled on the ground while I did so."

"Silvi, look at me."

She raised her eyes to her mother's.

"Tell me right now that you're not attracted to him and I'll take you to Uppsala myself."

Cold, like the winds from the glaciers, spread through her. It was hard to find her breath and she opened her mouth. If she just said the words . . .

She couldn't. Lifa would know she didn't speak the truth. She'd never have made the challenge unless she already knew the answer. Silvi set her jaw and looked back into the fire.

"I thought so. He is a fine man. He'll make a good husband for you."

"If I were looking for a husband."

Lifa sighed. "In spite of your years, you're still so young. You haven't lived yet." She leaned back in the chair. "If you go to the temple and become a *hóvgythiur*, what do you think the people who come to you would ask you?"

Silvi shook her head. She'd never thought that far.

"It won't be why some stars move and others don't. Or how to best color the runes. Or why the moon turns to blood at times. Those things are the questions of priests and kings. No, a wife will ask you how she can convince the gods to give her a child. A man will want to know which market he should go to this year to get the best prices. A young man will ask how he can get a girl at a nearby village to notice him. How will you know the answers?"

"The gods will tell me."

"The gods are often busy with other things."

Silvi stared at her mother. That was so similar to what Magnus had said to her at Haardvik.

"*You* must have the answers to the questions of life," her mother said. "And to know them, you must live them. Being at Uppsala is not retreating from the world. It is helping others live in it. You must understand it better than they do. That's why the young initiates travel with the older *völur* on their journeys, like I did. So that they'll learn and grow."

"They don't stay there?"

"No. We traveled in a group throughout the north. Unn, the *völva* who guided us, was so respected, we didn't need to fear anything or anyone. She was higher placed than even the jarls. Kings would rise from their seats in their halls so she could sit there. We traveled for months, seeing other peoples, other lands. And that's when we came to a village called Haardvik."

"You met Father there."

"Yes. I saw him and he was so handsome and fine. I think I fell in love with him then. But I was already an initiate. I knew what I wanted in life."

Silvi's skin tingled as Lifa smiled. "It sounds familiar, doesn't it? I left Haardvik behind to continue my studies. I never forgot him, though. The following year was the time of the great sacrificial festival that happens every nine years at Uppsala. Everyone has to come to it, or give something of value to those who do. I wondered if he would make the journey. His father was a powerful jarl, so it was likely."

"And he did?"

"He did. I saw him as he entered the temple with his family. When he looked at me, I knew. Right there, before Thor and Odin and Freyr, he walked to me and told me I was his. I had come to a fork in the road, just as you have. I chose the one where he walked, and I have never regretted it."

"Why haven't you told me this before?"

"Because you never needed to hear it until now."

"But the gods gave me the gift of visions. I had always thought to use that gift to serve them."

"The gods gave you the visions, not because they need them, but because people do." She reached over and took Silvi's hands in hers. "Marry Magnus. Go trading with him. You loved being on the ship so much, it was as though you were born to it. Live here at Thorsfjell. The people here build, weave, carve, create, bring beauty into a world that sorely needs it. In no place else will you find such peace. Even the temple at Uppsala bustles with people coming and going, and every nine years there is the blood and deaths of the sacrifices, both human and animal. It is a dark time. Here, you can walk with the things of the earth and sky, the winds and the land spirits. Give it, and Magnus, a chance. If you are not happy, then you know there's an alternative."

She gave her mother a sharp look, her blood running cold. Did Lifa know she had already thought of that? Of course she did. In other lands, women were the property, the chattel, of their husbands. They had no rights. But here, the gods had made women strong, giving them an escape from an unbearable marriage. Divorce. Any woman could divorce her husband and take her dowry with her. He didn't own it. She did.

With that, she would be free to do whatever she wanted, and no man would hold sway over her any longer. She'd already thought of it. With Lifa, in essence, sanctioning the possibility of escape, her nerves and fears calmed.

"I ask you not to consider divorce until a year has passed, Silvi. Give him a year. I want you to promise me that."

"What if there's a child?"

"You know the herbs to use to prevent that."

"But an entire year? It won't look good for either Magnus or me to go without having a child."

"It won't take that long."

"What?"

"Nothing, my love. It's all in the gods' hands."

Silvi nodded. Her stomach tightened. "I saw what Hakon's men did to so many of the women of our village throughout the winter. It was horrible."

"Oh gods, Silvi. Come here to me, my love." She took Silvi to the bed and sat down beside her, her arm around her. "I spoke to you of such things long ago. About the love of a good man. Of what passes between a husband and wife, the consideration and respect and, if they are lucky, the desire and even love. Do you think what Hakon and his men did is what Eirik does to Asa?"

"No. She'd run him through with her sword if he tried it." A tiny smile rose in her.

"And do you think your father would have done so to me?"

"No. You'd have threatened to put a rune under his pillow that would make him incapable. Of anything."

Lifa gave a soft laugh. "That's right. But we would never have to, because there was love. And they were and are good men—Ivar, Eirik, and Magnus. He loves you, Silvi. I see it whenever he looks at you. He will be gentle for your sake. Let him do as he will. It is his right as a husband, but he will make certain it is something you enjoy as well."

"And he needs the ships. He said so. For his people."

"That's right."

"Then everything rides on me. I met them, the people here. They were so warm and welcoming. The things they make are so beautiful. But they can't sell them unless their ships are safe on the fjord and the seas. Without that, Thorsfjell will fall and its people will become destitute." She turned to Lifa. "Eirik could lend him the ships, couldn't he? But he won't, because he knows including the ships in the bride-price will pressure me to marry Magnus and keep me from Uppsala. He never wanted me to go, and this is his way of stopping me. My conscience."

"Magnus is too proud to accept a loan. He wants his own ships and men. If any of the vessels were sunk, he would owe Eirik their value. He can't risk that. We raised you to care about others. It shines from you. It's what you are. Give it a year with Magnus. Promise me."

"All right. I promise."

"Then you'll marry him?"

"I'll marry him."

Lifa embraced her. "I'm so happy. I'll go tell—"

"No, Mother." She stood and brushed off her skirt. "I'll tell Magnus myself. Every other choice has been taken from me. This is one decision I can still make."

* * *

"Perhaps I should act like our ancestors did and just carry her off and wed her." Magnus wiped a hand over his face, then took another large drink of ale. "It would be easier."

"And start a war, as when people still did things like that." Leif leaned back in his usual chair in Magnus's meeting chamber. He propped his booted feet on the high table Magnus used as his desk. "You'd have Eirik and Rorik descend on you so fast, it would make Ragnar Lothbrok's siege of Paris look like a child's game played with wooden swords and toy boats."

"It might be worth it. What do I know of speaking about marriage to a young woman?"

"Not much, obviously."

He glared at his brother. "You're not helping the situation."

"Apparently, neither did you. I'm certain you handled it with all the delicacy and aplomb of a shield upside the head." He cracked a hazelnut in his hand and popped the nut into his mouth. "What will you do if you can't get the ships?" He reached for another one.

What would I do? He hadn't even thought of that, only of what he would lose if Silvi refused to marry him—Silvi. He had to get his mind on the right course again. Figure out a way through it all. For Thorsfjell, if not for himself.

"I could try to . . . what do they call it in the south? Court her."

Leif coughed, ejecting part of a nut. "It may happen down there where the sun has addled their brains, but not here. The entire family can come after you if they think you're a bit too interested in her. The longer a man can keep from seeing his prospective bride, the longer he can stay alive. Her family won't suspect any dalliance."

"Leif, where do you come up with this nonsense?"

"In the old stories. Of course, in them, if a woman doesn't consent, the marriage is always a disaster. Certainly teaches us mere men a lesson."

"I didn't kill Eirik for wanting Asa."

"No, but you thought about it."

"I don't think he's going to kill me over Silvi. He knows I'm talking to her about marriage."

"That's enough to assure him that nothing will happen between you."

"Leif—" A light knock at the door stopped him from throttling his twin.

Leif grinned. "And there's the army."

Magnus shot him a look as he stood. "Enter."

Silvi peeked in. "I didn't mean to interrupt. I can come back."

"That's all right." Leif rose. "I was just leaving. Don't want to get caught in the melee."

She frowned at him as he winked at her on his way out. "What did he mean by that?" She stood before the table.

"I rarely know with him. Please, sit. May I get you anything? Wine?" At least he hadn't been killing Leif when she'd opened the door. That would not have looked good.

She tilted her head to one side, her white-blond hair sliding over her shoulder. "I've never had wine before. I'd like to try it."

He knelt beside his chest and opened it. "Did Eirik never bring any back from his raids with Rorik?"

"He didn't come home much. Most of the winters, he stayed at Vargfjell, Rorik's holding. I suppose the memories of his dead wife and son kept him from returning."

Magnus set a bottle of wine and two glasses on the table. His father had brought the goblets home from Miklagard when he was very young. They were delicate and chased with silver, just like Silvi's eyes.

He cleared his throat. "The wine is made of a fruit that grows where it's warm. Not like here. We have to import all of it from the Rhineland." He poured and handed her a glass. Her hand trembled as she took it.

"I didn't know. It must be very expensive. I could have ale instead."

"It's well worth it." He met her gaze. "We only use it for special occasions."

"Except for Ingeborg."

He laughed. "Yes, except for Ingeborg. She swears it cleans a wound, though I would think water does just as well. But it works for some reason. Our warriors survive wounds that others die of."

He was babbling. Why was she here? He'd seen Lifa go into their room after Silvi had. What had they spoken about? He raised his glass to her and she did the same.

"Skoal."

She nodded and took a sip. Her eyes widened as she stared at the liquor, then she smiled. "It's very good. Thank you." She held the glass in her lap as she stared at it. With her pale skin, her slender body, her delicate hands, she looked as fragile as the glass.

"Silvi? I'm sorry if I upset you in the grove."

"It wasn't your fault, Magnus. You were nothing but kind. I just . . ." She took a deep breath. "I came to tell you that I'll marry you."

He wanted to grab her, swing her around, kiss her. Ride through the village, yelling, with his sword in the air . . . More like scare the wits out of her. His heart almost burst from him, but he calmed himself with an effort. He nodded.

"I'm glad of that, Silvi. I think we'll get on very well together."

He'd always had good relationships with willing women. Some, he'd even stayed with for a time. But he'd been so focused on his business and his responsibilities that he hadn't bothered to consider a wife yet. He'd always known it would happen one day. After all, he had a legacy to leave and needed descendants to remember his name. However, none of the women he'd been with had made enough of an impression to steer his thinking toward marriage. Until he saw Silvi at the battle for Haardvik. Through the smoke and the blood and the screams, she'd come, like a calm sunrise after a stormy night. And he'd known she was for him.

Now he needed to convince her of that. In spite of her agreement, she was even more pale than usual and she wouldn't raise her eyes to him. When she took another drink of her wine, her hand still shook.

He stood and came around the table. She stilled as he took the glass from her and set it aside. Kneeling before her, he caressed her cheek with one hand while taking her palm in the other. She drew in a trembling breath and her eyes gleamed too brightly for the dim light coming from the small window.

"I've never wanted anything as much as I want you in my life. Please believe me when I say that."

She swallowed. "Not even the ships?"

Smiling right now would not be a good idea. "Not even the ships. I would take you without them. But don't tell your brother. He'd probably kill me."

"Probably." She ducked her head, her glorious hair veiling her so he couldn't see her expression. "But that wouldn't solve the problem with Toke, so we'll just have to keep it between us. When will you have the *handsal?*"

"Most likely tomorrow, with three of Eirik's men and three of mine to witness it. The agreement for the dowry and the bride-price will stand as long as any of them are alive. It's between him and me. But this, Silvi, this is just between you and me."

Because he was kneeling, they were at the same level. He brushed back her hair and rested his hands on her shoulders. The strands were like the fine silk he brought back from Staraya Ladoga in the east. He would take the bolts of it out of storage, ells and ells of it, and dress her in it. Her skin under his hands was as the ivory he'd traded for, smooth and cool. He'd have his carvers make beads out of it and drape her in necklaces and bracelets. She was like something in a dream, a dream of Asgard and the light realms. How would he ever have the nerve to lie atop her and make love to her? He almost groaned as his body tightened. With a clenched jaw, he brought himself under control. Again. He would go slowly with her. Very slowly.

He brought his mouth close to hers, breathing her breath, giving her a chance to pull away if she wanted to. She remained still, in his hold, and bit her lip. It was so innocent, yet so enticing, he couldn't wait any longer.

He kissed her. No mere touch, like before on the cliff. Yet, he was careful and tender as he moved his mouth across hers, as though he was sipping the finest wine. He combed his fingers through her hair to hold her, as gently as he'd held the delicate glasses they'd drunk from. She was every bit as rare and beautiful. And as breakable.

Drawing back, he gauged her emotions. She put a finger to her lips. Color rose in her face, tinting her cheeks when she looked at him. He sat back on his heels as wonder filled her wide eyes.

"Maybe Mother was right."

"Your mother isn't who I'd hoped you'd think of while I kissed you."

She drew in a sharp breath. "I'm sorry, Magnus. I didn't mean—"

He touched her lips where her finger had been, stopping her. "I would imagine your good mother is right about many things. And if she spoke well of me, then I'm grateful I lived up to her opinion. I came into the longhouse after you did and saw her go to your room. She stayed in there with you a long time, I'm told. Did she force you to agree to this marriage?"

She shook her head. "No. That's not her way. She knows we all follow our own paths. For anyone she advises, she points out other ways they might take, and suggests what they may find there. It's their decision what they do. With her help, I saw this could be another way for me to help people, as I wanted to do at the temple."

Something inside of him sank. "So that is all this is? A way to help others?"

"It is the way I am, Magnus. It's how she raised me, to be like her. I agreed to this of my own free will."

At least she would be here, with him. And if she did not return his feelings just now, there was time for that as they built their lives together. He would make certain of it.

"Go now and see to your day. We'll meet again at the evening meal." He gave her a gentle kiss and she left, her eyes down. Something wasn't right. But she said she did this freely, and he had to take her at her word. He couldn't see Lifa browbeating her into it, either. Neither would Eirik. He'd been most adamant that the marriage be Silvi's choice.

He sat on his table and picked up the glass she'd drunk from. A little of the wine was left and he swirled it, watching the reflection of the silver tinted glass in the liquid. Perhaps it would be best to have the *handsal* this afternoon. To not wait and give her time to change her mind. It wasn't likely, but why take any chances? Then it would be done and he could hold a feast to celebrate tonight. The entire village would come.

He lifted the glass in a solitary toast. Soon he would be wed and would see her beautiful face every morning when he woke, instead of only in his dreams. With a smile, he drank the rest of her wine.

"Before these witnesses, you, Eirik, bond me in lawful betrothal. And with our hands joined, you promise me the dowry and to fulfill the whole of the agreement between us, which has been notified in the hearing of witnesses, without deception, as a binding contract." Magnus spoke the words in a strong voice so that none of the men who heard it could doubt his sincerity.

All of the men in his meeting room called out their agreement and the betrothal was sealed. Everyone slapped Magnus on his back and grasped his wrist in congratulations.

"Tonight, we feast. Don't drink too much until then." He laughed as the men filed out, heading straight for the beer. He held his hand up to stop Eirik and Leif. "We'll have the good drink in here. I keep it hidden for a reason."

They settled in their chairs with their cups, Leif propping his feet on Magnus's table as always.

"And so it is done." Magnus raised his cup. "Skoal."

"Skoal."

After they drank, Eirik said, "I spoke to Silvi to be certain this is what she wants. She assured me it is. She seems . . ." He paused, as if searching for the right word.

"Resigned." Magnus sighed. "I feel I'm interfering between her and the gods. Am I risking their displeasure?"

"Risking hers, perhaps. It has long been a dream of hers. An impractical one. It was never a possibility as long as my father or I were alive. If she has to marry anyone, and she does, I want it to be you. I know the manner of man you are and I have no concerns about that. If anyone is interfering in her dreams of the gods, it's me, and it'll be on my head. It's a chance I'm willing to take."

"Even your father didn't want her to be a priestess?"

Eirik snorted. "No. And neither does my mother, and she, of all of us, knows what it's like. It can be brutal and solitary. Even the initiation is dangerous. There are the sacrifices, the death and blood. Silvi thinks she can drift along in a dream there. But that's where the realm of the gods and the world of men collide, and the tempest can sweep away the weak."

"She's so fragile. How does she think she'd survive it?"

"Silvi? Fragile? I assure you, that's not the case. It takes enormous strength to withstand the power of the gods when they fill you. She has that strength. To hold the visions and the wisdom of the runes is more difficult in many ways than holding a weapon and a shield in battle. I've done both. The gods can be fickle. War? That's something we all understand. You live or you die. Give me the sword any day."

Magnus drained his cup and poured another draft. When Silvi and he had stood in the grove, and the storm had moved over them, she'd appeared to become a part of it, as though she were welcoming its majesty into her. Straight and proud, she'd faced it with no fear. She hadn't appeared so weak then, standing against the gale. Was it only around him that she was uncertain of herself?

"So when will the wedding be?" Leif stretched. "I want an excuse to drink myself under the table."

Magnus chuckled. "Since when do you need an excuse to do that? I don't think we have to wait. We delayed Eirik's wedding to Asa because we'd lost warriors at the battle and had to honor them with the *sjaund*. We have no reason to wait now. I'd say next Frigga's day."

"That's only five days from now," Leif said. "Shouldn't we invite Rorik?"

"It would take a long time to get a message there and back again." Eirik shook his head. "Besides, he's most likely already out plundering someplace."

"Or someone." Leif grinned.

"True." Eirik regarded Magnus. "I know you need my ships. Right after the wedding, I'll go to Haardvik and prepare them and bring them back. It might take a little time because I wasn't planning on sailing this year. Before we left to come here, I gave my men the order to start overhauling the ships, so they should be well along by this time. Do you have all the provisions you'll need for the week-long celebration?"

"I think so, even though it's early in the year. Usually we have weddings in the late summer when the crops are in, but we can't wait. We'll hunt, and I still have stores set by from the winter. We have honey from last year, so we can make mead."

Eirik winced. "At least I won't be the only one suffering."

"The tradition is that you drink it with her, not all the time."

"And when have I left her side? But she's not here now." He reached for the pitcher of beer.

Magnus joined in their laughter as Eirik refilled their cups. Five days. In only five days, Silvi would be his. He had to go to his storage buildings and find beautiful things to give her for the morning gift after their wedding night. With all the treasures he had collected throughout his travels, he should have no trouble finding enough to honor her. Through the years, he had gathered items from all over the world for this reason. Perhaps he'd bring Lifa with him, for she'd know what Silvi liked.

Then he had to make certain the women started baking and

preparing for a week of feasting. He'd have to send word to the neighboring jarls, inviting them to come.

Toke would, no doubt, hear of the wedding, and he would also hear of Magnus's new, powerful allies. Word of Silvi's dowry would echo through the fjord from here to the sea. With the ships and the warriors Magnus would command, Toke would find the game was changing along the Sognefjorden.

And now, Magnus held all the pieces.

Chapter Six

"You have many lovely things, Magnus." Lifa picked up a gold chalice. "You could have built a longship for what you have in here."

"I've never considered it mine. My father began collecting it so Leif and I would have morning-after gifts for our future wives and dowries for our daughters. I've added to this over the years."

"You're a wise man." She smiled as she ran her hand over a bolt of silk fabric.

She was still a beautiful woman. A feeling of calm followed her. Her light blue eyes were shaped much like Silvi's, and both mother and daughter had the same graceful movements. She still had too much to give. No woman like her should remain alone.

"Where's your bodyguard? I've never seen him apart from you."

"Nuallen knows I'm quite safe with you. He's enjoying your sauna." She sniffed a bottle of perfume. "He's been a great comfort to me since my husband died. The gods were right when they caused Eirik to save his life."

"I know he was your slave, taken when Rorik attacked his lands in Northumbria."

She set the bottle down and continued perusing the other items. "Eirik freed him for helping us win back Haardvik. He asked to be my guard. He takes it very seriously."

"I don't think he's stayed with you out of a sense of duty. Perhaps I speak out of turn, but with the way he looks at you, stays near you, it's obvious he loves you."

She gave him a calm smile. "I know. But I loved my husband and it is still too soon. Our time will happen. Nuallen is a proud man. He won't want to come to me with nothing, and right now, he has nothing. He is very deep minded. It is part of what draws me to him."

Magnus had sensed that Nuallen was, indeed, deep minded and a lethal fighter. It lay in his way of moving, his stance, even in how he watched the world around him. And he had guarded Silvi as well, all winter. For that, he would always have Magnus's deepest thanks, though he wasn't entirely comfortable with how attentive Nuallen was to Silvi.

"Do you see anything here Silvi would like for her morning gift?"

"She's a practical woman." At Magnus's dubious look, Lifa smiled. "In between visions. So many of these things are beautiful. What would she do with them? The material is too thin for our climate, unless it is made into something she wears for you in private. The gold plates are too soft to eat off of, and she's never worn perfume." She glanced sidelong at him. "Unless she would wear it for you. This fine linen, however, she could sew clothing with, for both of you. The soft leather would make beautiful shoes and gloves. And this white fur could be a warm cloak. She'd be dressed as befits a jarl's wife. A very powerful jarl with three warships. Yes, these are what she would like."

"No jewelry? Here are gold necklaces and rings."

"The rings for your wedding. She could use these silver broaches to hold her clothing. And these flat purple gemstones. Perhaps Eirik could carve runes in them for her and she could use them to cast with. They would be beautiful. And powerful."

"Then choose enough for yourself, Lifa, so that you may have a similar set. My gift to you for helping Silvi accept this marriage."

"It's not necessary, but I thank you. I'll choose them later." She narrowed her eyes and moved toward a small, ornate box. She picked it up and opened it.

He already knew what it held. A necklace of amethysts, carnelians, crystals, amber, lapis, and clear brilliant stones, all colors and shapes.

"Ah. Now this, she would want." She held it up to the dim light coming from the open doorway. "Where did this come from?"

"I don't know. It was one of the pieces my father brought back from his journeys when I was young. From somewhere in the distant East, I think. Or to the far south where there is only sand instead of ice." He chuckled. "It doesn't seem very appropriate for such a practical woman, though."

"This is not for her practical side. This necklace holds power. I felt it even through the box. It's very old, from a time so far past, we cannot imagine it. A time when the world was young. The power of the gods can channel through this. She would love it."

The power of the gods? Would that be wise? Lifa thought so, and she had knowledge of such things.

"Give her this at the first meal after your wedding night, then the rest later." She put the necklace back in the box. "There's a balance in all of life, Magnus. The goods," she said as she dropped it in his hands, "and the gods. Silvi must come to understand all this." She indicated the piles of treasure. "And you need to learn there is more to us than swords and silver. We live in this world, but we must please the next one. It is only when you merge these things together, that you'll have the balance you seek to become one with her."

What bride thought of divorce at her own wedding? If they had an overbearing family like hers, probably plenty of them.

Silvi watched from her seat on the dais as Magnus plunged his new sword, the sword she had given him at their marriage ceremony, into one of the longhouse pillars. It sank in deep and true, attesting to his strength and prowess with a weapon. Just as he would plunge into her.

Her stomach shot fire through her body. Was it any wonder? She had to calm herself, and her face hurt from the smile she'd worn all day. A smile she didn't feel.

Magnus had spared no expense to give her a wedding to remember. All the jarls and families from the entire region had come, and she'd heard their branch of the fjord was filled with ships of every kind. Everyone was dressed in their very finest clothing.

Married women of the village had steamed her in the sauna and rinsed her with cold water, washing away her old status as an unmarried woman while telling her of her duties as a wife. Lifa had brought her a new dress, deep blue, hemmed with tiny gems and belted with a beautiful woven ribbon. Two gold broaches held it at her shoulders. That Lifa just happened to have brought the dress with her only proved she and Eirik had conspired about this ahead of time.

Further proof came with the sword her brother produced for her to gift to Magnus at the ceremony. It was very fine and quite expensive. An exquisite weapon. He had to have brought it here from Haardvik.

She'd ridden to the sacred grove on a beautiful pure white mare, which Magnus had given to her afterward. He'd carried a hammer, which symbolized his mastery in their marriage. Eirik hadn't done this, probably because Asa would have hit him with it, but Silvi had no such recourse. His father's sword, which he'd given her in safe-keeping for their future son, had been no less beautiful than the one she'd presented him with.

All through the ceremony, as they'd exchanged swords and rings, she'd thought of another ritual—the initiation she would have gone through to become a priestess. It should have happened long ago. Her heart panged. Perhaps this was just a short detour on the journey to her true destiny. Perhaps, as her mother had said, she needed to learn the ways of the world so she might help others live in it.

The pain in her stomach faded. Only a year. She needed to live here only a year to keep her word to her mother. She would be a good wife to Magnus and a good mistress to the village. She would learn of the things that mattered to others. Perhaps, once the threat from Toke was past, she could travel with Magnus. Go on a ship again. At that, excitement filled her.

"I would give your bride-price all over again to know what you're smiling about, Wife." Magnus sat down in the seat beside hers. He leaned closer and his clean scent washed over her. "And this time, it's genuine."

She'd been so lost in thought, she hadn't seen him approach her. "I don't know what you mean, Magnus." She couldn't quite bring herself to say *husband*. It wasn't a word she'd ever thought she would use. "This is all so beautiful, the way the hall is decorated, the food you've had laid out, everyone cheering as you carried me over the threshold, into the longhouse. Any bride would be pleased."

"And when you handed me the bridal ale in the *kasa*, your hands shook and your eyes were moist."

"What woman wouldn't be moved on her wedding day, Magnus? All the rituals and traditions are so powerful."

He eyed her for a moment. "And yet there's one we haven't done that everyone is waiting for. Only then, will the festivities begin." He stood and picked up the hammer that he had carried back from the ceremony. She stayed seated, her heart pounding. The guests quieted and watched them.

Magnus laid the hammer in her lap with great care. He caught her gaze. She wanted to look away, but couldn't. His voice rang out, though it seemed he spoke only to her. "I bring the hammer to the bride to bless. On the maiden's lap I lay Mjölnir. In Frigga's name, bless our marriage."

Silvi listened as Magnus asked the goddess of childbearing to make their union fertile. While, in secret, she took herbs to prevent that. Her cheeks became cold, as though the blood drained from them. He studied her for another moment, then turned to the guests. "It is done. Now we celebrate."

A great cheer went up and everyone rushed to the tables set along the side of the hall, to grab food and drink. Magnus lifted the hammer from her lap and set it aside. He held his hand out to her.

"May I take you to get something to eat?"

Often, her stomach felt better after she ate; though, if she were going to survive the upcoming night, she would have to ask her mother to make her the tea with ginger she drank to calm the fire.

They walked together to the laden tables. Everyone crowded around them, laughing and congratulating them. Asa embraced her while Eirik pounded Magnus on the back, welcoming him to the family, again. Lifa watched her from the side and they gave each other a sad smile. If only her father had been here for this day.

The people around her strengthened her resolve. Haardvik's very survival depended on the agreement between Magnus and Eirik, but it went even further than that. She looked at their happy faces, young and old, weak and strong, jarls and farmers. Her heart opened to them. There were many she didn't recognize, for they came from other places. Through her, they all might one day know peace, to sail the fjord without fearing ambush and piracy. Magnus could take even more of their goods to market, not only for Thorsfjell but for all the villages on the fjord. With the warships, he could go farther and fetch better prices for it all. Everyone would benefit.

The ramifications of her agreement to this union had been so distant and unreal, just words in a marriage contract, something her brother and Magnus had agreed upon without her. But now that she could put faces to all the people it would affect, the weight of it shocked her. With only four words, *I will marry you*, she had impacted hundreds of people, making their lives potentially better. Could she have done the same at the temple, as one of many priestesses? Perhaps over her lifetime, but not like this.

Magnus filled her plate with all the finest foods, but their only beverage would be the mead they'd drink from the same cup. She ate as well as she could. She was the center of attention and couldn't dishonor Magnus by letting anyone suspect something was wrong.

He knew, though. It lay in his eyes. As the afternoon ended and the evening wore on, she couldn't look at him and not see the questions he wanted to ask. She listened to the music and to the insults the men hurled, each trying to outdo the others. Many of them had composed stories made of lies, to see who could tell the tallest tales. It came as no surprise that Leif won.

And when Lifa and the other women of Thorsfjell came to escort her to the bridal chamber, as she left she gave Magnus a smile for the benefit of the guests, their cheers and ribald teasing echoing behind her.

The women slipped her dress from her and arrayed her in her own hair, remarking how beautiful she was, how perfect. Magnus would be pleased. They helped her into bed and drew up the furs over her body, then busied themselves with putting away her clothes and jewelry.

Lifa took a cup from a servant and handed it to her. "Ginger tea. I thought you might need it."

"I do. Thank you." Of course her mother would know. She drank it down. "I don't suppose you sprinkled any runes under the bed to make him, oh, fall asleep right away?"

Lifa's mouth twitched. "No, but I might have put a few around for other reasons."

"No herbs in his drink?"

"No herbs in his drink." She laid her hand on Silvi's arm. "It will be well, my love. Let him do as he wishes, for he will be a gentle and kind husband to you. It's his nature where you are concerned. He cares for you so."

And that was the problem. To hurt a man as fine as he when she left him . . . She needed something stronger than the ginger tea. But it was too late. The voices of the men who escorted Magnus to her filtered through the door. Her mouth dried.

They burst in, Leif and Eirik in front, then Magnus. A group of men flanked him, bearing torches, laughing and joking. Lifa stood and moved slightly in front of the bed, like a mother wolf guarding her pup. They sobered when they saw her.

Magnus walked out from the group and focused on Silvi. "I have come to be with my wife."

"As is your right," Lifa said. "Let us witness you to bed and we will leave you be."

His gaze never left Silvi's. Her breath came hard as the men lifted off his shirt. She'd seen him like that when he'd sparred with Rorik, but she'd tried to forget how beautiful he was. It flooded back into her—his broad shoulders, corded arms, and his narrow waist. Then he stripped off his boots and his trousers and straightened.

He was perfect. All the women saw it and sighed. He bore a few scars on his chest and arms from past battles, and the wide scar crossing his lower abdomen, but they were marks of honor and only served to show that he was worthy of her. His legs were long and hard, and they weren't the only parts of him that were. Her cheeks heating, she looked away, then gave him another quick glance. Clad only in his gold torc and arm rings, he was primal, strong, a warrior born and bred. And she was his.

He walked to the bed and several of the men lifted the cover so he could get in. They made as though they wanted to get a glimpse of Silvi. It was all in jest, but he still glared at them as she shrank farther beneath the furs. He slid into bed beside her.

"We could always follow the old traditions and stay to make certain the marriage is valid." Leif winked at her.

"And die by my sword. Get out." Magnus's words were hard, but he grinned. Laughing, all the men and women left, carrying the torches. Lifa was the last to leave.

"Magnus and Silvi, may the gods bless this night and all the others of your marriage."

"I thank you." He nodded to her.

With a quick, encouraging smile at Silvi, she left and they were alone. He shifted so that he faced her, but she stared straight ahead. Her heart fluttered. She'd seen other men before, wounded men she'd helped her mother treat, or others who simply stripped and washed after they'd worked or sparred. None had been like Magnus. How could he . . . ? How could *they* . . . ? He was so large. Everywhere.

The women at Haardvik had screamed as Hakon's men had taken

them. Had they been hurt that way? But he wasn't one of Hakon's outlaws. She had to remember that. He was her husband.

His touch on her cheek made her jump. He turned her head with the tips of his fingers until she had to look at him. Her mother had said to do as he wanted, so she met his gaze.

He leaned over and kissed her. "We have all night, Silvi. You needn't be like the doe that has spotted the wolf."

"I'm sorry, Magnus. I know this is your right. I'll—I'll do whatever you wish."

He drew back. "I want it to be what you wish also."

"I do." She met his gaze. "I want to be a good wife to you and I know this is part of it."

"Do you understand what is to happen this night between us?"

"Of course. I understand there's a bit of pain this first time. You needn't worry about that. I'll lie quietly beneath you until you're finished."

"By the gods." He jerked away from her and speared his hand through his hair.

She pulled the furs up closer to her chin. What had she done wrong?

"I don't want you to just lie quietly while I have at you."

She stared. "You don't?"

"No." He got out of bed and went to the side table where a flask of mead and two glasses waited. He poured for both of them and came back. He handed one of them to her, but she didn't drink. After swallowing his mead entirely, he set the glass aside and climbed back on the bed.

Kneeling beside her, he took her hand in his. "I want. Gods, Silvi, I want us. I want for you to care for me as I desire you. I know I can't expect you to love me as I—" He stopped. "As I hope you might one day. Not yet. But at least I'd like desire between us. Passion even. I won't do anything against your will."

"It *is* my will. You're my hus—husband. I won't deny you your rights. The man takes the woman. It is he who must desire in order to . . ." She couldn't finish the sentence.

"The woman must desire also, or else she can be hurt. I could kiss you, touch you, persuade your body to desire mine. But I want more than that. I want your heart and mind to desire me as well."

Her throat swelled with unshed tears. He was so fine. Any other man would have been satisfied with less. Not Magnus. He deserved a woman who could love him, who could give him what he wanted. She'd never envisioned knowing the love between a man and woman. This had all happened so quickly. Not two weeks ago, she'd been certain of her destiny. It felt as though she'd been riding a fast galloping horse all her life, and without warning, it turned, launching her out of the saddle and into a future she never foresaw.

Could she ever be what he wanted, what he should have? She looked away as tears slipped down her cheeks.

He touched one of them with his thumb. "Are you so unhappy, then?"

She shook her head. How could she tell him her thoughts? He deserved so much better than she was. But then, he would be with another woman. Her heart stung.

"Go to sleep, Silvi." He sounded resigned.

She peered at him through her tears. "What?"

"I said, go to sleep." His voice softened as he took her cup and set it beside his. "I won't take you when I could hurt you. I won't have you lie still beneath me, letting me do as I want only because it is my right. When you can come to me with joy and desire, *then* it will be what I want. Not before."

He got under the furs and lay down with his back to her. She reclined against the carved headboard and watched his wide shoulders rise and fall with his breathing.

This was childish. Foolish. She was a wife now. She needed to be there for him, to please him. To love him? He deserved no less.

"Magnus?"

He turned onto his back and looked up at her. Taking her hand, he kissed it. "Go to sleep, Silvi. I can't make love to you while you weep tears I caused. We'll work this out. Not tonight, but perhaps soon. Until then, no one will know. I'll honor you as my wife and if I'm very lucky, one day you will honor me with your love." He turned over again, facing away from her.

Oh gods. She slid down beneath the furs as her eyes burned with more tears. She would likely get little sleep this night, but if she looked tired in the morning, at least everyone would think it was for an entirely different reason.

His body gave off such a welcome warmth. She shifted closer to him, almost touching him. His breathing hitched, as though he held it. Not wanting to disturb him, she stilled. His heat still comforted her and she snuggled deeper under the soft furs. The long day and her tumultuous emotions took their toll. Her body grew heavy with exhaustion and she closed her eyes, determined to try to sleep. Her mother would want to know her dreams this night, and she had to be able to tell her something.

Before, she would cry or scream out the pain that burned in her. Or she would bring forth the vision to comfort her. Now the island, her haven, was gone, and with the celebration still ongoing, she couldn't seek out her mother.

Lifa would be gone soon, returning home. She must find her own strength now. She should be able to come to her husband for comfort. But he was the cause of her pain and confusion.

No. This was her fault. Magnus was steadfast and solid. Even when she had so disappointed him, he'd still treated her gently. It was she who caused her own sadness and solitude on this night, and she who had caused his pain. She turned her face into the pillow and dried her eyes on the soft linen, welcoming the lethargy that drifted over her.

At least, for a time, she could escape this world in sleep.

She stood on the island beside the sea. The waves ran onto the sand as though trying to grab her and drag her back, but she moved away from them. She gazed along the golden beaches and up to the peaks of the verdant mountains. Light surrounded her and peace filled her. All those years she had seen the isle only in the distance, across a harsh ocean. Now, she was finally where she belonged.

Someone was behind her. She started to turn, but before she could see who it was, the island vanished from beneath her. Cold waters closed over her, plunging her into darkness.

Chapter Seven

The morning sun came much too early. It glared at her through the smoke hole in the roof and the small windows set along the side of the chamber. Silvi stretched, trying to get her limbs moving. Then she remembered, and all traces of sleep left her. She was a wife now.

She pulled the furs up over her head to hide from both that fact and the memory of the night. But there was no escaping them. How could she face Magnus again? His side of the bed was empty and cold, so at least she wouldn't have to right away. He'd awakened early at Haardvik. Perhaps that was his way and not an indication of how he felt toward her.

Women's voices drifted to her from outside the door. She peeked over the furs as Lifa walked in, the older women following her.

"Ah, good. You're awake. We've come to dress you for the day. Magnus has been up for some time." Lifa pulled the furs from her.

Silvie grabbed them back. Being naked in front of the women when it was late at night and dark was one thing. But in the morning light they would see the clean sheets. As she wrapped the fur around her shoulders, she glanced down. A little red smear marked the bedding. How?

She drew in a breath. Magnus must have cut himself and put his own blood there. He'd said no one else would know, and he'd kept his word.

He was so honorable. So kind and patient. Tears rose in her eyes, but she hid them behind the curtain of her hair as she slipped out of bed. The women laughed and commented on the stain as they dressed her in another fine gown. They brushed her hair, braided it, and put it up in the style that married women often wore. But she hadn't earned it. She was yet a maiden.

Lifa stood to the side, and when the women left, she sat down in front of Silvi.

"He was kind to you." It was not a question.

"Very." Much more so than she deserved. She bit her lip.

"Then what's wrong, my love?" Lifa touched the beautiful braids on Silvi's head.

She couldn't tell her mother about her failings. But she could tell her about the dream. Or was it a vision? Either way, her mother needed to hear it, as was tradition. "I had a disturbing dream."

"Tell me." Lifa straightened and raised her head, as always the rune mistress who dispensed wisdom.

Silvi told her the dream she'd awoken from during the night. "I had the isle right under my feet this time, but I lost it again. The gods were telling me I had a chance for it, for all I've ever wanted, then they pulled it out from under me because I married."

"Don't be so certain you know their minds, Silvi. They don't always speak to us in ways we can understand. Always question. Always wonder and look for another path, another meaning. Just as each rune holds many meanings, so do our dreams."

"Then how can we ever know anything? If all we do is question—"

"That is the beginning of understanding." She rose and held out her hand. Silvi took it and stood. Her mother embraced her. "Consider this. The gods did not abandon me because I chose to marry your father. Instead, they blessed me in so many more ways than I could have dreamed."

That was true. There was no one who walked closer with the gods than Lifa. And yet she had left the temple to marry, even after she'd studied there. How had she known that was the right thing to do?

Before she could ask, Lifa took her hand again. "Everyone is waiting on you for the morning meal. Magnus had the men clear out all the drunks very early so the servants could prepare the common room. Plus, your morning gifts are waiting."

She hadn't thought of that. The new husband gave his bride gifts in exchange for her virginity. She swallowed. How could he do this when she hadn't lived up to her side of the marriage? *No one will know.*

She glanced at her mother. Lifa would perceive something was wrong. She always did. But she said nothing as she led Silvi into the common room. It was as she'd thought. She must find her own strength. A piece of her childhood slipped away, forever lost.

The crowd parted before her, but she saw only Magnus as he walked to her. He was dressed in a fine tan shirt and tunic, his long legs clad in darker trousers. They'd slept in his chamber, so he must have dressed very quietly. And perhaps watched her sleeping.

He took her hand from Lifa's and raised it to his lips. "You are even more beautiful as my wife than you were as my betrothed."

She smiled her thanks, but couldn't speak past the fullness in her throat. They went to their places at the head table and servants brought them food. She had to eat. If she didn't, people would speculate. If only her stomach would settle. Magnus ate a hearty meal, while she chose porridge and cream.

After the servants cleared away the remains of the morning meal, others brought in boxes and chests. They placed them in front of the high seats.

"I hope you'll find pleasure in these things, Silvi. I give them all to you in token of your gift to me."

He meant her maidenhood. She sought his gaze, trying to see what lay beneath his words, but could sense no mockery. He took a small box from the pile and opened it. He drew out a necklace made from stones of many colors. It caught the light in a brilliant burst of radiance.

"This is my personal gift to you. Not for your virginity, nor for any monetary value you hold. It's simply for you." He settled it over her head, letting it drape down the front of her gown. "Your beauty is such that even this necklace cannot add to it."

The women in the room sighed while the men banged on the tables in approval. She took a shuddering breath.

"I thank you, Husband. I shall always wear and cherish this." She touched it. The stones felt warm beneath her hand, as though they'd already absorbed the heat of her body.

They went to the pile of chests and he showed her the other gifts of fabrics and furs, the broaches and jewelry. There was gold for her to use as she saw fit, and glittering, flat purple stones to make into a set of runes. The people called out their approval as Magnus opened each chest.

She was speechless. Such wealth. She'd known he was a successful trader, but this was more riches than she'd ever dreamed of. And it was all hers. She'd never aspired to such things. What would she do with it all?

Her head light, she needed to sit down. But there was one more thing he had to give her. He handed her a ring of keys. "These are the keys to the household, my wife. They show your authority over all things here. You hold the keys to all locks in the village." He lowered his voice so only she could hear him. "Just as you hold the keys to my heart."

If he'd taken his sword and cleaved her own heart in two, it would not have hurt more. How could he be so understanding, so patient? She didn't deserve it. Any of it.

She made it through the rest of the day with people of the village giving her gifts and wanting to speak with her. She was their mistress now, the wife of their jarl. Their problems were hers, their needs and welfare hers to see to as well. Nothing was the same any longer.

There was another feast that night, as there would be over the next week. Magnus drank more than she'd seen him do before. He wasn't drunk, though, unlike many of the other guests. He was too controlled for that. But he was quiet, and when, at the end of the evening, he held his hand out to her, his eyes were shadowed.

He managed to fend off the laughing men who wanted to come along and assist him again, and once they'd gained their chamber, he shut the door against the noise and merriment. The boxes and chests holding her morning gifts stood along the far wall. She could hardly bear to look at them all.

"Do you like your gifts, Silvi? Your mother helped me pick these things out." His voice held an edge she'd not heard before.

There was even more someplace? "You're very generous with me, Magnus. In more ways than only this." She regarded him. "You cut yourself this morning and dropped the blood on the bed. Why?"

"I told you. Only you and I will know about last night."

"And all this? I haven't earned any of it."

"For the same reason as I put blood on the sheets. What would you have me do? Refuse to give you the gifts? Eirik would declare war against me for dishonoring you so badly." He crossed his arms. "Unless we told everyone I haven't yet claimed my own wife. That I won't until she comes to me in desire, of her own accord."

"If the marriage isn't consummated, we are not truly wed."

"Perhaps that's what you'd like. I know you didn't want this, that you'd rather be someplace else. Perhaps you will hold out, never giving me what I want, until I tire of it and set you free. Then you can take all this and your dowry and leave. Is that what you think?"

She gasped at his harshness. But she couldn't speak the words to deny it entirely. The last part was exactly what she'd thought of. Until she'd met the people here and had fallen in love with the village.

"Of course, you'd beggar me and Thorsfjell. But you'd have your precious Uppsala."

She clenched her jaw. "If you think so little of me as to believe I'd do that to you or Thorsfjell, then we have nothing more to speak of. I've never had any use for material things. Not like you do. They're all you know, all you believe in. If I want to leave, I have only to announce in front of witnesses that I'm divorcing you, and it would be done. I don't need to resort to such games as you accuse me of."

"Then why don't you? There are enough witnesses out there."

"Oh no, Magnus. If you think I'll have it on my head to destroy this village and let everyone suffer, then you insult me. You made certain I fell in love with the people here. I feel their need for me and I've seen their faces, heard their voices. I know their names now and I've held their babes. You know I can't hurt them." All the submerged anger and frustration building in her since she'd been pressured into marriage poured out of her. "By manipulating me, you've made quite certain you can keep those precious warships and the power they bring you. That's all that matters to you. Swords and silver. I can't help but wonder if the reason you're so solicitous to me is that you're afraid I'll leave and take my dowry and all these things. You'd be willing to put up with anything as long as you can keep the ships you bargained for. Even me."

She turned her back to him. Magnus had the right to use the ships, but they were, by law, hers. As was all of her dowry. In spite of his fine words to her, was that all she was to him? A way to get those damned ships?

"You're welcome to them, Magnus. I hope they rock you to sleep every night. Because I won't."

"Why should I expect anything different than what happened—or rather, didn't happen—last night?"

She wouldn't deign to answer that. Still turned away from him, she stripped off her gown and shift, and climbed into bed without even taking her hair down. It would be nice to make a grand exit after a scathing remark, but where would she go? He could always leave and finish getting drunk with the other men out in the common room.

He didn't. As soon as she settled under the furs, with her back turned this time, his belt hit the floor and his clothing rustled as he undressed. The down mattress sagged under his weight when he got into bed beside her. After a moment, he tugged at her hair.

"What are you doing?" She tried to sit up, but he put a strong hand on her shoulder, pinning her on her side.

"Just taking your hair down."

"Don't be nice to me. I don't need your help." She jerked her head away from him.

"I suppose I'd better be nice to you, shouldn't I? After all, I need to keep on your good side."

"Too late for that."

"You said you would do as I say, didn't you?"

"That was last night. This is tonight."

"Very observant." His tone was dry. "Still, you did say you'd do as I wish and lie still. Do so. Lie on your stomach."

"Why?"

"So I can get to both sides of your hair."

He pressed on her shoulder until she lay facedown. The furs slid to her lower back. He combed his fingers through her hair, then along her scalp. It felt so good. She was unaccustomed to having her hair up. She'd always worn it undone or loosely braided down her back as befitted a maiden. It fell free over her skin as he ran his hands through it, making her sigh with pleasure. If he could do this just by unbraiding her hair, what else could he do?

"It seems you have a lot of experience with unbraiding women's hair." She buried her face in the pillow as he worked on the other side.

"Not too much. After all, married women wear their hair this way, and I can assure you I have no experience with them."

"I would hope not."

"I still don't." A touch of humor laced his voice.

She tried to pull away from him and sit up, but he put a hand on her back and kept her down.

"I'm not finished."

"I am."

"If I stop now, in the morning it will be sticking out everywhere. Just do as I say this one time and stay still."

She hesitated. "Just this one time, then."

"The gods forbid it should be otherwise." He chuckled.

It did feel very nice. He was so much larger and stronger than she was, she stood no chance against him. She relaxed back down, hiding a smile in the pillow. He continued to take out her braids, until he gathered all her hair in his hand and gave it a light tug.

"Stay like that."

"Yes, my jarl."

"That's better." The mattress shifted as he rose.

She turned her head and opened one eye to peek at him as he crossed the room to her pile of chests. He knelt beside one, the muscles in his legs flexing. His long hair fell forward over his magnificent arms as he rummaged in the chest. He fished something out, then stood. She turned her head back into the pillow before he caught her looking.

He knelt beside her on the bed again and took her hair in his hand. "This is an ivory comb I traded for in the East. I wonder how it would feel in your hair." He pulled it through, letting the tips of the teeth run along her spine to her lower back.

Her toes curled. The muscles in her back clenched as little lightning bolts shot through her body. He laid her hair between her shoulder blades, stroking it with the comb all the way down her spine. No man had ever touched her before, except for a quick embrace from Eirik. This was her husband. He had every right. In spite of his disarming her anger with his gentle, dry humor, she shouldn't be succumbing to this.

She fought the sensation rising in her belly. It was not like a newly laid fire this time. It was more like the glow of old embers at the end of the night. It spread within her until she couldn't resist any longer. She gave herself up to his care.

Was this foolish? Of course it was. He was an idiot.

Magnus ran the comb through her hair again, dragging it all the way down her white back. She was flawless, her skin unblemished. Her hair was as a webbing of ice on a frosty morning. It slipped through his fingers like water.

Why was he torturing himself? He was still angry and frustrated.

And his sweet, demure Silvi had claws. No doubt she was angry as well, and frustrated, but not in the same way he was. No, his ice queen was above such base desires. Or was she?

He passed the comb lightly against her skin again and a muscle in her back jumped. Her hands gripped the sheet she lay on. With a sigh, she nestled further into the mattress. Perhaps she wasn't as un-affected as she wanted him to believe.

He should just turn her over and, with gentleness and exquisite patience, persuade her body to accept his. He'd yet to even see her breasts. They would be beautiful, her belly flat, her legs long and perfect. He could bring such pleasure to that body, and find his own as well. Then they would see if she could lie silent and resentful be-neath him.

And in the morning, she would still believe he wanted her only for her dowry and the connections their marriage brought him. That she could even think it had shocked him. He'd said things he regret-ted. But if he apologized, she would think he wanted to placate her, and it might make things worse.

No, he wanted all of her, not just her body, although another part of him didn't quite agree with that. To be certain, he wanted her arms, her legs, every part of her wrapped around him. He wanted to kiss her everywhere, taste her, worship her. He wanted her to do the same to him, to enjoy him as he would savor her.

Swallowing a groan, he set aside the comb and, using the heels of his hands, massaged circles into the muscles on either side of her spine. From deep in the pillow she gave a little sigh, and he smiled.

He wanted so much more. He'd watched Asa and Eirik and the love they shared, overcoming so much pain in their lives. Their feel-ings had taken a long time, all winter, to grow and develop. He needed to convince Silvi he wanted her for herself. It wasn't because of what she brought to him, or because he was afraid she would leave and take it all with her.

He loved her.

It was as simple and as complicated as that. When he'd seen her on their wedding day, riding the white mare into the sacred grove, his knees had nearly buckled. He almost couldn't speak his vows to pro-tect and guard her, for the fullness in his throat. All that day, he'd looked forward to the night when he could finally sink into her. How-ever, one look in those luminous, resigned eyes, and he couldn't force himself on her. That's what it would have felt like, though she'd said it was her will.

Someone had given her questionable advice. Lifa wouldn't have made that kind of mistake, but could Silvi have misunderstood? Or, like Asa, had she been through something that had traumatized her? He glanced down at the scar on his lower abdomen.

Hakon and his scum had been at Haardvik all winter. Lifa had assured Eirik and him that the outlaws hadn't touched her and Silvi. The men were too frightened of such a powerful woman as Lifa, and she had told them that her daughter was a seeress. Not a lie, and it had worked. Silvi was untouched.

Until now. He massaged her shoulders. Who knew what she might have seen during the long winter nights? Whatever it was, he had to make certain she saw only him, felt only his hands, heard only his voice. And that would take time.

Meanwhile, he would gift her with beautiful things, show her his world, let her see him for who he was. He would allow his love for her and her love for the people of Thorsfjell ensnare her more and more. Then she would never leave them.

He paused. Her breathing was even and light. She was asleep. He bent and kissed her between her shoulders. So soft and warm. With a sigh, he pulled the covers over them both and, grimacing, turned his back on her. Again. There was only so much temptation a man could take.

In the morning he would find a maid to help her dress, who had the skills to braid her hair each day as befitted a jarl's wife. But at night . . .

At night, he would be the one to take it down.

Magnus watched Eirik and Asa embrace on the beach, where Eirik's great longship waited to take to the seas once again. A short distance away, Leif oversaw the men who were loading provisions on board.

Silvi stood at Magnus's side to see Eirik off. She'd been distant since their argument two nights ago. They'd moved through the celebrations and feasts together, yet not quite as one. No one else gave the impression that they noticed, though Lifa appeared to contemplate them. She was wise and wouldn't interfere. She and Nuallen wanted to remain behind while Eirik traveled to Haardvik to get the ships he had promised Magnus. The people here needed the advice Lifa could give them as a rune mistress.

Asa also chose to stay here while Eirik was gone. The wedding preparations had left her too little time to pack her carving tools and equipment. But that might not be the only reason she wanted to stay.

"Your sword hand must be getting itchy." Eirik grinned down at her. "Hoping a fight breaks out at the celebration among the guests?"

"It wouldn't surprise me." She disengaged from Eirik's hold and looked toward Magnus. "But that's not it. It's just a feeling I have. Toke has threatened you, Magnus. I wouldn't put it past him to strike just after the wedding, when everyone's guard is down. You'll be wrapped up in your new bride. The guests will be gone, we'll be tired, and the routine, so he thinks, may be relaxed. I'm certain he's heard by now about the ships that are coming and the warriors you'll have. He might get desperate and attack before you come to full power, between the end of the celebration and Eirik's return."

In the winter battle when they'd defeated the outlaws, Asa had realized the outlaws would attack from a different direction than they'd initially thought. Her realization of the diversionary tactic had given Thorsfjell the victory. She'd always had good battle-sense; he'd long ago learned to trust her.

"I've never let my guard down and I don't intend to start now." He crossed his arms. "We'll post extra guards day and night, as well as lookouts on the top of our mountain. I'll create a relay system to get messages down to us faster. We'll keep our weapons on us all the time, shields by the doors. Everything will be ready in a moment's time."

"Then I won't leave," Eirik said. "I'll have my second, Kjeld, take command of the *Wind* and go to Haardvik for the ships. Only the smallest number of men needed to sail the ship will go and the rest can remain here. The men at Haardvik already know my plans. They'll come when all is ready."

Magnus and he gripped each other's wrists. "I would be glad of your help. You fight like no one I've seen."

As Eirik nodded his thanks, Silvi frowned. "If Toke is such a danger, why hasn't anyone killed him yet?"

"He's a coward," Leif said as he approached them. "He rarely strikes, letting his men act on his behalf. He probably couldn't avoid the attack on us at the islands. They were lying in wait for someone weaker, and didn't figure on someone as strong as we are. They saw us, and he couldn't back down in front of his men. Still, he never left his own boats."

"They target the weakest villages." Asa ran her thumb over the hilt of her seax. "Then they slip away to some hiding place. Toke has a village, Bygvik, on the other side of the mountain, but he's rarely there and no one wants to slay the innocent people who have suffered so under his rule. In fact, some of the women and children have escaped to the safety of Thorsfjell over the years, like Fastny and Jarpi did. We wouldn't trust any of the Bygvik men to be here, but we couldn't turn away starving and abused mothers."

Magnus grimaced. "Many of us up and down the fjord have killed his men. But unless we slay him, he'll keep gathering more criminals to him."

"In the north, we make outcasts of those who break the law," Leif said. "Then we turn them loose on the land to survive or not. No one can help them for a set amount of time, and they have only a few safe places and no real options. Quite often, it's a death sentence. They have nothing to lose. Toke offers them shelter, food, and a share of the spoils, even though it's illegal. So they fight for him, not caring who they go after. Anyone who is weak is vulnerable. But he's gotten bolder, or more desperate . . . He needs to be brought before the *Thing* to answer for his crimes of giving outcasts shelter. "

Silvi had become even paler than she usually was. If anything happened to her . . . How could he best protect her?

He took her hands. They were so elegant and graceful, he didn't press them for fear of harming her. "Silvi, do you want to go back home to Haardvik until this is over? They could take you today. It would be much safer for you there."

She studied him for a moment. "No, Magnus. My place is here now, with you. My brother and mother are both here, and if they stay, I stay. Don't forget I grew up in a warrior's household. I survived the winter with men such as these you speak of. I may not be a warrior like Asa and Kaia, but I have my ways. I can cast over the land and find them if they come. I did so during the winter, and let Nuallen know. He didn't realize how I gained the information. He simply followed what I saw and slew the men. If I may suggest it, use him and his abilities while he's here."

"What do you mean, cast over the land?" Were those the visions she was supposed to have?

She took her hands from his. With her head up, she looked out over the fjord. "When Eirik and I were very young, we found that if we opened ourselves to our surroundings, we could sense things. We thought it was a game. It's how he found me after the outcasts attacked us and our father was killed. Perhaps it is the *landvaettir*, the land spirits, speaking to us. If something isn't right, we know."

"When Eirik stayed here during the winter, we searched the woods for the outcasts who attacked my people. He felt them before we saw them."

"I thought he might have lost the ability when he went raiding for so long with Rorik, but he didn't. He sensed me in our sacred grove last fall; and I, him. He used it again for you. Between him, your strategy and battle-skills, Nuallen's abilities, and my visions, I have every confidence you'll protect us. Also, don't forget, we have my mother. She has the runes, and the ears of the gods."

This was starting to sound like some tale from the ancient times. If everything Silvi said was true, then he would take it. He'd always depended solely on his sword and his strategic mind, but perhaps there was more than that. He looked up at the top of the mountain, Thor's mountain. Just because he'd never felt the things Silvi spoke of didn't mean he'd dismiss them out of hand. After all, the gods existed though he'd never heard them.

He'd seen what Eirik could do with both his sword and his senses. Eirik had been a true raider with Rorik, the most wild and powerful of them all. His brother-in-law was the most skilled fighter he'd ever seen. If Eirik believed in such things, then that was good enough for Magnus. Toke wouldn't fight in an honorable way, and there was no telling what he would do when he was backed into a corner.

Land spirits, gods, and visions. He just might need them all.

Chapter Eight

"That's fine, Thyri. It's nice to wear it simply again." Silvi patted her hair at the back of her neck, where the serving girl had woven it into a knot. "Now that the wedding celebration is over, I can dress comfortably."

"It's not so intricate, yet still proper for a wife." Thyri picked up the ivory comb and set it back in its box on the table. She was shy, never quite looking into anyone's eyes, but she knew her work and did it well.

Silvi rose as Thyri held out a gown to her. Being the daughter of a jarl, she was familiar with servants, though she'd always refused their assistance. She hadn't wanted the contact with them. However, now, as the *wife* of a jarl, she had to make certain allowances. It would reflect badly on Magnus if she didn't.

She had no experience with arranging her hair in the style of a married woman, so she'd been relieved when Magnus had found Thyri working in the cooking room.

"Where did you learn to do hair so beautifully, Thyri?" She slipped the dress on.

"From my mother, mistress. She served a jarl's wife when she was young. When she married my father, he brought her to Bygvik to live. I was born there. She died when I was young." She kept her eyes downcast.

"You came from Toke's village?"

"Yes, mistress. My father forced me to leave and come here to live a better life. He said it was too late for him, but that I deserved a chance. There are several of us here."

Perhaps that was why Thyri was so quiet and withdrawn. Who knew what her situation had been like? She must still miss her father.

Was there some way they could bring him here? After they defeated Toke, she would find out. She'd grown fond of the girl, though she didn't know her well yet.

"Thank you for your help this morning. Go and seek your morning meal before it's all gone. Even though most of the wedding guests have returned home, there are still many warriors to feed. They eat everything in sight."

Thyri smiled as she walked to the door. "Yes, mistress."

Silvi smoothed her dress. Another beautiful garment. At some point, her mother must have had these made for her and kept them hidden. Had the runes shown her this time? That her daughter would marry? If they had, then it was destined all along and there was nothing she could do about it. For now.

When she went out into the common room, Magnus was seated in his usual place. He preferred eating among the people instead of at the dais. Yet this morning he was alone. They'd sat on the high seats all week because of the guests, but now things were back to normal. For everyone except her.

She couldn't sit elsewhere when he was already eating, even if she preferred it. Tension still stretched between them. They went about their days like any newly married couple, visiting with people and entertaining the guests. They rarely spoke otherwise. Magnus must have told Thyri not to attend her at night, for she was never waiting in the chamber to help her, as she should have been. Instead, Magnus came in after Silvi was already in bed.

Each night, he undressed and sat on the bed beside her. He never said a word, but with his touch on her back, she knew he wanted her to lie on her stomach. Once she did so, he took her hair out of its braids, and combed it out until it lay around her. She drifted off as he massaged the tightness out of her shoulders. In the morning, she woke alone. And nothing was resolved between them.

Steeling herself, she went to the table and sat beside him. He nodded to her as Birgitta brought her usual breakfast of porridge and cream.

"I thought you would already be gone." She poured cream into the bowl.

"I'm meeting with Eirik and Leif soon to discuss our tactics."

"What do you have planned?" She nibbled her porridge.

"I wouldn't think you'd be interested in such things."

She put down her spoon before facing him. "I was interested enough when my mother, Nuallen, and I plotted to help overcome Hakon in Haardvik. I may not wield a sword, but that doesn't mean I don't want to know what you're planning. Nuallen thought enough of me to include me in his plans, and even listened to what I had to say. Imagine that." She picked her spoon up.

A muscle jumped in his jaw. "I'm deploying men in the heights of the mountain." He took a last bite of his sausage and swallowed it. "Bygvik lies that way, in the next valley. Toke avoids going there, so he could attack from any direction. My men can see all around the region from there. We have fast riders stationed along the paths to relay information to me. The bulk of the men are here, staying prepared. Above all, we have to guard Thorsfjell, no matter what."

She nodded. "Thank you. I'll visit Ingeborg today and make certain she's prepared to treat any wounded. My mother and I brought herbs and other remedies with us since we didn't know what we'd find when we arrived. I'll unpack them and take them to her. I'm certain she has many of her own, but Eirik learned things in his travels. He brought back medicines and treatments from far to the east."

"We learned of his knowledge when our cousin tried to poison Asa with Death's Cap mushrooms. He knew what it was and how to treat it."

"Thank the gods. With Mother's love of healing, she learned all she could from him. And then she taught me."

"I'd be grateful for any help you can give." He still didn't look at her, but his voice softened. It was a start.

Healing wasn't all she could do to help. She ate in silence while he sipped at a cup of buttermilk. The feeling between them was almost amicable.

She finished her porridge and pushed the bowl away. "I'm going to the sacred grove this morning, as well." With all the celebrations and people she'd been exposed to this past week, she needed to seek the gods and the comfort she found with them and, just as important, to be alone for a time.

Magnus drained his cup and set it down very gently. "May I have a word with you, Silvi? In our chamber?"

"Of course." His soft words raised her hackles. He was being too calm, no doubt for the benefit of those around them in the common room.

He ushered her into their room and shut the door with great care, then leaned back against it. "You are not going up there."

She raised her head. "You would deny me my time with the gods? I thought part of the reason you wanted me was because I can speak with them, since you can't. How am I supposed to do that if you keep me from what I must do? We need them now more than ever." She slashed the air with her hand. "Just because you don't believe in them, doesn't give you the right to deny me."

"I never said I don't believe in them. That's not the point. It's too dangerous for you to go there. Toke's men may be crawling all over this area."

"You have your own men watching and patrolling. I have to do this, Magnus. I feel that someplace between the wedding and all the celebrations, I've lost everything I was."

"Not everything."

She took a sharp breath, as though he'd hit her. "That's unfair. You're withholding yourself. You can come to me at any time. I told you I don't wield a sword, but that can change. And trust me, with you making remarks like that, it's sounding better and better with every moment."

His lips tightened as though he tried not to smile. Then he grew solemn. "All it would take is one man to get through my lines and find you up there alone. There's no such thing as a perfect defense."

He was right. She took a deep breath to calm herself. "All right, then. I'll take Nuallen with me."

"No." He crossed his arms and leveled a glare at her.

"Why not? He's more than capable of watching over me. He cares about me and I trust him implicitly." At Magnus's darkening expression, she stopped. Oh gods. It couldn't be.

"Magnus, he's in his forties, old enough to be my father." She bit the inside of her cheek. It wouldn't do to laugh right now, though it welled up inside her. Nuallen? He was a fine-looking man, but . . . *Nuallen*?

Magnus said nothing. He continued to lean against the door and gaze at her.

"He loves my mother."

At that, he sighed. "I know. But still. I'll go with you."

"You have to meet with Eirik and Leif."

"And you said you wanted to see Ingeborg. Why don't you do

that, and afterward come back here? I should be done by then and we can go."

She didn't want him to be there when she opened herself to the powers surrounding her. She needed stillness, both around her and in her mind. But it was the only way she was going up there, so she would just have to ignore him. "All right. I'll be back here before midday."

He inclined his head to her and left, closing the door gently behind him. If only, one time, he'd slam it. Like she wanted to.

He was being entirely too reasonable. Then again, he most likely felt he had to handle her like the finest imported glass or else she'd be gone, taking her ships and gold with her. Like all men, it was the only thing he cared about. Well, not quite the only thing. But he wasn't making it easy for her to accept him and this marriage. He'd said she had to desire him before he'd come to her. Or was that just an excuse? She sat down.

Every night, he combed out her hair. And every night he ran his hands along her back and arms and shoulders, relaxing her into sleep. But nothing more. Not even a kiss. If he wanted her, all he had to do was turn her over and . . .

He appeared to have been attracted to her, but had he changed his mind? It might be that with as pale and slender as she was, he'd decided that she didn't entice him after all. Maybe Magnus just hid it better because he wanted something only she could give him. Many a husband suffered a marriage and a wife he didn't want to gain a hefty dowry.

Prospective suitors had always kept away from her because of her visions and strange silver-gray eyes. They sought women who were strong and capable, who could bear them many sons. They wanted women who knew only how to handle households, children, and farming.

She understood those things, as well. But no one had ever looked beyond what they saw, to what she could do. She'd thought that a man's rejection would never bother her. After all, she'd planned to go to Uppsala and become a priestess. Yet, as she looked back, each time a man had made an excuse and his gaze had slid away from hers, it had dealt her a tiny sting. Rather than admit it, even to herself, she'd always raised her chin and steeled herself against feeling anything. She'd told herself it just didn't matter.

What if it finally did matter? Magnus was her husband. If he turned away from her in the night, it would be the ultimate rejection. When she'd known her marriage was inevitable, she'd assumed he would take her, albeit more gently than she'd witnessed during the winter. Then it would be done.

He'd said he wouldn't. Not until she desired him. She put her head in her hands. What did that mean? She knew about what happened between men and women, but she didn't *know*. What did desire even feel like? Was it the melting sensation inside her when Magnus smoothed his hands over her shoulders and back during the night? What would happen if, just once, she turned over and faced him? Would he do the same thing to her breasts? He was waiting for some sign from her, but what did she know of such things? And each day, they grew more distant.

Even though she was married, she might end up being alone with the gods in the end.

The island, her haven, was gone. It had vanished from under her and plunged her into the turbulent sea. She was still sinking. She needed to reach up to find the gods and reconnect with them, pull herself back into the light. Feel their breath on the wind, hear their words in the trees, find their wisdom, which the land itself would sing to her. Maybe then, she would understand.

No one would keep her from the gods. Not Toke, not his threats, and not even Magnus. Once, they were all she wanted. Now, they might be all she had left.

"I brought this for Silvi, but it's also quite useful for wounds." Lifa's voice carried to the street as Silvi walked up to Ingeborg's small house. "It comes from the sap of trees that grow in a land where it's always warm. It's as expensive as gold, though, so it should be reserved for those wounds that will not heal any other way."

Silvi leaned in the open doorway. She didn't want to disturb her mother and the healer if they were involved in discussing the cures Lifa had brought with them. Ingeborg saw her and motioned her in. A chunk of brownish-yellow resin sat on the main table.

"The myrrh." Silvi picked it up.

"What ails you, mistress?" Ingeborg studied her. "And what do you use this for besides wounds?"

"I have burning pains in my stomach." She placed it back on the table. "It's mostly when I become upset, though it can happen at other times as well. Eirik said he bought this from healers who were from a place called Arabia. There, the healers are called *saydalani* and they must be permitted by their rulers to practice their art. They believe illness is not caused by the gods, but by imbalances in the body itself. These imbalances can be treated with medicines."

"For Silvi, I make an infusion of this with water, then mix it with honey, for it is bitter," Lifa said. "I sometimes add ginger as well. It's helping her."

"I see." Ingeborg nodded. "How it is used for wounds?"

"You may make a lotion of it with wine and place it on the injury."

Ingeborg chuckled. "With the jarl's expensive wine, and this being as costly as gold, it would have to be an important wound. Or person."

Lifa smiled. "Perhaps it would be better, then, for his peace of mind, to mix it with honey, flour, beef fat, and butter, then apply it."

"Thank you, Mother, for bringing it." And if things kept on the way they had been with Magnus, she would likely need it. Soon.

"Eirik bought the myrrh with you in mind when he heard about its effects on the stomach. It's only right that it come here with you. If this does work, we can ask Rorik to look for it in his travels. In spite of his raiding, there are quite a few traders with whom he does business. After all, he has to sell his spoils somehow. With as many languages as he speaks, he should be able to find some when he heads east to Staraya Ladoga."

Perhaps even Magnus could search for it in his travels. With the longships, he would be able to venture farther than he ever could before. If it worked on wounds as well as Eirik was told, it could be very profitable to sell it here.

Silvi winced. Already she was thinking like a merchant. She needed the time with the gods to bring herself back to what mattered. And yet, more profits meant a better life for the people of Thorsfjell, and what could matter more than that?

She sat at the table and listened while her mother and Ingeborg discussed various treatments and compared the herbs they had with them. Lifa would be gone in a short time and Silvi needed to learn all she could. She'd always stood in her mother's shadow, but soon the light would shine on her alone, and she needed to be ready. At least Ingeborg was here, but the elderly woman was frail. Who knew how many more winters she could withstand? Then everything would fall to her.

She stared out the open door. She wasn't ready for this. For healing, for guiding a people, for running a village, for marriage. Her parents had taught her everything she should know about such things, but she never thought she'd need them. At times, she'd listened with only half her attention. Details had faded into the back of her mind long ago. That was for other women. Not for her.

Now, she would have to remember everything she'd been taught. The only thing she was confident about was her role in the spiritual guidance of Thorsfjell.

She sat up. *Oh gods, Magnus.* He was supposed to take her to the sacred grove. Had he been waiting on her all this time? It was his own fault, though, for wanting to come with her. It served him right. And yet, it was for her safety that he had insisted on taking her himself. Perhaps he did care a bit after all.

"I have to meet with Magnus." She rose as Ingeborg and her mother gave each other a knowing look. Frowning, she let out an exasperated sigh. "Never mind where your thoughts have obviously gone. I have to go to the grove, but he won't let me go alone."

"Not with the way things are right now." Ingeborg mixed a bowl of ground herbs. "He's right to guard you so. And perhaps you need to be there more for him than he needs to be there for you."

She didn't respond. Magnus said he hadn't spoken of his lack of feeling for the gods to anyone, not even Leif. It wasn't her place to enlighten anyone else to that. Instead she picked up the chunk of myrrh.

"I'll take this. In case I need it. Then I won't have to disturb either of you. I can powder and mix it myself." And she wouldn't let them know just how often her stomach burned her. Her mother knew it happened when she was upset or anxious. With Magnus and her being at odds about so many things, she might have more need of it than she wanted them to know. Besides, she could show it to him so he would recognize it while on his journeys.

When she entered the longhouse, the door to his meeting room was open, so she looked in. He sat at his table, speaking with Leif. When they saw her, they stopped talking and she stepped in. She set the resin on the table.

"Did you bring that to hit Magnus on the head with?" Leif leaned forward. "It won't work. His head is too hard."

Magnus sniffed it, ignoring him. "It smells interesting."

"It's called myrrh. Eirik can tell you more about it than I can, since he brought it back for us. I do know it's used in the eastern lands for healing wounds." She smiled at the sharp look of interest he gave her. "It's worth its weight in gold, but if you find it in the markets, it could be very lucrative in your trading. It also helps stomach pains. Its true value is in healing injuries. They don't fester as often."

"These aren't things I have any knowledge of. Nor does Ingeborg. We know mostly the herbs and plants we have here. What else did he bring back?"

"I can show you the herbs and spices that my mother brought with her. Then when you see them, you'll know to buy them."

"To us, they all look like dead plants." Leif took the myrrh from Magnus and studied it. "He might have to bring you with us to help with that."

To be back on the seas, sailing in a magnificent longship, the spray on her face, the sounds of the waves on the hull at night. With Magnus so close to her the entire time.

"This is mine." She plucked the myrrh from Leif's hand. "Unless we need it for wounds. Magnus, are you ready to go to the grove?"

"Yes." He rose. "What use is it to you? There aren't any wounds on your body."

Leif snorted, then ducked as Magnus tossed a wooden cup at him. She had to stop herself from smiling. They were acting like two little boys, and she'd never seen Magnus this way. He grinned as Leif headed out of the room, winking at her. Heat rose in her cheeks.

"Excuse my brother. He knows no subtlety." He looked at the myrrh, then her. "You have stomach pains?"

She edged her gaze away from his. "Anyone can have an upset stomach, Magnus."

"Yes." He came around the desk to stand before her. "And we have plenty of remedies for that. But you said pains. Eirik would have spent a great deal of gold on this. That's something he would do for someone very important to him who was hurting."

He didn't miss much. But then, trading in all the markets, he had to be skilled at such observations. She should have been more careful about what she said.

"I have some pains in my stomach from time to time. It's nothing. But Eirik worries too much and so he spent much more than he should have. Still, since he did pay for it, I'll use it. It might help." It already had, but she didn't want him to think much of it. Especially if he knew what caused those pains.

After she put the myrrh in their chamber, she joined him in the common room. He swirled her cloak around her shoulders.

"It's not cold here, but on the cliff, the winds blow more freely. I don't want you to take a chill."

She nodded her thanks. They walked through the village, pausing as people stopped Magnus to speak with him about different matters. He knew each of them, their concerns, their situations, and their families' problems. Of course, he had been born here, and had lived here all his life, being groomed for this responsibility; but it went deeper than that.

He cared. From the warrior who needed a new battle-axe to the young woman who wanted more wool to spin, he listened to each of them with great attention.

When they left the village road to start up the path to the grove, she smiled. "They depend on you for many things."

"It's the way of a jarl. We must be provider, judge, protector, and mediator. We represent our people to other men as well as to the gods. The welfare of all, from the highest-ranking warrior to the lowest thrall, is my responsibility. It's why Leif hopes I live to be a hundred years old. He doesn't want the title."

"Neither does Rorik, though he's more like a king as far as his power and wealth go. All he wants is to go on raids and enjoy the spoils that come of them."

"Sometimes I feel that men like Leif and Rorik are wiser than I am, but it was what I was born to." He took her arm to steady her as they rounded a sharp turn in the path. "I still feel like I fail them all in the most important way. I'm supposed to intercede with the gods for them. To conduct the rituals on the right days, and make the sacrifices that will please Asgard. I go through the motions, but that's all. The gods must know it."

"Perhaps that's why I'm here." They reached the top of the path and she stepped out of the trees. Did the gods feel she was needed here more than at the temple? There, she would be one of many. Here, she would be one *for* many.

He stopped, as though uncertain. She continued on until she stood in the center of the open space, facing the gap in the trees where she could see the distant mountains and ice. A cool wind picked up. Closing her eyes, she breathed deep of the sharp scent and cleared her mind.

A place inside of her opened out. She raised her arms and tilted her head back, welcoming the sensations spiraling around her. From the land, the sky, and the air itself, energies penetrated her, strengthening her. Her hands tingled and her legs tightened with the power coming up to her from the mountain itself.

Here, it was so easy to feel the gods. Thorsfjell, Thor's mountain, held his force. Though the sky was clear, the hairs on her body lifted as though lightning was about to strike. Letting go of the energies, she followed them out across the lands, feeling, reaching, skimming the life forces there.

Warm light lay behind her, in the direction of the village. It held peace and calm, joy and contentment. It came from the people who lived there. But tiny pockets of gray drifted across them, like shadows cast by small clouds moving above the land. One of the shadows veered toward her and settled around her. She studied it. She had to understand what it meant, why it covered her. Where did it come from? Envisioning light surrounding her, she thrust out with her mind.

The shadow churned into the air, streaming away from her. The others trailed after it. She followed them, back along the direction they'd come from, climbing over the peak of the mountain and into the next valley.

Bygvik stood in gloom. She saw only that, but it was enough. The vision faded. Still, she sought the touch of the gods.

Hear me. An essence enveloped her mind, brushing against it like a warm wave of recognition. It bathed her in calm certainty. She smiled, welcoming it as she would a cherished friend.

Protect our people, for they are mine now as well as Magnus's. Touch them through me, if that is your wish, and in time, let me show him your ways and your power. His heart is true, but it does not see. Show him who you are in a way he will understand.

The wind rushed against her, the chill driving away the warm acceptance that had wrapped around her. The connection broke and she opened her eyes. She gazed up at the peak rising above them, where a blanket of snow still lingered. A gust took part of it, sending it cascading into the sky and over the other side. That was where the shadows came from—and the largest one had aimed for her.

Her visions were rarely clear and direct. Often, they were symbolic and she needed her mother to interpret them. This one, however, she understood. She turned to Magnus. He hadn't left his place at the edge of the grove.

"There's a threat directed at Thorsfjell from Toke's village. You know this already, but the danger is already here. And much of it is aimed toward me."

He strode to her. "How do you know this? What did you see? Did the gods speak to you?"

"Not in words. I saw shadows, like those the clouds make. They crossed the mountain and settled in the village. The darkest one came over me."

Magnus grimaced. "Toke vowed he would destroy anything I held dear, and he knows I'm newly married. I'm sending you to Haardvik, or even Vargfjell to stay with Rorik. You'll be safer there until this is resolved."

She faced him. "I told you, I'm not going anywhere."

"You'll do as I say, Silvi."

"Why? I don't see you evacuating all the women and children, and yet the threat to them is just as great if we're attacked. Are you trying to get rid of me? Is that it?"

"What are you talking about? You're my wife. I want you with me. But it's more important that you be safe."

"I will be. There was a light that surrounded me and drove off the shadow. It must have been the power of the gods that shielded me."

"The only shield I know is the one I have on my arm in battle. And that's the only one I trust. Not some light in your mind from a vision."

"And yet, you're taking my vision as an excuse to make me go elsewhere. I guess it's good enough for that, but nothing else."

"Where is all this coming from, Silvi? It's obvious Toke is a threat to you and to all of us because of his vow. I'm not entirely immune to portents. They have their places. Eirik's rune readings were certainly accurate. I believe in them somewhat, but I don't depend on them. And that's the difference between us."

"There are more differences than just that, Magnus. Yet, in one way, we are the same. We want to protect Thorsfjell. You in your way, and I in mine. Do you know how my mother and I came to be at Haardvik throughout the winter?"

He blinked. "What does that have to do with this? Eirik said Nuallen helped you to escape, but Hakon's men found you and brought you back."

"That's what we wanted Eirik to believe. He would have killed us himself if he knew the truth, so we never told him. Nuallen did drag us out when the attack first occurred. But we went back."

"*What?*" Color rose in his neck as he stared at her.

"We returned there for our people. It fell to us. We knew at that point that my father was dead and we weren't certain of Eirik, though I thought I felt him nearby. Neither my mother nor I could leave the people to those outcasts, so we went back. Nuallen fought our decision, but he was only a slave at the time and had to obey my mother's word. Still, he could have escaped, and we couldn't have stopped him. He came with us to protect us as best as he could.

"We're Norse women, Magnus. We defend the homesteads when the men are gone in the summer. I didn't leave Haardvik even in the midst of such direct danger, and I certainly won't leave Thorsfjell now. And neither will the rest of my family. Or Nuallen." His face darkened when she mentioned the name. She sent him a good glare.

He crossed his arms. "Then I suppose I would have to fight all of you."

"That's right."

"And I'd probably have to tie you up and toss you on a ship in secret, at night."

"You could try."

His lips twitched. "Don't tempt me. It sounds too intriguing, and I'm not talking about tossing you on a ship."

He gave her a long look and she frowned. What was he talking about?

Spearing his hand through his hair, he turned away and focused through the gap in the trees toward the distant glaciers. "Does insanity run in your family?"

A laugh welled up in her, but she wrestled it back down. "Our ancestral sword was made from metal the gods threw down at us from the sky. I have visions, and my mother has the ear of the gods. Both Thor and Odin fight over Eirik. Then there's Rorik, which speaks for itself. There are his sisters. One wants to kill everyone, and the other is a *vargamon*, a wise woman who runs with wolves. What do you think?"

"That's what I feared." With his eyes closed, he pinched the bridge of his nose. "In the interest of not starting a blood feud between our families, I suppose I should let you stay."

"That, and my mother has a habit of putting runes in odd places to produce certain unsavory results. It's not wise to cross her."

"Nor you, I'm beginning to think."

She gave him her sweetest smile. How did he do that? Dispel any argument with his understated humor. It wasn't as obvious as Leif's, but it worked. She couldn't stay angry with him.

He dropped his arms with a sigh. "I suppose there *are* ways to win a war without swords and shields. I have a feeling I just lost another one."

"Is that what this is between us? A war?"

He came closer to her, but didn't touch her. "I hope not. And yet it often comes to that, doesn't it? I suppose when two worlds collide, there's bound to be friction."

"My world is your world, Magnus. You just won't see it. It permeates and underlies everything around us. It's as much a part of your world as all of this." She swept her arm around them.

He shook his head and raised his hand to brush her cheek with his thumb. "You were so—you had such a beautiful smile when you had your vision. You almost glowed. I wish I could understand such things. My existence is one of strength and power, for that's what I need to survive and to protect those under my care. Prayers that dance on the breezes and are as thin as starlight won't help me in battle or on the seas during a storm."

She put her hand on his, where it lingered on her cool cheek, and pressed her face into his palm. His skin was so warm compared to hers. "Perhaps one day, you'll feel the true nature of the gods. Their power and the strength of their words make us what we are as a people. But take care. If power is what you understand, then power may be what they choose to show you. And only the strongest can survive that."

Chapter Nine

Magnus slept.

Silvi had awakened when the radiance from the moon coming through the smoke hole in the roof fell on their bed. He was on his back, one arm over his head. The furs had fallen away and he was uncovered from his hips up.

He'd taken down her hair, as he always did, and combed it out until it lay like silk across her back. Then he'd massaged her shoulders until she slept. She usually remained asleep until morning. This was the first time she'd awakened before he did, and she turned on her side to watch him.

In sleep, he looked younger than his years. The cares and burdens of his position added strain around his eyes and mouth. Perhaps this was his true age. She didn't know. He was beautiful in a masculine way. His dark hair lay across the pillow, too tempting to resist. She touched it with her fingertips. It was much softer than she would have thought. The golden lights within it sparkled in the moon's rays.

His deep chest rose and fell, the curves accentuated by light and shadow. His abdomen was ridged and flat, but the scar slashing across it marred its perfection. She held her hand over it but didn't touch him. He had other scars, to be certain, from battle. But they were light. This should have killed him. Asa told her that many years ago Magnus had found their step-uncle, Hakon, trying to rape her. Hakon had wounded him before he'd escaped and Magnus had nearly died. This must be the scar from the wound.

Sorrow engulfed her. The thought that so fine a man could have died, twisted her stomach. Tears came to her eyes. She never would have known him. Never have married him. She would be someplace else now, perhaps even Uppsala. Eirik wouldn't marry her off to just anyone; he had chosen Magnus for her because of who he was. Honorable, forthright, protective.

For the first time, the thought of Uppsala didn't entice her. She'd always been able to envision herself there and it had brought comfort to her. Now this, this was comfort. This was where she wanted to be.

She touched his shoulder, so softly it should not have disturbed him. His skin was cool in the night air. However, he was a warrior and slept lightly. He stirred. She lifted her hand and he quieted. Careful and slow, she pulled the furs up over his chest. He shifted farther under them.

Holding her breath, she moved closer to him and lowered her head onto his chest beneath his raised arm. She rested her hand on his stomach.

His breathing hitched, then he lifted his head. "Silvi?"

"I hope so."

He didn't say anything. Had she made a mistake? She started to move away, but he lowered his arm, holding her to him. "Stay."

Snuggling closer to him, she smiled. "I thought you might be cold."

"We have half the furs I own on top of us."

"You're warmer than any furs."

He chuckled. "So are you."

She was? Her skin always stayed so cool. "Then can we keep each other warm?"

"Every night, if you like." He pulled the furs up so they both were nestled under them. He took her hand and kissed her palm, then kept hold of it against his chest. "In the moonlight, your hair looks like the first fall of snow."

"It's too pale. *I'm* too pale. Colorless."

"When I first saw you, you looked like you came from Alfheim, where the Light Elves live. I thought if I were to touch you, you might fade away into another world."

She closed her eyes and swallowed. "I won't fade away, Magnus."

He stopped breathing and she looked up at him. The question lay in his blue eyes. Turning her head, she kissed his chest over his heart, then eased onto her back. He raised himself onto his elbow, leaned down, and kissed her. It wasn't the brief, respectful kiss she'd come to know. This was a kiss of possession, his mouth sealed against hers.

He threaded his fingers through her hair and tightened his grip. It didn't hurt, but she couldn't move her head. And she didn't want to.

"Open for me, Silvi."

She didn't understand what he meant until he pressed on her jaw with gentle insistence. She gasped as he invaded her mouth with his. His breath became hers. She tasted him, matching what he did. Touching his shoulder, she ran her hand up under his hair as it fell down over her. He moved onto her, and put his leg over hers. She couldn't escape him if she wanted to. Breathing hard, he lifted his head. His eyes met hers and she smiled, though it was tremulous.

Letting go of her hair, he peeled away the furs covering her breasts and gazed at her. She wanted to wrap her arms around herself. Would he think she was too small, too thin? Men liked women who were . . . large. She wasn't. She wanted to shrink away, but his legs still trapped hers. He looked at her body, not speaking.

She brought her arm over herself, her cheeks heating. He took her hand in his and intertwined their fingers. Bringing her hand onto the bed beside her head, he held it there. He shifted so her other arm was beneath him. She was open to him and couldn't hide from his gaze.

"Magnus, don't."

"Don't what?" He kissed her between her breasts.

She drew in a sharp breath as the touch of his lips drove straight into her. "Don't look at me. I'm too thin and too pale."

"Too beautiful for words."

She shook her head.

"Silvi. Look at me."

At the tone of command in his voice, she did as he said.

"You're the most beautiful woman I've seen." He touched his mouth to the tip of her breast and she jumped.

She pulled at her hand, but he wouldn't let her go. He was so strong. It took no effort at all for him to hold her still, but he was gentle. She quieted.

"That's better. I can see we have a few nights ahead of us for me to make you feel what I want between us. If I can survive, that is."

"I don't understand."

"I know, and I'll change that. For tonight, let this be a start."

His kiss was like the finest wine, heady and sweet. He still held her in his tender grip. She didn't try to break free. Relaxing into his hold, she returned his kiss. When he ended it, he released her, then turned her so her back was to him. He wrapped himself around her, pulling her close to him, her back to his chest. He was so hard—everywhere. Even she knew what that meant.

He pulled the furs up over them again and kissed her hair. "Sleep now, Silvi. I'm not so certain I'll be able to, but you need to rest. You may not get many chances over the next few nights."

"I know you have needs. I can feel it, even now."

"I'd be disappointed if you couldn't."

She elbowed him in the ribs and he chuckled. "Magnus, it's not fair to you."

"Believe me, we'll make up for it. I want to be certain it's what you desire and that you're ready for me. I want your first time to be more than you ever dreamed of. First, you need to understand how desirable and beautiful you are to me, and I don't think you do right now. I'll show you. Later."

With him wrapped around her like he was, and the strange feelings his strength and mastery had given her, it wasn't likely she would sleep. And unless she missed her guess, neither would he.

Magnus yawned into his plate. He'd told Silvi to go to sleep last night, but he hadn't followed his own advice. Her breathing hadn't slowed until the early morning hours either. Why didn't he just take her? In spite of her insecurities about her beauty, she acted as though she welcomed him. Perhaps he should have asked if insanity ran in *his* family.

They had a lifetime together, though. In spite of his discomfort, a few days wouldn't make a difference in the long run. It might make a difference, though, in how she viewed him and how their nights would be from now on.

Anyone older than a young child knew what happened between men and women. Yet she still seemed so innocent. It warmed him that he would be the one to teach her. It also made him uneasy. He'd never had a virgin before, only lusty widows and willing serving women. They'd known better than to expect anything more from him, but he'd made certain they enjoyed themselves the same as he. So much more rode on this.

He wanted her to love him. It was as though he walked on thin ice, both emotionally and physically. Any misstep would lead to disaster. But she was far stronger than he might have thought. How many women would have gone back into a village filled with out-laws to help her people? Perhaps the gods did shield her. She must have inherited her strength from her mother.

He took a bite of his cold sausage. Some women liked it rougher, others enjoyed a more tender touch. She'd responded to his gentle but firm command last night. Perhaps that was the way to her desire. But he didn't want to order her, or pressure her in any way. It had to be her choice. Still, he could strike a balance and find the path to her heart.

He pushed his plate away and stood. He had things to see to this morning, and unless he wanted to be in pain all day, he needed to stop this line of thinking. Leif watched him from across the room, a half smile threatening. They were twins; Leif often knew what he was thinking with uncanny accuracy. He had that skill with anyone he watched, but with Magnus he had it down to an art. And he knew Leif. He was arming himself with quips at Magnus's expense. He wouldn't provide him with more fodder for his jokes.

Nuallen walked in the open doors, his arms full of sheathed swords. He tossed them on one of the tables with a loud crash and headed for the pitcher of ale on the sideboard. Everyone stopped talking and stared at the pile of weapons, then at him.

Magnus inspected them as Nuallen poured a cup of ale. "What are these?"

"Swords." He drained the cup.

Leif choked out a laugh as Magnus rubbed the bridge of his nose. "I can see that. Where did you get them?"

"From the five men up on the ridge. They were spying on us, so I slew them." He poured more ale as Leif and the other men in the room gathered around the weapons, all talking at once.

"Nuallen." Magnus raised his voice over the din.

"Is there anything left to eat?" He frowned at the empty serving platters from the morning meal. "Killing is hungry work."

"I'll find you something." Birgitta walked toward the cooking room.

Magnus cleared his throat. "Nuallen, suppose you start at the be-ginning."

"Not much to tell." He sat at Magnus's table with a sigh. "I thought to go above and see the lay of the land. Your men had been through there, but I saw other signs. Even more recent. I found one of

Toke's men hiding in the bushes, looking down into the village. I killed him and figured there must be more of them. There were. Not anymore." He smiled his thanks as Birgitta set a full plate of eggs, beef, and cheese in front of him.

"Five? You slew five men by yourself?" He sank down at the table.

Nuallen shrugged as he stabbed a piece of meat with his knife. "If you take them one by one, it really doesn't matter how many there are, does it? One or a dozen. It just takes a little longer and makes you hungrier."

"I had a lot of men up there. What were they doing? Picking flowers?"

"They did their jobs." He spoke around a hunk of beef, then swallowed. "But Toke's men timed their spying in between patrols. Quick in, quick out. They weren't trying to attack. They wanted to find out if we were amassing more warriors. That doesn't take long."

"Then we change our patterns. Stagger the patrols. Nuallen, you see things others don't. Would you take one of the horses and make the circuit of this side of the mountain?"

"Of course, but I'd rather go on foot. Not so obvious."

"However you wish. Leif, get word to the men. And find Eirik and Asa. We need to meet."

Leif sprinted out the door.

"I also saw signs that they'd been closer to the village, but not so recently. Sometime in the past week, I think."

Magnus slammed his fist against the table. "Then we forget defense. We'll go over the mountain and descend into their valley. Stop them before they come anywhere near here. Send them a clear message."

"I think five dead men is clear enough. I left them where I figure they're coming over the peak. But still, your thoughts are good ones."

"I need you to show us that place. Eirik's men should be back with his ships in a few days, and Toke will be watching the fjord and may want to move before that. It might make them reckless, but we won't be. Nuallen, I want you to sit in on our meetings and come to the mountain with us. I can use your eyes. If we're attacked, your first responsibility is to get back here for Lifa and Silvi. They may not want to leave, but at least guard them."

"My life is theirs. And it always will be."

He met Nuallen's emerald gaze. An understanding passed between them. He might not be quite certain of the Northumbrian where Silvi was concerned, but he was positive Nuallen would guard her with his life. And right now, that was all that mattered.

"Asa, you'll stay here with a group of my men to provide a defense in case any of Toke's men get through. As before, we don't know which way they'll come from. You commanded well during the winter battle." Magnus drummed his fingers on the table in the crowded common room. It was late, but they would be up and out well before dawn.

She nodded. "I wish Arne were here. I miss him. He always stayed near me during a fight."

"I know." Magnus gave her shoulder a quick caress. The huge bear of a man had given his life for Asa's in the winter battle for Thorsfjell. He had died a death they all wished for, though, and now he was drinking, feasting, and fighting in Valhalla. "Leif will stay here along with half of Rorik's warriors. Eirik and I will take the other half. That will give us enough between us."

"As long as it's Kaia's half that stays here." Leif grinned at the somber shieldmaiden.

Her arms crossed, she cast him a disdainful glare, then looked away. "I'd rather be closer to my ships anyhow, in case we have need of them."

"Then it's settled." Magnus rose. "Get some sleep, if you can, all of you. Dawn comes early this time of year. And we must be gone well before then."

He waited until the common room emptied, then he sank back down and poured another small measure of beer. Silvi was waiting for him, naked, in their bed. Her white hair would be up in its braids, lit by the moon's light coming in through the ceiling and the small windows. The furs would cover her, but he had planned on seeing all of her this night. Showing her how beautiful she was.

However, the coming battle was foremost in his thoughts. If he'd already taken her, he would sink into her this night and lose himself in her warmth, in case it might be for the last time. But he hadn't. He needed the entire night to awaken her body to his touch, and he didn't have the time. He drained his cup. Thoughts of strategy and battle movements must take precedence now. She was the daughter of warriors. She would understand.

He shouldn't go to their chamber. It wasn't as though he would get any sleep. He couldn't just leave her alone, though. She might be frightened. Everyone in the village knew he and his men would attack in the morning. He needed to be with her, if only for a little while.

He went to the chamber door, opened it quietly in case she was asleep, and stepped inside. Leaning back against the closed door, he stared.

She knelt on their bed, naked, her hair streaming down around her. Moonlight poured over her upturned face from above, making her skin gleam like a new sword's blade. Her eyes were closed, and her hands were on her thighs, turned up as though holding the radiance bathing her.

"Silvi?" He didn't move toward her. Was she having a vision? She wore the same sublime expression as she had in the grove.

"Already they gather for battle." She remained still, but her voice was strong. "They know. Somehow, they know we're coming. It is as I said before, the shadows are here even now."

He crossed the room and sat on the bed before her. "How do you know? Do you see them?"

She opened her eyes but didn't look at him. They sparkled a bit too much for the moonlight. "They have word we're gearing for battle. They'll be here before the morning."

"Silvi." He touched her face, feathering his fingertips across her translucent skin.

She focused on him and gave him a gentle smile. "I knew you were making your plans for the attack. I thought to help in my own way. Mother read the runes this night and saw it also. Sometimes, that helps me." She dropped her gaze to her body. Her hair covered most of her, but she blushed. "I was ready for bed when I felt the vision come on me. I didn't stop to dress."

"Your hair is undone." He ran his fingers through it.

"I know you always do that. The knots and braids can block the words of the gods. I wanted them to be as clear as possible. I wore it up the other day at the grove because it's expected of me as a married woman. In here, it wouldn't matter." Her eyes widened. "Magnus, how do they know what we're planning? Is someone here giving them information?"

"I don't know. If so, it must be one of the people who escaped here from Bygvik. No one who belongs here would do that. I'll have them watched from now on. I don't want to banish anyone who's innocent, but I won't risk Thorsfjell. I gave them a home. If anyone has betrayed that kindness, that person will answer to me."

He ran his hands down her arms. "Was there anything else? Did you see anything more detailed?"

She shook her head. "The dark places moved over the mountain from the village under the cover of night. The moon was low, so I know it was closer to morning." Her gaze drifted away from him as though she saw something that lay in another world. He waited.

"There were dragons in the skies. I saw them against the stars. Then one of them screamed and flames hurtled toward it. But another dragon swept its wings and put out the fire. The dragon was unharmed."

What does that mean? Asa's guardian spirit is a dragon. Could she be in danger?

"The ships." Silvi took his hand, pressing it. "Anytime I've seen dragons in my visions, they've meant ships. Could Toke try to destroy Rorik's longships that are beached in the fjord?"

"If he does, he'll find a nasty surprise. I'll send Leif and Kaia and some of the warriors to guard them. I have some men there already, of course. But we'll need more."

She shook her head. "Rorik would rather lose an arm, I think, than one of his ships. They're like his children, if he had any. If anyone even thinks of damaging one of them, they'll have his entire fleet down on them before the end of summer."

"Then maybe we should allow them to singe them, just a little. Rorik could do all our work for us." Perhaps some humor would comfort her. It worked when she was angry.

She smiled. "If he happened to come here, that would be nice. But I wouldn't count on it."

"Of course not. I think we can fight this battle ourselves. Toke's men plan to attack us before we attack them. When they climb up the mountain, they'll find us lining the peak, waiting for them. Nuallen knows where they've been coming over. And we'll have the advantage of the higher ground." He leaned forward and kissed her.

"Thank you for helping us. It could make the difference between defeat and victory. I'm just sorry we have to postpone the lessons I had planned for you."

"Lessons?"

"Yes. About how beautiful you are. How desirable. And how much I want you. Only after you learn those things can you go on to the next instructions."

"Oh?" She blushed again. "And what would those entail?"

He touched his forehead to hers. "You'll have to wait. And so, unfortunately, will I. I must wake Leif, Eirik, Asa, and the others. I told them to try to get some sleep, but there's no time for that if we're to be on the peak before Toke's men."

He stood and she climbed off the bed as well.

"There's no need for you to rise," he said as she reached for her dress. He glimpsed her breasts as her hair swung to the side. He clenched his jaw. "Someone around here may as well get some rest."

"Do you think I could sleep now? I have preparations to make. I have to wake Ingeborg and my mother, though she's likely already up. There are herbs to prepare, dressings to make, and poultices to mix. I hope we won't need them, but if we do, I want to be ready. You have your fight, Magnus, and I have mine." She put her hair up in a simple knot at the back of her neck.

"Then we'll go out together and rouse the others. Find Birgitta and have food brought out. This will be a long night and perhaps an even longer day."

He grabbed his sword where it leaned against the wall by their bed. When he turned around, she stood before him. She put her arms around his neck, pulled his head down, and kissed him hard, harder than he thought she could. He caught her to him and took over the kiss, deepening it. When he lifted his head, she looked up at him. Her eyes were moist.

"Please, Magnus, be careful. I know the Norns fate us to die at a certain time. Nothing can change that. But what we do in the meantime is what wins us word-fame and the gods' goodwill. No matter your fate this night, strike true and fight bold, for that's what matters."

"I'll be well. I'd fight the gods themselves to come back here and finish what I've started with you. Just listen to Nuallen and stay with him when he returns here. He'll guard you while I'm on the mountain."

She put her hand on his chest. "Remember, this is *your* mountain, Magnus. Not theirs. You are lord here. The power of Thor surrounds it, and it knows you protect it. The streams that flow on it are your blood. Its roots, so deep in the earth, are as your ancestors. The winds blowing from its heights are your breath. Trust in it, use it to your advantage. It will bring you home to me."

He gathered her closer to him, just holding her, his face buried in her hair. Who knew if her visions were real? But he couldn't take the chance and ignore the warnings. During the winter, Eirik had read his runes and had said that because Magnus had a tendency to hesitate to act, someone he loved suffered. It had happened long ago to Asa, then again with their cousin Estrid. It wouldn't happen again.

Never again.

Chapter Ten

One moment, Magnus knelt alone amidst the rocks and snow on the peak of the mountain. The next, Nuallen crouched beside him. The man was an enigma, but at least he was on their side. Thank the gods.

"Toke's forces are most of the way up. I counted about fifty of them, but I couldn't be certain."

"We have half again that number just here. That doesn't count the warriors in Thorsfjell and those on the beach, guarding the ships. We have the element of surprise and the advantage of the higher ground." He sat back on his heels and checked the seax hanging from his belt.

"It doesn't seem like enough men to mount an attack," Nuallen said.

"It may be all Toke could attract to him since the winter. We killed all his other followers when they attacked us. We don't have large armies like your country. Our forces are smaller."

Nuallen's voice was harsh. "You don't need larger numbers to be victorious. All men fear you as it is."

Eirik knelt on Magnus's left. "No foreign army has ever attacked us in our own lands, not even the Christian emperor Charlemagne, though he thought of it. He forcibly baptized and then slaughtered thousands of people of the northern tribes in a single day. We began raiding foreign lands to show him what he'd be up against if they tried that here. They've never invaded us."

"And with good reason." Nuallen stilled. "Stay here. I'll take a look. I thought I heard something."

He rose, took a step, and melted into the darkness. Even his weapons didn't make a sound. Magnus sighed. He'd have to find out how he did that. He passed the word along to be ready. His order flowed along their lines and the men unsheathed their weapons in a wave. They waited, as silent as the shadows around them.

Magnus's breath steamed into the cold night. He hadn't felt right leaving Silvi, but Asa was there along with his best men. They were guarding so many fronts that they'd had no choice but to split up. It would be the height of hypocrisy to pray to the gods now, when he had all but ignored them before. But if it came to Silvi's welfare, he had no pride.

Please Odin, Thor, let her be safe. And grant me the strength and skill to keep her that way.

Nothing. But then, that was how it had always been. What had he expected? A thunderbolt from the clear, star-filled sky?

Eirik narrowed his eyes. "The land doesn't feel right. They're there. On the path beneath us."

Magnus cared nothing for himself. His fate was sealed. For the sake of Thorsfjell, however, he was afraid. If anything happened to him, Leif would take over. In spite of what his brother said, he would be a good jarl. But Leif could also be killed. Then who would care for Thorsfjell? And Silvi. What would she do?

Magnus had never worried before. Was this what love did? Bring weakness like this? He drew a sharp breath, hardening his resolve. Or it could bring strength to fight for something more than his word-fame—his wife, his village, his mountain.

He knelt forward, listening. The chill air carried the sound of distant running water to him. The falls. What had Silvi said? That the mountain was his. To use it to his advantage.

Had the mountain spoken to him and he had finally learned to listen? "There are falls that run out of the peak from the melting snows this time of year." He pointed down to their right and Eirik nodded. "They're quite wide and rapid now. When Toke's men get here, we'll block off any path of retreat for them except in that direction. It will herd them right into the falls and they'll have no place else to go. Pass the word."

Eirik moved off to the nearest group of warriors while Magnus gave the orders to the men on his left to descend off to the side.

When they were in position, Nuallen stepped up beside him. "They're not far behind me and they travel in a group. Fools. It should be easy enough to surround and slay them."

"I'm sending men down now. They'll come up beneath them like a hook, and we'll catch them like struggling fish. We'll trap them between us and the falls, so they'll have no chance to retreat. But we have to time it just right."

"You'll be able to see them easily down below. With the moonlight and the light covering of snow, they'll stand out. If they look up, there's only darkness behind you. They won't see you against the sky until it's too late."

"My thoughts exactly. I've been on this mountain all my life, and even as boys Leif and I hid that way. Our parents would look for us at night when we were above them. They never saw us."

Nuallen chuckled softly. "Then I'll leave you to your games. I'll go down to the village. May your gods bless you."

"And may your Christ watch over you." Being a Northumbrian, Nuallen would be a Christian. "I trust you more than any gods or god to protect Silvi and Lifa."

He nodded. "With my life." And he was gone.

"We'll hear them when they find the bodies Nuallen left on the path." Eirik hefted his sword. "It should confuse them long enough for us to attack."

"I'm using the archers first. Don't give the signal to advance until after that. We'll shoot from above. Even if Toke has his own archers, they're aiming uphill. When we move, I'll be in the center. All the men will gauge their positions by how far they are from me, keeping the same distance. In that way, we'll maintain our lines." They waited.

Eirik tensed, then held up his hand. "Listen now."

After a few moments, panicked voices soared up to them from the path below. Magnus rose and stood on the edge of the peak, his sword in one hand, his shield in the other. The enemy milled around the bodies, gesturing and looking at them. Already they were in the net and they didn't even know it.

He called down to them. "Yes, they're dead. Care to join them?" As Toke's men scrambled to arm themselves, he nodded to his archers. "Now."

The bowmen stepped to the edge and sprayed their arrows down on the confused group. Screams followed as the men called for a shield wall.

"Again." He pointed with his sword. The archers rained down more arrows, but the shield wall stopped most of them. Time to move.

Magnus raised his sword. "After me."

Eirik ran at his side as they led the men down to the attackers' position. As a group, they used their momentum to slam into the shield wall, knocking many of the men down the path and slaying them. Others, to their credit, stood and fought. Magnus sidestepped a spear thrust, knocked the gleaming point aside, and gutted the man. Another attacker came at him. Grabbing him by the helmet, Magnus swung him hard, breaking his neck with a sickening crack. He let the body drop, looking for another opponent before the corpse hit the ground.

Hearing a sound behind him, he dropped to one knee and twisted, bringing his shield up. An outcast brought his axe down at the same time. The blade skittered off the wood, grazing his upper right forearm. Magnus brought his sword under his shield in a cross stroke, slicing through the man's thighs. He spun, rising, and dragged his blade back across his throat.

His gaze dipped to his injury as he stepped back from the body. Blood already ran down his arm. Not good. He raised it, not wanting his sword hand to become slippery.

"Let me see that." Eirik tore the sleeve, exposing the injury, then looked around them. "You, and you, guard us while I tend to this."

"Yes, Jarl." The men circled them, their weapons ready.

"It's only a scratch," Magnus said. "I can still fight."

"Of course you can. After I wrap it. You'll get blood on the hilt otherwise."

Eirik was right. He couldn't afford to have his sword slip at a bad time. "Use the material from my sleeve to bind it."

"No." Eirik pulled the sleeve out of the way and knotted it above his elbow. "With all that blood and gore on it?" He removed a piece of linen out of his belt pouch and cleaned the cut and the rest of his arm.

Magnus chuckled. "Always prepared?"

"We did a lot of fighting when I raided with Rorik. You learn things. Especially from the desert peoples." He dropped the cloth and got another from his pouch. "A clean cloth." He bound it around his arm. "They think it makes a difference in the healing. We tried it and the wounds don't fester as often. Not certain why."

He tied it off. "How is that?"

Magnus swung his sword. "Good as it ever was. My thanks." He nodded to the men who were guarding them and they moved off. He and Eirik followed them back into the melee.

Eirik cleaved his way through the confusion, never stopping, barely looking at the men he slew. A man came at him with a spear and an axe. Magnus started forward to help his brother-in-law, but Eirik knocked the weapons aside with a sweep of his sword and shield. He leaped inside the weapons' reach, driving the man back with his shoulder, then gave him a shove. The man fell onto a boulder, breaking his back. Eirik flipped his sword so that it pointed downward, and slew him.

Eirik and Magnus stayed together, watching each other's backs. Magnus deflected an axe blow, then countered with his sword. He slammed his shield into the other man's, knocking him off balance, then sliced deep into his axe arm as he flailed. He silenced the shrieks with one cut.

A movement to the left caught his eye. A man aimed his axe at Eirik, pulling it back for the throw. "Eirik!"

He dropped to the ground, dragging his shield over himself. Magnus shrugged off his own shield and threw it. The metal edge hit the man's throat, crushing it. Eirik rose and guarded him until Magnus retrieved his shield.

"Good of you to have practiced that move." Eirik grinned. "But it leaves you open."

"Sometimes, to use something you must be prepared to lose it."

They moved on, wading into the crush. Never mind the men trying to slay him; if anything happened to Eirik, Asa would kill him herself.

Magnus's men who had gone to the right came toward them, driving in front of them the outcasts who had tried to escape. Magnus yelled and his men divided. They picked off the nearest ones, but let most of the panicked outcasts run past them. Otherwise, the warriors of Thorsfjell might have been caught between them. They closed ranks, and the enemy, seeing the increased numbers, broke and headed straight for the swift-running falls.

Magnus slew a man who wasn't fast enough, then picked up speed as the enemy came within sight of the falls. Several of them tried to wade across. The waters swept them down the cliffs, their howls dying as they did.

The remaining men tried to surrender, but there was no court of law for them. There would be one verdict, one sentence. Magnus, as jarl, was the judge. He gave the order as they begged for their lives. If he allowed them to leave, they would only prey on other villages. There was no other recourse. His men moved in, their swords at the ready. He nodded. The mountains rang with their cries as they all died, cowering on the ground like the vermin they were.

"There are only two outcomes to any battle. Either one lives or one dies." Eirik shoved one of the bodies with his boot. "There are many kinds of death, and these men will never know the afterlife of an honorable warrior. They are truly dead and gone."

"I don't want these bodies cluttering up my mountain." Magnus turned his back on the pile. "In the morning, get them down to Toke's valley. Let their blood be a message to him." He raised his voice. "This is *my* mountain."

The men all banged their shields and cried out in agreement. He let the sound wash over him, swelling his heart. This was his birthright and nothing would wrest it from him. The rocks so firm beneath his feet anchored him here, the wind was his breath, the water rushing off the peak was like the blood in his veins. Was this what Silvi felt? The power? The strength of the land around him? He raised his sword, yelling out. All around him, the men joined in. Their voices echoed through the night, carried down into the valley on the cold air. Let Toke hear that. Let him understand. Let his heart freeze in fear.

As they stripped the bodies of weapons and jewelry, Magnus cleaned his sword on the tunic of one of the dead men. All men had a choice in how they lived their lives. These had chosen poorly.

He straightened and sheathed his sword. "I need a report on our dead and wounded."

One of his archers walked up. "One dead, eight wounded. I think the dead man was one of Rorik's."

"Oh, he'll want revenge from Toke for that," Eirik said. "Maybe not as much as for a warship, but he'll still want to collect."

"He'll have to stand behind me." Magnus picked up his shield. "As it is, we'd better get back to Thorsfjell. They may need us."

"Let's move, then." Eirik sheathed his sword.

Magnus called the men to him. Enough of them would stay to clean up and help the wounded return to the village. The rest would come with him now. He glanced back as they started toward the other side of the peak. It was a good day's work and the sun wasn't even up yet, though the east was starting to lighten.

But the battle might not be over.

Had her marriage to Magnus joined her to this place, the same as it joined her to him?

Silvi didn't need to wait for Nuallen to return to tell them the battle had begun. The mountain had already told the tale to her in the shifting of forces around her, the tightening of her stomach, the sensitivity of her skin.

Her mother sat at a table in the crowded common room, a pile of small wood pieces before her. Lifa was dressed in her full regalia, her fur cloak over her shoulders, her rune staff at her side. She carved Sowilo into a round of oak, then made a small cut on the palm of her hand. She dropped the blood into the symbol and murmured soft words.

Silvi left her and went into the weaving room, where women sat at the looms, waiting.

"Our men fight this battle in their way," she said to them. "And we fight it in ours to help. Just as the Valkyries and the Norns weave the fate of men, so will we turn the course of war on our looms. The Valkyries bind a warrior with terror or loosen that fear. Tie your knots in the weft to make the enemy immobile and unfasten them to free our men to slay. The warp strands are the *wyrd* upon the earth. Weave strength and peace upon it."

As the women worked, Silvi walked to those sitting by the walls. "Spin your distaffs, twining the strands of fate. Call upon the gods to aid us. Bind that into your threads, bringing victory to our men and safety to all who dwell here. For we are the weavers of destiny. While each person's death is his own, we control what happens until then."

She circled the room, encouraging, guiding, praying. This was her role, the one she'd always thought she'd play, but in a place far from here. And yet, did not the gods hear her wherever she was? Even wives and maidens such as these held power.

The hands of some of the women shook and their eyes were moist from fear for themselves and their men. Still they wove, still they spun. She encouraged them, seeking out those who were terrified, calming them.

"We are Norse. Even Charlemagne himself would not come here. He feared us. Our men sail the world, conquering all, knowing we're strong enough to protect what is ours when they're gone. Are we not the same as they are? The gods protect us and hear us, as well. The Norns are women, yet the gods of Asgard cannot thwart what they have woven. The blood of warriors flows in your veins. Feel it, use it."

She glanced toward the common room as the front door opened. Nuallen stepped in and nodded to her. Swallowing, she went to him.

Silvi spoke low. "It started?"

"It might be ended by now. There wasn't a very large force. Magnus will make short work of them. I passed Asa on the way in. Her men are patrolling the perimeter of the village. She said there have been no problems here."

"No. Leif and Kaia are down by the ships with half of Rorik's men, as well as some of our own. I haven't heard anything from them."

He nodded. "I'm going back out to help patrol the outskirts. But I'll stay near the longhouse so I can hear if anything is wrong. Do you feel anything beyond here?"

"A change in the land, in the mountain. Nothing close to here." She smiled. "It's rather like old times with me telling you if anyone is close to us so you can go out and kill them."

"Let's hope I don't have to kill anyone. If I do, it means they got too close for my liking."

"And for mine. The women are afraid, but they're strong."

Nuallen's green eyes sparkled. "They get that from you, Silvi. Don't you see how your gifts can be used here, among the people?"

"I'm beginning to. You sound like my mother. And my brother."

"If I sound like them, then I am honored."

"And persistent. Go now. I'd feel better if your eyes and ears listened to the night instead of to me."

"Yes, mistress." He gave a gentle, teasing laugh and left, but not before glancing at Lifa, his expression softening. She was still bent over her runes, her eyes closed as she spoke soft, arcane words to the gods.

Silvi returned to the weaving room. Would she ever know all of her mother's wisdom, the things she'd learned at the great temple? How much of her learning had come from the priestesses there, and how much had come from living life itself?

She walked to the great looms where the women worked, and leaned her forehead against one of the frames. *Let him be victorious. Let him come home to me.* Tangling her fingers in the threads, she closed her eyes. What would happen if he fell? Thorsfjell would go on, but could she? He'd become a part of her. She'd wanted to hold herself from him, to feel nothing for him, so that eventually she could walk away.

But each day, she'd discovered more of his fineness, his honor, his gentle caring for his people. And for her. She hadn't gone to him, as he wished, yet he'd still respected her. And each night, he touched her more deeply, if not her body, then her heart. With every stroke of the comb, and every brush of his hands, she'd opened more to him and their lives together. The desire for Uppsala had faded, even as the island in her visions had vanished.

There'd been someone on the island with her, though. If only she'd seen who it was. She could remember the feeling of joy when she'd felt him there.

Could it have been Magnus on the shore behind her? Was the island giving her to him? Could he be her true destiny? If he died this night, she would never know. If he died . . .

She turned her face into the weaving as tears filled her eyes. Once, she might have thought that if he died, she'd be free. Instead, she'd never hear his voice again, never see the humor in his eyes, never feel his touch in the night. He'd never teach her the things he'd spoken of.

Her stomach lurched and she blotted her tears on the cloth in the loom, lest the women see them and lose heart. She walked over to the corner where Asa kept her carving tools and sat down on the bench.

No, she would never be free again, no matter what happened this night. Whether he lived or died, it would make no difference in how she felt for him.

She loved him.

As the women worked, the sounds of the looms filled her head. Destiny wove all around her, the knots tightening and loosening, the strands binding Magnus and her together, intertwining them. There was no escaping it. No vows, no ceremonies, no dreams could hold her as this did. For it wasn't about something or someone beyond her. It *was* her.

She looked at her pale, slender hands. He'd said she was beautiful, but she knew better. She was as a piece of cloth left too long in the sauna—insipid and washed out. How could he love her? The longships she brought him were what he wanted. They would empower him, strengthen him, give him the world. That was what he understood. She could never stand beside him wielding a sword, as Asa did with Eirik. All she could do was this.

The women continued weaving and spinning. Who knew if it did any good? While he was out there with his weapons and his men, risking his life for them all, she was here, safe and weak, mumbling prayers to gods on another world. Which made more difference to the outcome?

The sounds in the room made her head hurt. She rushed out through the front door. She wouldn't be foolish and stray too far from the longhouse, but she needed an escape from the noise and the emotions of the others. To breathe the clear air and be alone for a few moments.

Dawn was coming, though the stars still filled the sky. She lifted her face to their gentle light. She tried to reach over the land, to feel what it would tell her, but her heart was too tumultuous. She couldn't clear her mind as she needed to. With a sigh, she gave up. News would come soon enough.

Usually women were out by now, drawing water from the wells, gossiping, taking clothes to be washed. But the street was empty and silent. As she looked up at the sky, she could almost imagine she was by herself, her mind was as calm as the morning air, and she didn't love a man who might never love her back.

"Silvi, is everything all right?"

She jumped at the sound of Asa's voice and took a deep breath to quiet her pounding heart. "It's fine. I just needed some air. Have you heard anything?"

Asa rested her hand on her sheathed sword. "Nothing yet. It shouldn't be too much longer though. If the battle was going to last long, Magnus would have sent someone back to get reinforcements. He hasn't. That's a good sign."

She breathed easier. "Have you seen Nuallen? He came out here a while back."

"Yes. He checked in with me before disappearing. He's probably watching us, even now."

"Probably." They shared a smile, but her stomach remained knotted. "Perhaps we could go up there. I could bring along medicines for wounds."

"Magnus knows what he's about." Asa put her hand on Silvi's arm. "I'm certain everything is well, but it may not be safe there yet. They'll bring the wounded here on their shields."

"Of course." She looked down the path leading to the valley. "Have you heard from Leif?"

"No. But then, they're playing a waiting game. We weren't certain of an attack on the ships, so they may not have met with any of Toke's men." She looked at Silvi. "I'm not disparaging your vision, but—"

Silvi held up her hand. "Sometimes I misinterpret them. Or they don't happen when I think they will. The gods aren't always clear. There may not be an attack on the ships tonight. But I couldn't take the chance and not say anything."

"I agree." Nuallen stood behind them. Asa scowled at him and slid her sword back into its sheath.

"Don't do that again." She hit his shoulder with her fist.

"Then pay closer attention to your surroundings."

"Why should I when you're out here?" She glared at him. "Sneaking."

He looked affronted. "I do not sneak. I use stealth. There's a difference."

"If you say so. You might find a blade in your gut no matter what you call it."

"It's nothing that hasn't been tried before. I'm going down to the fjord. I want to see what's happening there. If there were any more of Toke's men on the mountain planning to attack Thorsfjell, they would have done so by now using the cover of darkness, coordinating assaults on our various positions for maximum effect."

"You're right. I'll keep my patrols out there and come with you."

"I want to come as well." Silvi lifted her chin as they both stared at her. "I have a brother and a husband out there fighting, while I'm here, eating myself inside out with worry. At least let me do something. I can bring my healing supplies."

Nuallen and Asa looked at each other. "Very well," she said. "But we're bringing extra men with us. Get your supplies while I find them."

At least she wouldn't go too mad now. She went inside. Her mother had gathered all her runes and was placing them in their bag.

Silvi stopped by the table. "What have they told you?"

"Victory." Her expression was troubled. "But other forces move here. There are warnings of secrets and betrayals. Their message isn't clear, so I'll have to do more castings when all is calmer again. It might be that the fighting and death on the mountain are influencing the runes. Blood always draws the shadows."

A chill ran up Silvi's spine. Her mother spoke of shadows, and Silvi had seen them flowing across Thorsfjell. She hadn't told her mother of her visions, yet the runes had spoken of the same thing.

"I'm going with Asa and Nuallen to the fjord to see what's happening with Leif. I'm bringing my healing supplies."

Lifa stood. "That would be good. Ingeborg and I are ready also. When Magnus comes back, I'll tell him where you are."

When Magnus came back. "Have you seen that in the runes?"

"Only that there is victory."

Then Magnus and Eirik would return, for there could be no true victory without them. However, what the gods considered a victory and what they actually won, could be two different things.

Chapter Eleven

The ships were untouched.

The men who lay dead on the beach weren't so lucky. A small boat rested on the sand, no doubt the one they'd come on. Silvi had been right.

Leif met Asa, Nuallen, their men, and her as they all dismounted from their horses. "The marauders tried to come under the cover of darkness in this *faering*, but we heard the water against the hull. Fools should have beached farther up the fjord and come in on foot. Even then, we would have found them. They had torches ready to light to set the ships on fire."

Kaia, standing a small distance off, crossed her arms. "We should have sent their bodies back in the boat to Toke with their bollocks cut off to give him a message."

Leif paled, clearing his throat. "I think he'll get the message from Magnus up on the mountain. Besides, I want to keep the boat. They're too precious to waste. It's small, but it's worth having. The fewer Toke has, the better."

"That's true."

"See? We can agree on something."

She turned away without acknowledging his comment.

Silvi shook her head. Leif still had no idea what he was getting into with the shieldmaiden. What would it take to show him? The flat of a blade to the side of his head? She wouldn't put it past Kaia to try. Silvi should warn Leif about her cousin, but it likely wouldn't do much good. After all, Magnus had known about Silvi's visions, yet he'd still wanted to marry her.

For the ships. Rorik offered a handsome dowry for Kaia, but not one of his ships. She looked at the magnificent vessels.

"Why would Toke want to destroy Rorik's ships? Even he can't be so insane as to provoke Rorik. No one does that and lives."

"He probably thinks they're part of your dowry," Leif said. "He wouldn't know Rorik owns these. He hoped to destroy something Magnus owns, to stop him from challenging him on the fjord."

At the sound of hoofbeats, the warriors reached for their weapons, but they relaxed when they saw it was Magnus and Eirik. Asa ran to meet them. She jumped up onto Eirik's horse and landed in front of him, grabbing him and kissing him hard. He laughed and let her down before dismounting.

"Now that's a greeting that makes any battle worthwhile." Eirik put his arm around Asa and kissed the top of her head as she smiled into his chest.

Magnus leveled his gaze on Silvi as he swung down from his horse. She could breathe now. He was safe. He had a bloody cloth wrapped around his forearm, but such a wound would not be life threatening. He was dirty and spattered with blood, his arms corded with exertion, his hair sweaty and tangled. He was beautiful.

The look he gave her, though, was like a storm over the mountain. Instead of embracing her, he took her arm.

"I need to speak with you." He led her away from the group.

She snatched her arm from his grasp when they were out of the others' hearing. "Stop pulling at me. I can choose where I want to go."

He rounded on her. "That's obvious. Why are you here? You should be up at the longhouse, safe. I arrived there from battle, expecting a greeting like Asa just gave to Eirik, but you weren't there. Instead, you're wandering the countryside when the enemy might still be about."

"I had Nuallen and Asa and her warriors with me. They wanted to check on Leif and I asked to come. I was going insane staying inside, awaiting word. I thought if anyone here was hurt, I could treat the injuries. They're fine." The remark about Asa stung. Her beautiful sister-in-law was strong and brave. A shieldmaiden. It was easy for her to jump on a horse like that. And she was confident in Eirik's love for her. None of those things applied to Magnus and her.

"I have eight wounded. I need you in the village to help your mother and Ingeborg when they arrive. Instead you're here."

"What if Leif was hurt? You'd want someone to treat him as soon as possible, wouldn't you? I have visions, Magnus, but I don't know everything. Perhaps you need someone like your sister. Someone strong and perfect, who knows where she stands in her husband's eyes. Unlike me."

She strode away from him, back to her horse. He caught up to her.

"Where are you going?"

"To the village, where you want me, my jarl. Maybe someone there will appreciate my efforts." Seeing how loving Asa and her brother were knifed into her. She would never have that with Magnus. He looked at her and saw ships, not a wife.

"You're not going up there alone. I'm coming with you."

"Then I'll still be alone." She mounted and nudged the white mare into a walk. But she kept the horse to a slow pace so Magnus could catch up to her on his gelding. She was angry, not foolish. She needed someone to come with her in the event Toke had other men on the mountain. Because *she* wasn't a shieldmaiden.

By the time she started up the path, there were several horses behind her. She glanced back. Magnus rode in front, while Eirik, Asa, Leif, and Kaia rode in a line after him. More warriors flanked them. No doubt they all knew of the argument, for they hung back, well away from the anger radiating off of Magnus. Her mother's habit of using runes for nefarious purposes was starting to look better and better.

Her stomach twinged. Oh gods, not now. She was upset, and the pain often started then. She'd get the myrrh. And honey. And ginger. Might as well gather it all. She was going to need it.

"Sit down." Silvi pointed to a bench in the longhouse and glared at Magnus. The wounded were there. Ingeborg and Lifa still worked on the one serious belly injury as servants got them more boiled water. Eirik had taught Lifa of its use for cleansing wounds; Ingeborg, however, insisted on the wine. And leeks for the belly wound. Other women smeared honey and herbs on the cleaned cuts before wrapping them in linen they'd boiled.

"I'm fine." Magnus scowled at her. "Go help your mother and Ingeborg."

"I'll only be in the way. They have what they need. Everyone else is taken care of. Now I need to examine your arm. Sit."

"Yes, mistress." He sank down with a sigh.

"As you've told me on the rare occasions when I've done as you asked, that's better." She unwrapped the cloth, recognizing the way it was arranged. "Eirik did this."

He nodded. "On the battlefield. It was minor, but could have interfered with my sword hand. He stopped the bleeding. I really don't need this. You have other work to do."

"Stop being a child. You were like this after the battle for Haardvik. Just be still." It wasn't too deep and shouldn't need stitching. The gods help her if it had. He'd have been even worse, no doubt. She cleaned the wound again with cooled boiled water, then picked up a bottle of wine. He narrowed his eyes. She poured a good portion of it into a bowl, smiling at him.

"Surely this little cut doesn't need all that." His jaw was tight.

Still smiling, she dumped most of it on his arm. He jumped up, cursing and shaking his arm.

"The cut may not need it all, but I do." She drank the rest of the wine straight out of the bowl.

"You can pour some for me." He sat down, eyeing her. "I need it more."

"No, you don't. I'm having to put up with you. Now, let me get the rest of this done." She dabbed up the excess wine, then smeared the honey mixture over the cut. When it was wrapped, she stepped back. "There. I'll need to check it again tomorrow, but I've done all I can for now."

"I'll survive." He glanced at the empty bowl. "Perhaps."

"Just be glad it isn't a belly wound. Ingeborg is armed with her leeks." She glanced at his lower abdomen. The injury he'd survived long ago would have killed another man.

He got off the bench. "I need to see to my man, Egill, who was so badly hurt."

She followed him to where Ingeborg and Lifa were working on him. He was laid out on one of the tables, his tunic torn open. A horrible gash crossed his abdomen just under his ribs. Blood pooled under him. He was, thankfully, unconscious.

"Do you know if his stomach was cut open?" Magnus peered over Lifa's shoulder.

"I don't see any sign of it. Before he passed out, he ate a leek," she said. "So far, we don't smell anything. This will have to be stitched shut and then cauterized. He's lost a lot of blood. Perhaps too much."

"We'll do it now. Even if he's cut inside, the blood loss will kill him if we don't." Ingeborg took a needle and sinew out of a bowl of steaming water. "I've boiled this as Eirik said to do, though I don't see that it would make any difference."

"Shall I powder the myrrh?" Silvi would need it soon anyhow, for herself. Her stomach burned.

"Not for him." Ingeborg pulled the skin together. "Unless it looks like he's going to live. Then it would be worth the expense to use it on him."

Silvi winced. Ingeborg was right, of course, but it still sounded hard-hearted. However, one had to be practical about these things. She looked around the room where the wounded men lay on tables and the floor. They would live or die according to their fates, which the Norns wove before their births. All the healers could do was try to keep the injuries from festering. And wait. Perhaps the new techniques Eirik had brought back with him from the desert lands would work. They'd find out soon enough.

Silvi went to their chamber and shut the door. Between the battle, the waiting, the wounded, and her anger at Magnus, her stomach was on fire. She'd hidden it well enough while among the others, but in the privacy of the bedchamber, she grimaced.

The resin lay in one of her personal chests, wrapped in linen. It was sticky, but she scraped off a flake with her knife, and put the rest away. She needed hot water. There was plenty of that in the common room.

She rose to go to the door. Magnus stood there, leaning back against it, his arms crossed. He'd been so quiet, she hadn't heard him.

"Taking lessons from Nuallen in stealth?"

"I don't require lessons from him to see what my wife is doing." He looked at the piece of myrrh she held. "I thought they didn't need that yet."

She didn't want him to know she was in pain. He likely thought she was weak enough already. "Shouldn't you go wash in the sauna? You smell of battle."

"That's because I've just been in one. Actually, I came in here to get fresh clothing for after I wash. But I see you here, using the myrrh. Why?"

"It's always best to be prepared in case we need it. Because it's so sticky, it takes some time to steep. I can powder it early. We can always use it another time if we don't need it now."

"I see." He pushed away from the door and crossed to one of his chests. He rummaged through it and pulled out a clean shirt and pants. As he left, he glanced at the resin in her hands but didn't say anything else.

She sighed in relief. Strength and health were everything to their people. Even the women strove for the masculine ideal of fortitude, resilience, and endurance. Physical prowess defined them. They were taller and stronger than any of the other peoples they'd come across. They had to be, to survive in their brutal world.

That was why she'd always wanted to retreat from it. She wasn't strong, or vigorous. Her stomach was weak. At times, it seemed as though all the pains of the world burned inside her. Perhaps if Magnus had known about her imperfections, he wouldn't have married her. If only she'd thought of it then, but it was too late. In more ways than one.

She loved him and wanted him to regard her like Eirik did Asa—as a woman who could stand beside him with strength and bravery. An equal. She looked down at the resin in her hands. If she could hide the extent of her pain from him, perhaps one day, he would.

The common room was quiet, except for the moans of the man whose stomach Ingeborg was still stitching. Silvi poured hot water into a cup and grated the myrrh into it. After adding the honey and ginger root, she set it aside to steep. Lifa watched her, offering her a gentle smile.

Silvi walked over to her. "Do you think they'll all survive?"

"They should, but we'll have to see about Egill."

"If you need the myrrh, tell me. It might be a good opportunity to try it."

"I didn't think you were preparing it for him." She lowered her voice. "The pains are back?"

"Yes, but I'd rather no one know besides Ingeborg. I mentioned something to Magnus, but not about their intensity. The last thing anyone needs to learn is how weak I am."

"The last thing you are is weak, Silvi."

"Spoken like a loving mother. You don't see my flaws."

"The gods don't choose those who cannot stand up to their demands. That takes strength. Not the same kind that's needed to wield a sword or row a ship for days. I cannot do any of those things. Would you call me weak? If all of us were warriors, we wouldn't survive as a people."

"But you're not... flawed. Like I am. I don't want anyone to know the wife of their jarl has something wrong with her."

"Or, you don't want the jarl to know."

"He probably thinks I'm weak enough. Insipid. Like a turnip that has been boiled too long."

Lifa gave a short, horrified laugh. "Oh gods, Silvi, where is this coming from? You've never spoken like this before."

"I never needed to. It didn't matter. Before. Now it does. I fear I'll disgrace our family, and Magnus, if everyone knew. Promise me you'll say nothing to him."

Lifa brushed back a lock of Silvi's hair that had fallen loose. "My love, you're wrong in so many ways, I can't begin to reply to them. But I won't say anything. You made your own life when you married. I won't interfere in that. You'll tell him when the time is right. Just as you'll tell him you love him."

Was it that obvious? Then again, her mother could see things no one else could. She couldn't deny it, not to her mother. "All he sees when he looks at me are warships." She gave her a sideways glance. "And a boiled turnip."

Lifa's shoulders shook as she laughed gently. "Then I'll wager he's developed a particular fondness for turnips. You need only look at him to see it in his eyes."

So often, the only expression she saw in his eyes was anger. She smiled to hide the pain, both in her body and her heart. "I know of no man who looks at a turnip with particular joy, unless he's starving." Of course, if he continued to hold himself away from her, he might be starving in a completely different way. Then, maybe she would look good to him. "I need to take this mixture and lie down. It's been a long night."

"Go and sleep. I may do the same. We have several women watching here, and they'll let us know if we're needed." Lifa kissed her forehead. "No matter how far apart we are, remember my love will always be with you."

"I know. Sometimes, that's the only thing keeping me standing."

She took the cup with the myrrh mixture and brought it to the sleeping chamber, then drank it. The myrrh hadn't quite dissolved. A small lump lay in the bottom of the cup, but she'd swallowed enough of it. The honey and ginger should also help.

She took off her shoes and lay on the bed. Exhaustion weighed her down. She wasn't the only one. Her mother looked tired as well. They all were. No one should hold it against her if she rested for a short while. Then she should be about her day. The people of Thorsfjell needed her.

But the bed was too soft, the furs too comforting. Magnus, Eirik, Leif, and Asa had survived. They had defeated Toke's outcasts. Again. Thorsfjell was safe.

The pains in her stomach lessened and she breathed deep, snuggling into the warm nest of covers. She drifted, like a ship on a calm sea, and let herself go.

The endless ocean surrounded her. The island was gone. She was alone with only waves around her, the open sky above her. Yet, if she reached down with her toes, she could touch sand beneath her. She couldn't see it, but she could feel it. Was the island below her? If she stayed in contact with it, she'd be able to keep her head above the water.

Why wouldn't it rise? Why was it beneath the waters where she couldn't see it? How long could she go on like this before she grew too weak to stay afloat, and slipped away forever?

Magnus closed his chamber door behind him softly, trying not to awaken Silvi. She hadn't been in the common room when he'd come back from the sauna. But neither had Lifa or Ingeborg. Only a few of the village women were there, seeing to the needs of the wounded men. They'd said everyone was resting for a while. And he had hoped . . .

She was here, but he couldn't bring himself to disturb her. He went to the side of the bed and looked down at her. So beautiful. Her cool beauty, illuminated by the daylight coming in through the windows, took his breath away. She was like snow spread out under the sun.

Sighing, he took off his belt and walked to the table where he usually left it. A cup sat there. He set his belt aside and picked it up. Dark yellow granules sat in the bottom. He sniffed at them. Myrrh. There were other scents as well. He ran his finger around the inside and tasted it. Ginger and honey.

She'd said she needed the myrrh for the wounds. That could also be true of the honey. But not the ginger. That could help the stomach pains. Why did she need so strong a remedy? And why hadn't she told him? She wouldn't use the precious myrrh unless she needed it, when they had so many other treatments.

He set the cup down and stripped off his shirt. Between being up all night, fighting the battle, then the steam of the sauna, he wasn't certain if he'd found her awake, he could have made love to her. *That* would have to wait. Again.

Lying down, he turned on his back beside her. He tried to be still, but the mattress dipped and she rolled toward him. She roused with a frown, opening her eyes. They were glazed, as though she saw something beyond her. Then she focused on him.

"Magnus. Gods, I must have fallen asleep. I didn't mean to." She started to get up, but he took her wrist and she stilled.

"Relax. There's nothing you need to rise for."

"I need to see to the wounded men. And food. No one has eaten yet today. The common room is a mess. The tables need to be scrubbed." She pulled at her wrist.

He tugged back and she landed on top of him. "That's what we have servants for, and they're very efficient. My warriors are patrolling outside. Eirik, Asa, your mother, Leif, and even Nuallen are all resting. And so should you. We'll rise for the evening meal. Until then . . ."

He put his arms around her and settled her against his chest. She made a small protest, but when he didn't release her, she relaxed with a tremulous breath. He closed his eyes. This was what he'd fought for. This was what he'd spilled his blood on the mountain to protect. And she was worth it, every drop of it.

The scent of her hair filled him and he turned his face into it. It was still up in its knot, but he was too tired to take it down. As exhausted as his body was, though, the battle turned over and over in his mind. Something wasn't right.

He envisioned the mountain from above, as though he were a bird flying over it. His ability to do that had often let him see strategies others didn't. Toke's men had come from the valley, up through the pass, as expected.

As expected. The same thing Asa had picked up on during the winter battle. Either Toke was more of a fool than he'd thought, or something else was in the air. But what? He shifted. He needed to sleep, but not with this hanging over him. He should talk to Eirik, Leif, and Nuallen about this, but they'd be asleep by now.

"Magnus? Can't you sleep? Is your arm bothering you? I can get some herbs to help the pain."

He winced. He'd been keeping her awake. "I'm sorry. I'll go elsewhere. I can't sleep because of the battle. Sometimes, after we fight, I see it again in my mind, over and over."

She tried to sit up, but he held her tight against him. "Magnus, let me go. Turn over onto your stomach."

He did as she asked. "Why?"

"Because you help me fall asleep every night. Now it's my turn." She ran her fingers through his hair. "This is a mess."

He smiled into the pillow. "I washed it, but I didn't comb it."

She rose and came back with the ivory comb. He closed his eyes with a groan as she pulled it through the damp strands. So this was what it felt like. No wonder she liked it so much. His hair wasn't nearly as long as hers, but it still hung down his back. The comb ran against his scalp and over his shoulders as she worked out the snarls.

"There." She set the comb aside and scooped his hair to one side. Then she smoothed her hands over his back. Her fingertips brushed his skin as he buried his face in the pillow.

He grew hard, but was so fatigued, he couldn't have moved if he wanted to. This was sweet torture—to have her here, touching him, and yet he was at her mercy. He had no defense against her and he wanted none.

She placed her palms on either side of his spine and pressed them up toward his shoulder blades in small circles. "I'm not certain what to do. I'm trying to match what you've done to me."

"You're a quick learner. I may never get up again."

She gave a soft laugh. He surrendered himself to her hands, which was new for him. He'd always been the one in command, the one giving the pleasure. This single time, though, he could make an exception.

She massaged farther down his back to the top of his hips, just above his pants. Maybe he would make an exception more often. She had a healer's hands, after all. Soft, yet strong and certain. When she rubbed his shoulders, he arched his neck into her touch. No woman had ever done this for him before, but then, none of them had been Silvi.

He turned over, pulled her onto his chest again, and kissed the top of her head. "Thank you for that."

"I hoped you'd fall asleep, as I do."

"As long as you're in my arms, I don't think that will be a problem now." He pulled the furs over them both.

She smiled against his chest and snuggled closer.

He'd been too short with her this morning on the beach. When he'd returned from the battle and she wasn't here, anger born of fear had twisted in him. The situation was still too uncertain for her to be away from the village, no matter who was with her. Asa and Nuallen should have known better. In the future, he'd make certain they did. But he shouldn't have taken his concern out on her. He should have greeted her as Eirik had welcomed Asa—with joy, his arms open to receive her. Instead he'd been an idiot. That happened too often around her.

"I'm sorry, Silvi. I shouldn't have been upset with you this morning."

She only sighed, her eyes closed, her breathing steady and light. She was asleep already. No matter that she hadn't heard him. He would make certain she knew.

The battle still bothered him. Toke was out there somewhere, but right now, he had Silvi in his arms. He let go of everything else. His world became their chamber, their bed, and the woman he held.

That was all he needed, in this world or any other.

"It's a feeling I have in my gut." Magnus glared at Leif as his twin propped his feet up on his table. Magnus let it go. He had other battles to fight.

"Your gut's always been good enough for me." Leif yawned.

They'd finished the second meal, which Birgitta had served early since their morning had been so disrupted. The women were seeing to the wounded, except for Asa, who sat with Eirik, Nuallen, Leif, and him.

Nuallen was a mystery, and Magnus didn't like mysteries. The Northumbrian was a former slave and might harbor deep-seated resentiments toward Eirik for his enslavement. But Magnus couldn't argue with his abilities, and so far, Nuallen had used those talents to help them. Nuallen was skilled, no matter who he had once been. Magnus needed all the help he could get. This mess with Toke wasn't over yet.

"I've stayed awake thinking about the battle, and something keeps knocking at me about it. There weren't enough men to defeat us. Toke should have realized that. They came up a known pass. It was too predictable, too easy."

"I agree." Eirik leaned forward, setting his elbows on his knees. "Even though Silvi warned us about the timing, we would have seen them at some point with all the men we had up there. Even if they had made it closer to Thorsfjell by the time we met them, the outcome would have been much the same."

"Exactly."

"Might he not have done it to save face?" Asa held Eirik's hand. "He vowed to get vengeance because of his son. He made this attempt and it failed. He might figure that at least he tried and it should save him in the eyes of his men."

"If he has any men left," Leif said. "He's managed to kill off dozens of them between the winter and now. The ones left are probably fleeing like rats from a burning ship. It's as though he's trying to bring himself down."

"Or someone else is." Nuallen rubbed his jaw as they all looked at him. "I've heard everything about the winter battle that happened here. People, including Asa, saw a rider with the attackers, yet he didn't join the fight. He was also seen before that. If he was there again last night, we might not have noticed him in the darkness. He may be the one to tie this all together."

"If he has anything to do with the strategy they're using," Eirik said, "then he's a poor tactician."

"Or perhaps, a very good one. If he's working against Toke." Magnus drummed his fingers on the table. "But why would he do that if he's part of Toke's forces?"

"What I'm more concerned about is whether or not Toke is finished with his vendetta against you." Leif scowled. "He might be a coward, but his anger over his son is very real. He may come up with another way, an underhanded way, to seek his revenge. He did say he would destroy whatever you loved."

"That's Thorsfjell. He's already tried and failed twice." But there was also Silvi. Magnus met Leif's eyes, ice running in his veins.

Leif nodded. "He knows you have a new wife. Even if you didn't love her, she'll bear your children and that would make her valuable."

Magnus didn't bother denying his feelings for her. From the grin on Leif's face to the knowing looks they all gave him, it would be futile. "I should have made her leave here. I wanted her to go back to Haardvik, or even to stay with Rorik, to be safe. She wouldn't go."

"No more than any of us would. She may not be a shieldmaiden." Eirik drew Asa closer to him. "But she's still one of us. She has strengths we can't understand. Believe me, I've tried through the years."

"She's not to leave the village. All of you will make certain of this." Magnus looked at each of them, but fastened Asa and Nuallen in his gaze. "I'm not sitting back and waiting for Toke to make the next move. I'm sending men out to search for him. He has to be here someplace. If we kill him, the outcasts who flock to him for food and shelter will fade away."

"What of his people?" Asa frowned.

He'd already thought of this. It would increase his responsibilities, but he had little choice. "Bygvik will become part of Thorsfjell, depending on what we find there. We've already taken in a number of the women and children, and from what I've heard, the people in the village will be glad of a new jarl after Toke killed the old one."

Leif grinned. "New ships, a new wife, and soon a new village. Your empire is expanding, Brother. I'm proud of you."

"It's not my intention. I've only wanted what's best for Thorsfjell, and that's Toke's death. If having to take on a new village is the result, then that's what I'll do."

Silvi came through the open door, her eyes sparkling. "I heard what you said, Magnus. I don't know about the new wife or the new village, but your new ships are here. Your lookouts on the peak have seen the ships Eirik sent for, in the main fjord. They'll be here soon."

Everyone rose. Magnus nodded to Eirik. "It's barely been eight days. Your men work fast. Let's greet them."

The others left to prepare, but he held Silvi back. "I want you to stay here in the longhouse. It still may not be safe out there. It's better if you remain behind. You can see the ships another day."

She crossed her arms and his heart sank. Of course it wouldn't be that easy.

"I'm going. They're my dowry. I have the right. You and your warriors will be with me. The men continue their patrols. Toke is likely off licking his wounds in some dank place far from here."

"I wouldn't take a wager on that, and it's not worth risking you. You're staying."

"I'm going. Unless you plan to tie me up like you've threatened before. That's the only way."

His body tightened at that picture, but he ignored it. "You're making it sound more and more tempting."

She narrowed her eyes. "Then see what happens when you free me."

If he had his way, after he rendered her helpless, neither of them would go anywhere for the rest of the night. She would be so sated afterward, she would forget about revenge. He almost groaned. But he had ships to greet, and unless he wanted the entire longhouse to know about her defiance, he had to relent. This time.

He raked his hand through his hair. "Fine. But stay in the midst of us."

"Of course. I may be stubborn, but I'm not foolish."

To think he had once thought of her as shy and demure. It was becoming clear that, just as there were different kinds of warriors, so there were different kinds of shieldmaidens. It wasn't enough that his sister was one. He was married to another.

Chapter Twelve

They arrived at the beach in time to see the ships sail into their branch of the fjord. Three of them traveled in close formation while Eirik's great warship followed. The sails were lowered and the oars dipped into the still waters in perfect unison. Dozens of warriors rowed while others stood ready to jump into the shallows and pull the ships onto the shore.

Magnus's heart swelled. They were beautiful, long and sleek, their dragon prows rising in the late-day sun. They must have started out early at the mouth of the fjord to have arrived before dark, which spoke of the strength and skill of the warriors who crewed them.

He glanced at Silvi as she stood at his side. Her eyes were moist. These had been her father's ships.

"Remembering?" He took her hand.

She nodded. "So many times I watched my father leave and then return from his travels in these ships. I can still see him there, standing in the prow, lifting his sword in greeting while we stood on the cliff above. It's one of my earliest memories. Those ships brought him home safe, protecting us all. I was so proud of him."

"He was a man to be proud of. He left you a great legacy. And now that legacy has followed you here. They're still a part of your life, and they'll still protect you."

She smiled. "I hadn't thought of that, but you're right. I'm not losing them. They're staying here with me."

"You know that, by our laws, a woman's dowry is hers. A husband holds it in trust, but ultimately, she owns it. Those ships belong to you. I don't suppose you'd allow me to use them once in a while." His humor, such as it was, usually helped dispel any anger she had toward him. It was worth a try.

Her lips quirked. "What would I do with a longship? Asa would love them. She'd be sailing over the edge of the world tomorrow. But me? I'm not planning on needing them anytime soon, so you can use them for now." She crossed her arms and lifted her chin as she gazed out at them. "On one condition."

Oh gods. Here was her revenge. "What would that be?" He held his breath.

"I want to go with you when you take them out for the first time."

He exhaled. When she'd first come to Thorsfjell, she'd spoken of how much she'd enjoyed the voyage. "Of course. We'll only sail a little way down the fjord. It's too far to go to the sea and back. Two days' travel. But we can do a run for half a day, then return. Word will spread. Everyone along the shoreline came to the wedding and knows of your dowry. They'll see the ships, if they haven't already, and there's a good chance Toke will hear about it. He'll have his warning."

The ships slid onto the beach and most of the men jumped into the water. The shallow draft of the keel ensured the water would only be up to their knees at most. Magnus's men helped them haul the vessels farther onto the shore.

Magnus walked to one of the ships and put his hand on the forestem at the front. Not only was it carved to simulate the overlapping planking fastened to it, but ornate, interlaced patterns curved along it, testifying to the art and skill of the shipbuilders. These were vessels to be proud of.

"Rorik's family's shipwrights built these years ago." Eirik looked up at the sails. "My father bought them when I was very young. They are just as sound and seaworthy as they were when he first brought them home." He laid his hand on the forestem of the nearest one. "This is *Raven*. The next is *Sea Eagle* and the farthest one over is *Fire Serpent*. May they take you as far and keep you as safe as they did him."

"May Njord will it so."

"Speaking of which." Eirik smiled as his own ship, the massive *Wind of Njord*, slid onto the beach beside the others. Eirik's second-in-command, Kjeld, leaped off and came to them.

"The voyage went well. Everything was nearly complete when

we arrived, so it took only a few days to return." The tall, blond-haired man looked around. "The wedding celebration was still going on when I left. Did I miss anything?"

"Just lots of drinking, feasting, and a good battle." Eirik clapped him on the shoulder. "Take heart. The scum causing all the trouble is still out there. There'll likely be more fighting."

Kjeld grinned. "Thank the gods. I can always hope." He walked back toward Eirik's ship, yelling orders as some of the crew threw supplies over the sides to others on the beach.

When Eirik followed him, Silvi caught Magnus's arm. "Thank you for letting me come here. I wanted to see them as they sailed in from the fjord."

He gave her a sideways glance. "I had little choice in the matter. I don't know that I allowed it." As she stiffened, he touched her cheek. "But I'm glad you came. We'll take them out in a day or so, once we sort out the supplies and the men. For now, it would be best for you to return to the longhouse. We have a lot of unloading ahead of us before dark. We'll probably work until late. Take Asa and several of the men with you."

She smiled. "All right. I'll see you when you return."

"If we're too late, go to bed. Tomorrow may be busy. We have many new warriors to assimilate. And that will call for extra food and drink. A great deal of drink. I'm glad your brother is giving me gold to help support them for a while."

"It will be worth the expense in the long run."

"I know. If it takes down Toke, then the cost is worth it."

He helped her mount her horse. Asa, Nuallen, and a dozen of his best men joined her. As they rode into the valley, Magnus watched them. Any amount of gold and silver, no matter how much, was worth spending to protect her. He had already given her his heart. It would be nothing to give his life and all he possessed as well.

Magnus hadn't been able to sleep earlier, and now it was her turn.

Silvi lay awake, the moon's rays cutting into the darkness of the bedchamber from above. Ingeborg, her mother, and she had spent the evening tending to the wounded, especially the man with the serious belly wound. They had sewn it shut and cauterized it with a red-hot knife blade, but who knew what was happening inside? Some blood and fluid still leaked out, and if it was not better by morning, then her mother and Ingeborg had agreed to try the myrrh.

His moans rang in her mind. That could have been Magnus there. Or Eirik. It was only the grace of the *wyrd*, the fate, that had saved them. This time.

Magnus hadn't lessened his vigilance, so he must suspect Toke hadn't given up. There might be more fighting, more injuries, more deaths. It was never ending. This was why she'd wanted to go to the temple, where all was peace and calm. Weapons weren't even allowed on the sacred grounds. The horrors of the world didn't dare interfere with the power of the gods.

Love didn't exist there either. At least not the type she felt for Magnus. Was it worth the pain if she lived with him for years to come, loving him, and he didn't return it?

She shifted onto her back. He was there, standing in the rays of the moon, looking at her. His hair was windblown and his clothes clung to his body, still damp, no doubt, from the fjord waters. With the light sculpting the contours of his face and arms, he looked like one of the gods. Powerful. Beautiful.

She sat up, clutching the furs to her chest. Without speaking, he drew off his shirt and tossed it aside. He came to the bed and sat down beside her.

"You didn't take your hair down."

"I didn't think of it."

"Good." He leaned over and, cupping the back of her head, kissed her. "Lie down on your stomach."

She did as he said while he stood and pulled off his trousers. He was different tonight. Was it the aftermath of war? Had the battle stirred his warrior's blood so he needed to conquer her, as well? She wouldn't fight with him or refuse him. Not this night.

Naked, he went to the table and picked up the comb. She peered at him from the pillow and her own pulse raced as warmth spread between her legs. He came to the bed, but this time, he moved over her, straddling her thighs. His weight held her down, but it didn't matter. She was content where she was.

He loosened her hair from its knot and ran the comb through the strands. "I don't want any harsh words between us this night. Don't say a word unless I ask you something. Do you understand?"

"Then why can't you be the one to stay silent?" She glanced at him over her shoulder.

"Because then I couldn't tell you how beautiful you are, how soft your skin is, and how much I want you."

He couldn't mean those words. But if he spoke them, she could imagine he spoke the truth. His voice was harsh, low. It called to something deep within her and she nodded. She closed her eyes, giving herself up to him. When her hair lay smooth down her back, he set the comb aside.

"Turn over." He shifted so she could do as he said, then settled back on her thighs, keeping enough of his weight on his legs so he didn't hurt her. He leaned over her, his arms on either side of her. "Tell me you want me, Silvi. If you do, then it's the last decision you'll make tonight. If you don't, then I'll let you rest. It's your choice."

She wanted to cross her arms over herself, to guard her heart. "What kind of choice is it when you loom over me like this? You're rather intimidating."

"Whether or not you understand it, you have all the power here. The power to say yes or no. The power to give me joy or pain. You, alone, hold this night in your hands."

She ran her fingers over the bandage on his arm and up to his heavy shoulders. They were like iron, but they trembled as she caressed them. His gaze on her was intense, his body as still as a bow string when it was drawn back, waiting for release.

She let out her breath, and her doubts along with it. "Then, yes."

One side of his mouth curled up in a satisfied smile. Rising over her, he took her wrists in his hands and held them down on either side of her head, pressed into the mattress. His mouth slashed across hers and she returned his kiss full measure. She ran her leg along his thigh. He caught his breath.

He rained kisses down her jaw and neck, then dipped lower. Fire shot through her as he nibbled the inside curve of her breast and she arched against him. How could he create such magic with just his mouth? She pulled at her wrists, wanting to touch him, explore him as he did her. He didn't let her go.

Instead, he took her breast into his mouth, rasping the tip with his tongue. She was helpless to stop him, but she didn't want to. It felt too good to have him over her, touching her, awakening her. Warmth seeped through her, weakening her body. Her heart pounded. Even the air against her skin caressed her like a lover, leaving tingles in its wake.

"Magnus . . ."

"Hush. Say nothing. Do nothing. Feel everything." He let go of her wrists, but slid his hands down to her waist and held her still. His mouth left a trail of fire down her stomach to the juncture of her thighs.

When he touched her with his mouth, she gasped. She tried to sit up, but he held her in place. Then he ran his tongue along her tender skin, her most secret place, and she cried out, grabbing his hair. He ignored her and continued his sensual conquest.

She had no weapons, no shields against him. Ever the strategist, he would know all her weaknesses and vulnerabilities. He was the ultimate warrior and he had vanquished her. There was nothing else to do but surrender. Closing her eyes, she opened herself to him.

He turned his head and nibbled the inside of her thighs. Muscles quivered that she didn't even know she had. How was she supposed to just lie still and let him do as he pleased? Her body was formed of lightning, and she could no more remain quiet than could a storm.

Not caring if he grew displeased with her, she caressed his back with her heel. His wide shoulders held her legs apart, his hair spread across them. His hands spanned her waist.

Pressure built within her. It began low, then climbed throughout her body. She threw her head back, writhing. Why was this happening? Was this the pleasure her mother had spoken of? But there was more . . . Somehow.

He cupped her breasts, flicking the tips with his thumbs, and she fractured. She fell into a whirlpool of sensation, her body at its mercy. It swept her into a place she did not know, where all was light, ecstasy. And Magnus.

His scent washed over her. Her lids were heavy, as if she'd just awakened. Kissing his way back up her body, he painted her skin with awareness—of her unexplored desires, of forgotten dreams, of a new world of belonging. She was his, completely, in every way. He spoke to yearnings so deep within her, she'd never seen them, never knew they existed. Not even in her visions. How could she have known about them before this? There was only one way she could have found them—Magnus.

He moved over her, watching her, his eyes filled with a softness they'd not held before.

"Now, you're ready."

She almost couldn't understand his words for the whirlwind in her mind. "There's more?" Then she blushed. "Of course there is. You haven't sought your own pleasure yet."

"I fully intend to. But I'm bringing you along with me." He ran his hand between her legs and she cried out as her body clenched. "You have to trust me. There might be a small pain for a moment. But after this, there'll be only pleasure."

His eyes never leaving hers, he guided himself to her. She gripped his arms tight, expecting him to plunge into her hard, as she had seen done before. He lowered his mouth to hers, kissed her, and slid into her in one exquisite, sublime movement.

There was a slight pinch, then it was only fullness, completion. Motionless, he studied her. "Beautiful. Passionate. Mine." He ran his hand over her face as though he'd never seen her before, his eyes alight with joy. "Wrap your legs around me." As she did so, he gathered her hair in his hand and held her with it. He supported his weight on his other arm and pressed into her.

"Are you all right?"

"Oh yes." And she was. As he moved inside her, the pressure built again. This time, she understood it and welcomed it. She met his thrusts, embracing him with all she was, burying her head in his chest. His head tilted back and his hair flowed over his arms and shoulders, dark as the shadows around them.

He let go of her hair and took her wrists. He raised them above her head and held them there with one hand. With his other hand, he cupped her cheek, his touch gentle. "I think you want this. It's the way I am. In this way, we're made for each other."

What did he mean? His hands tightened on her wrists, but not so much that it hurt. Just enough so she understood his control over her. She pulled, trying to free herself, to touch him as he had caressed her, but he held her, moving faster and harder, his eyes boring into hers. Heat rushed through her, like an inferno engulfing a pyre. She was on that pyre, the flames sending her up to the gods themselves. Like a flurry of sparks, she rose up into the darkness, brilliant and burning. And he was the wind lifting her.

"Now, Silvi." At his command, she shuddered around him as he poured himself into her with a groan. The sparks dissipated in a radiant burst.

He collapsed onto her, then shifted off of her, freeing her wrists. Rolling onto his back, he brought her with him so she lay on him. His heart beat under her ear, his breathing matching hers. Even though they were no longer joined together, they were one.

"Now, you're truly mine. In the eyes of both the gods and men." He kissed the top of her head. "You're so perfect for me, Silvi. Your body fits mine, and your gentleness complements my strength. You gave yourself so completely into my care, that I can give in to my true nature with you."

She raised her head to look at him. "You said something like that earlier. I don't understand what you mean."

"I'm a warrior, Silvi. I take. Yes, I trade and barter for what I need instead of raiding, but I still win. I still want to be victorious over the other merchant I'm trading with, getting the better bargain. I made the arrangement with your brother with the intention of winning. You. And I did. Now you're mine, and what is mine, I keep. It's my nature to control and conquer, the same as any of our people do. In here, I want you in my care, doing as I wish so that I can give you all the pleasure I can. I sense in you the counterpart to me. That you want me to guide you and show you all the ways we can come together."

"There are other ways?" She slipped to his side and rested her chin on his chest.

He chuckled. "Oh yes."

"And you want me to do as you say."

"It's a dream I have." He grinned.

She gave his arm a light smack. "Magnus, I've gone my own way much of my life. I always knew I was separate, destined to tread a different path. It is not easy for me to follow a course that others lay out for me."

"I've noticed that." He took her wrist and ran his thumb along it. "Just in here, Silvi. Out there, you'll drive me to drink, no doubt, and make me pull my hair out until I'm bald. I'll be forever chasing you across the mountain as you flit just out of my reach.

"But in here, when it's you and I alone, let me be as I am. Let me bring you to new places you've never dreamed of. If not, then neither you nor I will know true completion. If you let me care for you as I want to, and do as I wish, then there's no place we cannot go, no mountain we cannot climb."

Making love with him had been like nothing she'd ever imagined. Even with everything her mother had told her, she'd only hinted at the pleasure, the stars, the fire that had poured through her. Or was she the only one who felt that way? If the love in Asa's eyes when she was with Eirik was any sign, she wasn't alone. Maybe she should talk to her, wife to wife. She didn't know Asa well, but she was family now. Talking about this with her mother would be mortifying, but Asa was of an age with her and newly married as well.

Magnus brought her hand to his mouth and kissed the palm. "Remember what I said. You hold the power. When you're strong enough to give yourself to me completely, and trust me, then everything I do is for your pleasure. I'll do nothing to harm you. Ever."

"And what do you get out of this?"

"You."

She blinked at him. *And ships.* But she didn't say it. "This night you gave me the choice. You're my husband and you have the right to me. You gain only what you already hold."

"Your body, yes. I have the right to that. Did I take it before now? Even though I could have, and none would have faulted me for it? No. Because I want so much more with you and from you."

He gathered her closer. She rested her head on him with a sigh.

"I've given you much to think on this night. We should sleep. In the nights to come, I'll make it easier for you to decide. I promise."

"And of course, you'll be very diligent to do everything you can to help me come to the conclusion you want."

"Of course. Never let it be said I shirked my responsibilities to be a helpmeet to my wife."

She smiled, but as she moved, a twinge caught her. She was a bit sore. Would there be any other signs that she had lost her virginity?

Shifting, she saw a dark spot on the sheet. Magnus looked at it as well.

She winced. "You don't think the washerwomen will believe I had two wedding nights, do you?"

He pulled her back down with a laugh. "I think my, oh, exertions just now, opened the wound on my arm again and it bled a bit. We'll have to change the bandage in the morning."

"And it will be miraculously healed by tomorrow night?"

"Maybe even by morning." He nipped her hand and brought it to his chest, keeping hold of it.

"I hope you heal fast, Magnus."

"Oh, I will. Believe me, for this, I will."

As the three longships neared the mouth of their fjord, Silvi leaned on the dragonhead prow. Magnus stood behind her. They'd spent the day sailing in the main fjord as Leif and their men studied how the ships responded to the wind and the currents. It was critical to understand how each ship handled at a moment's notice, in the event they were attacked. Magnus seemed pleased and Silvi smiled with pride. After all, the vessels represented her and her family.

They sped into their own branch of the fjord and approached the shore. The three ships slid up onto the beach together. As the men jumped off to help pull the vessels up farther, Magnus swung his leg over the side and vaulted off.

He stood in the water and held out his arms, grinning. "Trust me?"

She narrowed her eyes. "Not when you have that expression on your face. But if I jump off by myself, I'll end up soaked anyhow." She edged off the side and landed in his arms. "Just once, I'd like to leap off like I'll wager Asa does."

"When you wear a tunic and leggings like she does, you're welcome to try." He walked with her onto the sand and set her on her feet.

She stood to the side as he issued orders and made certain the ships were secured to the great boulders used for mooring. When he was satisfied all was the way he wanted it, he helped her onto her horse. Leif joined them, along with most of the men, and they headed into the valley.

Before they reached the path leading to Thorsfjell, a rider on a small, shaggy horse galloped toward them.

Magnus signaled her to stay with him. "It's the sheepherder. He keeps the flocks farther down the valley."

The rider, a round-faced, heavy man, stopped in front of them. He panted as though he'd run all the way instead of the horse.

"What is it, Ofeig?"

"The sheep, my jarl. They're dying. It only now started happening. I was heading for the village to tell you, but I saw you riding here."

"Did they eat something poisonous?"

"I check the pastures all the time, Jarl Magnus. My boys do, as well. We make certain nothing could hurt them."

"Let me see them." They all looked at Silvi as she spoke. "Many of the same things that poison people also poison animals. And often, the remedies are the same. I know of such things from my mother."

"Take us there, Ofeig." Magnus urged his horse forward and she followed, the others taking up the rear.

When she saw the dead and dying sheep scattered over the pastures, her heart fell. She rode to the nearest sheep. Magnus swung off his horse and helped her down. She knelt beside the animal. It was still alive, but it trembled, and its breathing was hard and shallow. Putting her hand on the inside of its hind leg, she felt for its pulse. The heartbeat was slow. A memory tickled the back of her mind.

She went to the next sheep. It was dead, vomit by its mouth. She studied the contents, pushing it with a stick. "Oh gods. This makes no sense." She ran to another one that was still alive, opened its mouth and reached inside. Short, dark, needle-like leaves came out on her hand as she pulled it free.

Magnus helped her up. "What is it?"

"Someone has given them yew plants to eat."

"That only grows in the south. Not here."

"I know. Someone did this purposely. The dried plants are just as deadly as the fresh ones are. If the yew was collected and dried late in the year, it's even more toxic."

"How long ago would they have done this?"

"Not long at all. It works quickly. An animal can be standing one moment and dead the next. Because many of these sheep are still alive, I'm hoping they didn't eat as much and have a little time. Also, the younger sheep are more susceptible." She regarded the distraught sheepherder.

"This isn't your fault. Do you have a cooled fire where the wood is burnt and blackened?"

He wadded his shirt in his hands. "Yes, mistress. The fire I cooked on last night. It burnt down and I haven't restarted it yet for tonight."

"Bring me as much of the charcoal as you can."

He waddled off to his horse and Magnus motioned to two of his men. "It'll be faster if you go with him. Don't wait for him. Get back here with it as fast as you can."

Leif looked down at the sheep as Silvi knelt by it and stroked it. "Toke?"

"Any other outcasts would take them to eat." Magnus grimaced. "Why would he do this? He vowed to destroy what I love. And that's not sheep."

With a wicked glint in his eye, Leif started to speak, but when Magnus shot him a hard look, he glanced at Silvi and shut his mouth.

"He can't think this would hurt us financially. We have other pastures, other flocks."

"Which we'd better watch." Leif crossed his arms. "The warriors are going to love this. Guarding sheep."

"They'll do what I tell them to do."

"Yew can poison people as well." Silvi stood. "If Toke tries this with sheep, he could poison the grain stores. Or people in the outlying farmsteads. There's also the cattle and horses." She glanced at her own white mare, which one of the men held. It was the mare she'd ridden to her wedding, and Magnus had given it to her afterward. Her blood ran cold. "Don't let the horses graze here. We don't know if any of the yew dropped on the ground."

She walked to several of the other sheep. What else could she do until the men came with the charcoal?

"Magnus, can your men pick up the living sheep and bring them all here to one place? It would make it easier and faster to treat them."

He spun to his nearest warrior. "Do it."

It was all Silvi could do not to smile as the massive, tough fighters gently hefted the sheep under her watchful eye and set them on the ground in a group. When they were finished, Magnus's other two men returned with the charcoal.

"I need help to get this done as fast as possible." She showed them what she wanted. "Break up the pieces as small as you can and shove them down their throats. I don't know how much, but just keep giving it to them until we run out. That will have to do."

Between the cursing of the men and the bleating of some very irate sheep, they finished quickly.

"I'd feel better if we had more charcoal to give them." Silvi petted one of the sheep that was trying to stand.

"When we get to Thorsfjell, we'll gather all we can from the cooking fires and send others down here with it." Magnus helped her up. "You can tell them how to give it. Right now, I don't like being out here in the open with so few of us."

"Neither do I," Leif said. "We should return now."

When Silvi mounted her horse, she looked back. Ofeig was seeing to the sheep. They might still lose some of them, but perhaps they'd be fortunate. This time. Their livestock and people were spread out over a large area. Even with the additional warriors Eirik had sent them, there wouldn't be enough of them to guard everyone everywhere.

She was no warrior, but it was clear, even to her, that Toke was attacking them on more than one front. What did he hope to gain with this?

After they dismounted at the longhouse, Silvi searched for her mother. She was with Ingeborg in the healer's small house, an assortment of herbs spread on the table between them.

"I don't know of anything that will keep a child from being born too soon," Lifa said.

"I've tried a few things on Droplaug, but I'm not certain if they're helping her." Ingeborg shook her head. "She still bleeds from time to time. We'll have to keep a close eye on her. We have several women in the outlying farmsteads who are with child, but no others are having difficulties." She looked up at Silvi. "Here's your daughter. Come in, mistress."

"Did you enjoy your sail with Magnus?" Lifa indicated a space on the bench beside her. "I remember how beautiful those ships were when your father came home in them. They were his pride."

"I know, Mother. But something else has happened. When we returned, we discovered that someone has poisoned the sheep in the valley with yew. Magnus thinks Toke did it. I gave the ones that were alive charcoal from the shepherd's cook fire. I didn't know what else to do."

"You did right." She looked at Ingeborg. "It doesn't grow here. Someone must have brought it from the south."

The elderly healer frowned. "Any merchant can get any type of substance in the markets, whether it's herbs or powdered poisonous minerals, even from distant lands. It's all available for the right price."

"And if it's from far away, we might not recognize it or know the antidote for it." Lifa sighed, her face set. "Toke's tactics may have changed from the kind of battle men conduct, to one that we women understand. And in some ways, that's far more dangerous."

Chapter Thirteen

"I had thought to leave in two days, but now I'm not so certain I should." Eirik stroked his jaw. "Toke is likely out of men, or nearly so, and he may be getting desperate."

Magnus had called a meeting between Leif, Eirik, Nuallen and him. They'd gathered in his private chamber, for he didn't know who might listen and report back to Toke.

"The sheep weren't his real target," Nuallen said. "They're a means to an end. What that end is, we must figure out. I'm sworn to follow Lifa wherever she goes. If she leaves for Haardvik, then I must go as well. I would rather stay and see this through. You may have need of my, ah, talents."

"Which are?" Magnus gave him a hard look.

"If you need them, you'll know."

Magnus narrowed his eyes but didn't pursue it. He'd thought the man was an enigma, but that didn't begin to tell the tale. "Eirik, I have so many men here now—my own, the warriors you've lent to me, and Rorik's. I think you can head back to your holding. You're just establishing yourself and shouldn't be gone too long. But if Lifa would consent to stay, it might be for the better. Then I'd have Nuallen's help. Whatever *that* is." He shot him a look. "And we'll have Lifa's help as well. Not only her abilities as a healer but also a rune mistress."

"Silvi can read the runes just as well as our mother. Only she didn't study at the temple and she wasn't initiated into the rank." Eirik crossed one ankle over his knee as though he was settling in for a long talk.

"That's not entirely what I'm referring to." Magnus took a deep breath. "The *Thing* will take place in a few weeks at the mouth of the

Sognefjorden. The jarls of the region will be there. I want to bring charges against Toke. I need all the weapons I can get, and to have someone of Lifa's stature there—"

"Women can't speak at the *Thing*," Eirik said.

"Lifa's rank is above all laws, all social positions. Kings step aside for her and give up their seats so she might sit down. Even if she's not allowed to speak, she'll stand at my side, and that will make an impression."

"It won't hurt your reputation that you're married to her daughter," Leif said.

"That's right. I'm also concerned about Silvi. She seems to be adjusting well to this life, but we might be in for rough seas ahead, especially since Toke's tactics have changed. Having Lifa here could help her."

"Silvi's a woman grown and married," Eirik said. "She can make her own way."

"Yes, and Lifa hasn't interfered with us in any way, which is as it should be. I respect her for that. I can handle what happens between Silvi and me. But what happens between Silvi and the world may not be so easy. I don't understand what she sees and hears in the grove, or her link with the gods. She relies on those things, and I can't walk beside her there. Lifa can. She supports her in ways I cannot."

"I think you give my sister too little credit." Eirik uncrossed his ankle and leaned forward. "I've told you how strong she must be to hold that link between the gods and her. Believe me, I've tasted it myself. It's not for the weak. Still, if you feel that our mother, and Nuallen, will be a help, and if they choose to stay, I won't disagree."

Magnus looked at the Northumbrian. "Nuallen?"

"I'll be glad to remain, as long as Lifa is here. I'll feel relieved knowing I can keep an eye on Silvi as well."

"That's my right." Magnus leveled his gaze on him.

"Of course. But are not more eyes better?"

"It depends on where those eyes are focused."

Leif stood. "I'm up for a game of *tafl*. Eirik?"

"Gladly." He followed Leif out of the room.

Magnus didn't look away from Nuallen. "I appreciate that you guarded Silvi over the winter. But that ended on our wedding day."

"And if I see a danger to her, shall I not protect her?" He didn't blink.

"I don't intend to leave her alone long enough for it to become a question."

Nuallen's lips curved in a half smile. "Good. Remember though, the greatest danger doesn't always come from without. You've fought all your life with swords and ships and shields. That's all you know, all you prepare for. As the battlefield changes, so must the strategy. Even if a leader doesn't know how to wield all the weapons needed, he should have the wisdom to call on those who do, no matter what lies between them. Keep that in mind."

Nuallen rose, straightening his tunic. "Speak with Lifa. See if she's willing to stay. If she is, then for Silvi's sake, I'll guard your back. There may be those, even here, who will try to put a blade in it."

Magnus couldn't find Silvi anywhere. He'd asked Ingeborg, and she told him Silvi had come by just long enough to give her the myrrh to make into a powder. Egill's belly wound was no better, so they planned to try the resin on it that night.

He checked their chamber. It had been a long day and he hoped she was resting. He could always help her relax even more. Only Thyri was there, straightening the room.

"Thyri, have you seen my wife?"

The young woman jumped, flushing. Her eyes were red, as though she'd been crying. "Jarl Magnus, the mistress said she was going to the sauna."

He smiled to himself. That was even better, provided there were no other women there with her. "My thanks."

Thyri nodded, not meeting his eyes. Unlike many of the other serving girls, who'd tried to catch his attention in the past, she'd always avoided him. The woman who'd accompanied her from Bygvik, Mardoll, stayed with Thyri a great deal; perhaps Mardoll was a relative. Thyri never looked happy around her, though. He would have Birgitta look into it. He had other things to worry about. He wouldn't have noticed, except Thyri's situation might affect Silvi. With the possible threats to her, he had to be vigilant.

The next day, Magnus spoke to Birgitta outside, where none would overhear them. "I want you to be very careful and not let on that you're watching Mardoll and Thyri. I'm not certain they've done anything wrong, but someone from this village poisoned those sheep. My men have been watching the perimeter. They'd have no reason to notice anyone going into the valley from here. At least not up to that point. Now, nearly everyone is suspect."

Normally, he wouldn't explain himself to a servant, but she was almost family. She needed to understand the weight of what was happening.

"I'll keep an eye out, Jarl Magnus. They spend a lot of time in the cooking rooms, so I can pay attention to what they say. They don't get along very well, for all that Mardoll stays near her. I know Thyri leaves in the night sometimes, though. I always thought she was seeing someone here. You know." She blushed.

That was a good piece of information. Perhaps it would be wise to have Nuallen follow her one night. The man was a shadow.

"Let me know when she does, even if it's in the middle of the night. Wake me."

"I will, Jarl Magnus." Her eyes moistened. "First it was the mistress Asa during the winter who was being threatened. Now it might be the mistress Silvi and the whole village. It used to be so quiet here while I was growing up."

"I know, Birgitta. And it will be again. Do you know where Lifa is?"

"Yes, Jarl. She's in the common room. I think she's planning to check on Droplaug, the woman who's having problems with her pregnancy. She's waiting for some of the men to escort her."

"My thanks." He left Birgitta and went inside. Asa and Silvi spoke together in a corner. What was that all about? Sometimes, it was better not to know. Lifa sat alone at the table where the *tafl* board was set up, sipping a cup of ale. He walked to her. "May I speak with you?" At her nod, he sat down across from her. The board looked as though Asa and Leif had just finished a game. Pieces lay strewn about like a slaughtered army. Asa had won again.

"Eirik and Asa will leave this morning. Are you going with them?"

She sighed. "It will be difficult to leave my daughter, but she must go her own way, with you at her side."

"Would you consider staying longer? What you say of Silvi is very true. But there are other matters to consider. I need Nuallen with me. He has ways of fighting unlike anything I've ever seen. I could use him in this mess with Toke. I need every advantage, and that includes you."

"Oh?"

He picked up one of the scattered game pieces and set it in its place. "Ingeborg is very old. I wanted her to move in here where it's warmer in the winters and we can watch over her better. She won't come. I fear we'll have need of her services before this is over with Toke. I'm not certain she has the strength for it."

"My daughter is very well trained in healing."

"I'm aware of that, thank the gods. But your knowledge must be even more extensive, and she still has much to learn from you. We're fighting a battle I don't fully understand. It may involve weapons other than swords and ships. I could use a little of the gods beside me."

She tilted her head to one side, studying him. "And the *Thing* is approaching soon. I've heard you're considering bringing charges against Toke for unlawfully attacking you. Twice."

"I can only prove the attack on my ships when we returned from the wedding, but I hope to gather more information in the weeks ahead."

"And it would help your standings to have me with you."

"A rune mistress of your stature would be to my advantage, yes." She saw too clearly for him to dissimulate. "And I could use your knowledge of the runes."

She narrowed her eyes. "You don't believe in such things. The gods don't touch you."

His blood froze. How could she know this? He'd told no one but . . . Silvi. He'd trusted her discretion.

"I've seen it, Magnus. The gods have whispered it to me in the night. Don't you think that I, who have their ears, wouldn't know when someone doesn't hear them? No one else said anything. They didn't need to."

He looked down at the board, at the patterns in the wood. He picked up another piece and set it in its position. "It's always been this way. Silvi says I'm too steeped in the things of this world, but it's all I know."

"Perhaps it's not so much that you don't hear them, as they haven't deemed you ready. They'll call to you when they choose to, not before. In a way you'll understand."

Then, perhaps, one day he could walk beside Silvi in the grove and feel what she felt. They could come together finally, completely.

He looked into her compassionate, pale blue eyes. "Then will you and Nuallen stay for a time? I'll take you back to Haardvik once I've brought Toke to justice. One way or the other."

"Will you challenge him?"

He studied a carved playing piece before placing it on the board. "I'm considering it. Over the winter, Eirik read my runes. He said I hesitate too much and that it will cost me someone I love. That's happened before, and I've vowed it won't happen again. And yet, in this, I need to weigh all considerations. I want to bring my charges against Toke at the *Thing* and let those assembled hear and vote on them. If they find in my favor, I'll have more standing to challenge him. They'll want him to pay restitution, but it will be up to me to collect it. He won't pay, so I'll have the right to go after him then."

"We can't just attack our neighbors for no reason, though with all the blood feuds we have in our land, you wouldn't know it." Sitting back, she took a breath. "It's good, then, that I'm not packed, even though the ship is due to leave so soon, isn't it?"

He chuckled. "You're a wicked woman, Lifa."

She smiled. "The runes told me to stay. To help as I can. I also want to see where this leads. They've spoken to me of a time of darkness and treachery. They're unclear on many matters, and I want to try to work with them to shape what is to come."

His mouth dried. To hide his consternation, he finished setting up the *tafl* board before he spoke again. "And will you stand with me at the *Thing*? Even though women can't testify there?"

"You'd be surprised what I can do, Magnus. I've had kings back down based on my words alone, and avert their eyes. I'll stand with you. That will speak louder than even the gods themselves. Very few people know of Silvi, or that she's my daughter, for she never left our lands. It could work to our advantage. Quite often, surprise is the best weapon. And as you said, we must use every one we can."

The relief washing over Magnus shocked him. He'd never put much store in anything other than his warrior's abilities, the weapons he could hold, the strategy and tactics he could form in his mind. He'd always approached warfare in the light of day, on the open seas, with all the subtlety of a war cry. The rules had changed and he needed to change with them. He picked up the tiny king and placed it in the center of the squares.

The game board was widening, and now he finally had all the pieces he would need to win.

"Magnus says such words to me and I don't understand what he means." Silvi watched him as he spoke with her mother. He'd said he was going to ask her to stay and, no doubt, he was doing so.

"What kind of words?" Asa sipped at her ale. "They must be interesting considering how red your cheeks are."

Silvi put her hands to her face. "Is it that obvious? This is difficult enough. I can't ask my mother. But you're near my age and just married. It's to my brother, though, so I don't want to know too much. Magnus wants me to make a decision about us, but I'm not certain what he wants."

"Don't forget, we're speaking of my brother, as well. Without going into too much detail, tell me what he said."

"He spoke of his true nature, of how he could have that with me. He said something about control, I think of me, and of doing what he wishes to give me pleasure. He said I have the true power. He holds my wrists sometimes." She looked down, unable to continue.

"Granted, I'm not very experienced at all this myself, but Eirik has been diligent in showing me what pleases him. We're often on equal footing in this since he knows I keep my sword by the bed." She grinned. "There are times when I want to explore the possibilities, shall we say? Magnus has always been very powerful. He's had to be because he came to the title so young. He controls everything here, all matters of his life. It's what he's accustomed to. And I think it sounds like he wants that to extend to you."

"To me?"

"Of course. You're his wife. Men want to think they possess us, and we are theirs. It's not so easy in our land. We're very strong. And we hold many weapons against them."

"But I'm not strong. I'm not like you, Asa. I don't have a sword beside the bed."

"I can always get you one. Besides, you have runes, and that can be far worse, from what I've heard. He's giving you the choice. It's your decision. That's what he means when he says you hold the power. Eirik has told me that when he takes me as he wishes, his one desire is to see to my pleasure. It's his entire focus and responsibility. I think Magnus feels the same."

It would make sense. He did see to her pleasure before his own. This could be interesting.

"It's very freeing, actually." Asa took another sip of ale. "He does all the work and you get all the pleasure."

"When you say that, it doesn't sound so bad."

"Oh, it's not bad at all." She raised the cup, then drained it.

"I thought I was supposed to just lie there while . . ." She blushed.

Asa made an effort to swallow, then coughed. "Where did you hear that? Unless he tells you to, no. I don't think that's what Magnus has in mind. Just do what you feel is right. Follow your heart. He loves you and—"

"Loves me?" What was she talking about? If he did, wouldn't he have told her by now? He loved the ships. She could see it when they were out on the fjord. But her?

Asa frowned. "You've been married for how long, and he hasn't told you?"

"Perhaps there's nothing to tell."

"He's been shield-struck since the first moment he saw you in Haardvik. Odin's eye, Leif would love this. He'd never let Magnus live it down if he knew. Leave it to my brother to forget this tiny detail. If we weren't going back to Haardvik now, I'd tell him a thing or two."

"Don't." Silvi grabbed Asa's hand across the table. "Don't say anything to him. He can't know what we've been speaking of."

"Oh, don't worry. I'll let him stew in a cauldron of his own devising. Serves him right. I might give him a good kick in the rear, though, as I leave. Hit him in the brains and get them working again." She stood. "I have to go. I think all our things are loaded, and Eirik is probably waiting for me outside. Just try what I said with Magnus. And if you ever need a sword by the bed, send word and I'll bring you one myself."

"What did she kick me for?" Magnus rubbed his backside as they watched *The Wind of Njord* pull away from the beach. Onboard, Eirik and Asa stood together, his arm around her, as their men rowed toward the main fjord. Asa waved at them, smiling.

"I wouldn't know." Silvi waved back.

He crossed his arms and stared down at her. "You and she were talking together for quite a while."

"The same as you and my mother. I'm not accusing you of plotting anything with her."

"She's dangerous enough all on her own. Like mother, like daughter?"

She stood on her toes and kissed him on the jaw. "You'll see."

"I don't like the sound of that."

"You just might like it. If you're good." She walked to her horse. He followed and helped her mount, then narrowed his eyes at her.

"I should keep you here until you answer me."

"I wasn't aware you asked a question that required answering. My mother is waiting for me. She's asked me to go with her to see Droplaug, who may lose her child. She wants me to be prepared in case she's not available when Droplaug needs help."

He mounted his gelding. "I thought you knew about childbirth."

She urged her mare forward and Magnus's men fell in line behind them. "I've been to many of them, yes. Thanks to my mother's good advice to the women, all of them have been successful. A very rare thing. Droplaug didn't seek help right away. Ingeborg told us she's had three other miscarriages. Maybe she feels it's fated by the gods, so she's been despondent. Anyhow, my mother asked me to come with her."

"You're taking at least ten men with you. I can't come. I have a meeting with those who crew my ships. I should have gone to the markets a long time ago. What with the battle for Haardvik, and this trouble with Toke, I haven't been able to leave."

And their wedding. He didn't say it, but he didn't need to. "Will you go before the *Thing* takes place?"

"There isn't enough time. It takes many days to get from here to Kaupang. I can send one of my *knörrs* with my best traders, and one of my warships to guard it. At least that will get the season started. That will leave us two of the longships to carry us to the *Thing*."

Lifa, Nuallen, and the warriors were waiting for them when they reached the top of the path.

"Did everything go well with their departure?" Lifa stepped toward a waiting cart.

"Yes." Silvi steadied herself with her hands on Magnus's shoulders as he lifted her down from her horse. Just once she would like to try swinging her leg over her horse's neck and leaping off like she'd seen Asa do. And, quite likely, land on her face. She sighed.

Magnus gave her a quick kiss, then walked toward the longhouse. She and her mother climbed into the open cart. It was more seemly for a woman of Lifa's rank to travel that way. To keep up appearances, they would both ride in it. The men fanned out around them, Nuallen on horseback, riding ahead.

When they reached the small house nestled in the woods, Nuallen helped Silvi and Lifa from the cart.

"We'll stay outside to watch." He eyed the open door where they could hear a woman crying from within.

"Of course you will. This is women's work." Lifa led Silvi inside.

The house was dark. The weeping came from the bed, where Droplaug was curled up, holding her stomach.

They approached her and Lifa put her hand on the woman's forehead. "Do you still feel pain in your belly and back?"

"Not since you gave me the willow-bark tea," she said. "I know it's dead inside me. It hasn't moved in two days, and I'm still bleeding."

"How much?" Lifa lifted the covers.

"Just spotting, but it's getting worse."

"I see. Where's your husband?"

"Out getting wood for the fire. He should be back soon."

Lifa took Silvi aside and spoke low. "He shouldn't have left her. This is very serious."

"She'll lose the child?"

"I think so. She's had nettle tea and raspberry-leaf tea for weeks now, but it hasn't helped. She's still cramping, fevered, and her nausea went away some time ago. If the child isn't moving, that's a disturbing sign. I also tried painting runes on the palms of her hands—Fehu, Berkano, and Perthro. Nothing has helped."

"How long will it be?"

"I don't know. It could be tonight, or in several days. There's no way to know. I hope, for her sake, that it's soon. It would be better for her. Then she can recover."

"To conceive and lose yet another child?"

"Ingeborg will have to speak to her about using herbs to prevent conception. She may not like it, but she can't have this happen again. She could die. Are you using the herbs yourself?"

"Yes." She and Magnus hadn't even mentioned children yet, but every man wanted a son to come after him. She looked at Droplaug.

The woman was strong and healthy. Silvi bit her lip. How could she carry and bear a child, as slender as she was?

Lifa crossed to the other side of the room to make more of the teas.

Silvi followed her. "Will she ever be able to have a child? Would she have a better chance if you were here?"

"Ingeborg and I spoke at length about her treatment. Ingeborg did everything I would have done. She's an excellent midwife. Sometimes these things aren't meant to be. I've seen women who couldn't bear the child of one man go on to have children with another. It's a mystery."

Silvi gave the tea to Droplaug, then sat and comforted her while Lifa straightened up the room. She felt so helpless, but she had to act positive, as her mother had taught her. Men's voices filtered in from outside, and Droplaug's husband came in. He was a fine-looking man, but his face was haggard with fear and concern for his wife.

Lifa motioned him to the side. "Knud, I'll ask one of the men to stay here with you. If anything changes, send him to me. I'll be here as soon as I can."

"I will, mistress." His reddened eyes went to his wife as she moaned.

"Give her the teas as I instructed you before. I made them fresh just now."

"There's nothing more you can do?"

"It's in the hands of the gods now, Knud."

"So far, the gods have held nothing in their hands for us."

Lifa touched his arm. "They have given you each other. The love between a man and woman. That's more than many people have in this world."

He looked down. "I know, mistress. And if there's a choice to be made between my wife and the child, I cannot lose her. Even if we don't have any children, she is my life."

Silvi met her mother's eyes. Lifa wouldn't tell him the child was likely already gone. "I understand."

They left, with one of the men remaining behind. In the past, she'd often felt as though she was living in her mother's shadow, but now she was glad of it. At least her mother was staying for a time and could take care of this. Silvi could not. It was heart-wrenching enough to see what Droplaug was going through emotionally. When the time came for the birth, how much worse would it be?

At the temple, she never would have had to see this. She looked out at the forest as the cart moved along toward the village. *The temple.* She had to stop thinking of it. She wasn't there and most likely never would be. Instead, she was here, in the midst of war, treachery, and the natural order going horribly wrong.

Two other women in the area were close to giving birth, and their pregnancies were progressing well. When the time came, which would be soon, she'd attend them, leaving her mother free to help Droplaug. That much, she could do. She wasn't made for the harshness of this world, and yet, the gods had seen fit to put her here instead of allowing her to dwell in the shelter of the temple. She closed her eyes.

If only she knew why.

When Silvi returned to the longhouse, she went into Magnus's and her chamber. Birgitta had said he was down on the beach, seeing to the shipment of goods for the markets. He might not be back until later. She kicked her shoes off and lay down on the bed. The day had taken all her strength, and she had some time before the evening meal.

Droplaug's grief turned over in her mind, not letting her rest. She rose and took out the bag of runes from her chest. Sitting on the bed, she opened the bag and sifted the carved wooden pieces through her fingers. She envisioned a sphere of pure light around her that would keep out any dark influences, then let her thoughts flow free.

Would the runes speak to her? Would she understand what they had to say? Her mother was trained for this, not her. But she had learned at her mother's knee all her life. Though she didn't call on them often, they did hear her.

One of the runes felt warm and she drew it out. Berkano. It lay reversed on her hand. She sighed. The gods were being obvious today, which was no help.

The door opened and Magnus came in. He stopped when he saw her on the bed.

"I remembered a seax I wanted to send with the ships to Kaupang." He went to one of his chests and lifted the lid. "Casting? I thought that was your mother's talent."

"I know the art as well. I can do a casting for you, if you'd like me to."

He rose, carrying a sheathed seax. "Eirik already did that this past winter and told me more than I care to know. Unless you can tell me the best trading routes and where to get the highest prices this season, I can do without it." He crossed to the bed and gave her a kiss on her cheek, then left.

She looked down at the rune, and pain welled up inside her. He'd appeared preoccupied, but still, his brusqueness told the story. She had tried to help him, but he didn't need it. The ability to see and to foretell were all she had to offer him. That, and her healing knowledge. If he didn't need her, then at least the people of the village did. Everywhere she went, they asked her questions, wanted advice, spoke to her of their troubles. And *they* listened.

What lay within her were the things he didn't understand. She turned the rune over in her hand. Berkano-reversed signaled miscarriage. But it also indicated a series of choices and that there would be difficulties until she made a decision.

She ran the pad of her thumb along the symbol. If she sought her visions, the gods might clarify what this meant. She didn't want to risk it. She might find herself back in the sea alone, her island only a whisper of sand beneath her, with nothing to hold on to ever again.

And, like Magnus, she didn't need the gods to tell her that.

Chapter Fourteen

"Mistress, wake up. Please." Birgitta's voice was far away. "It's Droplaug. Her husband sent for help. She's having the child."

Silvi came awake with a start, her heart pounding. "Oh gods. Where's my mother?" She jumped out of bed and grabbed her dress.

Birgitta brought her shoes to her. "Your mother and Ingeborg left to help another woman who's having a baby. She lives down at the far end of the valley."

She slipped her shoes on. "My husband?"

"The jarl and Leif are staying down at the holding near the beach for the night. I sent for them all, but it will take time for them to come."

Silvi stopped. "There's no one here to help her but me." How was she going to do this?

"I'll come with you, mistress." Birgitta raised her chin. "I've seen a few births."

"Not like this, you haven't. Still, I can use your help. Where's Thyri?"

"I don't know, mistress. She isn't here."

Why was everyone gone this night, of all of them? "Come, then. I'll need you."

The stable lad, Sjurd, had horses ready. The warrior who had stayed behind at Droplaug's house, and brought the news of the impending birth, waited for them. They cantered out of the village, the moon lighting their way.

She couldn't think of what she would face once she arrived. She must think only of Droplaug and what she would need. There was no chance to save the child, but she had to save the mother. If she concentrated on that, perhaps she could do this.

She *would* do this. She could panic later. Right now there was no time for that. Knud stood outside, watching for them.

"It's the child. It's trying to come, but she won't push. She's given up."

She swung her leg over the neck of the mare and landed on her feet. She rushed to the door. "Knud, stay out here. My mother may come soon." *I hope.*

They hurried to Droplaug. Blood and fluid covered the bed where she lay, but she wasn't moving. "Oh gods, no." Silvi cupped Droplaug's cheek and her eyes fluttered open. They didn't focus.

Silvi breathed again. At least she was alive. She lifted the covers and checked her, then examined her stomach. A slight contraction rippled through her.

While Birgitta blotted the sheets with cloths, Silvi took the mother's head in her hands and looked into her eyes. "Droplaug, you have to listen to me. The child needs to come out. You have to help it or you'll die."

"That's what I want." Her words were faint. "I can't keep a child, so this is the only way. If I die with him inside me, then he'll be with me always. I won't lose him like I did the others."

Silvi gasped and looked at Birgitta. The serving woman's eyes filled and she went back to her task. If only her mother were here. She'd know what to do, what to say. Why had the gods done this to her? Her stomach roiled as the pain flared.

This wasn't about her. Right now, all that mattered was Droplaug. Not her, not the gods, not the *wyrd* itself. Silvi swallowed past the lump in her throat and tapped Droplaug's cheeks until she looked at her.

"Listen to me. You will lose this child." The woman cried out and shook her head. Silvi stopped her and made her focus again. "You must live. Fight for your life."

"No. What good am I? I can't even give my husband a son. All men want that above all else. He needs a wife who will bear him fine sons. I've told him that, but he won't divorce me and he won't let me leave him. He says if I divorce him, he'll force me to remarry him."

"You love him."

"Yes. He's such a fine man, he deserves a son. I want him to have what I cannot give him."

"What he wants, Droplaug, is you. Do you know what he said to my mother and me when we were here earlier? He said if there's a choice between you and the child, he wanted us to save you. Even if you can never have children, you are his life, everything to him."

"He said that?" She grasped Silvi's arm.

"Yes. How would you feel if he died?"

"It would be like my own death."

"Then what will he feel if you allow yourself to die?" She took the woman's tearstained face in her hands and spoke very clearly. "It would be no different. Will you do that to him? Will you break his heart? Would you have him mourn both a wife and a child? You must be here for him so he's not alone in his grief. You are so much more than just your womb, Droplaug. There is a vast, incredible world out there. And there is a loving, warm world here for you and Knud. He wants to be in that world with you, no matter what. Please, please stay here with him. With us."

Tears ran from the corners of her eyes. "For Knud, then, tell me what I must do."

Silvi met Birgitta's hopeful gaze. "Push. Wait for a contraction and push as hard as you can." She changed places with Birgitta, going to the foot of the bed while the servant stroked Droplaug's hair. This was it. Her mother wasn't here yet and they couldn't wait.

A contraction came. "Push, Droplaug. Now."

The woman screamed and pushed, her face red, her body taut. In a few more contractions, Silvi caught the small, still body in a blanket, cut its cord, and wrapped it quickly before Droplaug could see it. She nodded to Birgitta, who went to the door to call Knud.

He came in, his eyes moist. "I heard her scream. Is she . . . ?"

"She lives. But not the child. I'm so sorry." She gave the bundle to Birgitta to take outside.

He went to his wife's side, but as Birgitta passed him, he put his hand on the blanket. "What was it?"

"A son."

His face screwed up with grief, but he composed himself with an effort and sat on the bed. "Droplaug?"

She opened her eyes. "I failed you again, Knud."

"No. Not you. The Norns have said it is not meant to be. But I have you, and that's all the joy I need. We'll make a life together, just you and I."

With a weak smile, she nodded, then her eyes closed.

He rose and went to Silvi. "Will she live?"

"When my mother gets here, she'll examine her. But I think so. There was much blood and she still has to pass the afterbirth, but other than the child, everything else seemed to be as normal as could be expected."

"Knud?" Droplaug's weak voice drifted to them from the bed. Trying to smile, he sat beside her and bent over her, holding her hand.

Birgitta came back in and Silvi met her at the door. "I need to go outside for a few moments. Watch to see if she passes the afterbirth and call me when she does."

She stepped out into the night. Magnus's warrior nodded to her and moved off, keeping watch. She pulled water from the well and washed her hands and arms, then sank down on a bench by the house and leaned her head back against the wall. She had only just gone to sleep when Birgitta had awoken her. With almost no rest, and the emotional drain of the ordeal, her muscles were like water, exhaustion climbing through her.

There was no guarantee Droplaug would survive, but what was it her mother had told her so often? There was always hope where there was the will to live. All the years of her mother's teaching, not only of what to do, but of what to say, had come to fruition. She'd found a strength she didn't know she had. She smiled. And she'd finally jumped off a horse and hadn't killed herself.

The sound of horses and a cart came to her. Her mother was there. The pain still burning in her stomach subsided. With a groan, she made herself rise as they pulled up. Nuallen lifted Lifa down.

She indicated the small bundle on the ground outside the door. "It was a boy. Droplaug lives, but she hasn't passed the afterbirth yet."

"I'll tend to her." Lifa embraced her. "I'm so very proud of you, Daughter."

Silvi nodded and her mother went into the house. Nuallen sat down on the bench.

"Come here, Silvi. You're going to fall down if you keep standing."

She settled beside him and he drew her head to his shoulder. "Rest for a time. I'll keep watch."

She smiled. "You always have." It felt so good to let everything go, finally. Her mother would have things well in hand inside, and Nuallen was keeping guard over them all. She closed her eyes and let the day drain away.

* * *

"I'll take her back to the longhouse."

Magnus's voice woke her. Rousing, she looked up. He stood before the bench, his arms crossed, his face set. She pushed away from Nuallen, but he pulled her back to him.

"Get on your horse and I'll hand her up to you. She's beyond exhausted." He picked her up as Magnus mounted his gelding.

"I can walk. Put me down. I can ride my own mare."

"Nuallen can bring your horse back to the village."

Nuallen lifted her up into Magnus's arms and he settled her across his lap. He wrapped his cloak around them both. She snuggled against him. In her rush, she'd forgotten to bring a shawl and the night air was cool.

He nudged his horse into a walk and she sighed, leaning her head on his chest.

"You won't believe what I did this night."

"I know. You saved Droplaug. Nuallen told me everything before you woke."

"Not that." The warmth of his body seeped into her and it was too much work to tell him about how she'd finally dismounted like Asa did. The rest was the will of the Norns.

Magnus's strong arms held her close against him, and his powerful legs cradled her. She breathed in his scent, her body melting even more. She should think of letting him have his way more often. This was so much better than riding her own mare back to the village.

He didn't let go of her even when they arrived at the longhouse. The stable lad, Sjurd, held the gelding while Magnus threw his leg over the horse's neck and slid off, still carrying her. It was late, so no one was in the common room except those who slept on the benches against the walls. None of them stirred as Magnus walked with her into their chamber. He set her on her feet and reached for the bead closing the neck of her dress. She stepped away from him.

"Thank you, but I can undress myself."

"I'll undress you if I like." He unfastened the bead button at her throat. "Be silent."

His jaw was set, his eyes hard. He was angry about finding her sleeping on Nuallen, but he had to know she was drained and this wasn't the time to confront her about it.

She didn't look at him as he slipped the gown to the floor. She wore only her linen shift.

"Tomorrow, you will rest. There will be no healing, runes, visions, gods, or running through the cold night, half dressed. Do you hear me?"

"I hear you, Magnus. But I have duties and responsibilities. Several of the women have ailing children. I have herbs to prepare."

He wrapped one arm around her and put his other hand on her mouth. She tried to remove it, but he was too strong. She subsided, glaring at him.

"You will rest, Silvi. Or I'll tie you to the bed, and trust me, there won't be much rest for you then." He dropped his hand and stepped away. Her eyes narrowed. Was that what Asa was talking about? Then he would truly control her. His perfect body was a column of leashed strength as he came toward her. Power, so primal and male, rolled off of him, awakening her traitorous body.

"I thought you were spending the night down at the fjord."

"No sense in riding all the way back down there now. Before I left to get you, I asked Birgitta to have a meal ready for us. I'll return when it's light. For now, you're mine. I have to be certain you obey me. For once."

She shot him a look. "Yes, my jarl."

"That's better."

"I think I'll take Asa up on her offer."

"What would that be?"

"Never mind." A sword beside the bed would change his high-handed ways. If she could lift it.

Magnus answered a knock on the door and took a tray from Birgitta. He set it down on a table beside the bed. His gaze swept her body, his eyes dark. Her muscles tightened as he took her hands in his.

"Since you're so tired, I'd thought to feed you myself, giving you only the choicest of morsels, a tiny sip of wine to relax you. But I suppose you can do without all that."

Her knees threatened to buckle at the depth of his voice sliding over her. "Perhaps I'm more tired than I thought."

He ran his thumb over her wrist. "I wouldn't want you to go hungry. For anything. It's my duty, and pleasure, to see to your needs in all ways."

Gods. She swallowed as he let go of her hands.

"If I take that shift off, we'll never eat. To bed. I'll get our meal."

She cast a glance at him over her shoulder as she walked to the bed. Sinking onto it, she watched him undress, then he retrieved the plate of food. He came back to her, his body moving with his warrior's grace.

"Birgitta gave us a nice meal." He put the plate on the bed between them and picked up a piece of roasted beef. Setting it against her lips, he smiled, his eyes twinkling. She took it, careful to nip at his fingers before he could withdraw them.

"Ungrateful woman." He ate a piece himself, then offered her a slice of honeyed carrot. "Nicely, or you'll get nothing else this night."

She tilted her head to the side. There were certain merits to going hungry in order to teach him a thing or two. She took the piece of carrot gently, then sucked at his fingers to get all the sweet sauce off of them. He narrowed his eyes at her, but she only gave him a shy smile as she chewed.

"Mead?"

"Please."

He tipped the cup to her lips with care as she drank, eyeing him over the rim. "May I have more beef, please?"

"You have but to ask." He fed her another piece, holding it as she tried to take it.

She licked his fingers. He caught his breath and released the morsel.

"I don't know what's worse—your teeth or your tongue."

"I suppose that depends on where they are. And what they're doing."

He bowed his head and groaned, pinching the bridge of his nose between his fingers. "This is one meal where I might be hungry after it's done."

"I still am."

He looked at her from beneath his hair. "I don't know. You're torturing me on purpose. I don't think I'll reward you for that. I should, in fact, take you over my knee."

What? "Am I, then, a child to be treated so?"

Eying her breasts through the thin material, he shook his head. "You're anything but a child. But I would enjoy teaching you a thing or two about behaving."

The room became warmer, even though no fire burned in the brazier. Her breath came short, and a liquid sensation flowed deep within her. With a shaking hand, she picked up a piece of meat and held it to his mouth. He took it with great care, watching her.

Death had visited them. But they'd defeated it, wresting Droplaug into life. Even if it wasn't Droplaug's time, she'd had a hand in the woman's survival. A need for an affirmation of life burned in her. The knowledge that they'd come through the fires of the *wyrd* and emerged victorious swelled in her. She was alive. The sensation coursed through her, carried on her blood, the very essence of life itself. And what would be more life-affirming than to come together with Magnus?

She leaned forward and kissed him. He tasted of the beef she'd given him, rich and savory. Moving her lips across his cheek, she whispered to him. "Teach me."

He leaned back to look at her. "Are you certain? After tonight?"

"After tonight, I need to feel you inside me. I need your arms around me, holding me, letting me know we overcame death. In spite of the loss, we live, and Droplaug lives. We must grasp life with both hands, Magnus, for it may fade like the sun in the winter. And we cannot know when it will happen. While we're here, while we have each other, let us come together. Because we live."

He cupped her face in his hands. "I have always clung to what is mine, Silvi. I don't know why that is. These past days have taken much from me and I cannot know how I'll be this night. Whether it's the gods taking a child, or Toke attacking me in ways I don't understand and can't plan against, I feel that everything around me is spiraling out of control. Just as you need to feel your life to its fullest, I must try to control what I can. I have always been that way. I don't think you understand. I fear what I may do."

She took his hands from her face and held them. "I don't. I don't fear what you will do to me. You've always had to control everything around you, yes. But it has been so you can protect Thorsfjell, its people, me. You want to shield us, and to do that, you must wield your authority, your command. The people have trusted you all these years, and you've seen them safe and well cared for. Would you do no less for me, your wife? I trust you, Magnus."

He closed his eyes tight, holding her hands to his lips. After a moment, he stood, bringing her with him.

"Raise your arms." She did so. "Keep them there." Kneeling before her, he lifted her shift over her thighs and followed it with his mouth, kissing and nipping at her skin.

Her muscles quivered. She drew in a sharp breath, wanting, needing to touch him. But his words held her arms where they were and she tilted her head back. He laved her skin with heat. His head was on a level with her breasts and as he raised the shift over them, he took one in his mouth, pulling at it.

He flung the garment up over her head, tossed it aside, then grabbed her wrists and pulled them back behind her. With one hand, he held her captive as he took her breast with his free hand and caressed the other with his tongue. She pulled at her wrists. He tightened his grip, not enough to hurt her, but enough so that she stopped resisting. He was too strong.

A thrill flashed through her, of shock, excitement, tinted with just a touch of fear. Not of Magnus, but of the unknown, like what lay beyond the edge of the world. And yet he must have sailed these waters before and knew the right course. She would travel any sea with him at the helm.

He released her wrists, rose, and swung her up in his arms. His face was grim, his eyes hard. But he laid her on the bed with exquisite gentleness, gazing down on her. Swallowing, she bent one knee in a vain effort to shield herself from the male power pouring from him. He was very aroused, his muscles corded as though he had just come from battle. His long, dark hair flowed down his chest, cascading over the slabs of muscles there like the falls coming down from the mountain peaks.

Climbing onto the bed, he urged her to lower her leg. "I want you open to me, Silvi. Don't think to shield your beauty from me."

Beauty? She knew better. But with the look in his eyes as he swept her in his gaze, she could almost believe it. He slid his hands over her breasts, her stomach, and down to her thighs. His breathing came hard and ragged as he slipped his hands between them. Parting her legs, he sat back.

"I don't want you to hurt your hands by holding on to the headboard. The carved wood can be sharp." He moved over her, keeping his weight on one arm. With the other, he brought one of her arms up over her head and held it there. "Keep this here." He brought the other one up to match it. "I expect you to stay like this, or I'll have to tie you. Do you understand?"

Her cheeks heating, she nodded. He swept his fingertips over her face, his gaze following them. "I wonder if you do."

He kissed her, hard and deep. She almost lowered her hands to run them through his hair and hold him to her. But she didn't want to disappoint him. He nibbled her neck, then moved lower. When he reached her breasts, she started to lower her arms, unable to keep from touching him. Before she did, he spoke without lifting his head.

"I have warned you. Not again."

She placed her arms back over her head. He continued his sweet torture on her breasts. The urge to hold him made her grit her teeth. She looked up. The headboard had intricate open knotwork patterns. She grasped the wood and held on. The pressure stung her skin, but she increased it. The small amount of pain drove down into her body, spearing into her core. At that moment, he nipped her on the inside of her breast.

Letting out a cry, she arched up against him. The sensation burst over her. It lapped against her, like waves on the shore of her island.

Magnus stilled. "Silvi? Oh gods, I didn't hurt you, did I?" He moved up to her. "I forget how delicate you are."

She smiled and took a deep breath at the pleasure still pulsing through her. "I didn't cry out because it hurt, Magnus."

His eyes widened. "Oh." Then he looked up at the headboard. "I told you, I didn't want you to risk hurting yourself."

She tried not to smile though her heart pounded with what she was about to allow. "I'm not certain I can keep from touching you, Magnus."

He dropped his head to her chest and spoke through his hair. "Are you saying what I think you're saying?"

"Perhaps I have more of the explorer in me than I thought. I want to explore with you."

His voice was muffled, but she heard him. "I must have done something to please the gods at some time in my life."

She laughed and lowered her arms, ruffling his hair. It might be the last time she would be able to do so for a while. He rose off of her, then dipped down to kiss her.

"Don't go anywhere."

"I won't. I think you'll make certain of that." She smiled up at him.

He rolled off the bed and went to their chests lining the far wall.

He hesitated, staring down at them. "I don't want to use anything that could hurt you."

Turning onto her side, she propped her head on her hand and studied him as he knelt. He was so powerful, he could break her without even thinking about it. But he was her husband, and he had said that if she were to give herself into his care, it would be for her pleasure. She had to trust him. No doubt he'd done this before and knew what he was about.

He returned to her, holding a silk sash Eirik had brought back from the East for her. After urging her onto her back, he straddled her and took her hands in his. "Are you certain? I told you once that you hold all the power here. Everything I do, everything I want, is for you to enjoy."

Her head grew light. "I want your pleasure as well. And if this gives it to you, then yes, it's what I want."

"This gives it to *us*." He leaned down and kissed her. "Thank you for your trust." Still, he paused. He looked uncertain.

"What is it?"

"You must know that I've had . . . relationships before."

"Since you weren't a virgin, I assumed so."

He cleared his throat. "It has never meant this much to me, Silvi. I feel like an untried boy with you. We have the rest of our lives together. If I don't do this right, it could come between us."

"How do you think I feel, Magnus? I know I'm not as strong and vibrant as other women. I don't know if I'll please you, or be enough for you. I don't want to be compared to others in your past and found lacking."

He frowned. "What are you talking about, Silvi? Surely you must know how beautiful you are. How exquisite. There can be no one else like you. No one else for me. The others are shadows next to you. They fade away in the light of your splendor."

She closed her eyes as his words poured through her. Did he speak of love? The men of their lands often would not say the words, lest they fall under the woman's spell. But hadn't he shown her?

Looking up at him, she longed to tell him she loved him. Would that give him even more power over her? The words climbed in her, but fear followed them. What if he didn't want to know? What if this was all he wanted between them? He had married her for her dowry, after all. She had no doubt he cared for her and wanted to give her pleasure, but that was an ocean away from love.

Uncertainty still shone in his eyes as he watched her. Not the same as hers, but she grew uneasy. Misunderstandings happened so easily between them. Not this night.

"Magnus, I need for you guide me in this. You want control, so take it."

His jaw tightened. "Perhaps you need it as much as I do." He twined the sash around her wrists and knotted it. "It's not too tight, is it?"

"No. It's fine." More than fine. The snugness reassured her, made her feel secure. Now she was in his care and she would find out what that meant. As Asa told her, she only needed to let go and be free.

He tied the long end to the headboard so she lay exposed to him. Settling his full weight on her, he pressed her into the mattress. He rained kisses along her neck and between her breasts. Not touching them, he moved downward between them, nibbling and feathering his lips over her skin.

She pulled on the sash, but it didn't give. Her breasts ached for his touch, but she could do nothing about it. Raising her leg, she ran her heel along his leg, up toward the top of his thigh.

"You're setting a fire you may not be able to put out."

"Then let me burn." She already was. Her heart pounded, her skin was damp and she needed him in her, a part of her.

"Very well, then." He rose up and flipped her over. Drawing her hips back to him, he pressed into her hard and fast. She cried out and met his thrusts. He held the back of her neck with one hand, keeping her as he wanted. She gave in to his dominance. All her being centered on him. His strength called to the deepest aspect of her. He was the consummate warrior. He took, and what he took, he kept. Her.

He brought her to the brink, then withdrew, turned her over, and entered her again. With his hands hooked over her shoulders, he gripped her, holding her to him as she wrapped her legs around him.

They moved together as one. He held her hair and tilted her head back, exposing her throat. He controlled her completely and she gave herself up to him, body and heart.

She flew free.

He shouted and poured into her. A wild ecstasy hit her so hard that pain speared through her along with it. They intertwined together, twisting everything she was so that she sobbed with the power of it.

Magnus collapsed on top of her, then rolled off and lay at her side. Shocks of pleasure continued to uncoil within her and she shuddered. After a few moments, he shifted onto his side and looked down at her. "Are you all right?"

"Very." She smiled at him.

Lowering his head, he kissed her, then reached up and tugged at the knot. "Let me free you."

"You already have."

"Oh gods, Silvi." He gathered her to him. "The first time I saw you, I never thought . . . I never knew anything could be like this."

"Nor did I. Believe me." She could never have known about this if she'd gone to Uppsala. Priestesses weren't always celibate, but even if she had chosen that path, Magnus would not have been with her. And that made all the difference.

He pulled the furs up over them and settled her against his chest. "With all we'll have to face in the coming days, Silvi, know that I'll be with you, protecting you, caring for you, and standing at your side. In all ways, at all times."

She rested in his comforting embrace. She would always listen to the words the gods wove in the trees and the waves, but this was what she wanted. Not the chants of prayers to unhearing wooden statues. Not the blood of sacrifices. Not the solitude of her visions and the reverence of people who didn't know her and who stood in distant awe of her.

This. Warmth, passion, using her gifts to help the people she knew and loved. And Magnus. Closing her eyes, she listened to the sound of his heart. She could no longer deny that she wanted to stay here with him, loving him, and perhaps one day, bearing his children.

And perhaps, one day, if the gods smiled on her, he would love her as well.

Chapter Fifteen

Leif took a sip of ale. "Who do you think is coming here in the longship?"

"I don't know." Magnus drummed his fingers on the table. One of his men had given him a message that they'd spotted a ship sailing into their branch of the fjord and he'd sent men to meet it. Leif and he waited in his private room for those aboard to arrive at the village. "It has a dragon's head on the bow, so it must belong to someone of high rank. At least a jarl."

"Right. No king would come here."

"I hope not. We'd spend too much gold on food and wine."

Leif chuckled as one of the men opened the door.

He stood aside. "Hoskuld, envoy to the Law-Sayer."

Magnus and Leif rose as the man swept into the room. He was large, obviously a former warrior, and still had a commanding presence.

"Jarl Magnus. I greet you in the name of the Law-Sayer, Yrian."

Yrian was a powerful man who presided over legal matters for the entire region. Magnus nodded toward a seat at the front of his table. "Will you have wine, Envoy? You must have sailed far."

He sat down. "It is a long way up the fjord, Jarl Magnus. But you may want to hold the wine. I do not bring glad news."

Magnus sank into his chair and met Leif's gaze. "What brings you here?"

"The *Thing* will take place in less than two weeks. I trust you will be there?"

"Of course."

"First, a complaint has been brought against you, to be heard by the assembly. It concerns the killing of an heir to property, a grievous offense. He does not claim murder since it was in the open, but it is still grave."

"Toke Gudrodson."

"Yes. He claims that you willfully drowned his son while the boy was unarmed. He was Toke's only heir, and so it is a potential financial disaster for you and your relations."

So this was Toke's revenge. It would be easy enough to dispute; Magnus had many witnesses. "I won't argue my case to you, Envoy. It took place in battle. However, I'll come and give my evidence and let all free men hear me."

"That is well. But there's another matter he brings forth." He looked uneasy. "He accuses your wife of practicing the dark arts. If she is found guilty, she can be executed by drowning in the bog."

The blood drained from Magnus's head.

Leif stood, his fists clenched. "That bastard attacks us, poisons our sheep, tries to burn Rorik's ships, and he dares to spew such lies?"

The envoy's eyes widened. "Rorik? Of Trøndelag? Gudrodson must be insane."

Magnus's vision turned red. To attack him was one thing. But Silvi? Beautiful, sweet, innocent Silvi? She would have to stand before all of the free men, unable to speak, for women could not testify at the *Thing*. This alone would hurt her beyond measure.

He rose and slammed his fists on the table as heat roared through him. "And I accuse Gudrodson of attacking my ships without provocation. I also accuse him of waging war on this village and its people. Again, without cause. He killed our livestock, terrorized all the villages and ships in this part of the fjord, and gives shelter to outcasts. I want him to stand trial for these grievances."

"Very well, Jarl Magnus. I will let the Law-Sayer know."

"What exactly did he say my wife has done?"

"He would make no statements, but assured us he has proof."

"And my wife is to be slandered on the word of a known marauder."

"If it is true, then it is no slander. If it is false, then all will know it is so, and you'll receive compensation." He stood. "With the meeting being so close, there's much to be done, and I must visit other villages along the fjord. Gather your witnesses, Jarl Magnus. Bring your wife. And may the gods stand at your side."

After the envoy left, Magnus hurled his cup against the wall, shattering it. "The whoreson! It isn't enough that he accuses me of killing his son, but he has the bollocks to drag Silvi into this."

Leif eyed the pieces of the cup. "He did say he would destroy all you cared about. He probably knows he can't truly touch you. There are too many witnesses to what happened. But Silvi? That's another matter."

"He was too cowardly to say what evidence he has to support his accusations. So it will be difficult to defend against them when we don't know what they are ahead of time."

"We can most likely start with the sheep. I would say that's why he had them poisoned. To say that her dark magic did it."

"It was obvious someone gave them yew."

"Yes." Leif thought for a moment. "But does he know that the yew was unmistakable? Something isn't right here."

"Of course something's not right. Silvi's accused of the dark magic. That's what's not right."

"I mean beyond that. The sheep were poisoned, and the evidence was too plain. We're attacked, yet the tactics involved were so inept, it was as though they wanted to lose. Some dead sheep hardly constitutes evidence for evil powers."

Magnus rubbed his forehead. "I wish I could think straight. Gods, how am I going to tell her? And Lifa. I don't even want to think of what she'll do."

"Yes. This affects her, as well. And Eirik. Runes will be flying. And not the good ones either."

"We have to make plans. I want Lifa here when I tell Silvi."

Leif nodded. "And Nuallen. If we're making plans, he'd better be part of them. We have to find this evidence Toke says he has. And unless I miss my guess, Nuallen may be just the one we need to do it."

"I don't understand how this could be. I don't even know what the dark arts are." Silvi stared at him with her large, silver eyes. Tears misted them. He wanted to go to her, hold her, tell her nothing would happen to her. But with her mother, Nuallen, and Leif in the room, it wasn't the right time. After they'd formed a plan, and he and Silvi were alone, he could comfort her.

"Sorcerers can use their talents to harm others." Lifa's voice was low, her face hard. "They can cause stillbirths in animals as well as people. They can poison from afar, cause the ground to shake and rivers to flood. They do not heal and achieve the good we do. They are destructive and dishonorable. To link the darkness with me is a grave insult and I intend to answer this myself."

"Women cannot speak at the *Thing*." Leif took a drink of his beer. They all held cups, for they needed the fortification.

"I will speak if I see fit. They may not listen, but I will speak the truth. I know the Law-Sayer, Yrian, from long ago. He is fair and respects my rank. He'll at least allow me my say, though it is not traditional."

"Be that as it may, we need a reserve plan." Magnus regarded Nuallen. "Thyri has not gone out again at night?"

"Not since the night Droplaug gave birth, but Birgitta told me she brought out her shawl and laid it on her bed today. Apparently she does this beforehand so she doesn't risk waking anyone. I'm not waiting for Birgitta's summons, though. I'll stay outside, watching all night if I must. And I'll wait the next night if necessary, until I can follow her."

"At this point, only find where she goes and see who she speaks to. We don't want to strike before we get more information and know the best way to handle this."

"Agreed."

"Come to me as soon as you return. Birgitta will let me know that you've left, so I'll wait up for you."

"It may not be until morning. She said Thyri usually doesn't come back until nearly dawn."

"Nevertheless, I doubt any of us will be sleeping much until this matter is resolved. Are you certain you don't want anyone else with you?"

Nuallen smiled and it wasn't pleasant. "I can follow you so closely in the dark I could touch you, and yet you'd never know it. Others would only jeopardize my success. I'll go alone."

"As you will. What we've said doesn't leave this room, not even to speak of it to each other, except for Birgitta. We cannot be certain of anyone else."

After everyone agreed, Leif and Lifa went out into the common room, but Magnus shook his head at Nuallen, then took Silvi's arm and held her back. "Wait for me in our chamber." She nodded and left, not looking at him.

"Do you think you can do this? I'm accustomed to meeting my foes on the seas and on the battleground."

Nuallen shot him an amused look. "I realize that. Your people are not known for their subtleness in war. But I was trained in these ways, so yes, I can do this." He stood. "Just as Leif is skilled at assessing people, so am I. Silvi is falling over the edge of her world right now. You may try to reach for her to help her, but don't be surprised if she strikes your hand away. She may blame you for this, for marrying her into this life. She was so set on being a priestess."

"Eirik and her mother agreed she shouldn't go to Uppsala. She'd marry someone, and it turned out to be me."

He chuckled. "Yes—you, Eirik, and Lifa thwarted her dreams, and if it weren't for that, she'd be safe at Uppsala. She'll blame all of you. The three of you are in very deep trouble."

That was obvious when Magnus walked into their chamber. Silvi stood with her arms crossed, her head lowered, facing away from him. He embraced her from behind. Her body trembled and she was stiff in his arms.

"We'll prove him wrong, Silvi. Trust us."

"I trusted my mother all these years to send me to the temple to study. I trusted Eirik to love me enough to allow me my dreams. Instead, they betrayed me and forced me to come here."

"And to marry me, I know."

She shook again, breaking away from him. Sinking down on the bed, she curled into a ball, holding her legs tight to herself. "See what this world has brought to me, Magnus. This is why I wanted no part of it."

"Or of me?"

She rested her forehead on her knees. "You are the only good part of it. And the people here. What will they say about me now?"

He sat beside her but didn't touch her. "They'll stand with you. All of them. You've done so much good for them, healed them, and given them advice and wisdom."

"And this is how the gods reward me. I had just given up my desire to go to the temple, and remain here. Now, the gods punish me for abandoning them and turning to physical pleasures and the ways of Midgard."

"You can't know that, Silvi. They set you on this course, to come here for a reason. We need you here. They saw that."

She didn't raise her head. "Who are you to speak to me of what the gods want?"

"I may not hear them as you do, but I can see their hands in this. There has to be a reason for it. Trust in them and trust in me."

"I did that and see where it has taken me."

"This is only one step. What matters is where the journey ends."

"With my death. How can we prove what I didn't do? How can we prove something that few others understand? The people who vote on issues are all farmers and jarls and free men. They are just as afraid and in awe of the unknown as anyone. They attack what they don't understand."

"And once we find out what Toke's evidence is, we'll counter it with common sense of our own, spoken by the plain people who know you well. *Our* people. I intend to bring as many of them as I can to testify to what you have done for them."

"It may not be enough."

"Then we'll get more evidence." He put his hand on her shoulder.

She shook it off. "I need to be alone. I was always that way, all my life, and I was happy. Leave me be."

"I'll leave for now, Silvi." He kissed the top of her bowed head. "For I have much to do. But there's one thing you can be certain of. Though the gods desert you, and your dreams flow away from you, while I live, you will never again be alone."

"Thyri met with a young man, about her age." Nuallen stood with his arms crossed in front of Magnus's table in the meeting room. He had darkened his skin with some substance, and had not washed it off yet. "It was a distance from here, to the northeast, in a heavily wooded area. She wasn't pleased to see him, though. They argued, though they kept their voices so low, I couldn't hear what they said. He gave her a small pouch, which she didn't want to take. When she left, she passed very close to me and I could see that she was crying."

"That doesn't sound like a lover's tryst."

"Not like any I've experienced." He gave a thin smile.

Magnus didn't question the statement. "We need to see what she brought back. Perhaps that will provide a clue. We can't alert anyone else." He considered their options. "I'll ask Silvi to call her into our chamber to help her with something. In the meantime, Birgitta can go through her things and look for the pouch. Depending on what's in there, if we confront her with it, she'll have to tell us the truth."

"I have methods, but they're nothing I would use on a young woman. However, if it's for Silvi's welfare, I might make an exception." He inclined his head to Magnus. "With your permission."

"Let's take one oar stroke at a time. I'll ask Silvi to call her to help her. Then we'll see what Birgitta finds. If we all confront her, I don't know of any young woman who wouldn't give in to a group of warriors standing before her."

"It depends on what she has on the line."

"Then we'll just have to find out, won't we? And offer her something far more valuable."

Magnus and Nuallen waited in the common room, a pitcher of ale between them. Silvi barely acknowledged him when he went to speak to her, but she did send for Thyri. No matter how upset his wife was, she had to realize the importance of all this.

He watched the door to the cooking rooms, where many of the serving women slept for the warmth. In spite of how positive he'd tried to sound to the others, his own uncertainty ate at him. Unless he could prove otherwise, Silvi was in grave danger. All because of him. No. He set down his cup. Because of Toke.

When Birgitta came out, his heart pounded. She walked toward him with a platter of sausages balanced on one hand, and set it before him. "Mardoll is watching. The pouch is under the plate."

He nodded to her and stabbed a sausage with his knife. Nuallen did the same, holding the plate as though to steady it. The pouch came away in his hand and he dropped it in his lap. After Mardoll left, he gave it to Magnus. When they finished eating, Magnus and Nuallen went into his meeting room. Leif joined them and shut the door.

"We have to be fast, lest Thyri returns to her bed before we speak to her and finds it missing. She may flee." Magnus opened the pouch. White granules filled it. "What do you make of it?" He passed it to Nuallen.

He smelled them but didn't touch them. "No odor. It looks like a mineral of some kind. There are so many poisons from other lands we can get in the markets, it's hard to say. I would wager that if we ask her to take some of it, she'll tell us everything."

Magnus took back the pouch. "Remind me never to get on your bad side."

Nuallen's face was grim. "That would be Rorik. He's the one who attacked my holding in the first place, leading to my enslavement. My war will be with him one day."

"I wish you luck with that." Leif shook his head. "Some of that family's insanity may have rubbed off on you."

Magnus hid the pouch in his hand and walked to the door. "Let's go speak to Thyri."

When they entered the bedchamber, the servant was brushing out Silvi's hair. Magnus's body tightened at the sight. It flowed down her back like spun silver, gleaming in the morning light. She was his. No coward, no man, no assembly would ever take her from him.

Nuallen remained by the door, and Magnus walked up to Thyri. There was no point in dragging this out. He showed her the pouch. "What's in this, Thyri? Nuallen followed you last night and saw you receive this from a young man in the woods."

Thyri turned pale and dropped the comb. Glancing at the door, she backed away, but Nuallen crossed his arms and met her panicked gaze. Leif stood at Magnus's back.

"It's—it's from Oleg. I've known him since we were younger, and he's sweet on me. He said it will make me want him, but I wasn't going to take any of it. I was going to get rid of it."

"If he's sweet on you, then he wouldn't give you anything that would harm you, would he?" Magnus looked at Silvi. She was even more pale than usual and sat unmoving, her hands kneading her skirt. He tried to catch her eye, to comfort her, but she wouldn't acknowledge him. He crossed to a pitcher of water and poured some into a cup. "Thyri, why don't you try taking some of it and we'll see if it works? I'm certain any of the men here would like to give some to their women and make them more willing." He held out the pouch and the cup. Nuallen stepped up beside him.

She looked back and forth at all of them, then crumbled to the ground, hiding her face in her skirts. As she sobbed, Leif shrugged. "You were right, Brother. We must be more intimidating than I thought."

Magnus reached down and dragged her up to stand before them. "I want the truth, Thyri. What is this and what were you supposed to do with it? I want you to tell us everything. Now."

"I can't." She sobbed. "If Mardoll even knows you're all in here with me, she'll kill me and Toke will kill my brother and father. She watches me all the time and might come in here. If she sees all of you . . ."

They looked at each other. Magnus gave her to Leif to hold, and he knelt before Silvi. He touched her cheek, but she drew back. "Silvi, I need your help. Do you understand?"

"I'm angry with you. Not stupid."

He hid a smile. "Angry is all right, as long as you do something for me. For all of us."

"What."

"We need Mardoll to leave the longhouse for a time. Can you ask her to go, in a way that won't arouse her suspicions?"

She didn't answer at first. Then she sighed. "I could ask her to go to Ingeborg and get some herbs that must be freshly ground. She'll have to wait for them."

"That would be fine. Will you do that?"

She nodded and left. He returned to Thyri, and Leif continued to hold her by the arms. She wept and pleaded, but they ignored her until Silvi came back in. "Mardoll's gone to the healer's house. She doesn't suspect anything."

"Thank you. Now, Thyri, Mardoll isn't coming in here. What's in that pouch?"

Her face collapsed and tears ran down her cheeks. "I don't know its name, but Toke got it in the Far East. It comes from a rock and they use it to kill people. He wanted me to put it in the bucket that people use to draw water from the well. It would make them sick, like they had eaten something rotten. But it might also kill them."

"Why is he doing this? What does he hope to gain?"

"He wants revenge on you for his son. Also for being more prosperous than he is. He wants Thorsfjell for himself. That's why he had the outcasts attack you last winter. He sent me here to spy on you and then to do things that look like the dark arts. He wanted the blame to fall on the mistress, so you would lose her."

Leif shook her. "We took you in, gave you shelter, a home. This is what you do to thank us?"

"I had no choice." Her legs gave out and Leif set her in a chair, then stood back with Magnus and Nuallen.

Magnus slipped the bag inside his belt pouch. "What did you mean when you said Toke would kill your father and brother?"

"That's why I had to do as he said. He's hiding my brother, Rollo. He's only fifteen.

"If my father and I don't do as he says, Mardoll will kill me and Toke will kill my brother. He's forced my father to lead his outcasts or he'll slay all of us. My father never meant any harm. He's a good man. When Toke slew the old jarl and took over Bygvik, he found out my father had been a raider once and had his own ship. Toke took the ship, and then my brother, and used him against all of us. Mardoll is a relation of Toke's and will do as he says for her own gain. He gives her things and supports her. He sent her here to be certain I do what he wants.

"I'm so sorry. I had no choice." Her expression hardened as she looked up at them. "But now, if I can tell you anything to help you, I will. I want revenge on Toke for what he's done to us."

"Tell us of your father." Magnus sank down on the bed.

"He's a skilled fighter. He didn't want to attack you. I've heard it said that whoever led Toke's forces must have been very foolish and inept. He's not. I'm certain he meant to lose those battles, deliberately misdirecting the men. He knew you'd defeat them, but he still could tell Toke that he tried. It would, at least, keep him from killing my brother."

"What of my wife? Do you know how he intends to accuse her of the dark arts?"

"Oleg is very proud that Toke trusts him. He brags of things. He told me Toke plans to say the mistress's dark ways caused the sheep to die. Mardoll forced me to give them the yew. She was watching me. But I made certain some of the leaves stayed in their mouths so you could see what it was and try to help them. He's going to use Droplaug's stillborn son, saying Silvi caused it, that the child died as it came from the womb because she touched it."

"And he wanted you to use this poison and say the sickness and deaths are Silvi's fault."

She nodded, and sobbed again. "I wasn't going to do it. I was going to tell Mardoll that I tried it and it didn't work. Toke is also going to say the mistress brought down snows on his side of the mountain, to kill people. Mardoll saw her sitting on the stillborn child's grave, and everyone knows that's how sorcerers make the ground shake and the rivers flood."

"He's using our misfortunes to his own advantage," Leif said. "As well as lying outright."

"I know." Magnus couldn't trust Thyri, but he might still need her. He regarded the other men. "If we can get the boy back here to safety, it would take away some of Toke's leverage. Thyri, do you know where your brother is?"

"No, Jarl. But Oleg has a sack of food with him when he meets with me. He might be taking it to Rollo."

"All right. You have to understand that we can't quite trust you any longer. You'll be watched very closely from now on. If you do as we say, we'll be able to rescue your brother and father. But you have to be true to us."

"I understand, Jarl Magnus." She left the chair and fell to her knees in front of him. "I don't care what happens to me. You can sell me into slavery for what I have done to you. But please rescue my brother. He's blameless in all this."

"No one is being sold here." He pulled her to her feet. "We've never dealt in slaves. My rescuing your family gives me more leverage against Toke. It's a means to an end. Understand this, Thyri: Nothing is more important than my wife's safety. Nothing. Not me, not my brother, not even Thorsfjell. If you betray me, you'll wish I had sold you off."

Now he had the information he needed. The missing pieces were on the game board and all he had to do was move them into place. Toke would be on the run; but, like the pursued king's piece in *tafl*, once he reached the end of the board, he would have no place left to go.

He shoved her away and nodded at Leif and Nuallen. "Tonight, we plan."

Chapter Sixteen

Silvi hid a tiny smile behind her cup. She hadn't felt anything other than pain in the week since the envoy had come. Since the unthinkable had happened. The smile felt foreign.

Sitting at a table in the common room, she sipped her milk. It was all she'd been able to stomach these last seven days. She'd used so much myrrh for the pain in her belly, her mother had stopped her from taking any more of it. The darkness she'd been living under since finding out about the charges against her had begun to lift only in the past two days.

Magnus paced the room, striding out the front doors and back in again. He wasn't accustomed to waiting. He'd always charged into the fray, leading his men in their battles. Not this night.

All their plans were coming to fruition. Even though they involved only the warriors, Magnus had insisted she sit in on all their sessions. It had helped. Seeing what they were doing for her sake, how they were fighting for her reputation and her life, had given her heart and hope. Magnus hadn't worked at all on his own defense, only hers. It made her uneasy, but every time she'd mentioned it to him, he'd told her not to worry about it.

She hadn't sought her visions, or the runes. Let her mother do that. It was all dead to her. She'd always thought them a gift, but now they were a curse.

"What's taking so long?" Magnus sliced his hand through his hair. "They should all have been back here by now."

"They had to travel a good distance." Lifa sat at another table with her runes spread out before her. "All the signs are good ones. The gods smile on us."

"If they did, we wouldn't be in this position to begin with." Silvi shot her mother a glare. Although she'd started to come to terms with what had happened, resentment still simmered in her. If it weren't for Magnus, her mother, and Eirik, the gods would indeed be pleased with her. But they weren't, and this was the result. Now Leif was stealing ships from Toke, and Nuallen was out chasing some boy across the mountains to find Thyri's brother. All of them were in danger.

"The gods don't change what people do, Silvi." Lifa turned one of the runes over and studied it. "They do help us overcome the misfortunes we have."

She didn't reply. Thyri had met with Oleg a few days ago, and then again, this night. He let her know when he wanted her to come to him next, so Magnus and his group had been ready. Toke had left for the *Thing*, so they'd had to move fast. Right after Thyri had told them of Toke's plans, Magnus had ordered Mardoll locked away so she couldn't do any more damage, or harm Thyri. Leif and Kaia took the small *faering* to Toke's fjord to kill whoever was guarding their vessels, and steal them. Then, no one could go after Toke and warn him about what was happening there.

Nuallen went with Thyri to follow Oleg. They could only hope he led him to Rollo. If he didn't, when Toke's men found the ships missing, they would kill him.

Magnus stayed behind to coordinate their plans so the timing would be right. His inactivity was wearing on him. Thyri was curled up in a little ball on a side bench, tearstains on her cheeks, lost in her misery. She'd returned a short time ago saying that Nuallen had sent her back and then followed Oleg. They'd heard nothing since.

Voices drifted to them from outside. Silvi jumped up as Leif and Kaia came in. He was grinning, and even the stoic shieldmaiden looked pleased.

"Toke's ships are gone from their beach." Leif took the cup of ale Birgitta brought him.

"And so are the five outcasts guarding them." Kaia smiled and Silvi stared at her. She was quite beautiful when she wasn't contemplating killing someone. Then again, her joy may have been because she *had* just killed someone. "We hid the ships in a small cove to the west of the entrance to your fjord. We felt it would be better than bringing them here. Stealing ships is not honorable."

Leif shrugged. "We're only claiming them a little early, is all. When the assembly finds in favor of Magnus, he'll challenge Toke, and kill him. Then, by law, he'll gain all of Toke's property. The ships will belong to Magnus anyhow." He drank down the rest of his ale.

Birgitta brought out a platter of meats, cheese, and dried fruit. Behind her, Nuallen strode in.

"I didn't want to come in the front door in case there was a problem." He nodded to someone in the cooking room. A young man stepped out. He had long, wavy brown hair and gray eyes, like—

"Thyri." He held out his arms and she leaped off her bench and ran to him. They embraced hard, their faces buried in each other's hair.

"Rollo. I thought I'd never see you again." Her voice was thick.

He held her away from him and ran his thumbs over her tears, drying them. "I know. I wasn't certain I'd survive either. They said if I tried to escape, they'd kill you. I didn't know what to do. There were four of them guarding me all the time. I couldn't get away, and even if I had been able to, I couldn't risk them hurting you." After giving Thyri a kiss on the forehead, he walked to Magnus.

"Jarl Magnus? On our way back here, Nuallen told me all that has happened. If you need another sword, I'll pledge myself to you. Now and always." He looked embarrassed. "But I'd need a sword first. Mine was taken."

They all laughed. Even Silvi smiled. He was a tall, strong young man, not yet grown into his maturity, but the promise of it was there in the set of his shoulders and the pride of his bearing.

"First you need to recover, Rollo." Magnus indicated the food. "Take what you want. You must not have been fed much."

"No." He took a plate and piled on the meats and cheese.

"And Nuallen, I suppose Toke has four fewer men."

Saying nothing, the Northumbrian inclined his head.

"What of the boy you followed?"

"I don't kill unarmed youths, barely into their first beards. I waited until he left."

Magnus regarded them all. "Tomorrow, we leave for the *Thing*. We'll keep Rollo and Thyri hidden until the right time. Toke will want to keep their father close to him, so he should be there. We'll find him and let him know we have them and he needn't fear for them. Toke will have no more leverage against us, and the truth will be told. Like tonight, we must hold back our strike until the right time. Then we attack with every weapon we have."

They raised their cups with a shout. Thyri held on to Rollo, smiling through her tears. After they'd drained their ale, Magnus came to Silvi.

All through the past seven nights, he'd done nothing more than hold her. At first, her resentment kept her turned away from him. She couldn't look at him or touch him without anger building in her because he had destroyed her dreams, and perhaps her life. Still, he'd gathered her to him, keeping watch over her while she'd slept. In the daytime, he'd planned and strategized to save her. Following his lead, all the villagers had come to her, supporting her, lending whatever help they could. Love surrounded her from all of them. She'd seen she wasn't so alone any longer.

Last night, in bed, she'd needed to hear his heartbeat, so she'd rested her head on his chest, her arm over him. He'd stroked her hair and it had reminded her of better times with him. Sensual times. She'd finally slept through the night for the first time since this nightmare had begun.

Now, he gazed down at her, his eyes filled with hope, and held out his hand to her. She placed her palm in his.

Near the mouth of the Sognefjorden,
western Norway

The *Thing* at the south side of the Sognfjorden represented the territories of Sogn, Rogaland, Hordaland, and all the fjords from Stad in the north to Egersund in the south. So Silvi was not surprised to see Eirik's magnificent ship beached there. Her heart filled with relief to know he'd be with her.

A storm had followed them down the fjord, as though the gods were urging them along. Whether that was a good omen or not, Lifa wouldn't say. She'd only contemplated the clouds with a thoughtful expression. With the wind at their backs, Magnus pulled their ships onto the shore beside Eirik's huge vessel. Magnus had brought only the *Sea Eagle* and the *Fire Serpent*, though Kaia had followed with both of the ships and crew Rorik had lent them. A show of force and splendor never hurt. For Magnus to bring four warships and the warriors to crew them would send a message to everyone there, especially Toke.

204 • *Sabrina Jarema*

"How are we going to find Eirik in all this?" Magnus shielded his eyes with his hand as he peered out over the land.

As far as Silvi could see, tents and booths had sprung up everywhere and crowds of people milled about. People were negotiating marriages, making treaties, conducting business, and settling feuds. Everyone wanted to make a good showing. They built booths for their groups and wares, each one more splendid than the last.

"I'll find my brother." Silvi hadn't reached for her abilities in some time, but this was as natural to her as calling out to him. She closed her eyes. Eirik and she had connected over the distance since they were children, and it gave her a feeling of home, safe and welcome. Her visions, however, she avoided. She didn't want to know what they would tell her. Unlike this, visions came from the gods, and she wanted nothing to do with that now. Perhaps never again.

Warmth touched her mind and she smiled in relief. "He knows we're here and he'll come."

Magnus said nothing about it. He directed the men as they unloaded the ships. She'd brought all her finest clothing and jewelry, including the necklace Magnus had given her after their wedding day. She was a jarl's wife and had to appear and conduct herself like one. She was also Lifa's daughter, though few knew that yet. She would go before the assembly with her head high, even if her spirit was huddled in a darkened corner, bloody and weeping.

She watched the crowds and saw her brother striding toward them. She ran to him and he caught her up, enfolding her in his arms. His scent, so much like home, enveloped her. Drawing back from him, she watched Magnus as he approached them. Eirik and he grasped each other's forearms.

Eirik's face was grim. "I've heard rumors since I've been here."

"Yes. We need to talk."

Nuallen lifted Lifa off the ship and set her on the shore. She was dressed in her full regalia, and as she walked to Eirik, the people who had gathered to see the vessels drew back to allow her to pass. A breeze whipped her fur cloak aside, showing the gems covering her blue gown.

"Mother." Eirik inclined his head to her. In the presence of so many, it would not be wise to show too much familiarity. "How are you?"

"Angry. Very angry." A stronger gust hit them all. She raised her voice and pointed east. "And the gods have followed us here."

The crowd gasped and retreated. Silvi hid a smile. Of course her mother couldn't control the weather, but she knew how to make a good show of it. Then again, one could never be quite certain where Lifa was concerned. Still, a rune mistress of her stature had disembarked from Magnus's ships, and word would soon spread throughout the *Thing.*

"Come with me," Eirik said. "Asa's waiting at our camp and we've saved a place for all of you."

Even though they'd left Thorsfjell before light that morning, with the clouds overhead it was nearly dark by the time they'd sailed all the way down the fjord. With everyone working together, they set up their camp and tents before night fell.

Silvi stared into the fire as Magnus sat down beside her and put his arm around her. Eirik, Asa, Nuallen, Lifa, and Leif joined them. Their men patrolled the perimeter so no one could come close enough to listen to them.

She blinked away tears as Magnus told Eirik and Asa what had happened since they'd returned to Haardvik. Hearing it all again brought back the pain in her stomach. She trembled, her muscles taut to the point of discomfort. Magnus stroked her back as he spoke and she leaned into him. While it was true that if he hadn't married her, her life wouldn't be threatened, it was Toke who had done this. Not Magnus. She saw this now. He was her one chance. At life, and at love.

"I've considered our options." They all turned their attention to Nuallen. "I swore to protect and guard Lifa, and through her, Silvi. I don't hold to your legal system. If Silvi is found guilty, then Magnus, I ask that I may use one of your ships and take her from here to my homeland. I have allies there who would harbor her and keep her safe. No one could touch her there."

"A Norse woman would be welcome there?" Leif shook his head. "We're not exactly well liked in your land."

"I have a great deal of power and influence there. It will be so, if I wish it."

Magnus tensed next to her and held up his hand. "Three things. First, she will not be found guilty. Second, we know nothing about you. To us, you are but a freed slave with unusual talents. You have no reason to love us."

"At least not most of us." Leif glanced at Lifa. She blushed.

Nuallen's expression didn't change. "My hatred is aimed toward

Rorik. I have told you that. He's the one who attacked my lands and wounded me. If I harbored any hatred toward you, I think you've seen I could have wreaked my revenge all too easily, many times over. I have not. Lifa saved me, and so did you, Eirik, after a fashion. When Rorik would have thrown me overboard because I was dying and wasting provisions, you stepped in and stopped him."

"It wasn't so altruistic. I saw you as a strong man who might make a good slave. And then the sun turned black when we were at sea. The gods stopped us."

"How do you know it wasn't my God who did so? Besides, you've told me that in the Far East, they've learned it's only the moon passing in front of the sun. To answer your other concern about me, in Northumbria I have the title of earl, equivalent to your own jarls. I have vast holdings and lands, and many men fought for me. I have two sons and a daughter, all of your own ages. My wife died many years ago giving birth to my daughter."

They all stared at him. Silvi met his green gaze. "Then why haven't you returned there? Eirik offered to send you back."

"I hope my children have taken my place, since I must be thought dead and they would inherit. But we have many greedy and envious neighbors, and I fear they may cause trouble eventually. I'll have to return sometime to see to my affairs. It might well be, though, that I'll choose to live among you after all is settled at home."

Of course. Silvi smiled to herself. Her mother could never live in Northumbria. They were Christian there and she would be accounted evil, according to their beliefs. She would never give up their gods or try to be anything other than what she was. If Nuallen wanted to be with her, he would have to remain here. By the same token, she, herself, might be reviled if he took her there. Did she have no place to belong in this world?

"I'll be able to retrieve some of my wealth, which I hid from Rorik. With it, I can establish myself among you. I would no longer be beholden to you. I have many allies, men I've fought beside, and for. They'll give Silvi shelter, should she need it. I have but to ask."

He took a drink of ale. "Now, you said there were three considerations why I couldn't take her to safety. I hope it's not a reason so foolish as jealousy. Or, God forbid, honor. That has killed far too many people in all lands."

"We have no morals such as you Christians believe in," Magnus said. "We know neither good nor evil, nor do our gods. But we do have honor and word-fame. Both live on after us, and it's all we leave behind for men to remember us by. As jarl, I'm responsible for taking care of my people. As a husband, it's my duty to protect and care for my wife. I am also accountable for everything she does, according to our laws. And that is why, if the gods withdraw from us and she's found guilty, I will take on her punishment in her place. I will be drowned so she might live."

Pain knifed through Silvi. In shock, she wrenched away from him with a cry that tore from her heart. She rose on shaking legs as the others all spoke at once. She didn't listen to them.

"You won't do that, Magnus. I won't allow it. You've done nothing wrong." Tears choked her and she could say nothing more.

He stood and took her in his arms. "You haven't done anything wrong either, Silvi. It makes just as much sense for me to die as it does for you."

She tried to push away from him, but he was too strong. "It's because of how I am. I'll walk into the bog myself, Magnus, rather than let you do this. How can you think I'd be able to live without you, knowing you died because of me?"

"I would have died because of Toke's lies. Not you. If I went into battle and was killed defending Thorsfjell, and thus you, would it be any different?"

"You know it would be."

Leif cleared his throat. "Since I don't want to be jarl, I think we'd better win. When we plan a battle, we plan for success, not defeat. We believe we're already victorious. The time has simply not yet come to claim it."

"So that's why all of you are mad on the battlefield." Nuallen took another drink. "No one here will die. Leif's right. We need to plan. Now."

Magnus let go of her, but only to urge her to sit beside him again. Asa moved among them, pouring more ale.

No matter what their laws said, he didn't have to sacrifice himself for her sake. Unless he loved her. She covered her mouth and bowed her head as she tried not to sob again. Surely the gods wouldn't be so capricious. She'd always done what they wanted, always loved and served them. Except recently. And they'd let her know their displeasure.

She had to find a way to appease them, cajole them. Staring into the fire, she nodded. Of course. A sacrifice. When one desired something from the gods, one gave a sacrifice. She'd never been able to offer up animals to them. What else could she give? There was gold, treasure, many other things one could use. What would be worth as much as their lives?

She caught her breath. Herself. What greater offering could she give? She'd promise to give herself to the temple and serve the gods the rest of her days in exchange for Magnus's safety and her own life. She'd have to divorce him, though. And it would break her heart.

How ironic. That which she had once planned because she so desired it, would become a sacrifice of last resort. If it saved Magnus, it was worth it.

Let nothing happen to Magnus. For if we are victorious, I will give him up and serve you, as you always wanted. Just let him live.

A calm settled over her, as though the gods heard her and approved. It was done. Closing her eyes, she leaned into him, to feel his warmth, his strength. Soon, she would never feel them again.

Magnus drew her closer. "We have only tomorrow, for the trials will take place the next day. Thyri needs to go through the area near Toke's camp and try to find her father. She'll have to wear a hooded cloak so no one will recognize her. She'll point him out to me, and Kjeld will speak to him, for no one here knows Kjeld. He'll let her father know that she and Rollo are safe. If we can get him to testify as to what Toke has been doing, it should go a long way toward discrediting him. Rollo can also testify. Thyri, unfortunately, can't since she's a woman, but I think with all the other witnesses we have, and Thyri's father, it should be enough."

What other witnesses? He'd brought the men who had been with him in the sea battle. They had come to testify as to what had happened when Toke attacked them in the islands off the coast. But what others?

For the first time in over a week, the pain in her stomach subsided, another sign from the gods they were pleased with her decision. She relaxed, drinking in the calm certainty that filled her. Sometimes the gods brought one back around to the path one had originally followed. Her life would be no different, after all, from what she had always dreamt.

Except now, she dreamed of Magnus.

* * *

Silvi walked through the collection of booths with Nuallen. Lifa was with several other rune mistresses, and no one would dare threaten them, so he'd felt it was safe to leave her. Kjeld, Eirik's most trusted warrior, walked ahead of them. He'd been raiding with Eirik for many years, but had been away from Haardvik when Hakon had taken over. Thyri, wearing a hooded cloak, led the way through the crowd.

Neither Magnus nor Leif could make contact with Thyri's father, Ketill. He was probably being watched. However, no one from Toke's village knew Kjeld. He'd come to Thorsfjell with Eirik and Asa, but he'd stayed down on the beach with the ships. Even Mardoll hadn't seen him. And what could she have said about him if she had? That he was tall, had long blond hair and blue eyes and was quite handsome? That would describe so many of their men. He was the best choice to speak with Thyri's father.

They followed Thyri as she wandered from booth to booth. People sold all manner of goods—herbs, carvings, fine weapons, household items, weavings, cloth, and many things from far away. Poets told their kennings and the audiences tried to figure out what their flowery phrases meant. Harpists played music, and skalds told tales. There was much food, more drink, and brawls erupted everywhere.

It was her first *Thing*. If only she could enjoy it all. But the dread of the trials the next day kept her on edge. Even if they were victorious, first she had to stand before all the free men, undergoing their scrutiny. It would be a disgrace, a nightmare she might never forget.

Thyri slowed until Kjeld caught up with her. They spoke, then she moved off, browsing the tables of wares. Silvi and Nuallen did the same. Kjeld approached an older man with Thyri's wavy brown hair. He had dark circles under his eyes and stood bowed over, as though he had a great weight on him. He was looking at leather work, and Kjeld stopped beside him and picked up a belt. They spoke together, as though discussing the piece. Thyri's father stilled, but gave no other indication of what Kjeld had said. He nodded, then shifted as though to look at something else on the table.

Thyri lifted her head just enough for the light to shine inside the hood. Her father looked away, but not before Silvi saw the brief flash of joy on his face. Kjeld paid for the belt. He left, walking back toward them, but as he passed, he nodded.

"Good," Nuallen said. "He'll help us."

Silvi frowned. "Just because Kjeld nodded to us, doesn't mean that for certain."

"Look at Thyri's father." He stepped in front of her so it wouldn't be so obvious, and she peeked around him.

Ketill was watching as his daughter returned to their camp. His eyes were bright, as though he tried not to weep. Then he walked off in the other direction. He had a spring in his step and a straightness to his back.

"Let's get back to the camp and see what he had to say."

When they returned, Thyri had disappeared inside one of the tents with her brother. Magnus was pouring ale for Kjeld, Leif, and himself, and when he saw Nuallen and her, he filled more cups.

"He'll testify." Magnus handed them their drinks.

Kjeld swallowed the ale. "I asked him if he wanted revenge against Toke, and explained that we have Rollo and Thyri and they are safe. It wasn't until he saw her that he agreed. He's very wary, which is understandable. In fact, he wondered if we were holding them to force him to testify, however I said that wasn't our way, but Toke's. His concern was the safety of his children, and he said he would testify only if we gave them sanctuary. I told him that was a given, so he agreed. He already knew about the charges against you. I don't know, though, what he plans to say. There wasn't time to find out."

Magnus poured him more ale. "All we need is for him to testify that Toke made unprovoked attacks on us, harbored outcasts, and forced Thyri to poison the sheep and try to contaminate the water to make it look like sorcery. The first two are enough to make him outcast, and the other things should help exonerate Silvi. It shows he had this planned."

"But what of the stillborn child?" Silvi swirled her ale in the cup. Milk would have been better, but it was in short supply there. And ale, at least, was more of a food than beer, so she'd get some nourishment from it. She still couldn't eat.

"Knud is coming in one of the *knörrs* today to testify to his wife's problems in childbirth, and to explain that this all began years ago. Ingeborg told him months ago that the child likely would be born dead like the others. She can't testify, but he can."

Magnus set down his cup and went to Silvi. Enveloping her in his arms, he looked down at her. "It will be all right, Silvi. I promise.

We're innocent. The gods have given you to me for a reason, and I have a feeling they're standing with us."

She pressed her cheek to his chest. "So do I, Magnus." But not for the reason he thought. For what the gods gave, they also took away.

"I would be with you this night." Magnus put his arms around her from behind as soon as they walked into their tent.

She ducked her head and gave a dry smile. "In case this is our last?"

He kissed the back of her neck, then turned her around to face him. "You know better than that. Lifa said the gods followed us, and for the first time, I believe it. I want to affirm that you're mine, to show them I won't allow anything to come between us."

She leaned against him, drawing from his strength. "They have a habit of not listening to us at times. But this night, let there be no doubt." Even though she would go to Uppsala if they were victorious, the gods would know that, while she served them as promised, her heart would always be reserved for Magnus alone.

He smiled. With gentle hands, he took down her hair and combed it through his fingers. She shuddered at his touch, the hairs on her body lifting. The noise and laughter outside faded away until only they existed.

He slipped off her gown and shift, and she helped him with his clothing. They sank onto the pile of furs and he drew her under him. His face was grim as he looked down at her. Trying to smile at him, she studied every angle of his eyes, his mouth, his body. To remember him. For if they lost, she'd brought with her the strange powder Thyri had at Thorsfjell, and she'd take it. She could not allow him to waste his life for her. And if they were victorious, then she had to keep her word and go to Uppsala.

Either way, this might well be their last night. Her eyes filling, she clung to him and urged him into her. She needed him inside her, to feel his strength around her. But he held back.

"You need to be ready for me, Silvi."

"I am, Magnus. Please."

He kissed her, his body joining with hers. Grasping him with her legs, she tilted her hips to meet him, burying her face in his chest. His scent, the iron of his body, the warmth of his skin, all this she would have to take with her—wherever she was after this, with Freya at Folkvang or with the priestesses at Uppsala. Either way, the gods would take her from Magnus. From the only love she would ever know. Tears slipped from the corners of her eyes and he pulled back to look at her.

He touched her face. "Why?"

She shook her head. "There are no words for what I feel. Just make love to me."

"Always, Silvi. Always."

Chapter Seventeen

Silvi had dressed in her finest gown. It was blue, Odin's color, and she wore the necklace of stones and crystals Magnus had given her after their wedding. More crystals and amber beads hung from her broaches, and Thyri had done her hair in dozens of intricate, coiled braids. She'd hidden the tiny bag of poison-stone powder in her belt pouch. If she were found guilty, she'd swallow it before anyone could stop her. She didn't know how much would be lethal, but if she took all of it, it would solve that problem.

The area where the assembly conducted business was roped off, but all the free men who voted stood around the outside. A storm threatened overhead, but it had held off for the past days as though even the gods would not interfere. All morning the assembly had heard complaints, feuds, and accusations, and had rendered their verdicts in the traditional way, by brandishing their weapons to indicate assent.

Lifa stood with a group of other rune mistresses and masters. They all bore their staffs and regalia, watching the proceedings with dispassion. Silvi and Magnus remained with Eirik, Asa, Leif, and Nuallen. Late in the night, the free men of Thorsfjell had arrived in Magnus's remaining *knörr,* among them Knud and Droplaug. Testimony of craftsmen, farmers, and huntsmen wouldn't have the same weight as that of higher ranking men, but they would be heard and could still vote. That vote was equal to any, even a king's. They all stood behind Magnus's group, along with his warriors.

The Law-Sayer, Yrian, stepped into the center of the area. He was, perhaps, in his thirties, tall and red-haired. "We will hear the accusations of Toke Gudrodson against Jarl Magnus Sigrundson."

Magnus kissed her, long and deep, then walked to the Law-Giver.

Her head swam with her husband's kiss and his power. He was splendid, dressed in a brown tunic, light-colored shirt, and black trousers. His heavy gold torc lay around his neck and he wore matching twisted-wire wrist cuffs. Silvi's heart swelled with pride, for he looked every inch a jarl. He raised his head with disdain as Toke approached. An older man, Toke had a grizzled beard, unwashed hair, and his clothing was worn. As he stopped before the Law-Sayer, he glared at Magnus with hatred.

"Ketill is the only one who stands with Toke, except for a few of his poor villagers." Eirik pointed with his chin.

"Of course," Leif said. "All his allies are outcasts. They certainly can't come here."

Yrian tapped his staff against the ground and all quieted. "Three things are at issue in this matter. First we will hear the accusation Toke Gudrodson makes that Jarl Sigrundson killed his son, who was heir to his property. Gudrodson, give to us your testimony."

"In the spring, I was returning from a trading journey at the time of the Ostaramoon, in my two *knörrs*. I was just within the islands at the mouth of the Sognefjorden when Jarl Sigrundson attacked me with his two boats. He killed my only son. He did so with his shield, striking him. The dark powers of his wife, no doubt, had entered into the shield, and my son was struck dead instantly."

"What say you to this, Jarl?"

"It is true that I killed his son, but it was in a battle Gudrodson initiated. We were returning from my sister's wedding to Jarl Eirik Ivarson in Hordaland. We had been following Rorik of Vargfjell up the coast, under his protection, for he is now family to me through marriage."

"Good to make that point," Eirik said, as men around the circle murmured. "It shows the power he has behind him."

"Toke waited until Rorik's ships were well away from us to attack from behind the islands. We moved until our backs were to the sun and Gudrodson would be blinded by it. If we wanted to destroy Toke's ships, would we not have used Rorik's fleet to do so instead of engaging Toke in our *knörrs*?"

Again, all the men surrounding them spoke among themselves, nodding.

Magnus waited for the discussion to subside. He stood calm and patient while Toke fidgeted. "The battle was nearly done, with our victory assured, when my brother, Leif, called out from my other ship. We've fought so often together in the past, I knew what he was warning me about. I ducked and brought up my shield, using the wind to catch it and strengthen my blocking move. It hit the boy before I even looked at him. He went over the side. I realized how young he was and tried to reach in to save him."

Yrian held up his hand. "You would save the son of your enemy?"

"I did not know who he was. Only that he was not even in his first beard yet. He wore mail, which dragged him under."

"You lie." Toke clenched his fists. "I saw you lean over the side and hold him under so he would drown."

Yrian frowned. "Which story is it, Gudrodson?"

Toke froze. "I don't understand what you mean, Law-Sayer."

"First, you told us that your son died when Jarl Sigrundson's shield touched him because of a dark spell his wife placed on it. Now you say he held him under the waters so that he drowned. It cannot be both."

As Toke stammered, Magnus spoke. "I was not yet married to my wife and had only just met her before the wedding. She barely knew me at all, and in fact, did not think much of me." The men in the crowd laughed. "I need no spells to give me victory, or to kill an opponent. The gods smile on the brave, not cowards."

"I have the right to challenge you for that." Toke's face turned red.

"Yes, but you won't. Instead you use others to do your fighting for you. Your son was on my ship, fighting, but you were still on your own vessel, moving away from the fray. You were foolish enough to allow him to wear mail for a sea battle. That is what killed him. Ran pulled him under. When she desires a man, no one can gainsay her."

Magnus crossed his arms. "Gudrodson says he was returning from a trading journey, but that would have still been too early in the year. He was lying in wait for any ship to come into the fjord, as is his habit. He hid until Rorik's fleet passed, then struck. He, alone, is to blame for his son's death. At least the boy will enter Valhalla, unlike his sire."

Toke cursed, spraying spittle, but Yrian stepped between them. "Gudrodson, do you bring with you any witnesses?"

He stepped back. "No, Law-Sayer. All the men who were with me are out trading."

"All the men who were with him are outcasts." Magnus chuckled. "They cannot come here, of course, or their lives are forfeit."

Yrian nodded. "And do you bring with you any witnesses, Jarl Sigrundson?"

"Yes. I bring my brother, and all the men who were with me in my two ships."

"Let them come forward."

They came into the area and stood behind Magnus. Their hair was washed and combed and they were all dressed in their finest clothing and jewelry, as the law demanded, making an impressive showing. One by one, they gave the same testimony while the winds from the coming storm rose.

Then Leif stepped forward and Yrian looked from him to Magnus. "I did not know you had a twin."

"I am Leif Sigrundson. I need not repeat what the others have told you except to say that I had to stop my brother from going into the waters after the boy. He searched so deep, his head was almost beneath the waves. I had to grab his belt and haul him back to make certain Ran did not see him and take him for herself. She had more than enough dead men to choose from that day. Toke's men. She did not need another.

"Our father taught us to use our surroundings to our advantage in battle. Positioning ourselves so that the sun shines in the eyes of our enemy, using the high ground to strengthen our charges, and using the wind behind our shields to augment our strikes—all these things we have learned. My brother only used what we were taught, and that is why we have always been victorious in battle. Few pirates on the seas will engage us. They are too wise, but it would appear Toke is not."

The crowd yelled their approval, banging their fists on their scabbards.

Yrian raised his hands. "We have heard the testimony of this matter. What say you all? Do we find that Toke Gudrodson's accusations have merit in this case?"

No one called out. Toke stared at Thyri's father and the other villagers. They hung back, looking down, but Ketill stood with his arms crossed, silent. Toke narrowed his eyes at him, but he only raised his head and met his glare.

"Or do you find that Jarl Sigrundson was within his rights when he killed Gudrodson's heir?"

The men in the crowd all raised their swords, axes, knives, and spears, brandishing them with a great shout. Silvi sagged against Eirik, weak with relief. They'd found for Magnus. Her heart could pump again.

He smiled at her. She acknowledged it as Asa embraced her. The men all filed out of the center of the circle, to join the crowd again, but Magnus remained behind.

Yrian called for silence. "Jarl Sigrundson, the assembly has found that you are held blameless in this matter and therefore you and your relatives do not owe him any *wergeld*. Do you wish to make any charges concerning his attack on you?"

"No, Law-Sayer. I have other charges pending against him that are far more onerous. It is true that I lost men. However, it was in battle. I have no doubt I will receive my due from him after this is concluded."

"Well spoken. Then we will continue." He addressed the assembly. "We will now hear the accusations of sorcery Toke Gudrodson makes against Silvi Ivarsdottir, the wife of Jarl Sigrundson. Let her come forward."

She tried to walk, but her legs wouldn't move. Everyone stared at her. She looked at her mother across the area and Lifa inclined her head to her with a slight smile. Then she raised it, her pride blazing from her as lightning flashed against the mountains in the distance. Silvi swallowed and took a deep breath. She was her mother's daughter. And her father's, who had been a great jarl and warrior. She'd made a promise to the gods and they had answered her. They would not have accepted her vow if she were going to die this day. Strength poured into her body as she straightened.

Magnus came to her and held out his hand, his eyes shining as he gave her an encouraging smile. She placed her hand in his and walked with him to the Law-Sayer. When she stopped, she turned to Toke. No man had ever been able to look into her eyes except Magnus and Eirik. Toke glanced at her, then backed away.

"She tries to curse me with her strange silver eyes."

"Silence." Yrian studied her, but she stood strong. "You will remain with your wife, Jarl Sigrundson?"

218 • Sabrina Jarema

His love? It felt as though the lightning in the distance shot through her. She stared at him, but he didn't look at her. Shaking, she observed all the men around her. They were silent, weighing everything that happened. She tried to calm herself, but her heart still pounded. She wanted to be sick.

Magnus had not let go of her hand and he pressed it. She gripped his fingers as the world wavered. For a moment, she was going under the waves. He was reaching down to her from the light and air. She shook the vision away and focused hard on her surroundings. Now was not the time for it.

"Toke Gudrodson has brought a charge that Silvi Ivarsdottir has practiced the dark arts, and in doing so has wrought havoc and death on her village and his."

What lies would he tell now? Some of his villagers were with him. Would they testify falsely for him? How could she counter that?

The crowd murmured around her. Her cheeks heated, but she pressed her lips together.

"Present your case, Gudrodson."

"Yes, Law-Sayer." Kneading his shirt, he spoke to the assembly. "Jarl Sigrundson has long been stealing away the women of my village for the use of his own men. Some of them have managed to return to me and they have told me that his new wife, this woman, is a sorceress and has brought great disaster to our valleys."

She looked up at Magnus, but he didn't react to this slander. He just watched Toke, his face calm, as though he listened to him discussing the weather.

"List the offenses she is said to have committed," Yrian said.

"The dark powers surrounding her have struck down livestock in the valleys. Many sheep have died for unknown reasons, both ours and theirs. This was no natural occurrence since there were no marks upon their bodies. My villagers will testify to this."

"In the right time," Yrian said. "Continue with the facts."

"A child died when she touched it as it was being born. Two other infants who were born at nearly the same time have lived and are thriving. She was seen the day after that, sitting on the grave of the dead child, mouthing a spell."

Silvi gasped, the pain of the child's death still fresh. She had tried so hard. How could he twist it like this?

"We all know that sorcerers move the earth by sitting on graves. The next day, an avalanche took the lives of a man and woman who lived in our valley. Also, many people in both villages have become ill from drinking the water in their wells, and it is feared that she has tainted them."

She fought back her tears. Unable to take any more, she tapped Magnus's arm and he leaned down so she could whisper to him. "Why aren't you saying anything? How can you let him lie like this?"

His lips just brushed her cheek before he spoke. "It's not the right time. I'm letting him dig his own grave deeper and deeper with every word he says. Then I'll push him into it."

That calmed her a bit, but she still had to stand and listen to his lies. Magnus caressed the palm of her hand with his thumb.

"Her powers have caused buildings to catch fire and strange creatures have been sighted in the mountains near our villages. All these things have happened since she came here and married the jarl."

Yrian tilted his head to one side in question. "Why would she do this? She married a wealthy jarl, and that is her home now. Why would she try to destroy it?"

"For revenge, Law-Sayer. It was well known in Thorsfjell that she did not want to marry the jarl. She was most unhappy about it, but her family forced her into it to align themselves with Jarl Sigrundson, a very successful merchant."

In the crowd, Leif gave a short laugh.

Toke's jaw tightened, but he continued. "To hear the woman I spoke to tell it, the jarl's wife wanted to go to Uppsala instead, to be a priestess with all the prestige and rank that entails. And yet, she was forced to become only a wife."

Yrian considered Magnus. "I see no great hardship for any woman to marry such a man. So then, Gudrodson, tell us which of the priestesses practices the dark arts at Uppsala—the *völur*? The *seith-kona*? The *blótgythiur* or the *hóvgythiur*?"

"I—I don't understand, Law-Sayer."

"It becomes apparent that you don't understand much, Gudrodson." Many of the men around them laughed. Yrian addressed Magnus. "It this true? Did she want to go to Uppsala rather than marry?"

220 • *Sabrina Jarema*

"Yes, Law-Sayer. Since she was very young."

She caught her breath. Why did Magnus say that? It gave credence to Toke's accusation and made it sound much worse.

"I see." Yrian pondered this. "It seems to me, if she is a sorceress, the last place she would want to go would be to the temple. She would be slain if they discovered she practices such destruction as you say. Who there would welcome her, Gudrodson? Who do you accuse of being immersed in the dark arts at the temple?"

"I—I know not of such things, Law-Sayer." He turned red again.

"I thought not. In any event, bring forward your witnesses to your words."

Toke turned to Ketill and the villagers of Bygvik, but they stood where they were. He motioned to them. "Come here, Ketill, and give your testimony about the poisonings, the illnesses and deaths, and the creatures you have seen."

Ketill crossed his arms. "We know nothing of these things, Law-Sayer."

Toke strode toward them. "What do you mean? That's why you're here. Speak, as we agreed. Or are you afraid to say anything lest the sorceress place a spell on you, as well?"

"We agreed to testify to your lies because you held my son and daughter under threat of death if we did not."

The crowd erupted and Toke shouted at Ketill. "I do not hold your son or daughter, you whoreson."

"He speaks the truth. For once." Magnus raised his voice so that all could hear him over the shouts. "I hold them now. For their safety." He nodded to the group from Thorsfjell.

Thyri and Rollo stepped from behind Magnus's warriors. Screaming, Toke rushed toward them. Several men from the crowd surged forward and stopped him, gripping him as he cursed.

"I believe you have no witnesses, then, Gudrodson. What do you answer, Jarl Sigrundson?"

"I answer that my wife is no sorceress, but a healer, a rune reader, and a woman whom the gods have blessed with beauty, intelligence, and their wisdom. If I may make my statements to counter his accusations?"

"Proceed."

"My thanks, Law-Sayer. Gudrodson sent two women, Thyri and

Mardoll, to my village under the pretense of their fleeing from him. Many women have done so to escape him. I have never captured women as Gudrodson has charged. Thyri is Ketill's daughter. Mardoll was to kill her if she did not do as Toke wanted. She was forced to give yew to our sheep, thus poisoning them. But she left leaves in their mouths so that we would find them, administer a cure, and save the ones we could. Thanks to my wife's knowledge of healing, most of them lived.

"As to the stillborn child, the mother, Droplaug, has lost other children in the same way over the past few years, long before we knew of Silvi or her family. Months ago, our healer woman told her this child was not well either and that she would likely lose it. The child had already ceased to move in the womb before my wife saw her."

"Do you have a witness to this?"

"Yes." Magnus nodded and Knud came forward with Droplaug.

"I am Knud Ulfrson. It is my son who was born dead." Droplaug hung her head as he spoke. "The gods have shown us that my wife can never bear a child. We know that now. This began years ago, shortly after we were wed. We have had three other stillborn children. It has been a source of grief for us. Now, for Gudrodson to use our misfortune for his own lies..." He glared at Toke. "May the gods strike you down. It was only the love and the words of Mistress Silvi that saved my wife from dying. Droplaug didn't want to live. She wished to die with the child still within her. The mistress came that night because our healers were helping other women bear their children. The child was already dead, but she spoke to my wife and convinced her to try. To live for me."

He gazed down at Droplaug. "Because of the mistress, I have my wife with me now. She saved her. We won't try again. We want to foster children who have lost their parents to illness and war. We have so much love to give a child and it seems the best way for us."

Droplaug looked at Silvi and smiled, tears streaming down her cheeks. "My thanks, mistress." In spite of her fears, Silvi returned the smile. For them to adopt children would be perfect.

"Very well, Ulfrson." Yrian inclined his head to them. "We have heard your testimony."

As they returned to the other villagers, Magnus spoke again. "*If the ground shakes on their side of the mountain, it must mean the gods are displeased with Gudrodson. All has been quiet on our side. Thyri was ordered to put this poison in the buckets of the village wells." He reached into his belt pouch and pulled out the tiny bag.

She stared at it. "How?" She narrowed her eyes at him. "When?"

"While I kissed you before I walked out here. Do you think I don't know you by now, my love?" He turned back to the assembly. "Thyri could not bring herself to do it. Her hesitation allowed us to discover the poison, and she told us of Gudrodson's plot. Only then did we understand why all this was happening. She told Oleg that she had used the poison on us and burned some of our buildings, but this was false. He must have passed the word to Toke. He does not even know it didn't happen, which proves his lies. We did it to buy time to rescue Rollo, who had been held captive.

"When I killed his son, Toke swore to destroy everything that meant anything to me. And what means the most to me is my wife. He targeted her, even though it's against all our traditions and laws to attack the women of our own land. He threatened the lives of Ketill and his family to manipulate them, and wreak vengeance on me. But they are safe now, and he is exposed."

"Do you have any other witnesses who wish to speak?"

"The men of Thorsfjell, Law-Sayer."

"Then let them come forward."

One by one they spoke, telling of how she had helped them, healed their wounds, read their runes, cured their ailing. They spoke of her gentle wisdom and giving nature, and of how she had been a good wife to Magnus, all that a jarl's wife should be.

Silvi's throat swelled as tears filled her eyes. She hadn't realized how much the people of Thorsfjell loved her and how much she had helped them. Magnus gazed down at her with pride, his eyes shining. When the last man had spoken, Yrian banged his staff on the ground.

"We have heard from all witnesses—"

"Except one other." Lifa moved out from the group of rune mistresses and masters. "I wish to speak. Will you hear my words?"

Toke, still held by the men, shook his head. "No woman can testify here. It is forbidden."

"You will be silent. I speak the laws here." Yrian bowed his head to her. "Lifa, you know it is not traditional."

She gave him a warm smile. "And, Yrian, you know I am not traditional, either."

He chuckled. "That is true."

"My rank puts me outside of the norms of society. The gods have chosen me to speak for them all my life. How is it that men will not hear?"

He considered, his head lowered, but he still kept her in his sight. "Very well, then. You may speak for the gods. I'm not certain the men will weigh your words in their deliberations, but that is their choice whether or not to do so."

"That is all I can ask." She stepped beside Silvi and Magnus, her head high. The rising wind whipped her hair as the storm grew closer. Another flash of lightning hit the mountains in the distance and she pointed at the sky. "The gods walk among us now and hear our words, see our thoughts. Know that I am the rune mistress Lifa of Haardvik." A wave of soft exclamations washed through the crowd. "Many of you have heard of me and that I was trained at the great temple at Uppsala by the *völva* Unn herself. My name goes before me in honor and I leave wisdom in my wake." She leveled her gaze on all of the assembly. In the distance, a roll of thunder echoed down the fjord. "I tell you now that Silvi is my daughter, and if the dark arts had taken her, I would slay her myself as we stand here."

She met Yrian's gaze and, without looking at Silvi, returned to the others. They surrounded her in solidarity. Knowing her mother, she had timed her statement for when the thunder would come after the last lightning strike.

"We have heard the accusations against Silvi Ivarsdottir and listened to the witness testimonies. I ask you now, how do you find? Is she innocent?"

A great shout went up and she flinched. As the lightning lingered overhead, weapons flashed when the men raised them in assent. Magnus lifted her up with a laugh and all the villagers and warriors of Thorsfjell ran into the circle, cheering.

She clung to him, unable to stop the tears. She sobbed against his chest as he drew her to him, weak with relief. The gods had kept their promise to her. Hands patted her and held her, and for the first time, she welcomed the touch of others. Their love flowed into her, comforting her, supporting her, and she turned to them all. One by one, they embraced her, and she them. Her throat was too full to speak, but she didn't need to.

"There is a third matter to be heard between Jarl Sigrundson and Toke Gudrodson."

As the people of Thorsfjell returned to their places, she wiped her eyes and stood again beside Magnus. Toke waited off to the side, sullen, hatred pouring off of him. Two men stayed by him, guarding him.

"Jarl Sigrundson, you have accused Toke Gudrodson of attacking your village without provocation on numerous occasions. And that he harbors outcasts, a serious offense. Please state your case against him."

As Magnus described the attacks over the winter and the battle on the mountain peak, she barely heard him. It was hard to believe the nightmare was over. She was afraid to move for fear she would wake and the day's outcome would be only a dream. But Magnus was warm and strong beside her, and so real. They were safe and alive. Soon, the gods would demand their payment. She'd have to tell Magnus that she was leaving him. She closed her eyes against the continuing pain in her stomach.

Called to testify, Ketill spoke of how Toke had forced him to lead the outcasts in the attacks against Thorsfjell, in fear for his children's lives. He related that Toke had come from the far north and killed their jarl, taken over their village, recruited outcasts from the surrounding areas, and mistreated the people.

"I once had my own ship, which Toke has now. We came here in it. But in my day, I led my own men and fought many a battle, so I have some knowledge of tactics. I made certain the outcasts lost each attack on Thorsfjell. I had to make it seem as though I followed Toke's orders, for the sake of my children, but I had nothing against Jarl Magnus. If he slew all the outcasts, so much the better. Their lives were forfeit anyhow for leaving their safe places, and there would be fewer of them to threaten our women and daughters. Toke told me the fight on the mountain peak was only to throw Magnus off course and make him think it was his one attempt to exact revenge for his son's death. Then he might not make the connection with everything else that was going wrong until it was too late. My daughter and I, we fought him as well as we could, Law-Sayer." He smiled at Thyri, and she returned it with tears.

"My thanks." Yrian turned to all the free men. "You have heard their words. What say you? Do you find for Jarl Sigrundson?"

The crowd shouted, their weapons raised against the dark sky as Toke yelled in rage. Yrian waited until the tumult died down.

"Toke Gudrodson, you have been found guilty of unprovoked attacks and of harboring outcasts. Your sentence is permanent outlawry, to wander the lands without shelter or support until you die."

The men grabbed him as he tried to lunge for Magnus.

"If he is set free to wander the lands, Law-Sayer, there's nothing to stop him from gathering more of his kind and wreaking more death and destruction on innocent people. It is my right, if I am not satisfied with the outcome of a trial, to seek redress in my own way." Magnus lifted his head, his eyes hard. "Therefore, I challenge you, Toke Gudrodson, to the *hólmgang*. In three days' time, we will meet with swords and shields, and fight until the blood of one of us flows beneath our feet."

Chapter Eighteen

Silvi said nothing to Magnus as they all returned to their camp. How could he make such a foolish challenge? They were exonerated. They would both live, and yet Magnus planned on risking himself in this duel with Toke.

The threatening storm had passed by and was dissipating. Already word was spreading among the people attending the *Thing* that the gods must have been pleased with the outcome and were showing their pleasure in the beautiful sunset that shone down the mouth of the fjord.

They had almost reached their camp when they heard Thyri and Rollo's names called out. Ketill ran to his son and daughter and they embraced with a glad cry. Thyri wept as Ketill held her and Rollo. The young man was already taller than his father.

Ketill came to Magnus. "My thanks, Jarl Magnus. I don't deserve your help, but my children . . . Whatever happens to me, please give them a place."

"They'll live with you in Bygvik. For when I defeat Toke, it will become mine. I'll need someone to see to it and guide its people for me. Thyri and Rollo can return there with you in the ship Toke commandeered from you."

He fell to his knees, thanking him, but Magnus raised him up. "Norsemen kneel to no one, Ketill. You will earn back your honor. Now see to your son and daughter. You have much to speak with them about."

As they walked into the camp, Leif said, "Was that wise, Brother? He was in league with Toke, whatever the reasons. Can we trust him?"

"I'll have my own men at Bygvik to keep track of him. I just gave him back his children and his dignity. He has much to thank me for. Time will tell us what manner of man he truly is."

"What of Mardoll? She's still at Thorsfjell."

"She came with Toke from the far north. Let her go back there. I know a merchant who makes runs up the coast and he can take her back to her people. If she is seen near here again, her life will be forfeit."

Leif nodded. "I never did hold with executing women, of course, or enslaving them, so that seems a wise choice."

"And now, I need to speak with my wife." Magnus looked down at her. "She is entirely too quiet."

"A warning if ever I knew one." Leif sauntered off toward the table where they kept the ale pitchers.

Magnus led her into their tent and shut the flap. "You're upset about the duel."

She spun to face him. "Why shouldn't I be? We escaped death and dishonor and now you want to fight a man who you know won't fight fair. He has nothing left to lose. He'll try anything, any revenge on you for all of this."

"And that's why I challenged him to the *hólmgang* instead of the *einvigi*. There are rules and witnesses that way."

"None of which will mean anything to him. He won't care if he dies, as long as he takes you with him."

"And do you think so little of my fighting skills that you fear what such a coward could do in the duel?" He crossed his arms, his voice hard.

"I fear what he will do beforehand, what treachery he'll plan."

"Guards are watching him to be sure he's in the appointed place at the appointed time. He won't have the chance to plot anything."

"Don't underestimate him, Magnus. Do you think he showed all his weapons? Or might some of those outcasts be here, unseen, to do his bidding? He had to have had men to crew his ship."

"I have four shiploads of the finest warriors in the north. We're well guarded, and they'll be with me when the time comes for the duel. There's a place set apart for these things, and with the Law-Sayer there and all the witnesses, he won't have a chance to try anything."

"I hope you're right. It's your life if you aren't. You must guard against many attacks, but he needs to be successful with only one of them."

"He won't be. Did you see the storm and how it faded after the verdicts? The gods have walked with us this day. Even I could feel them around us."

"Yes, they are pleased, but perhaps not for the reason you think."

"What reason, then, Silvi?" He went to her, but she backed away from him.

"The gods can be fickle. They are like distant relatives who must be appeased and bribed. Then they'll smile on us. I had to ensure they would stand with us, Magnus. That takes a sacrifice."

"Of what? An animal? Gold or silver? I could have given whatever you needed to perform the ritual."

She closed her eyes so she wouldn't see him when she spoke the words. "I gave them what they wanted, Magnus. Me."

He didn't say anything and she had to look at him. He went very still, a question in his eyes. "You? You promised them your life for our victory?"

"Not my life. I told them I would go to Uppsala and serve them for all my days if they influenced the outcome of the trials. They held up their part of the offer. I must uphold mine."

"What did you do?" He strode to her and grabbed her arms. "Why did you bargain your life away? Our life together? Does it mean so little to you?"

"No, Magnus. It means everything to me and that's why I did it. A sacrifice is just that. It must be important. There is nothing more precious to me than my life with you. Gold and silver mean nothing. All the beautiful things I have would have no weight with the gods, because they know it all means so little to me.

"My life with you is the only thing I care about. The only thing I had to offer. I couldn't take the chance we would lose and you would die for me."

He thrust her away from him. "Not so much a sacrifice, I think. It's what you've wanted all along, to go there. You waited until I defended and cleared you, and now you use this as an excuse to make your dreams a reality. The gods must be laughing at me."

"It's not like that." She tried to go to him, but this time, he stepped back. Her heart was tearing apart inside of her. His color was high, his jaw set. She had never seen him like this before. "I did it to save you. To save both of us."

"And you didn't think to trust me to do that myself. You don't think I can defeat a piece of scum like Toke. You don't consider me able to defend you against his lies. Perhaps he has had his revenge after all, as he planned all along. He's caused me to lose the one thing I love. You."

She sank down on a chest as he strode out of the tent. Crossing her arms over her burning stomach, she rocked. Sobs tore from deep within her and a heaviness weighed down her chest. Hatred flared in her for the gods she had once loved, for herself, and for this world that was slowly destroying her. Magnus was all that made this life tolerable, and now he was gone. Let the gods take her, then. They would find her empty to them. To everything.

The vision hit her like a sword strike and she cried out in anger. She needed nothing from the gods, but she couldn't block it. *Birds, tiny and vicious, attacked Magnus from a stand of trees. He raised his shield . . .* It ended as quickly as it began.

She looked up as Magnus came back in with Eirik, Leif, Asa, and Lifa.

"Tell them, Silvi. Tell them what you have told me. Then speak the words, if you can. For I cannot."

She swallowed, the memory of the vision still soaring around her. The words came hard. "When Magnus said he would be executed in my place if I was found guilty, I made a promise to the gods that if they stood with us and gave us victory this day, I'd give myself to them, to serve them all my life. I had to be certain Magnus was safe. That he would live." She met her mother's wide eyes. "I must keep my word. I know, Mother, that I promised one year, but I have a larger vow to keep. I must go to Uppsala."

Tears shielded Magnus from her, but Silvi stood and faced him even though he was only a blur. "I divorce you, Magnus, in front of witnesses. My dowry, I leave with you. I will take only what I brought here with me." The words tore from her throat, leaving it raw. "But first, listen to me, Magnus. I have had a vision—"

He slashed the air with his hand. "I have listened enough to you. Tell your visions to the gods. They're all you care about."

Lifa tamped her staff on the ground. "You will listen to her, Magnus. This last time."

He pressed his lips together, but gave a short nod.

"I saw you approaching the woods, a sword and shield in your hands. From within the branches of the trees, dozens of small birds with long, sharp beaks flew down and attacked you. You raised your shield to defend against them, but I saw no more. Somehow, Toke will attack you, Magnus, in a way you do not expect."

"So, I am too weak to fight Toke. I am too feeble-minded to defend us at the trials. And now you say I must fear little birds. That he will send them to peck at me."

He shook his head and turned to Eirik. "Take her from here in the morning, to Uppsala, since it's all she ever wanted. Take her, her ships, her dowry, all of it. For she takes my heart as well. I'll have no need of them any longer."

He stormed out and Silvi sank down, sobbing. Warm, strong arms enfolded her as Eirik, Asa, and Lifa surrounded her on the ground. She buried her head in her mother's chest, curling up into her pain.

"My brother is an idiot." Leif's disgusted voice sank into her. "I'm going to beat some brains into him. Or out of him." The tent flap rustled.

"We'll leave in the morning," Lifa said. "We'll go to Uppsala."

"What?" Eirik sounded frustrated. "We're just going to let this happen? Not be here to back Magnus in the *hólmgang*?"

"For now." Lifa lifted Silvi's face so she would look at her. "Magnus doesn't need the distraction when he fights. Silvi needs time to think, to understand. The gods need to speak with her and tell her what they truly want, and there's no better place for that than the temple where the gods walk. Magnus must come to terms with this as well, and fight the duel. In the end, all will be as it should be. You know, Eirik, even in war, one retreats for a time from the battlefield in order to rest and regroup, then returns. There's no dishonor in that."

"Very well, Mother. But I'll leave the ships here. He may have need of them and will have no choice but to take them. Besides, he'll get to Uppsala to take Silvi back much faster in a warship than in a *knörr*."

He smiled at Silvi, and she tried to return it. At least she still had her family. But soon, all she would have would be hard, dead wooden statues, empty dreams, and an even emptier heart.

* * *

Magnus stood on the shore, scowling at the two ships.

Damn Eirik. He'd left them behind, knowing they'd be a link to Silvi. He couldn't leave them for anyone to take. They were far too valuable.

"I'm surprised they don't burst into flame with how you're looking at them. Did they do something to offend you?" Kaia had walked over to him and he hadn't even seen her. She'd been directing the men loading supplies on her ships.

"No. It's nothing."

"Are you certain you don't need my help any longer? I can stay until after the duel this morning. Just in case."

"My thanks, but you must have other places to be this summer. I have my own men, and once I crush Toke, there won't be any more threats to us."

"I like your attitude. I've enjoyed my stay at Thorsfjell. With weddings and wars and poisonings, it certainly wasn't boring."

"No, it wasn't. Where will you go now? Back to Vargfjell?"

"No. Rorik is overdue. He would have sent word to me that he returned and where he wanted me to go next, but I've heard nothing. He was supposed to raid with Ragnar Lothbrok up the Humber river. As weak as the people are there, he should have amassed another fortune and been back by now. He has important matters at home to see to. I'll go to Haardvik and wait for a time. He'll put in there once he's made the crossing, and it's closer than sailing all the way to Vargfjell."

"Or then again, you might be offering to stay because Leif is here." He glanced sideways at her.

"Men have died for insinuating less than that." She smiled. "But you have one duel already to fight this day, and the blood loss might make you weak. You have to relieve that cursed *nithingr* of his head. I'll grant you mercy. For now."

He inclined his head to her. "My thanks, shieldmaiden."

She sobered. "Just remember that he *is* a *nithingr*, without honor, disgraceful, and a coward. He had some sort of crew for his ship to get here. Where are they? Watch for treachery."

She stalked off, shouting at her men to hurry with the provisions. He drew a deep breath and walked back to camp. One reason he'd brought such a show of force was that he'd already thought of the outcasts Toke brought with him. Ketill had told him he'd had twenty men on their ship. They couldn't show themselves, and that was the problem. They were hidden somewhere, no doubt ready to strike if it went badly for Toke at the trial. As outcasts, they didn't want to lose their only source of shelter and support.

Silvi had warned him of the same thing. He hadn't wanted to listen to her. The words of the divorce she'd spoken were still ringing in his head as she'd told him of her vision. He hadn't wanted to hear anything else.

And he hadn't wanted to think of her these past three days. But memories of her crept into his mind—her beautiful silver eyes, her sweet smile, the way her lips parted when he brought her to her ecstasy. She was his. He'd known it since the first moment he saw her. She was the light to his dark, the water to his thirst, the way to something beyond himself. He'd gone into the trial with the same confidence with which he went into war. He had already won. He just never dreamed she wouldn't feel that way as well.

He couldn't stop thinking about her vision, and now Kaia, a warrior, warned him about the same treachery. He'd be foolish not to heed them. Regardless of what Leif often said, he wasn't an idiot.

Come the time when he went to the *hólmgangustadr*, place of duels, he would look to the skies, and the trees. Then, only when he had vanquished the enemy who had torn his life apart, would he look into his heart.

Magnus walked at the head of his group of men, Leif at his side. The *hólmgangustadr* was just beyond the stand of trees ahead. Toke should be there, guarded to make certain he didn't run. Magnus still didn't trust the situation. He searched beneath the trees as they approached the combat area, but the shadows there were too dark to make out any shapes.

He hesitated, and the men behind him stopped. Silvi had said she saw tiny birds with long, sharp beaks. They hadn't come from under the trees, but in them. *In them.* Of course. He almost smiled.

He motioned to the five bowmen behind him and they came forward. He addressed them all in a quiet voice. "Archers. In the trees. No one would see them on the way in, and neither would we until it's too late. When I give the signal, drop and form a shield wall. Bowmen, shoot from behind us into the trees. Let's see what prey we flush."

"Yes, Jarl." They continued on, positioning themselves as they walked. Then, when they were just within range, Magnus dropped his hand. They knelt and slung their shields forward, forming a solid barrier in front of them. The bowmen remained standing, protected by the shields, and shot a volley of arrows into the trees.

Several men fell, screaming, out of the trees onto the ground. Others jumped down and ran. Magnus and his men chased them, slaying all they found.

As they surveyed the carnage, Leif clapped him on the back. "You saved Silvi's life, and now I suppose she's saved yours. I think you need to go and thank her in person."

"After I slay a coward. He thought to take her from me, but not even the gods will do that."

Magnus walked into the clearing. The Law-Sayer and twelve men who would witness the duel sat to the side. Toke stood, his face white, as he saw them coming. Magnus stopped in front of him. "You still try to have others fight for you. Now, shall we do this the honorable way?"

He approached Yrian. "In the woods you'll find a number of dead men. They were archers, hiding in the trees to ambush us. No doubt, they were the last of his outcasts and they died like the *nithingr* their leader is."

As the men around them grumbled at the outrage, Yrian nodded at Magnus. "How did you know about them?"

He grinned. "The birds, Law-Sayer. The birds warned us."

Yrian stroked his beard. "Do you, then, wish to continue with your challenge?"

"Of course. The fight only loosened up my sword arm." He rolled his shoulders. "My blade has tasted blood this day, but it thirsts for more."

"Very well. Let it begin."

The men guarding Toke pushed him toward the area designated for the duel. A square of cloth about the length of two men was laid within the boundaries, with three lines etched into the ground around it. It was roped off at the outer boundary, with a hazel post at each corner.

Toke held one sword and had another on a cord attached to his wrist in case the first one broke. Magnus chuckled. He would never have the chance to use the spare. As was their right, Toke had three shields, held by a man outside the square. Magnus had brought only one sword and one shield. It was all he needed. When Toke saw this, it would further unnerve him.

"Neither of you may step outside of the bounded area," Yrian said. "If one of your feet touches outside the ropes, you will be considered to have yielded, the mark of cowardice. If both feet touch the exterior, you'll have fled, the mark of a *nithingr*. The duel is ended when blood touches the ground."

They faced each other. The other men and witnesses stood outside the square. Toke sweated, his eyes darting as though he looked for a way out. Magnus waited. Toke was already nervous and the longer he could draw it out, the more likely Toke would be to make a mistake.

"So your little pale wife cast her spells on the assembly also. Does she whisper her dark words to you as she lies beneath you? After I kill you, perhaps I'll find out. Except I'll cut out her tongue first to stop her magic." Toke sneered as he moved from side to side.

Magnus didn't react. He affected a bored expression, though he was focused on every shift of Toke's body. "We didn't come here to talk. Your words are the lapping of waves on a distant shore. Let us finish this."

"Why don't you try for me, then? Or do you only slay children?" Toke glanced to one side in a feint, then charged. Magnus raised his shield and Toke slammed his blade into it, trying to shatter it. Magnus didn't deflect it, taking the blow full force. The blade bit deep. He twisted the shield, bending the sword so that it stuck fast.

Toke held on to it a moment too long. Magnus jerked him forward and drove his blade into Toke's stomach. They were face to face as Toke's wide, disbelieving eyes bore into him.

He spoke so the words were only between them. "For Silvi." He ripped his sword to the side and shoved him away with his shield. Toke dropped to the ground, screaming, mortally wounded. He tried to grasp the sword still hanging from his wrist.

Magnus snapped the cord and threw the weapon out of his reach. He stood over him. "You are not worthy of Valhalla. I did not drown your son, Gudrodson. I want you to take that to your death."

"It is no matter now." Toke gripped his stomach as blood pumped out of it, spreading underneath him. "Though I will not see him, he is feasting with Odin, a warrior grown, as he should have lived to become."

He breathed his last and lay still. Magnus faced Yrian. "The rules state that the duel ends when blood touches the ground. I believe the requirement has been met."

"And so it has, Jarl Sigrundson. I declare you the victor. You will take possession of all his property."

The men came forward, congratulating him. He stood looking down, his sword dripping Toke's blood. He was anything but victorious. Toke had still taken his revenge, still taken the one thing that mattered. The one thing he loved.

But he would rectify that. And in the end, though he would have to fight the gods themselves, in the end he would win . . .

Silvi.

The Great Temple
Uppsala, Uppland, Sweden

"There it is, Leif."

Magnus reined in his horse, borrowed at an exorbitant price in Birka, and gazed at the massive building. Leif, next to him, whistled through his teeth.

The temple stood in the midst of a vast plain, a towering, complex structure, with many gables and staves. Around the top of the roof hung a glittering chain, said to be pure gold. It was set there so that all who came would see it from a distance. A massive tree grew beside the temple. It was always green, though no one knew what kind it was. Perhaps the god who had built the temple, Freyr, had brought it from Asgard and planted it. Mountains surrounded the plain, and in the distance, groves of trees stood. Ancient burial mounds rose nearby around the valley.

"Remember, we can't bring our weapons onto the sacred ground." Leif checked his sheathed sword. "I imagine there will be a place where we can leave them."

"No doubt. I wasn't going to leave my sword on the ship in Birka. We still had to ride through Sigtuna and all the way here."

"Nor I."

"Besides, I don't need weapons to convince Silvi to come back with me." He grinned. "Maybe a little rope. But not weapons."

Leif frowned. "Rope? You would force her? If I'd known that—"

"Of course not. Just a little reminder of our nights together."

"For once, I don't know what you're talking about."

He gave his brother a dubious look. "You mean you've never? With a willing woman?"

"What? Why would a woman want that? Odin's eye, Magnus, that's as bad as someone with a sheep."

"Forget the damned sheep already. I still don't know where you hear these things."

"You talk of *me* hearing things."

"Listen, Brother, if you want that shieldmaiden, you'd better start thinking of rope, yourself."

Leif gave a short laugh. "I'll just use my charm and wit to win her over, as I do all the women I've been with."

"Both of them?" Magnus studied him for a moment. "Just keep beyond the reach of her sword and you should survive."

"I'd like to keep her well within the reach of mine." He winked.

"In that case, when we get back to Birka, we'll look for some nice silk sashes for you."

"Me? Do I look like a woman, to want such things?"

Chuckling, Magnus rode on while Leif grumbled beside him. They'd traveled many days by ship, then had ridden here, leaving their men behind with the two warships in Birka. They were sick of each other, but their journey was at an end. At least, until they had to return. Then Silvi could keep them from killing each other. If he could win her back.

He and Leif descended into the valley. People walked throughout the temple complex, some clad in the regalia of the priests and priestesses, others dressed as Magnus and Leif were. As they rode up to the temple and dismounted, a priestess greeted them.

"You must not bear arms in this sacred place. If you will give me your weapons, I will take them in peace and you may retrieve them when you depart. Keep your knives to eat with."

With reluctance, they handed over their swords and seaxes. She took them with a small bow, then walked to another small building.

"That wasn't easy."

"No. But if we're not safe here, where else would we be so?" Leif took a deep breath. "Let's go inside."

They entered the temple. The ceiling rose to the highest rafters, gold ornaments hanging from it. Gold glittered everywhere around them: on the walls, the statues, and on the underside of the roof itself.

"I think we're safe enough." Leif craned his neck as he studied the ceiling. "If anyone attacked us, they'd be more interested in all this treasure than in us."

A beautiful woman, dressed in the robes of a priestess, came to them. "How may I help you, travelers?"

"I'm Jarl Magnus Sigrundson and I've come to speak with Silvi Ivarsdottir. Is she here?"

"I will ask Unn to come and speak with you. She will know."

"My thanks." As she left, he spoke low to Leif. "At the trial, when Lifa introduced herself, she said she was trained by Unn. That must have been many years ago. Can she still be alive?"

"I remember her saying that. She also said Unn was a *völva*, so there's no telling how old she might be." He looked deeper into the sanctuary. "There are the gods."

Magnus spun. Three large wooden statues stood in front of the far wall. They were up on a pedestal, offerings of food and valuables placed before them. Magnus drew closer. Thor was in the middle, with his hammer, Mjölnir. On either side of him were Odin with his spear, Gungnir; and Freyr, the god of lust and happiness. It was obvious what he was armed with.

Perhaps if he had brought a sacrifice of some sort, it would help. But the gods had already taken all that meant anything to him. He had never thought to bribe them in the past. He had always done for himself.

"Jarl Magnus?"

He turned. An elderly woman had come in, flanked by several young priestesses. She stood straight, and was clad in regalia much like Lifa wore when she wished to show her rank.

He went to her and inclined his head. Leif joined him, doing the same. Her braided hair was white, her eyes were clear and blue, and her skin, though wrinkled, was luminous. She shone with a calm joy, and must have been very beautiful in her youth.

"I welcome you to Uppsala. I have been expecting you."

"Did Lifa tell you we would come? Is her daughter, Silvi, here?"

"No one needed to tell me. And yes, Silvi is here. She is well and safe. But you are not."

He tensed. "What do you mean? I'm in excellent health and if I'm not safe, I'll need my weapons."

She put a hand on his arm. He stopped. The calm that came over him shocked him. All the responsibilities, worries, anger burning in him, faded away.

"Stay here for a time. See what we are, what Silvi is. She has told me, these past few days, everything about herself, you, and much of what lies between you. I have given her no advice, for I needed to meet you and speak with you as well. Will you have wine with me?"

"I would be honored."

She motioned to the priestesses standing behind her, and they left.

"I'm going to wander the grounds. Worship some gods." Leif winked. "Or some goddesses."

Unn smiled. "Surely the gods must have been pleased when they created you both, to make two of a kind."

"They liked me best," Leif said. "Magnus was the afterthought. They copied my good looks. He was just lucky." He followed the women out the great front doors.

She laughed, low and full. "He is delightful."

"Not if you have to travel with him for days."

Still laughing, she led him to a side room. After inviting him to sit in one of the chairs, she poured wine for them, then handed him a glass. It was rimmed in silver, very rare and expensive.

"Skoal." She sat, raised her glass with a twinkle in her eye, and they drank. The wine was excellent. She was very different from what he'd thought a *völva* would be. And yet, hadn't she once been a young woman, possibly much like Silvi?

He set down his glass. "How shall I call you? I don't want to give offense by my ignorance."

"Just Unn. It is who I have always been and always will be. There is no need for more than that." She regarded him for a moment. "Let us not dissemble. There's no reason to since Silvi told me what happened between you at the *Thing*. Silvi promised herself to the gods. She feared you would take on her punishment if she were found guilty, so she made a bargain with them. She was so upset, she did not think it through well enough."

"Yes. She didn't think of us, or of how we could not win because of what she did. If the accusations went against us, one of us would die. If we were victorious, we would still lose each other. I thought if she knew she was safe, it would relieve her, that it would make her see how much I love her. Instead, my decision to offer my life in place of hers drove her to this." He indicated the room around them.

"You were angry."

"Of course. I was finally going to give her the life I wanted to, with the peace and calm she needs. I dragged her into marriage with me and, in doing so, brought my troubles with Toke into her path. I defeated him by heeding her warning. Maybe she should be here, in Uppsala, but I cannot give her up so easily."

"You say you cannot let go, and yet you did."

"My anger forced me to do so. Now that I've had time to think, I'm here to win her back, no matter what promises she made. If she still wants me, and I don't give her a choice whether or not to return with me, then she cannot be forsworn to the gods. Their anger will fall on me. But I, at least, will have her back. I'm already estranged from the gods anyhow."

She smiled. "We'll leave that for the moment. Why do you think you cannot let go of the things in your life? Why must you control everything around you, including her?"

To his shock, heat rose in his cheeks. He hadn't blushed since he was a young boy. "She told you of that, did she?"

"She didn't have to. I heard it in the words she did not speak. Magnus, you came into the title of jarl very young. You were well trained for it, but it was sudden. Your father left you his legacy, Thorsfjell and all of its people, and his trading business. You had to hold on to it with both hands, afraid to lose it. If you control it, you need not depend on anyone else or risk someone failing you. You feel that same need to possess Silvi, but she's like no other woman you've known. She has always traveled her own path. You don't want her to slip through your fingers.

"And yet, you did let go of her. You say it was because of your anger, but was that truly the reason? Or did you see that she needed to come and find out for herself if she belongs here?"

"I think it was because of my anger, Unn. I felt nothing else."

"I wonder. You may think that's the reason, but is it? Did you know to look within yourself to ask why? Even a rune cannot read itself."

"It doesn't have to. It knows its own nature by what it is."

"True, but every symbol has many meanings, especially when it's paired with another. Sometimes it takes someone well versed in them to see both, and catch the truth between them." The look she gave him was one of wisdom, woven with humor. Her mouth turned up at one corner.

He sighed. "I should know better than to debate such things with a *völva*. It doesn't change, though, that I'm ready to defy the gods to bring her back with me."

"That's not anger, or possessiveness. That is love. Let me ask you this. If she doesn't want to leave with you, if you go to her now and she refuses, would you force her? Could you keep her, knowing she wanted to be elsewhere?"

He tilted his head back, gazing at the ceiling. "If she still wanted me, but wouldn't be with me because of her promise, I would take her. But if she, herself, did not want to, apart from that, then no. I could not. For her sake, not for mine."

"Neither would the gods expect her to stay, Magnus. Do you think they want her here if her heart is no longer with them? Remain here for a time and learn, where you don't have people, responsibilities, and battles pulling at you. Let go of all those things that have drowned out the gods' voices. You have so much to learn of love and of the gods. Let Silvi teach you about both. She has lived in your world. Perhaps it's time you live in hers."

Chapter Nineteen

Silvi lifted her face to the late spring sun, letting the warmth flow over her like the small measure of peace she'd found here in Uppsala. Magnus was alive; she'd have known if he wasn't. She fingered the necklace he had given her, unable to bring herself to remove it. She was alone, standing in one of the sacred groves ringing the temple. There was peace here, but still she was empty. The gods walked here, though she didn't feel their footsteps as she had at the sacred grove in Thorsfjell. They spoke their wisdom in the storms, but she couldn't hear them as she had when they approached Magnus's mountain. When Unn performed the ancient rituals, the gods were as leaves moving in the winds that drifted across the plains.

She didn't belong here. She missed the mountains, and the chill air blowing down off the peaks. She needed to hear the boisterous people as they went about their days, flowing in and out of the longhouse. The scent in the air here wasn't that of the newly planted herb gardens outside of the cooking rooms.

She'd poured her words out to Unn, her mother's mentor. Now she saw where Lifa got her calm wisdom. The *völva* shone with serenity, but Silvi would never find that here. Not without Magnus.

Uppsala wasn't her home. Thorsfjell was. The people there loved her and needed her. They'd told her so as she was boarding Eirik's ship to come here. All of them had met her at the shore and asked her not to go. They had offered her their own homes to stay in if Magnus did not want her to be there. He would relent, they'd said. A love like his for her could not be denied for very long.

Could she return there, even if he no longer wanted her? Could she be one of the people, working with them, healing them, reading their runes? Could she watch as he took another wife and had children with her? Every time she saw him, would his eyes blaze with the same anger as they had that horrible night?

To never feel his arms around her, hear his heartbeat again, or revel in his strength as he took her to her ecstasy . . .

She closed her eyes.

The vision wavered, just out of her sight, as though it asked to come to her. Perhaps now she could hear the gods and understand.

The sea surrounded her. She could not feel the island beneath her. In the distance, a longship sliced through the waves, coming toward her. A great dragonhead rose from its prow, shields gleaming along its sides. It grew closer, but she couldn't see who guided it.

The waves pulled her under. Only the dark waters were beneath her. No island at all. "Silvi." She looked up as a hand extended down from the sunlight above her. She reached for it . . .

"Silvi."

Magnus stood before her. At first, he seemed part of the vision, as though he belonged there. But the sun and the breeze drove away the remnants of what she'd seen. She blinked at him.

"You defeated Toke. How is it you're here?" Her heart pounded with her relief. He was so much more beautiful, so much stronger than she could hold in her mind. It had always amazed her each time she saw him anew.

"It was a very short duel. In a matter of moments, his blood touched the cloth. There was a bit more than is usual because he was dead. But if I've lost you, he's still victorious, by taking you from me. I had to come here. Speak to you. Unn told me where you were." His lips curved. "After I assured her I wasn't going to throw you on my horse and ride away with you."

"You—you would want to do that?" What was he saying? She took a breath that was filled with hope, and kept it within her.

"I always hold what is mine, Silvi. Surely you know that by now. But now I understand why that is so."

"And am I yours?" She held his gaze.

"You are. Just as I am yours. I need to hear you say it. It's your choice." He watched her with such longing in his blue eyes that her own filled with tears.

"I am, Magnus. I'll always be yours."

He strode to her and gathered her into his arms. She lifted her face for his kiss. It sealed her to him, as though they would never again part. When he ended the kiss, she grew weak with desire as she looked up at him. He wiped a tear from the corner of her eye with his thumb.

"I love you, Silvi Ivarsdottir. I was willing to give my life for you to prove it. That will never change. Whether it's in battle, or against the entire world, I'll always protect you. That's something you must understand."

"I do, Magnus. I was so afraid for you and for us. I trusted you, but I couldn't trust those who would judge us. I couldn't see beyond that and I made a promise I shouldn't have."

"Unn wanted to speak with you about that. We should go back to the temple. She's waiting."

"Whatever she says, I've already considered returning to Thorsfjell. I wasn't certain how you'd react, but I couldn't leave our people. Or you. Even if you married someone else, I couldn't live anyplace else. It's my home."

"As though I would even think of another woman. You slew me from the first moment I saw you. There was no shield, no weapon, no strategy I could use to defend against it. I was conquered from the start. No hope." He smiled down at her.

She reached up and kissed his jaw. "Where there is love, there is always hope." As his eyes widened, she shook her head. "You must know by now that I love you, Jarl Magnus. I didn't want to tell you before, fearing you only wanted me for my dowry. It would be too painful to know if that was true."

"I required those things, Silvi. But I wanted *you*. In the end, I realized I need you more. No ship, no gold, no measure of wealth means to me what you do. It all fades in the light of your beauty and kindness."

His kiss was power and passion, a glittering chain binding them together. Lifting his head, he searched her eyes. "Unn said I need to live in your world for a time. I don't want to come together with you until I can stand beside you in it. Until I can know what you know, feel what you feel when the gods brush you with their hands. Perhaps they brought you here, knowing I would follow. I was meant to be

here with you so I can finally hear them, and so fulfill my role as jarl
through them. Then they can bless Thorsfjell."

"Oh, Magnus, they blessed it when they made you jarl."

He took her hand and together they walked back to the temple. A
lightness filled her that no prayer, no ritual could match. Unn waited
for her at the front doors.

"Magnus, a small house has been set aside for you and Leif. Go
and refresh yourself from your ride. When you're done, come back
and we'll have the evening meal, all of us."

He walked to where Leif flirted with a pretty priestess.

Silvi followed Unn to her room. The *völva* sat down while Silvi
perched on the edge of a chair across from her. What would she do if
Unn said she had to keep her vow to the gods?

"So, he did come to you, as I said he would." Unn's eyes sparkled
with mischief.

"Yes. And he said he loves me, as you foretold."

"I didn't need the runes to tell me that. With every word you
spoke when you told me of your life with him, I saw it. Did you tell
him of your feelings?"

"Yes. He was very happy."

"Yet still, you question."

"I don't question him or what he feels for me. I question what the
gods will want me to do, for I promised them I would serve them
here."

"Perhaps you already have, for you drew Magnus to this place,
where they want him. They can speak more clearly to him now, without the noise of his life deafening him to their words. As to your bargain with them, let me ask you this. Who dictates the time of our
deaths?"

"The Norns. They decide, as each child is born, the moment of his
death."

"And the gods cannot stop it."

"No one . . . can." She drew a sharp breath as the truth hit her.
"The gods can't change the time of anyone's death, not even their
own during Ragnarok. If the Norns had decreed that either of us died
at the *Thing*, even the gods couldn't have altered it."

"That's right. You haven't seen it because of your fear and sorrow.

They had nothing to do with Magnus's victory. They could not accept your vow because they had no say over the outcome of the day."

"Then why did I feel such peace when I made the promise?"

"You've always wanted to walk your own path. And you thought that path led you here. But your brother forbade it, as did your mother. They pressured you to marry Magnus. You went from being under your father's control, to Eirik's, then to Magnus's. With the stillbirth, the threats to you, and the trial, you felt events were swirling around you, taking you with them, giving you no choice in the matter. When you made the promise, it was the one time you believed you controlled your own destiny. You had chosen your path once again, having some say in what would happen. You could sway fate. That gave you the sense of relief you felt."

"And yet, I controlled nothing."

"In a way, you did. You came here. You needed to find out if you belonged at the temple, and I think you've found the answer. Child, the gods don't want anyone here who doesn't wish to be here. Who cannot give of herself freely and with joy. I told your mother this when she fell in love with your father. He was a fine man. And even now, these eyes aren't so old that I cannot see that Magnus is the same."

Unn took Silvi's hand. Her skin was as soft and thin as a bird's wing, but her grip was strong. "Stay here with him for a few days. Let him see this place through your eyes. Show him that the power emanating from the temple is what makes us what we are as a people. Let him understand that to hold the visions and survive the touch of the gods as you do, takes great strength."

"They haven't touched me in a long time. I wouldn't allow it. Today, I let them speak to me, and they showed me another vision like those I told you of."

"Of your island."

"Yes. Only this time, a longship with a dragonhead on the bow sailed toward me. I went beneath the waves and there was nothing below me. As I sank down, I heard Magnus call to me and I saw his hand reaching toward me. I tried to grasp it, but then I woke and he was there. I've always thought the island was Uppsala. But I'm here now, and yet it was still gone."

She laughed. "Oh, Silvi, the island you've seen all your life isn't Uppsala. It's Magnus."

Silvi gasped at Unn's words, her blood racing through her.

"The gods have shown him to you since you were young. Just as you drew closer to the island, so you were growing closer to him in time. He will be your refuge in the tempest of the world. It was only when you refused to accept him that the island disappeared. Now, he has come to take you with him. I think when you are his, with all the love between you, your island will return to you."

Her breath trembled as she drew it in. How could she not have seen it? "Then the gods are telling me to go with him?"

Unn patted her hand. "Your heart is telling you to go with him. Listen to it. For the gods dwell there and they always will. And now, through you, they will live in Magnus as well."

The storm walked across the plains on legs of lightning.

Silvi stood with Magnus, watching it come toward them, her hand in his. She was not afraid of the lightning. If it was her time, nothing could change that. It was the creed of the warriors, giving them courage and the will to show their strength to the gods without fear. And now, it was within her as well. For Magnus was with her, and always would be.

In the week since he had arrived, she had shown him all the wonders around them, the groves where they prayed, the springs where they threw the offerings, the tree that never lost its leaves. They attended the rituals when the sacrifices were made, and climbed the burial mounds. Long into the nights, they spoke of the ways of the gods and the powers of the runes. At times, he'd wandered through the valley, alone. He'd said it was so all he'd hear was the sound of the wind in the trees and the singing of the waters as they flowed past him.

With no responsibilities, they'd had time to talk. He told her how her vision had warned him of Toke's treachery, and how he defeated him. He described the places he had traveled to and the lands he had seen. One day, he'd promised, they would travel the seas together. But for this time, they were content to simply be.

He brought her hand to his lips and kissed it. "I always thought power lay in gold and silver, but it doesn't. It lies in the land, the mountains, the seas we sail on. They are a part of us as we are of them. The gods imparted their strength into this place and that force spreads to everything, including us.

"Our land is cold and gives us little, but it's made us strong warriors. As jarl, I had to perform the rituals for my people, but I never felt them. Now, when I climb my mountain to the sacred grove, I'll remember that everything I am comes from there. And I want you beside me. I understand the strength that runs in you to stand in the force of the gods, as you do. When they come across the snows and glaciers toward us, we can face them together."

"They come." Unn spoke from behind them and they turned to greet her. Leif stood to the side. She pointed to the storm, her head high. "They show their approval of you with their presence. May they bless you in all things."

"Then marry us now," Magnus said to her. "I would show them that I take Silvi for my own. Not hidden in a house, or in the darkness of a temple. But here, beneath the sky, so they will see it."

"Now?" Unn gave a knowing smile.

"Now?" Silvi's jaw dropped, the breath shocked out of her. "But my family—"

"Has already seen us wed once. I don't want you slipping through my fingers again. I want to proclaim you mine in front of the gods themselves." He drew close to her and whispered, "Or, to make certain I have you, I can use a certain silk sash I found in our bed after our last night together at the *Thing*. I brought it with me. Then you'll certainly be in my care."

She knew what that meant. His voice sent warmth throughout her body, melting the deepest part of her. She swallowed and looked at Unn. "Now."

The *völva* laughed and took their hands in hers. "Leif, you may stand as witness. Magnus, will you promise to love and protect Silvi for your lifetime, to live with her in joy and laughter, and to honor her for all your days?"

"I already have, and I always will."

"Silvi, do you marry Magnus freely, in the sight of the gods, with all happiness, giving yourself into his care?"

"Yes, Unn, I do." Smiling at Unn's choice of words, she leaned up to Magnus and whispered loudly, "As long as you untie me in the morning."

He choked back a laugh as Unn gave Silvi a stern look before grinning. Leif looked the other way, his cheeks turning red.

"Then before the gods, I say that you are married. You may kiss— Never mind."

Magnus had already grabbed Silvi with a laugh and slanted his mouth over hers. His kiss was so demanding and possessive, she could hardly breathe. She gasped for air as he straightened. He didn't let go of her, keeping her under his arm as he faced Unn again. She watched them with a smile, then cleared her throat.

"Magnus, since you're sharing a house with Leif, you may have mine for the night. I need to go contemplate the mysteries. Leif, please escort me back. I'm not certain they're going to make it to the house. It's more than my old heart can take."

"You'll outlive us all, Unn," Leif said as he offered her his arm.

She took it. "Such a powerful shield arm you have, Leif. Let me tell you of a warrior I loved far back when I was beautiful. He looked much like you. I have a lovely granddaughter descended from him."

"I'm certain you do, Unn. And you're still beautiful." They walked away toward the temple complex.

Magnus grinned down at her. "Shall we prove Unn right?"

"A nice warm bed, glasses of wine, and soft furs sound much better to me than the hard ground and getting soaked in the rain."

"Very well. I'd still like to see you naked under the stars. There's always our sacred grove. Or one of the longships anchored in the fjord one calm night." He cupped her face in his hands. "I owe you a true wedding night. And I always pay my debts."

She turned her head and nipped his palm. "I'd be happy to collect." She laid her head on his chest and he drew her closer. When she'd come to the temple, she hadn't brought her herbs to prevent a child, thinking she wouldn't need them. She was right. If a child came of this night, then it was meant to be. A brave little boy, just like Magnus. During the winter, she'd had a vision about Eirik. Magnus had stood behind him, though she hadn't known who he was yet. She'd seen that their blood would mingle, and so it would—through their children.

"What are you smiling about?" He brought her hand to his mouth and kissed it.

"Just dreaming of the future."

"You have all night to do so, Silvi. And every night after that. As long as I'm in those dreams with you."

She snuggled into him, and he settled her against his strong body, shielding her from the rising winds. Unn spoke the truth. Magnus was the island in her visions, and he was, indeed, her haven in a tempestuous sea. Of that, she had no doubt. "I think I always have dreamt of you, Magnus. Now I know I always will."

The village of Haardvik
Hardangerfjorden, Hordaland, Norway

People lined the cliffs and the shoreline as Magnus guided the *Fire Serpent* closer to the beach. Leif followed in the *Sea Eagle*. The two ships Rorik had loaned them were anchored just off shore, which meant Kaia was there as well. Silvi waved, her heart filling with joy as she saw Eirik, Asa, Nuallen, and her mother waiting to greet them.

When they were close enough, the men of the village caught the ropes the crew tossed to them, and pulled them onto the beach. Magnus leaped off and turned to lift Silvi down. But she laughed and jumped off herself. Her skirt was soaked, but it was worth it.

As soon as she cleared the water, Eirik grabbed her and swung her around. "I was certain you couldn't escape him for long."

"If only you knew, Eirik." She laughed as he gave her a quizzical look, but Asa just grinned.

Lifa embraced her, her face alight. "So, can we plan another wedding?"

"We're already wed again, Mother. Unn did it for us."

"Oh." She looked disappointed for a moment, but then she brightened. "Well, we can still have the celebration. We'll need more beer, the hunters will have to go out for game, and we'll have to start baking. I have to gather the women. We'll send to the outlying farmsteads and invite everyone. I'll have the servants start more cooking fires and brew barrels of ale." She hurried off toward the village, talking to herself. Nuallen looked at all of them, shrugged, and followed her.

"The celebration is the best part anyhow." Leif sloshed onto the shore from his ship.

Magnus clapped him on the back. "Maybe we should be planning your wedding instead." He nodded toward Kaia, who stood off to the side, her arms crossed. She rolled her eyes and stalked away.

Leif grimaced. "I'd like to live to see my nieces and nephews."

In the longhouse, Lifa already had food set out and plenty of ale and mead. Silvi sat at her old place at one of the tables as the warriors who had been on Magnus's ships filed in and headed for the drink. Many of the servants and villagers she'd known all her life greeted her. But Haardvik felt different now. Or, perhaps, she was the one who was different. The pains in her stomach had subsided. Unn had told her the discomfort had happened because she'd never accepted her life, and the sorrow had eaten at her. Before, Haardvik had been her entire world, and her dreams lay elsewhere. Now, her world and all her dreams were centered in one place with one love. Much of the pain was gone, in more ways than one.

Magnus talked with Eirik as Asa sat down across from her. "So, I take it you won't need any swords by the bed?"

She laughed. "I don't know if I'd go so far as to say that. Maybe a small one, just in case."

"I'll see what I can do."

A servant ran in and stopped in front of Eirik. "More ships, Jarl. They're not passing us by. They look like they're coming here. I think they're your cousin's ships."

"Rorik? Where has he been all this time?" Eirik led the way outside.

Kaia was already on the beach when they got there. "He has only three ships with him. He said he was taking four. Gods, I hope he didn't lose one of them. They're like his children. There's no telling what he'll do."

The ships came in under full sail, ramming onto the sand. Parts of them were blackened and damaged, their sails torn. Rorik, in the lead ship, leaped out, cursing.

Silvi tapped Magnus on the arm and he leaned down to her. "I don't think his journey to Northumbria went well. He's going to be livid, and it takes him a while to calm down. Days, sometimes. And when he sees Nuallen, we may have a small war on our hands."

"What do you have in mind?"

"I know a place we can go to escape the carnage."

"Lead on, then. I'd much rather listen to your sweet whispers than his ranting, anytime."

When they entered the sacred grove, he chuckled. "This is where you berated Rorik and me for fighting."

"Yes." She put her arms around his waist. "And you said you couldn't feel the presence of the gods here."

"I remember." He looked across the clearing. "But now, I do. They walk in the movements of the trees. Their voices carry on the wind, and they speak to us in everything we are." He gazed down at her. "Before we left Uppsala, you told me of your visions, and of what Unn said to you about them. What do you see now?"

She rested her head against him, closed her eyes, and let go.

The golden sands of the island stretched away from her as she stood on the beach, the calm seas lapping onto them. Above her, glittering halls, like those of Asgard, rose on the sides of the verdant mountains. A gentle breeze blew over her, carrying a comforting, familiar scent. She turned. Magnus stood there, his eyes filled with love. He held his arms out to her. She went into their shelter and rested her cheek against him, listening to his heartbeat.

She opened her eyes, the island fading back into the sacred grove at Haardvik. Magnus still embraced her, and she smiled up at him. "You're there now, just as Unn said. I think you always were. It just took me a while to see you."

"I love you, Silvi. I'll always be your haven. No matter what life brings, no matter where we go, I'll be at your side, standing between you and anything that would harm you. I've won so much more than I ever thought I would. Victory over Toke, peace for Thorsfjell, safety for the people of Bygvik. You."

"And my ships." She gave him a teasing smile.

"And your ships. The *Raven* is guarding the *knörr* on its trading voyages, but we still have the other two. Where shall we go? To distant lands? To sail the sea that has no tides? When we went through Birka on our way back here, we didn't see much of it. Shall we go there and find out what treasures it holds? Or to Kaupang, or Hedeby?

Even Staraya Ladoga across the Baltic?" He took her face in his gentle hands. "Anyplace you want to go, anything you wish to see, whatever I can buy you, is yours. Tell me what you want."

She placed her hands over his. "You. I want only you. All the treasure in the world is wherever you are. My love for you is all I'll ever need." Rising up on her toes, she kissed him. "Take me back to Thorsfjell, Magnus. Take us both home."

If you enjoyed *Lord of the Mountains* be sure not to miss the first book in Sabrina Jarema's Viking Lords series

LORD OF THE RUNES

Keep reading for a special look.

A Lyrical e-book on sale now!

Chapter One

Village of Haardvik
Hardangerfjorden, Hordaland, Norway
Late fall, 850 AD

She stood before him like a flame-haired Valkyrie—strong, proud, a warrior.

Not as she had been in life.

Eirik Ivarson had seen his dead wife in his dreams before, but in them, she was always as he remembered her—gentle and too weak to survive their brutal world. Her soft blue eyes would gaze at him with reproach like she blamed him for her death, sending her to dwell forever with the goddess Frigga. She'd been right.

But this dream was different and as he struggled to cling to it, she spoke.

"Why do you sleep, husband, while your kinsmen die?" Her eyes darkened into a deep brown as though she was sullied by passing so close to the earth. The vision turned as crimson as the blood that had gushed from her and carried her away from their life together. A scream split his sleep apart.

He tore himself awake and reached for his sword before he even opened his eyes. At least he was still dressed, having fallen across his bed well after midnight, passed out before he'd hit the furs. Head spinning with the mead he'd drunk, he staggered to the door of his small chamber.

Another cry cleared his thoughts. He eased open the door and took in the state of his father's main hall. An unfamiliar warrior, an outcast from the looks of him, stood over two cowering serving girls.

Another servant lay in his own pooling blood beside them. The attacker raised his sword and the women shrieked again.

Yelling to divert the man's attention, Eirik bounded across the room. He swung his blade as the invader turned. They clashed, flesh to flesh, iron to iron. Eirik's momentum smashed them into the wall and the outcast's head cracked against it. Dazed, he paused for an instant. It was all Eirik needed.

Using his forearm, he struck the upper edge of the intruder's shield into his face. His nose shattered. Eirik pushed the shield aside and whipped his blade across the man's neck. Blood arced down his body as the attacker fell.

He knelt beside the fallen servant. "What has happened?"

"Outcasts invaded us at dawn." The older girl tried to rise, but her knees buckled. "Even now, they fight outside. This one hacked his way in, though we locked the doors as the mistress bade us."

As he helped her to her feet, the sounds of the battle he'd slept through because of his drunken stupor came to him from beyond the damaged front doors. His blood rose again. But he couldn't just rush outside and join the fighting. He had to know what he faced. "Where's my father? My mother and sister?"

"Jarl Ivar fights. And the thrall, Nuallen, took the mistress and your sister to try to escape to safety."

He gave a quick nod. "May the gods will it so. Find shelter for yourselves." He ran to the entrance before they could answer. Stepping outside, he entered a world of war.

The attackers outnumbered them several to one. His father's warriors engaged them with bravery, but too many of the valiant men lay dead in the yard. Livestock ran free and two of the outbuildings burned. Villagers screamed and tried to hide, but many were already cut down.

While he'd lain insensible from his celebrations, his people had been dying. His family, his everything. He swallowed his shame. This was not the time.

The familiar stench of fear and bodies in their death throes seared his nostrils. He breathed deep of it to fortify himself. Confidence welled up in him. Now he was in the world of warfare he had chosen three years ago, the world he'd left behind when he'd returned here.

He ran through the yard, searching for his father. Three of the attackers fell to his assault as he went. A shield lay on the ground and he grabbed it as a man rushed toward him. Their blades met in a burst of sparks. The other man staggered back under Eirik's superior power, crying out. Most of them had to be outcasts, with little more than the element of surprise on their side. They were no match for him. Eirik hit his opponent's blade, driving him back farther until the invader stumbled and nearly fell. Using the delay, he swept the battleground for an instant with his gaze.

There. His father stood in the midst of the melée. On the ground, the bodies of his warriors surrounded him. They had guarded him to their deaths, but now the jarl struggled alone against two men. They came at him, one from the front and one from the back, toying with him. Eirik's heart swelled with molten rage. He had to get to him. Ivar was sick. Weak.

Eirik struck his opponent's shield again. His sword fragmented. He thrust the blade's jagged end under the shield, into the man's thigh. Hooking his hand under the lower edge of the shield, he yanked it toward himself, pivoting it on the outcast's hand. The upper edge tore into his opponent's throat, dropping him. Eirik leaped over the body, roaring to his father to disengage, to break off. But the noise of battle drowned out his voice.

Weaponless, and using only the shield, he battered his way through the tumult, yelling. The crush of men impeded him and desperation clenched his gut.

The outcast behind Ivar hefted his axe and threw it at the jarl's unprotected back. The blade hit hard and deep. Eirik skidded to a stop. The chaos around him receded into a pinpoint centered on his father.

The jarl stood for a moment, looking around himself as though he wished to remember his land while he was in Valhalla. Then his gaze fell on Eirik and he straightened. He smiled, holding out the ancestral sword, Star Slayer, like an offering to him. Then his eyes rolled back and he drifted down, still clutching the weapon. He lay still.

"Father!" Eirik's voice was high and thin, as it had been when he was a young boy calling for his sire in the night after a terrible dream. But this was no nightmare from which to awaken. Grief, sharp as a dagger, plunged into him and twisted. His breath came hard, his eyes filling.

"Hakon, how much silver do I get for killing a jarl?" The outcast grinned down at Ivar's blood-drenched body.

The silver-haired coward who had distracted Ivar from the front moved off, laughing, stalking other prey.

The clash of blades behind Eirik jarred him from the shock of his father's death. He spun.

One of his father's warriors fought a marauder. While Eirik had stood useless and staring, the man had shielded him from an attack. The warrior dispatched the outcast with a quick strike of his blade to the gut, and turned to Eirik, raising his dripping sword in a salute.

"Jarl." He offered the weapon to Eirik, hilt first. Eirik drew a deep breath at the title, then took it with a nod of thanks. Lifting an axe from his belt, the warrior moved off to intercept another attacker.

Jarl. He was the jarl now. These men were no longer his father's men, but his. So many of them lay around Ivar's body, having given their lives for him. But they had failed. And so had he.

The bastard who had attacked Ivar from behind rushed to the body, put his foot on the jarl's back, and pulled his axe blade free. It came out, covered in bone and flesh. He focused on the fine blade still gripped in the fallen jarl's hand. With a smirk, he slid the axe into his belt and reached down for it.

Pain shot through Eirik, as though he himself had been struck. He surged through the battle, toward his father's body, screaming his rage. He flipped the sword in his hand and threw it, point first, at the whoreson. The marauder raised his shield to deflect it, but the impact knocked him off his feet. He rolled away and came up, pulling the axe from his belt.

Eirik reached his father and pried the sword from his hand, keeping an eye on the outcast. Ivar had no further need of the weapon. Already the Valkyries circled and soon he would feast with Odin. Star Slayer, the sword of their ancestors, the symbol of the jarl and of all they were, was his now.

He tamped down the agony that threatened to release his fury. This adversary was a fighter, and Eirik needed his wits about him to do battle.

His eyes cool and assessing, the coward hefted his axe and threw it. It hit Eirik's raised shield. His father's blood spattered over his face. The metallic smell tightened his muscles. As he lowered the shield, he shook the axe free. The man unsheathed his sword and came at him.

Eirik met his blade with his own, the shock of it driving his breath from him. He slammed his shield into the man, knocking him back. He followed with a blow from his sword. The outlaw answered in kind.

Eirik's thirst for revenge gave him strength. He drove his father's killer backwards toward the fjord cliff with blows from his sword and his shield. As they neared the edge, the man glanced back and his eyes opened wide in realization. Eirik threw away his shield and, gripping his sword with both hands, struck the man's shield with the pommel. The damaged wood fractured.

Following through, he swung hard, slicing the man's belly open. The outcast tipped backward, silent, his gaze hard and resigned at his own death. At the instant he went over, he grabbed Eirik by the belt and yanked.

They fell together. Eirik tried to twist around, to dive in head first. But he was tangled with the body when they hit the water.

Cold like a thousand knives stabbed him. The water closed over him and crimson darkness surrounded him. His head swam and his blood slowed in his veins. He fought the cold and the ache of smashing into the fjord, though the man's body had hit the water underneath him, saving him from the full impact. He had to stay awake, couldn't succumb to the cloying call of death tugging him deeper. He fought his way clear of the corpse. They'd fallen in a shallower area near the cliff, so he kicked off from the bottom. Bursting into the light, he took a deep breath and looked up at the rock wall above him. The sounds of battle and the smell of smoke drifted down to him. He swore in frustration.

He needed to get to shore before he passed out or froze. The current carried him farther down the fjord. He stroked toward a small inlet where the shoreline wasn't so steep.

The bottom rose under his feet and he stumbled onto the thin strip of land. Shivers racked his body and he fell to his knees. Lying down, he sprawled on his back, gazing up at the mountain towering above him. The battle was too far away for him to hear it. The taunting quiet of the sunny morning was almost painful.

Who were these invaders? Why had they attacked? He had to get back home, to continue the fight. His father was dead and he was jarl now. They were his people and they needed him.

He'd come home from his journeys when he'd heard his father

was dying, setting aside the pain of his past to assume the mantle of responsibility as the heir. But many of his father's warriors had dispersed to their homesteads for the winter, never dreaming they would be attacked so late in the year. If he hadn't been too drunk to hear the beginning of the battle, he might have saved his father. He'd failed them all.

If only Thor would give him the strength to continue, to rise up and resume the fight for his home and his people. He touched the gold hammer pendant at his throat. But he could only close his eyes, his body stiffening with cold and pain. His head spun with hatred— at his enemies, the fickleness of the gods, and at his own weakness.

Darkness pulled him under and he closed his hand . . . On nothing.

His heart paused. In the waters, when he'd fallen, he had lost his family's ancestral sword.

Cold. He was so cold. It held him in a tight embrace as though he had descended into Hel itself. Had he died and lost the chance for Valhalla because he no longer held a blade?

He opened his eyes. The mountains still rose overhead, but the sun had moved behind them and he lay in shadow. How had he lost an entire day? His clothes were still damp. He needed to find warmth and shelter before the sun set. The late fall night would be frosty and in his condition, he would likely be dead by morning.

What was happening in the village? He couldn't just walk in there and find out. If the outcasts had won, he would be killed, and no one could go get help.

Groaning, he sat up. He ran his hands through his hair and scooped it back behind his shoulders. When he tried to stand, the stiffness in his muscles made him sink back down again. Cursing, he made another attempt. This time he rose and swayed.

He had no weapon, no fire-starter, no food. Nothing.

Forcing his legs to move, he climbed up the steep side of the mountain so he could look down into the village and see what was happening. He knew these woods as the outcasts did not. He could evade them if need be.

The sun had moved farther down in the sky, and the air had grown cooler by the time he reached the narrow ledge. He sat down, still unsteady, and studied the village.

Strange men roamed the streets. No women or children were about.

Two buildings stood smoldering, but the main hall, the granaries, the smith's shop, and the other houses had not been touched. As if the outlaws had planned it that way. This was no complete devastation. It had been calculated to take out the jarl, his warriors, and enough people so they could mount no further defense, yet leave the village itself relatively undamaged.

Eirik's blood ran cold through his heart. They intended to take the village for themselves and overwinter there. Men of their ilk had no homes, and the season of storms and snow was nearly upon them. They needed the shelter, the food, and supplies the place held.

They would be there all winter, along with survivors from the village. But what of his mother and sister? Had they succeeded in escaping? If they were still there, he would have to rescue them first.

Whatever the circumstances, he had to find help. Even if he could get to his other warriors who had dispersed for the winter, there weren't enough men to fight so many outcasts. He needed numbers, fighters who were seasoned, strong, and fearless. Like those he had just traveled the world with, fighting beside.

Looking to the north, he cracked a dry smile. He had access to hundreds of the best warriors in Norway. It would be a long, dangerous journey to get to them. Because of his failures, the gods were challenging him to redeem himself. He would see this through.

Wincing, he rose and climbed down and to the east, around the flat land where Haardvik was. As he moved, he opened himself to the woods, the air, the sounds of everything around him. He'd done it often enough when he was still young and full of belief in the gods, relying on the ways his mother had passed on to him. She'd taught him to be one with the things beyond what he could see and hear and touch. But then he had put all of that behind him, embracing instead the sharp reality of steel and the calm certainty in his own prowess.

Now, weaponless, he would have to depend on what lay within him, even if he had rejected it long ago. The forest closed in around him, the darkness of the twilight covering him. The spirit of the land had never left his heart. It remembered him.

A twig snapped, too near. He pressed himself against a tree. The sound of horses walking through the leaves came to him and he stilled.

"With that white hair, the little bitch won't be hard to find."

The outcasts spoke of his fair-haired sister. His heart sank. They had seen her, knew of her, and were looking for her. His sword hand fisted. They rode past him, making crude comments while he flattened back against the tree trunk. Holding his breath, he waited until they were gone. It went against everything he was to allow them to live, but he had no weapons. Even though he could kill without them, the sounds would bring others and he would be outnumbered. Stealth, not engagement, was his best course now, for they didn't know he had survived and that would gain him an advantage.

A flash in his mind made him pause. So familiar and sweet. He reached for it and the image of the sacred grove crossed his awareness. Of course she would be there, waiting for him. He moved a short way up the mountain to the clearing where his ancestors had worshipped the gods for centuries.

"Silvi?" He kept his voice low.

His younger sister stepped from the trees, leading a horse. Sacks, blankets, and a sword hung from the saddle. The dark hood of her cloak fell back and her white-blond hair blazed like a beacon. "There you are." She dropped the reins and held out her arms.

He strode to her and crushed her against him. "I sensed you in my mind, like we used to do when we were young."

"Mother knew you were still alive." She leaned back to look up at him. "She sent me to find you."

He didn't ask how they held the wisdom they did. Such gifts from the gods were best left unquestioned. "I heard Mother's thrall tried to get you to safety. What happened? Where is she?"

Silvi gently broke his hold on her, stepping away. She could never touch anyone for too long a time. As gentle and sensitive as she was, living in the world was too painful for her. She kept herself apart, from fear of taking on the sorrows of others.

Her gaze darted away from his. "The outcasts caught us and brought us back. By that time, the fighting had stopped or else we might have been killed before they learned that Mother is a rune mistress. She swept into her chamber and put on her regalia, her blue cloak, fur boots and gloves, her glass beads. And of course, she had her rune staff. When they saw her come out, they nearly shat themselves."

He smiled. "They had no way to know they would tangle with a woman of power. Her rank will see her safe. But what of you? You're not initiated." It was well-known what happened on raids, and his breath caught.

She gave him a slight smile, her strange silver gaze sad. "No man looks twice into my eyes, Eirik. Except you. I will be well. The runes have said so."

"The runes." He laughed, short and harsh, anger curling through him. "What good are they? Did they warn you of this? Did they warn me of—"

"They *did* tell us. Of Father's death. Mother saw it weeks ago. Since he was ill with the wasting disease, we thought they were fore-telling his death from that. We had prepared ourselves for it. Not for this." Her pale eyes filled and she turned away.

Whether she wanted his touch or not, he wouldn't let her grieve alone. He pulled her against his chest and she leaned back, shaking in her silent sorrow.

"And we no longer have Star Slayer. Father wielded it and it was lost in the battle." One of her tears splashed on his arm.

"I had it," he said. "I took it, still warm from his hand after he died."

"Then you do have it." She whipped around to face him.

The hope in her eyes cut him as no blade ever could. "I lost it. I slew the *nithingr*, the coward who killed Father, but he pulled me over the fjord cliff with him and we both plunged into the water. When I hit, I must have been knocked senseless for a moment. I dropped it. It's gone." He didn't want to look at her, but he did.

Her eyes lost focus for a moment and he held his breath, waiting for what she would say, what the Sight would tell her.

"Then it's beneath the waters, safe from those who would defile it with their touch. Hidden." She looked at him, her gaze clear and sharp once again. "As you must be. No one must know you're alive."

"I know. Were you able to find out anything about them?"

"Their leader, Hakon, plans to stay here for the winter. In the spring, he's going to take revenge on his own family, who he says betrayed him years ago. They live in the *fjells* to the north, where the glaciers are. Then he'll take their wealth and homestead for himself."

He'd been right. That was why they hadn't destroyed the village. "I'll journey to Vargfjell, Rorik's holding in Trøndelag and get his help. In the years I've been fighting and raiding with him, I have come to know him well. As our cousin, he won't let this outrage go unanswered. It's a matter of family and honor. He has great wealth, more than most kings, with four-and-twenty longships, and the men to crew them. Several hundred of the best warriors follow him. When he dropped me off here days ago, he was to head home for the winter. I'll go to Vargfjell, and return here with him to have our revenge. Then, I vow, I'll retrieve Star Slayer from the waters and we'll rebuild our village and our lives."

Her eyes widened. "To get the sword—that's impossible. It's said the fjord bottom follows the mountains down to the depth of a hundred man-lengths. Even the god Njord might not be able to find it, though he rules the sea."

He shook his head. "In the waters below the cliff, there's a shallower ledge. I know it from when I was a boy. I pushed off from it to gain the surface today. If the sword fell with me, there's a chance it rests there still. If it was thrown out farther, it's in the depths and Njord is welcome to it. For it means the gods have chosen to take it back from us."

She bit her lip as she studied him. "Mother has doubted your sanity ever since you dove off the cliff in your youth. She might be right."

He took her hands, his fingers enveloping her small, slender ones, and pressed them. "Don't you see, Silvi? That blade has been passed down to us from the early times, when the gods walked with our ancestors. It's a link with all we are. It gives us the right to bear the rank of jarl. I have to try to get it back, or how can I take my inheritance? I won't accept the title if I don't retrieve it, for without it, I'm not worthy."

Silvi slipped her hands from his. She looked into the growing shadows and her eyes became distant again. He braced himself. Why had he been cursed—no, blessed—with a sister who had the Sight? "When you find the sword again, it won't be for the reason you think. And you'll give it up for the sake of a woman a handful of days later."

How could that be? "It would mean I've given up Haardvik, and that will never happen."

The gelding pricked his ears and lifted his head. Another horse nickered not far off in the woods. If theirs answered, it would disclose their location and he would have to fight, bringing all the outcasts down on them. He would never make it away from the fjord to find help. He locked his gaze with Silvi's and they moved back into the shadows of the trees. He reached for the sword hanging from the saddle, steeling himself for battle.

But Silvi set her hand on his arm and shook her head. She whispered to the horse, cupping her hand over his muzzle. He closed his eyes and chewed, relaxing. Harsh voices threaded through the trees. Eirik tensed, still gripping the hilt.

Three outcasts rode through the sacred grove. They were dirty and unkempt, their weapons bloodstained with the lives of his people. But though his gut screamed to slay them, he could only let them pass.

As they vanished into the woods, he released the sword—his father's personal sword. He raised his brows in question.

She touched the scabbard. "Weeks ago, when Father knew he was dying, he told us to leave the sword for you, not to burn it with him. We'll send him to the afterlife in the flames as is his right, no matter what the outcasts say. We have a fine sword for him so that when he fights tomorrow in Valhalla, he'll be well armed. Even now, he drinks with the gods." She sniffed as her eyes moistened again.

"Drinking and fighting, his two favorite things." They shared a slight smile, then he took Silvi by the shoulders. "There's no time to waste. The bastards infest the woods and it's only a matter of time before they find us. We have to leave now."

"No, Eirik, I must stay here. They said if any of us leave, they'll kill one villager for every measure of the oil lamps that we're gone. Even knowing this, Mother sent me, and we've likely lost one or two of our people already since I left to find you and get these supplies to you. I can't stay away." Her voice shook.

His stomach tightened as though he'd been punched. How could he leave his beautiful, otherworldly sister here? "You did well, Silvi." He kissed the top of her head, letting none of his turmoil show. And yet, she was right. "Father would have been proud of you and Mother. We cannot allow the welfare of a few to overshadow that of the many."

"Already we have lost over ten warriors and as many villagers."

So great a number? His jaw tightened with rage, but he couldn't falter. "I may not be back until the spring, even if I can get through to Rorik now. Though the sea stays free of ice in the winter, most of his men will have dispersed to their homesteads, as many of ours did. And he will have beached his longships to repair them in the season of storms. We'll likely have to wait, as will you."

"I know, Eirik, but we won't be idle. Swords are not the only weapons we have, for the mind is also powerful. These men are ignorant and superstitious. They'll fall prey more easily to fear. Mother and I will use that to our advantage."

"Be careful. Fear may be a weapon, but any blade can turn on the one who wields it. Unease makes men dangerous. Let them eat and drink until they are so fat they cannot walk and so drunk they cannot think. It will make their bellies a larger target for our blades when we return to slay them." He drew her into his embrace. "I should just throw you on the horse and take you from here."

"Then they would come after me and discover you. This way, you can travel unimpeded. It's for the best." She pulled back from him. "Besides, Mother had a vision that I would one day be at the great temple in Uppsala." She waved her hand toward the clearing. "Does this look like Uppsala to you?"

He gave her a smile he did not feel as he pulled her hood up over her hair. "No."

"Then I will survive to go there to be one of the *hóvgythiur*, as I've always known I am destined to be. Now go. And may the gods watch over you."

He gritted his teeth. She would never be one of those temple priestesses if he had anything to say about it. "The gods will be too busy watching over you to worry about me. I've fended for myself quite well without their intervention. All I need is my own skill, a good sword, and a fast ship."

Instead of chiding him for such talk, as she always had, she gave him a kiss on the cheek. "I'll watch for the lengthening of the days and imagine that, somewhere in the world, there is still light."

He tightened the girth of the horse's saddle. When he turned back, she was gone, disappearing before he could weaken and take her with him. He slammed his fist into the trunk of a nearby tree and the pain centered him. What manner of man was he to leave his own sister behind? But she knew, as he did, that it was for the good of their people.

With the darkness of the coming night settling around him, he changed into the dry clothing she had brought him, mounted, and rode into the sacred grove. Reining in the horse, he looked at a solitary rune stone that stood at one end, as it would for centuries more. In the center of the carving stood Yggdrasil, the World Tree, and runes traced around it, made by his own hand. He didn't need to read the words he'd chiseled into the stone. They were seared into his mind.

Eirik carved this stone in memory of his wife, Sela, and their son who never drew breath. May Thor consecrate these runes.

Everything. He would leave everything behind. All he knew and loved. It wouldn't be the first time. But he would return, whether the gods willed it or not. And when he had exacted his vengeance, he would carve a rune stone to honor his father, so that he, too, would never be forgotten. For Eirik had failed him, his family, all of them. This day. But come the spring, he would not.

Voices erupted from the south, in the direction of the village. Had Silvi allowed them to see her, to draw them away from him? He fought the impulse to go to her. She made the sacrifice for him, and for their people. If he went after her now to protect her, everything she had done, as well as the deaths of the villagers, would be in vain.

He set his jaw. It would *not* be in vain.

He turned the horse to the east, where tomorrow, the new day would begin.

photo by Charles Bowles

Sabrina Jarema lives near Ocala, Florida, the Horse Capital of the World. She has a herd of fat, lazy Arabians on forty beautiful acres. She also breeds and shows white German Shepherd dogs and currently has several Grand Victrixes taking over her house. She's joined by a menagerie of tortoises, turtles, birds, fish, and cats. To avoid farm work as much as possible, she loses herself in the worlds she creates through the novels she writes, her art, music, dollhouses, and jewelry. She has worked as a professional fantasy illustrator and has written fantasy romance for many years. Recently, she has branched out into historical romances set in the early Viking era. She is currently writing the Viking Lords series, a family saga set in Norway during the ninth century. She is an active member of the Tampa Area Romance Authors chapter of the Romance Writers of America. Please visit her website at www.sabrinajarema.com to enjoy her art, music, writing, jewelry, and all the other visions the night brings to her.